ILE D'OR

ALSO BY MARY LOU DICKINSON

One Day It Happens

ILE D'OR

a novel by
Mary Lou Dickinson

Mary Lou Dickinson

June 4, 2015

inanna poetry & fiction series

INANNA Publications and Education Inc.
Toronto, Canada

We gratefully acknowledge the support of the Canada Council for the Arts and the Ontario Arts Council for our publishing program.

We are also grateful for the support received from an Anonymous Fund at The Calgary Foundation.

Cover design: Val Fullard
Interior design: Luciana Ricciutelli

Library and Archives Canada Cataloguing in Publication

Dickinson, Mary Lou, 1937-
Ile d'Or : a novel / by Mary Lou Dickinson.

(Inanna poetry and fiction series)
ISBN 978-1-926708-13-3

I. Title. II. Series: Inanna poetry and fiction series

PS8607.I346I54 2010   C813'.6   C2010-902244-0

Printed and bound in Canada

Inanna Publications and Education Inc.
210 Founders College, York University
4700 Keele Street, Toronto, Ontario, Canada M3J 1P3
Telephone: (416) 736-5356 Fax: (416) 736-5765
Email: inanna@yorku.ca Website: www.yorku.ca/inanna

In memory of Beryl and Geoff — and a childhood on the frontier.

This is a work of fiction. My family and friends will nonetheless recognize from whence some rivers spring.

Je me souviens
Quebec automobile license plate

*

"There are strange things done in the midnight sun
By the men who moil for gold..."
—Robert W. Service

Prologue

THE LAST GOLD *rush in Canada occurred in the Abitibi region of Quebec. By the 1940s, there were rugged mining camps scattered through the area where prospectors had staked their claims. Flying overhead at night in a small bush plane, a pilot would see lights like diamonds sprinkled in the bush.*

One of these villages was called Bourlamaque, after a general in Montcalm's army. It was connected to a larger town, Ile d'Or, which was the commercial centre. No markers told when you left one and entered the other, but the residents near the shaft in Bourlamaque were glad to live in the log cabins that were built for the miners with Anglo money.

In the 1980s, word was that the one operating mine left in town was soon to close, that the gold was too expensive to mine, that there wasn't enough of it any more. For a while, there was rumour of a buyer. The people of the town were worried. Some were anxious that dust and noise and the sight of an open pit would be too much for them. But there were even more who wanted the changes because of jobs the mine would continue to provide.

1.

MICHELLE DUFRESNE WAS standing near her father's grave in the cemetery on the outskirts of Ile d'Or when a man with a duffel bag slung over one shoulder walked between the tombstones toward her. She hadn't seen him in town before, so she was startled when he waved at her.

"Hi, Michelle," he said.

It was then she noticed that his face was somewhat familiar, but she couldn't place it.

"You don't know who I am, do you? I'm Nick," he said. "Nick Petranovich. Remember those dances at the Rialto when we were teenagers?"

Her face went white. Nick Petranovich was older than she was and she'd had a crush on him. It had surprised her when he'd asked her to dance and talked to her as if she were his age. But she wouldn't have thought he'd remember that. And she hadn't seen him since he went away to university in the 1950s. She'd heard he'd become a doctor, had a family, divorced *and* — she'd read his obituary just over a year earlier.

"But, but," she stammered.

She'd thought that he would have been in his late forties by the time of the untimely news. She didn't know if he'd been in an accident of some kind or if he'd had a heart attack. Or maybe it was cancer. The death notice didn't specify and among the charities named for donations, none were ones that suggested anything. She backed away slightly to look at him more closely.

"The obituary in *The Northern Miner*," he said, brushing his hair back with his free hand. "Yes, I can see you might be startled." He smiled.

"I don't understand," she said.

"Well, the newspaper got it wrong. Can you imagine how that felt?

I had to write and tell them I wasn't dead."

Michelle kept staring at him as if unsure what to believe. He was blonde in his youth and now his hair was almost white, but still thick and unruly. There were lines around the edges of his eyes and mouth and his face was thinner than she remembered. The same dark eyes, always intense. It surprised her that after all these years he still wore the same style eyeglasses. The black frames that had made him look so studious in high school might be a slightly different shape now, but that was all.

"You're quite handsome for a dead man," she said finally, recalling a quirky rhythm to their youthful banter. "How could that have happened anyway?"

He laughed. "Oh, you know, a lot of people left here to go to school or university or some job and never came back. It's easy enough for someone to wonder what a person they once knew is doing now and before you know it, a distorted story gets reported as factual. They hadn't checked it out."

Michelle nodded, noticing that he was studying her speculatively.

"You look great," he said.

Her outfit was one she had bought in Montreal for a customer and then decided to keep for herself. A striped blue wool poncho over a vibrant purple pantsuit. She was aware the colours enhanced the dark hair that still fell to her shoulders, the green flecks in her wide, hazel eyes. Even with the poncho covering her long, slender waistline, she could see he noticed something about her appearance that perhaps surprised him. The memory of a teenager he once knew who was now a woman?

"What are you doing here anyway?" he asked. "I thought you left just after high school. I didn't think people came back once they left."

"There were reasons," she said, a frown crossing her face. "I did come back and I live here now." Her hands trembled slightly as she realized she did not want to reveal too much to someone she hadn't seen in over thirty years. "What about you?"

"Well, I didn't come for the hot springs," he grinned.

As if there'd ever been a spa. You might come for the hunting and fishing, for the skiing or the curling, for the opportunity to go underground in one of the old mines that was no longer in operation. But he'd managed to make her smile again.

"My parents are buried here," he said. "There's a stone on the other side of the highway." He pointed off into the distance. "I had to come and look," he said, then added quietly, "I'm not sure why, maybe to know about myself."

That wasn't what she thought about when she came out to visit her family's graves, something she did more often of late. She needed to feel connected. To tell her mother or her father stories and to listen to the wind whisper through the trees as if they were answering her questions. It was awkward that they were buried on opposite sides of the road.

"Did you fly in?" Michelle asked.

"I drove," he said. "The roads are good now. It gave me a chance to stop in Haileybury where I practiced briefly when I finished my internship. My car is parked just outside the entrance to the cemetery. Yours must be the Chevy."

She nodded.

"So what do you do here?" Nick asked.

"I own the dress shop down beside the theatre on the main street. Chic Choc."

"I bet that's a thriving business."

"It does all right," she said coldly. Was he mocking her? She'd loved to dress up as a child, and as a teenager had started sewing, but he probably never knew that. "I like helping people choose what suits them." And they liked her sense of colour.

"Didn't you inherit The Flamingo?" he asked, his eyes seeking an apology for any unintended slight.

Her father had opened The Flamingo in the early days of the town. His first job had been as a dishwasher at the mine cookery. Then he worked underground. They said he got the money for the club from high-grade, so named for the quality of the ore. Some men smuggled high-grade up in their black lunch buckets, but to manage enough of it to open a nightclub? He was never apprehended for anything. It had always been a mystery to her how her father had come up with enough money to open the club. She knew clearly now that it was these suspicions around her father that had caused some children to stop speaking with her then. Even though she hadn't seen Libby Muir, the mine engineer's daughter, since they were both teenagers, it still hurt that Libby had been one of them.

Well, too bad! she thought. The mine never promoted any French man above foreman in those days. Her father was damned if he was going to put up with that. He built a nightclub where everyone could gather. And it was a popular place.

"My mother inherited it," Michelle said. "But I guess it wasn't a business for a genteel Englishwoman. She sold it."

"I think your mother adapted to the north, Michelle," Nick said, as if he knew her mother well. But he would have. They'd all known each other well in the small town Ile d'Or was then.

"You mean the way she wielded a gun during hunting season?" Michelle asked. "She hunted partridge, you know."

"I wasn't thinking about the hunting, but yeah, that, too. I just meant that she always seemed comfortable out there on the curling rink, ski- ing on the trails, shopping in the general store. She was friendly to me, you know. The little Ukrainian kid with the accent."

Michelle laughed. "She had an accent, too." That very British inflec- tion she'd retained. "Not one that would have been very popular up here in those days with either the French or the English."

He glanced away, and then took another tack. "Do you have chil- dren?" he asked.

"They're grown up now. They've moved away, like we did. Elise is married and lives in Montreal. I don't hear from Dawn very often. I don't know where she is right now. Maybe in Toronto." She paused, embarrassed to have said that much. Toronto was Dawn's last address after the ones in London, Paris, Frankfurt, and Heidelberg. When on the Greek islands, she'd left no address. The other ones had turned up unexpectedly on a letter asking for money, on a postcard saying she was fine. Once she described the snow falling outside a window somewhere in France and wrote that it reminded her of her childhood.

"I'll be a grandmother very soon," Michelle added. "In January. When Elise has her first baby."

"Young grandmother," he said.

She changed the subject quickly. "Where do you live now?" she asked.

"My practice is in Toronto," he said. "But, for now, I will be living out of this duffel bag. It's time for reflection. I can tell you, a busy practice in psychiatry doesn't grant you that. And often it doesn't give you the satisfaction that you're doing anything useful either. Oh, I see some of my patients getting better, but I'm tired. I think maybe I'd like to be a hunter like your mother, but I'd go after big game."

"Are you going to shoot elephants for their ivory tusks?" she asked, surprised at the way she had fallen in so easily with his teasing. "I don't know if that type of hunting is allowed any more."

"Well, it probably isn't. But it doesn't mean I can't fantasize."

"I suppose if you're a psychiatrist, you'd know more about that than the average person."

"I might know more about it in general," he mused. "But now I'm looking at what pops up for me in particular." As he stepped back and shifted the weight of his bag, any hint of a smile had left his face.

The graves extended for a few neatly laid out rows with lines of trees between them. A few plants and the grass were well tended. In the other cemetery on the opposite side of the road, the Protestant one where her mother was buried, weeds and grass had been allowed to grow wild. Michelle tried to keep her mother's grave neat, but she couldn't take care of the entire surrounding area. She always felt there was something more she could have done to spruce it up, but she never quite managed the perfection she envisaged.

Nick's expression softened as he watched her. "It's good to see you. Would you have time for dinner while I'm here?" he asked.

"I'll make time," she said, hoping she didn't sound too eager. "How long are you staying?"

Nick shrugged. "I'm not sure," he said. "For as long as it takes, I guess."

2.

NICK CLIMBED UP the side of a rock that was covered in moss and pine needles to peer out across the trees toward the mine in the distance. Earlier there would have been Mayflowers growing in the crevices and, after that, blueberries. Soon everything would be covered with unfathomable depths of snow. It was in rocks like these, deep inside the earth's crust, that veins of precious metals had been found by early prospectors and later dug and blasted out by underground miners like his father. Had it not been for the gold, the town would never have existed. Nor would there have been children who found this particular rock at the side of the road across from the company houses. He recalled coming here to hide, thinking it was his rock, only to discover an empty Coca Cola bottle and a package of matches, indicating someone else had discovered his secret spot.

The head frame of the mine, holding the cables for the cage that went underground, stood out above the trees and Nick could see it clearly. He also heard the throbbing sound that came from the mill. This was often where he had waited to see his father come across the path from the mine. Roman Petranovich came up from underground, covered in black grime, his hard-hat with the small light on it tipped just slightly back on his head. Black lunch-bucket under his arm. Nick shared this with Michelle; both Maurice Dufresne and Roman Petranovich had worked in the depths of the earth. His father for much longer.

It was just before the war that Roman uprooted his family and brought them to Canada from the Ukraine. Nick was two years old at the time. His father could tell that war was coming. They would be safe in Canada. So Nick was told as he was growing up. Everything was left behind the day his father announced they were leaving. At first the family went to Manitoba where Roman Petranovich farmed for a couple of years. But those were lean times and Roman finally left to look for work in the mines around Kirkland Lake and Ile d'Or. When he found underground work in the Quebec bush, he brought his family over from Manitoba. Nick was four by then and his sister, Jeannie, was an infant. The baby their mother had been expecting when they left the old country was stillborn.

They moved into a house in Bourlamaque, down the street from the mine engineer, Walter Muir. Nick's mother grew vegetables in the backyard where she often talked to Nick and Jeannie in Ukrainian. She never learned English, but Mrs. Muir always greeted her as she headed toward town from her house further up Champlain, near the bush. Nick often saw the two women smile and gesture at each other. Unlike so many who were married to men who worked on surface at the mine, Mrs. Muir was friendly to everyone and didn't seem to notice that his mother was different. Mollie Petranovich had embarrassed him with her thick accent and her almost nonexistent English. Now he felt sad about that. Not long before she died, he realized how much he loved his mother. This woman he had been so ashamed of would have done anything for her children. He'd loved Marie that much, too, albeit in different ways, but now they were divorced.

Marie, he thought. *How could that have ended so badly?* His experience of love was laced with regret.

He'd met Marie at a fraternity party when he was studying medicine at university in Montreal. One of his friends was a Delta Sig and sometimes they caroused and danced at the frat house until long after midnight. Marie had been with his friend that night, but Nick had also danced with her.

"Would you mind if I called her?" he'd asked afterwards. Nervously. "Well, not really, I guess," his friend had shrugged.

Marie hadn't looked that interested in her date that evening and hadn't hesitated to accept Nick's invitation. There were sparks between them. A few months later they were engaged and right after graduation, he from medicine and Marie from sociology, they married. Their first year was spent at an internship at a hospital in Michigan; afterwards they went to northern Ontario for a *locum tenens* in general practice. Nick didn't think Marie, who'd always said she'd prefer to live in Montreal rather than anywhere else, would want to leave the lakes and the ski trails once she settled in Haileybury. Gradually he realized from her yearning comments that she wanted a different kind of future. One with more time and more prestige, more money.

At the end of the *locum*, he took up a psychiatry residency, circulating through the hospitals of downtown Toronto. It wasn't Montreal, but they'd made the decision together to move south from Haileybury to Toronto for the residency.

During the placement, he worked even longer hours than in the northern *locum*. Marie did not make new friends quickly or easily. Home alone with their toddler, she'd been morose and had begun to be more critical of him. To his discomfort, it escalated.

"You're such a cold fish," she'd said more times than he cared to remember, something he'd never been able to fathom. Always more demonstrative than Marie, he'd frequently returned home with bouquets of flowers or a bottle of wine. A box of chocolates. He loved her. Hadn't she known that? It was hard to imagine her now in Texas, married to another man. The twinges of depression that had led him back to Ile d'Or sent tendrils twisting through him. Anger around women who were separated or divorced had alerted him that this hiatus was necessary. He could joke about this anger all he wanted, but it was an underlying truth he would have to surmount somehow. So he'd managed to arrange for a month's break quite quickly. Longer would have been better, but not possible on such short notice.

By the time of the divorce, his daughter had her own flat on the top floor of a three-storey brick house in midtown Toronto. Just before Nick left on this trip, he'd been there for a late supper with Diana, hummus and pita bread with a salad. Grateful that he and Diana were close, he was startled when she'd become exasperated and said she'd never met such a self-absorbed person in her life as her father. That hurt.

"Don't use any labels from the DSM," she'd said. "I'm fine, thank you."

"I'm sorry, Diana," he'd said. "I guess everything's been getting me down lately. I haven't meant to be remote." At twenty-one, she often seemed self-absorbed herself, going off to clubs and bars, drinking and dancing, but he didn't say so.

Nick leaned down to pick up something in a crevice of the rock, an empty Mars bar wrapper, reminding him that this place wasn't any more his own fiefdom than it had been in his childhood. There must be a whole new generation in Ile d'Or who knew nothing of his family. His sister, Jeannie, was now living in California and both his parents were long dead. But he was also sure there'd be some people who'd never left. He supposed if he stuck around, there would be a lot of questions about why he'd come. He knew only it had something to do with his parents' graves in the cemetery by the side of the highway.

A mass of curly, dark hair popped up on the other side of the rock. A boy of about ten climbed to a flat spot. He looked like a startled bear cub when he spotted Nick, and he stooped down low until he was hidden behind the peak of the rock again.

"It's all right," Nick said. "I won't eat you."

"What are you doing here?" the boy asked, approaching warily. He spoke in French. "Why aren't you at work?"

"I used to live here." Nick shoved his hands in his pants pockets, reaching for some gum or candy.

"Where do you live now?"

"Toronto." He couldn't find anything to offer this child he already thought of as a nuisance.

The boy let out a breath that sounded like a mixture of a burp and a sneer. "Where did you live when you lived here?"

"On that street we can see from here. On the corner of Champlain." Nick gestured toward the town.

The boy pulled out a package of Du Maurier cigarettes.

"You're too young for those things," Nick said.

"None of your business."

"I suppose it isn't."

The boy lit the cigarette and started puffing. He didn't inhale so much as pull his cheeks in so his whole demeanour was that of concentration. Then he drew himself up to his full height and looked Nick right in the eyes.

"Where are you staying, Mister?"

"You know the old bunkhouses on the main street? I'm staying there."

"Pay me something to show you around." The boy was cocky now, sure of himself.

"I know my way around. I used to live here, remember?"

"I bet you don't know where to gamble," the boy said, his eyes grazing over Nick's frame. "Or where the whores are."

"Do you?"

He listened to the adults and he knew everything, he said. Some kid. Should be in school. None of his business, Nick's.

"So where do I go to gamble?"

"I'll show you. Ten bucks."

"That's too much."

"Too bad," he said. "That's the price."

In his day, a kid that age would have delivered newspapers. Or maybe run more lucrative errands for prostitutes or high-graders and Nick hadn't known it. Anyway, he'd say good-bye and go back to town, buy a newspaper. A beer. Something.

"No, thanks."

The kid shrugged.

Next time, Nick could sense him thinking. *Something else will hook the Anglo.* Ultimately that's what became of the *Hinglish Polacks*. They were all Anglos. What would his mother have thought of that?

3.

MICHELLE LOOKED FOR an old photograph album in a chest in a corner of her living room. In the album were pictures of her childhood friends and schoolmates. She couldn't find one of Nick Petranovich. He'd been enough ahead of her in high school that the yearbook for her graduation wasn't any help. A niggling question intruded that she knew was ridiculous. He was an attractive man and she was lonely for male company. He'd be around for a few days at most and would move on again. Last thing she wanted was to set herself up for disappointment.

Besides did she really want to have a man in her life again? She recalled how smoothly the early dates with Dominic had gone. She'd met him at a party in Montreal where she was studying fashion. Very quickly he'd told her she was wonderful and he courted her with chocolates and flowers, intimate dinners at the best restaurants. He'd told her he wanted to spend all his free time with her and didn't want her to see anyone else. She had thought that meant he truly loved her. She was still so young then. It wasn't until they were married and he demanded she not see her girlfriends anymore that she became uneasy. He would phone from his job at the fire hall often, having told her to wait for his calls. Not as if he cared about her, more as if he were watching her every move. Nothing in her childhood had prepared her for this behaviour, not even the arguments between her parents she'd overheard that going to different churches had sometimes elicited.

Michelle, distracted by this thought of the ongoing battle between her parents, laughed out loud. Imagine that irrepressible little French guy who was her father meeting the tall English girl, Elaine, overseas during the war. When they fell in love, it must never have crossed their minds how difficult it would be for her in a Catholic and French environment. It must have been such a relief to find love in those war years. But those differences had created an ongoing struggle that affected almost every aspect of their family life. Her father, the papa Michelle had thought was almost perfect, regularly attended Sunday mass at St. Luc's, the Catholic church, in the early days of his marriage. For a while, he'd insisted she and her older sister, Francine, go with him. Later, when he'd stopped going there himself, she and Francine often went to the small Anglican church in Bourlamaque, St. Andrew's, with their mother. Built of wood, it was set next to a stretch of fir trees and rocks. Michelle fidgeted in whichever church they attended. Francine was disdainful of both churches and hadn't hidden that. She would sneak off instead of going with either parent. For the only time in her life she could remember, Michelle had briefly been their model daughter. Then Francine was killed in a car accident when she was only sixteen and was buried in the Catholic cemetery. Michelle was the only one left now.

Later, lying in bed, Michelle lay awake pondering why Nick's unexpected arrival in Ile d'Or was unsettling her equilibrium. She didn't think that seeing him would really ease her loneliness. If anything, when he packed that duffel bag and left town, she would probably feel even more desolate. She listened for the sound of the blasting. Because it happened at the same time every night, it had always reassured her. Even as a child. And she always fell asleep just after. But not tonight, when she needed her rest. In the morning, she had to go into the shop early to start unpacking orders for the next season. The Christmas season would soon be over and November wasn't too early to think of lowering prices on some of the fall and winter merchandise. As soon as that sale ended in January, spring colours and materials would go onto the racks. Next to raising her children, this store, which allowed her to use her flair and creativity as well as her business acumen, was her greatest pleasure.

When finally she slept, Michelle dreamed of a time when she was still married and living in Montreal, when the girls were young children. A night when Dominic, drunk, broke the door down to get into the house. He was arrested, but was released shortly after. There were court orders, but that didn't stop him. She awakened screaming.

As she rolled over in the bed, it seemed the wall facing her was the pale blue of the first apartment she and Dominic had shared. It was only when she got up and walked from room to room, observing the clock flickering in the kitchen and the photograph albums still out on the dining room table, that she felt calmer.

When Michelle left Ile d'Or and went to Montreal, she didn't intend to return to the north, to live there ever again. It wasn't en route to any-where she wanted to go. But when her father died, everything changed. Her mother seemed so small afterward, as if she had shrunk four or five inches, retreating into herself. It would help, she said, if Michelle could come back, manage the business. It just happened to coincide with the time when she wanted to be as far away from Dominic as possible. After the times he'd tried to choke her, she had never doubted she was in danger. While still in Montreal, she'd hid at a girlfriend's apartment with the children because she was afraid he would carry out his threats to kill her. The only place she could think of to go was Ile d'Or and, anyway, her mother needed her. Many times she'd vowed vehemently never to return to the north and he knew that, so she hoped he wouldn't look for her there. It was a tough town under the surface, not a place she'd wanted to raise her children. But after a while, its familiarity made it seem like it had been a good idea to return home. She loved her shop. And her customers trusted her. On days when she felt almost like a stranger in spite of her early experience of the town, that made all the difference.

4.

LIBBY MORLEY STOOD at the window overlooking the street, sipping the last of her coffee. Soon a taxi would pull up in front of the house to take her to the airport. Everything was quiet with the calm of early morning in the city. Her son, asleep in a room above, had wished her "bon voyage" the night before with a heartiness she treasured. Her daughter, with some of that same enthusiasm that was only slightly quieter, had called her.

Any sane person would be heading in another direction, Libby thought. Montego Bay. Acapulco. The Algarve. Anywhere but Ile d'Or. But ever since Libby had heard Michel Tremblay and Roch Carrier read to a crowd at Harbourfront in downtown Toronto, the trip north had become inevitable. On that evening, just a little over two weeks earlier, there were long moments when she stopped hearing the words. Instead, in the inflection of both men's voices were the familiar cadences and sounds of her childhood. French accents that had existed on the periphery of everything for her. Sounds that brought back the crunch of high-buckled galoshes on hard-packed snow. The sight and feel of potholes in gravel roads and the flaming red and yellow leaves of autumn. Spring rivulets turning to mud as ice melted.

I want to go home, was the message all this evoked in her.

A pull so strong she hadn't been able to resist it. She might be Elizabeth Morley now, but for almost two decades she had been Libby Muir. And the home that now drew her was the town where she'd spent her childhood. The town where her father, Walter Muir, had been the mine engineer. His office had been 'on surface', behind a metal link fence that separated the property from the company houses and the rest of the town beyond them.

Libby walked down the front steps from the verandah just as the man with light brown skin and dark hair stepped out of the airflight car. He wore a navy blue uniform and his stomach protruded slightly over the belt of his trousers. He took the suitcase from her, the one with the green pompon her mother had once attached to the handle.

As the car headed down Spadina toward the Gardiner, the first snow of the season began to fall, delicate flakes melting on the windshield.

"Where are you flying?" the driver asked.

"North," she said.

Long ago, she'd read Thomas Wolfe's novel, *You Can't Go Home Again*. Even then, before she had really left the north, she'd felt the nostalgia that would one day propel her to return. So strong was the longing now that soon after hearing Carrier and Tremblay, she'd bought a ticket. Would her childhood home still be there as vividly as it was in her memory, separated from the bush at the edge of town by a gravel road? Their house had had white asbestos shingles, dark green shutters and a porch roof she could climb onto from her window. The mailing address was c/o Alpha Mines, Bourlamaque, Quebec. It was a company house, as were the log cabins the miners lived in at the other mine in town, which meant her father had rented it from Alpha. For many years, Libby's father paid twelve dollars a month for the house; later it was raised to twenty-five.

One year her father had the mine carpenter build a garage covered with green insulbrick in the bush across from their back yard. He parked their new red Desoto there. Libby learned to drive before she was sixteen in the car that preceded the Desoto, a two-toned blue Nash.

Further down the street, around the bend before it hit the main street, were the Dions and the Paquins. The Petranovich family lived two doors away. The son, Nick, was the oldest. Then there was Jeannie. It had surprised everyone when Jeannie married Libby's brother, Wally, because she was older than he was. They'd met in California where they still lived and sent news of their wedding after it happened. Libby almost never heard from them. She recalled how much she'd hated it when the Dion boy called her younger sister, Sheila, and Jeannie Petranovich the *Hinglish Polacks*. Back then it seemed all the kids who weren't French were lumped together.

Across the backyard and a lane was the bungalow where the Dufresne family lived. She'd been friends for a while with the girl who had lived there. The girl's father, Maurice Dufresne, worked underground. The men were taken down into the depths of the earth in a cage. They spread out through dark tunnels to rock faces where they drilled holes for dynamite. After the blasts, they piled the splintered pieces of rock that were blown out into the tunnel in trolley cars that were carried on lifts up to surface. Sometimes there were still sticks of dynamite in the rock that would go off and kill someone. It was dangerous and dirty work for the men who worked underground to make a living from gold.

"You have family there?" the driver asked.

Family there? These words were the only ones Libby heard and she pondered what constituted a family. Although she suspected everyone she once knew would be gone, if there was anyone at all left they would be family, she thought. That was how it was in the north, the town so far from any large centres, none less than a day's journey away then, that it was too far to see relatives very often. You built your connections where you were, her mother had often said.

"Not any more," Libby said in answer to his question, thinking about the house on rue Champlain again. Icicles had formed on the inside of her bedroom window on long, cold winter nights. Something else, too, reverberated. A dream about a black stallion galloping toward her across a green meadow. The horse slowed as he drew nearer, a young girl with dark eyes and hair clinging to his mane. Libby longed to ride him, but her legs seemed to have turned to cement. The horse picked up speed again and galloped off toward a lake. She heard a high-pitched wail in the distance and ran toward it. As she came over a rise in the meadow, she saw the horse sinking in quicksand. The girl was on a rock, crying for help. The neighing was a piercing scream as the horse kept sinking.

"How do you get there?" the driver asked, the cab now speeding along beside the lake.

"Via Montreal," she said abruptly.

It was not like the good old days. Everyone took the train then. It was the only way to get in or out of Ile d'Or for most people. In the days when train routes and radio signals were the only things that connected the whole country.

"I come from Pakistan," he continued, not seeming to notice that she might be either disinterested or distracted. All his brothers had also come to live in Toronto. "The connecting flight from Karachi was in Paris."

Why hadn't she bought a ticket to Paris? Libby wondered. Late fall might not be the time to visit there either, but clouds and drizzle wouldn't have kept her from walking from l'Arc de Triomphe right

across the centre of the city to Place de la Nation. She knew about
rain from her visits to her sister, Sheila, in Vancouver. She had no
trouble visualizing Paris in that kind of dull, grey weather. She could
have wandered along the Seine and bought magazines from one of
the stalls or sat in small cafes and sketched the people. The buildings.
But that wasn't where she'd felt compelled to go. She had to admit to
not having any sound reason for doing what she was doing, but she
knew she had to.

"Only my sister is still in Karachi," he said.

By the time they reached High Park, she knew about his five brothers
as well as the sister in Pakistan. She was easily drawn into conversations
with strangers. Whether she liked it or not, Libby took after her mother
in some ways. Sometimes she liked the similarities of this penchant for
conversation and sometimes she would recall incidents when her mother
had embarrassed her. Particularly when, as a shy child, she would as
soon have remained invisible. Instead her mother had drawn attention
to both of them with some exuberant gesture. Still, she'd grown closer
to her mother in the years since her father died.

The sky lightened as the car sped along the shore of Lake Ontario,
past billboards, past Grenadier Pond. Alarms would be sounding,
blinds opening and letting in slits of light, traffic would gather mo-
mentum as the city sprang into the rhythms of another day. Toronto
was home now insofar as it could be when another landscape was so
deeply embedded.

Soon she would be there, Libby thought. With only forty minutes
between flights, she hoped her bag would arrive in Ile d'Or at the same
time she did.

"It will be enough," the agent had assured her, but she worried when
boarding for her plane was delayed.

Businessmen, dark-suited, filled the lounge, glancing at their watches.
Their newspapers were open to stock market quotations. Finally with
all passengers settled and belted, the aircraft rumbled toward the run-
way. When it stopped for another plane to land, Libby glanced at her
own watch, aware by the time they were aloft that her forty precious
minutes had dwindled to twenty.

As the ground receded and the shadow of the plane on highways and
fields gradually became smaller, she thought about the dream again.
About a horse sinking. She'd dreamed it over and over. And never

recounted it to anyone. Maybe in going back to Ile d'Or she would be able to confront what had happened to cause the dream. Maybe she would stop feeling that she was guilty of something.

She reached into her bag for the magazine her son, Paul, had given her. She hoped he'd marked the page for her to read. While looking for a turned down flap, a photograph of Dan Robinson surprised her. There he was, standing beside a cabin not unlike the ones in early photographs of Ile d'Or. She read the caption — *Dan Robinson in the bush*. She didn't know that he'd been on expeditions like the one she began to read about. There must be endless things she didn't know about Dan. A tall, bearded, black man, whom she'd met only a few months earlier at a party, she'd watched him quietly surveying the room. Aware that his gaze stopped when he noticed her, she was surprised when he headed in her direction. His was a face she'd seen in newspapers, magazines, on television, once at a meeting — a lawyer concerned about human rights. Now he was also a politician, the only black alderman on City Council.

"Elizabeth Morley?"

She'd nodded, intrigued that he knew her name.

"I liked your show at the Moritz Gallery," he continued, his voice a low, embracing rumble. Her watercolours were dramatic, he'd said. Her colours vibrant. "There's a distinct style emerging."

"I'm working in acrylics, too," she'd said, hiding her astonishment that he'd been following her work.

"Dan Robinson."

"Glad to meet you, Dan." His articles in the press and commentary on the radio had often made an impression on her.

He seemed to take a long time to call but, when he did, she'd readily accepted his invitation to have lunch with him.

The plane began to descend toward Montreal. As the ground rushed to meet them, Libby was relieved to think she'd make her connection after all. But as they rose abruptly, she held tightly onto the arms of her seat, feeling the way she had the one time she'd been on a ferris wheel. The suddenness of the wheel rising, then cresting before taking the plunge down again. When the pilot announced they would circle while another plane landed, she sighed. It would be impossible to make her connection after all. And by the time they arrived at the terminal, it was only sixty seconds to take off time.

Nonetheless, Libby ran frantically through the airport to the gate announced by the attendant just before her flight from Toronto landed. When she arrived, her mouth was dry and her face as brilliant as a boiled lobster.

"The passenger from Flight 400 has arrived," the man at the desk said into a telephone. To her, "It's all right. You can stop running."

The suitcase, Libby panicked. Where was her suitcase? Probably still in the hold of the other aircraft.

"Don't worry," the man said.

As the plane flew north, Libby's eyes were drawn to the shimmering lakes below. Likely the same scene her mother had looked upon forty-six years earlier, returning to Ile d'Or after the birth of her first child. Elizabeth, soon known as Libby. She'd heard her mother's stories about the small bush plane picking up a high-grader en route. He'd sat beside her in handcuffs while she held onto her baby. It was a full day's journey then, by train, by boat, and finally by plane. Through and over vast expanses of trees, rock and water to what was in those days the far north. A place where babies were born out-of-town, expectant mothers going away to stay with relatives in Montreal or Toronto for a few weeks because the two medical beds in Bourlamaque were reserved for mine emergencies. They went to Ottawa, and Rouyn or Noranda also. Now the trip from Montreal to Ile d'Or was as quick and uneventful as a subway ride in Toronto from Finch to Union Station.

On the way into town in a taxi, Libby saw a new, glass-fronted city hall and unfamiliar tracts of ranch-style bungalows. It was a mystery to her where the money came from that kept Ile d'Or alive as the gold must surely be running out by now. When she reached her hotel, she struggled in halting French to explain to the receptionist about her lost suitcase. She was glad she had packed an extra sweater, a toothbrush, and her sketchpad in her small carry-on bag.

"Ah oui, Madame."

There was a later flight and it would arrive then. The woman smiled and handed Libby the key to #407, a room that turned out to have sloping floors, stark yellow walls with chunks of plaster missing, and a light bulb hanging from the ceiling on a single black wire. She'd chosen this hotel because it was closest to the mine and the company houses where she'd lived. It surprised her how shabby it had become.

Although she wasn't tired, she lay down on the thin mattress on a bed with an iron frame. A low rumbling sound permeated the room. The mysterious muted thunder from somewhere deep within the earth she recalled from childhood. What was it like down there? she'd wondered, even more aware of the silence when it stopped.

Startled by a loud noise on the street below, Libby stood up and went to the window. Peering out, she saw a small crowd gathering around a car that had bumped into a pole. It appeared no one was injured and she figured by the time she reached the sidewalk, it would be quiet again. She wanted to go for a walk, to find some of the old familiar places.

As she stepped out through the hotel's main door, a man who appeared to be the driver was talking to a policeman. After looking them over briefly, Libby glanced toward the centre of town. There was plastic over the foundation of one house, cardboard in the windows of another. A man's white jockey shorts and some blue sheets hung on a line. When she turned toward the road to the mine where her father had worked, she saw the large black, iron letters that spelled out *Ile d'Or* at the edge of town. The same letters she'd climbed as a child.

A path had led through the bush, past a playground and the manager's large shingled white house, to the mine. Libby's father's office had been on the second floor of the main building. He'd worked at a drafting table, drawing precise lines labeled with his careful printing. When he went underground, it was to deal with mechanical problems and emergencies. She wasn't allowed to use the telephone that was in their kitchen for more than a minute or so at a time and not often.

"The mine might call," her mother said.

"He's the best damned engineer in the north," was how she often heard her father described. "That Walter Muir."

Drunk or sober.

It was hard to imagine how he achieved such precision with the bottle he sipped from that he kept hidden in a brown paper bag in a drawer. He drank Crown Royal straight in those days and he smoked pack after pack of Sweet Caporals, his fingers a rust colour that came of chain smoking and that gave his teeth a telltale yellowish tinge.

Off at an angle Libby noticed a lane where rocks jutted up between two slumping buildings covered with brown insulbrick. In spite of solid new houses she'd seen driving in from the airport, everything felt tentative, as if it could disappear in a moment. Except the rock and the bush and the grey slime left by the mine. Despite what had happened, she wished Dan were with her to see the rock at the centre of everything. Why hadn't he told her he knew this kind of country?

Turning back toward town, she came to a nightclub on the main street where she'd had her first drink. The Flamingo. It was the one rumoured to have been built with money made from selling gold smuggled out of the mine in the 1940s. High-grade, her father called it. The real thing, not the pyrite or fool's gold she and her friends sometimes found in rocks in the bush.

Even someone who wasn't actually working in the mine could find others to bring small bits of high-grade ore out, it was said. There would be subtle pressure.

"Your kid has to walk to school," the outside man might say quietly to one of the underground workers. And it was known that the mob was involved, dark figures off in places like Buffalo and New York City. Any smart miner knew what it could mean if you were once involved in high-grading and tried to back out of it.

So the illicit trade could happen whether a man worked underground or not, although there always had to be *someone* on the inside. It was Cathy McNab, the mine manager's daughter, who had finally filled Libby in on these sordid details. Her own father, Walter Muir, had expressed his disapproval that she played with some of the children who lived on mine property, but he hadn't explained why very well. She was afraid to ask what the repercussions might be for her. They were left implied.

Libby looked at the pink flamingo in the window, under a large pink sign that extended out over the street. It looked the same as when she'd had her first drink there, a rum and coke, in her teens. When her mother found out, she was horrified. But her father said not to worry so much about it, that when Libby went to university in Montreal in the fall she'd drink there anyway.

Some postcards in the window of early log cabins and aerial views of the mines distracted her and Libby decided to buy one later for her son. As she moved away from the window, a hand grasped her shoulder and she turned around to see a face that didn't seem to have aged at all.

"You must be a Dion," she said.

She would recognize those features anywhere. He wasn't Guy, the young man who had courted her almost desperately as a teenager. The man she now thought of as her first love. But reminiscent of Guy, this man, aside from a small tattoo under his ear, looked like his father.

5.

WHEN LUCIEN DION awakened that morning, one colder than any yet that fall, he'd had a premonition of something about to happen. It was more than sensing the first snowfall or ice beginning to form around the edge of the lake, but that was all he could have told anyone. He pushed back the green sleeping bag he slept under now that he'd moved out to the cabin on Lac Leboeuf and pulled on a pair of socks. His jockey shorts were on the floor beside the bed on top of the white T-shirt he wore under his sweater. Susan would be horrified if she could see how he lived now. Pulling on his underwear, he headed for the bathroom.

As he stood in front of the mirror, he shivered at the prospect of winter alone, of winter without Susan beside him in the bed. She'd slept on the left, one arm down over the side, while he curled around her with his right arm raised over his head. Sometimes he'd reached out to hold her. He still reached for her in his sleep and groaned when he woke up to find he was holding onto a pillow or part of his sleeping bag.

Since Susan left, she'd only written to give him forwarding addresses. Every three or four weeks there was a new one. Once he called her and she asked him not to call again. Over twenty-five years of marriage and she didn't want to talk to him. He bit his lip and brushed his cheeks with his hands, wiping away tears. Then he pounded his fist on the counter around the sink.

"*Maudit, tabernacle.*"

As he drove into town, Lucien fiddled with the radio until he found a station he liked. What did he have to do at the pharmacy? Maybe he could leave ordering new supplies for the cosmetics section to Charmaine now. She was young and inexperienced, but she'd learned quickly. He thought of the highway at the other end of town that went south through endless miles of bush unbroken before Mont Laurier by more than an occasional motel or cabin on a lake. Or a gas station.

It hadn't changed much since the first road was built, except that the part that was gravel when Lucien was young was paved at some point after their family's first trips out to the Laurentians and Montreal in the late forties. As a child, he'd watched the tops of trees until he was mesmerized, birch against pine, poplar against pine, branches reaching toward the sky.

Nor was the town very different, except most of the English people were gone and there were new houses at the far side of town, near the water tower, and on the road to the airport. If you'd lived in Ile d'Or all your life, as Lucien had, it was hard to imagine why anyone would ever leave. The local politicians had shown some foresight in attracting business to an industrial park and developing the airport for flights to the far north so that commerce went on even when some mines began to close down. If you did leave, as many of his contemporaries had when they married or found work elsewhere, it seemed they wondered why anyone stayed. For Lucien, moving somewhere else was inconceivable. Even after Susan took the bus to Montreal, leaving behind only a note and some clothes she no longer wanted.

That note had been on the kitchen table when he came in from the pharmacy only a three months earlier, her words on the paper rising like a cold wave to encompass him. His jaw had become tight, as if caught in a vise that extended right around his head. He swore now as he visualized her final words. *Feed the dog.*

Braking, Lucien pulled over to the side of the road on the outskirts of Ile d'Or and put his head down on the wheel. It was at least ten minutes before he was ready to drive again.

In town, Lucien parked in front of the nightclub with the pink flamingo on the overhead sign. It was the first nightclub in town. Now there were others, modern and with better entertainment. All the same, the old timers, of whom he knew he was one now, still went into The Flamingo for a beer, or something stiffer, after work. He merely glanced at the sign as he got out of his car and headed for Pharmacie Dion, the store his father had owned until his death. And when he died and left everything to his two sons, Guy, too far-gone with the booze to give a damn, had wanted nothing to do with the business.

As he was about to turn into the pharmacy, Lucien saw a woman looking at the postcards in The Flamingo's window. She looked familiar, yet he knew she was someone who didn't belong in the town. A visitor.

A tourist. In November? Who would come to Ile d'Or in November? And that feeling of some impending event heightened. He knew this woman from somewhere.

"Elizabeth," he said, reaching out to put his hand on her shoulder. "You are Elizabeth Muir, aren't you?"

"You must be a Dion," the woman said.

"Lucien," the man said.

"Lucien?"

"Yes."

"*Mon dieu*, but you're like your father."

6.

LUCIEN LOOKED JUST like Monsieur Dion had thirty years earlier when Libby worked in his drugstore for a summer. A handsome man with a square face and lines that came from laughter, Monsieur Dion was like someone who always anticipated good weather. He was as jovial and outgoing as Walter Muir, when sober, was quiet and introspective. Libby had watched him with curious anticipation, waiting for him to say something unexpected.

"You want to run the shop, Libby," he once said. "Just brush up on your French a little."

"So you still live here," Libby said, smiling warmly at Lucien.

"In a cabin out on Lac Leboeuf," he said. "When my father died, I took over the store. I'm on my way there, but I'd like to have coffee with you. I haven't had my breakfast yet either. Will you join me?"

Libby nodded. "How's Guy?"

Lucien lips were pursed and his eyes narrowed into slits that seemed designed to avoid scrutiny. "He's dead," he said. "Last year." He turned away abruptly and went into the store beside the nightclub. The sign, repainted in white with black letters, still read Pharmacie Dion.

Libby watched him through the window, a numbness making its way through her throat and stomach. How could Guy be dead? If there was one thing about Guy she recalled vividly, it was his curious eyes darting so that he wouldn't miss anything, his need to know what was going on everywhere. How animated he always was. Full of life.

What would Guy make of her now? Her reflection in the glass of the store window, long gold earrings thrust through her ear lobes on small fishhooks, looked out of place here. Although her mid-length brown winter jacket, pulled from her closet as the warmest she owned, seemed to fit into what anyone here might wear. She watched flakes of snow flutter down through bare branches to the road without really seeing them.

When Lucien returned, they walked to a restaurant further down the block where so long ago Libby and Guy had eaten French fries and gravy washed down with large glasses of Coca Cola. Lucien held the door open and gestured at a table near the window where she sat in the chair he pulled out for her.

"Why did you come back?" he asked. "You haven't been here for years."

Libby shrugged. "Maybe that's why," she said, almost as if she believed what she was saying. "It's been too long."

"How long are you staying?"

"Just a few days."

His eyes swept over her face, down to her hands on the table. "Are you married?" he continued in French as he had from the moment they first recognized each other and began to talk.

"I was," she said. "What about you?"

His hands shook as he pulled out a blue package and lit a cigarette. "My wife just left me and went to Montreal." He inhaled deeply and blew the smoke off to the side.

Libby didn't know what to say, so she was quiet. It was a long time since Barton had walked out on her, since her own hands had started to shake at the very mention of marriage.

"Do you have children?" he asked finally.

She nodded. "And you?"

As she listened to him, she felt a reprieve from any conversation about what she was doing here, about the breakdown of her marriage with all the questions that elicited. About why. No, for a while they would talk about their children. She would tell him about Rosemary now living in an apartment she shared with a friend and Paul at home probably tempted to have the wild parties she'd said were "off limits."

"Sorry, Paul," she'd said. "Not more than one friend at a time."

Her mind wandered as she thought of her children until a loud clearing of the throat caught her attention. She looked across at Lucien.

"They're all living away from here now," he was saying.

And she could tell that she'd missed things she couldn't ask about now. How many were there in his family? Were they boys or girls? What were they doing? She supposed she could ask him where they were as he'd just told her none of them were in Ile d'Or any more.

7.

A S MICHELLE DROVE toward the dress shop, up the street from The Flamingo, the car radio was playing. Leonard Cohen sang in one long drone that sent shivers through her, an icon who had pierced the barriers of her existence, moving her into an appreciation of English lyrics she usually reserved for French songs. She thought Nick might understand.

She was surprised to find someone already waiting at the door to Chic Choc when she parked in front of the shop. It was Charmaine, the young woman with a friendly smile who worked in the drug store.

"*Est-ce que la robe est arrivée?*" Did the dress arrive? Charmaine asked as Michelle walked across the sidewalk. Fair hair pulled back, immaculate makeup on her eyes and lips, Charmaine was becoming a good customer.

Michelle smiled and waved Charmaine into the shop as they exchanged the usual pleasantries. Both of them spoke in French. Since her mother died there was little occasion for Michelle to use English. She hadn't visited her mother's grave in a while. Maybe it was time. Although she had been to Francine's and her father's only the previous day. What would it have been like if her sister had lived? Nothing would have been the same, but she had no idea how it would have been different. Except her mother's sadness would not have happened, the blank stares that Michelle began to encounter from the time they heard about the accident. And her Pa's anger, which acquired a new dimension then. It simmered for days on end and then there would be an explosion. She'd learned to come in late or stay away when she could feel that coming. Maybe it wasn't so surprising she married young. She wanted to get as far away from her family, and the north, as she could then. For a while, she'd succeeded.

"It's in the back waiting for you," Michelle said. A special dress she'd picked out in Montreal, one with two thin shoulder straps holding up a low-cut top that would have the men lining up for a dance on New Year's Eve. It was dark midnight blue with a sheen and a few beads sewn into the bodice in a delicate pattern. "Come try it on."

"The dance is at The Flamingo," Charmaine said.

"Yes." That was where it had been held for years. Proud of the spirit at his club, her father had started the tradition of a New Year's Eve dance. Although he'd often told her he wished he'd called the nightclub The Flamenco.

"I should have listened to your mother," he said. Elaine had told him that Flamingo sounded tacky. "She told me about the wonderful Spanish dance and I didn't pay attention."

Instead he was stuck with pink swizzle sticks with flamingos on them. And flamingos everywhere inside the club. At least no one had put any of the pink birds on his grave, Michelle thought, smiling to herself.

Her father had met her mother in Edinburgh during a blackout, which was his story. An English girl from Bristol, he'd said. He was supposed to be meeting a blind date and he had her picture, but he said when he spotted this girl in the beam of the tram scanning the crowd, he tossed the photograph in a nearby bin, strode toward her, and gallantly asked her to go out with him. She was in the army, too, a payroll clerk or something. They saw a Colonel Blimp movie. Later he liked to tell the story of her mother being very shy until she met up with this Frenchie from Canada. They were married on a Sunday, the day before he left for France, the first wedding in England on a Sunday in twenty years. There had to be a special request by wire to the pope.

"Are you going?" Charmaine asked.

"Going? Going where?"

"To the New Year's dance."

"I haven't thought about it yet." Michelle wasn't sure why as she still knew almost everyone in town. Ever since she'd delivered the local weekly paper as a child. In those days, the Dion family lived in a shingled house just beyond the company houses. The next one was where the Mitchells lived. Coming back onto mine property, the green house next door to the Mitchell's seemed a smaller version of one of the bunkhouses closer to the mine, with a lot of rooms. There were so many people in that house, she couldn't keep them straight. Just as she was getting to know who one was, someone different would pay her. They talked to her in French or heavily accented English and she said thank you or *merci* when they handed her the money. She figured they all worked either at one of the mines or at the lumber mill.

Charmaine pulled her boots off before taking the dress and entering the change room. Soon her jacket and skirt were flung over the top of the door, her stockinged feet peeking out from underneath where there was an open space. When she came out, she stood in front of the mirror, pulling the bodice up so that it fit snugly over her breasts. Michelle stood behind her and adjusted the material over the young woman's hips.

"I don't know," Charmaine said as if she were visualizing herself at the dance and finding the image wanting.

"It needs to be shortened a bit," Michelle said, measuring in her mind's eye the younger woman's appearance when this one small task was accomplished. Stunning, she thought, although she knew Charmaine couldn't see that yet. "Do you want me to pin it up?" she asked.

As Michelle pinned up the hem, Charmaine began to smile. She, too, could see now how well the dress suited her. It dawned on Michelle in that moment that she was content here. Her childhood recollections were of a world that still felt safe, it was true. She hadn't been aware of the rugged nature of the town then, or that there might be places that were different. Until her mother counted airplanes for the Distant Early Warning line, recruited by the government during the Cold War to look for signs of an impending attack from Russia, it hadn't dawned on Michelle that there might be dangers somewhere out in the world that could affect her. In the winter, she'd imagine she was an Eskimo, living in an igloo. As children, she and her friends hollowed out spaces in the huge snow banks the ploughs left and these became homes or forts. Huddling down behind or inside the snow banks, she could visualize husky dogs pulling sleighs across large, empty expanses. When she skied, she strapped on her skis at the back door and headed out along trails to get across town. No one ever thought a bear or a cougar or some other wild animal might attack. This was how they moved around. Deeper in the woods, the prospectors wore snowshoes.

So once again, Michelle became a northerner. Once again she lived in a town where the neighbours all likely knew what she was doing. It used to bother her, but now it had its advantages. She didn't think they knew how often she went to the cemetery and stood beside her parents' graves where, two years after her return, her mother had also been buried, though on the opposite side of the highway from her father and Francine. People often don't grasp that you have a relationship with your parents that continues after they die, she thought. Her picture of them as well as her relationship to them kept on changing and evolving. What troubled her seemed to alter over time as she understood them better. And her visits at the cemetery had both strengthened and calmed her.

She was often told it had been a brave decision to leave Dominic. She'd known she had to; what would the kids do without a mother? So, with Elise and Dawn in tow, gradually she fit into the life of the town, which had become a thriving northern community. The airstrip was used by planes flying to the hydroelectric development at James Bay, the industrial park flourished, and although some mines closed, there always seemed to be others opening.

"What do you think?" Charmaine asked, gazing intently into the mirror as she turned to inspect herself from every side.

Michelle wished momentarily that she was young again, with endless choices still waiting to surprise her. Waiting for the dance on New Year's Eve with great expectation, ready to whirl around the floor. Perhaps she'd have a date, perhaps she wouldn't. Either way, she'd be aware of all the people around the floor watching her, admiring her.

"Wonderful," she said, smoothing the dress at the back.

"How long would it take for it to be ready?" Charmaine asked.

"Does it feel like the right length now?"

"*Oui.*"

"Only a day or two," Michelle said. She finished pinning the dress up all around now that Charmaine had decided, measuring first with a dressmaker's ruler and pressing a small rubber bulb that sprayed white powdered chalk on the hem line to make sure it was even all the way around. Charmaine went back into the change room and handed the dress to Michelle through the door.

Michelle put it on top of her sewing machine. If business was slow, she could start hemming the dress that afternoon. If she were busy, it would wait until after she closed the shop in the evening. But the more she could do now, before the season was really underway, the easier life would be as the festivities took over.

When Charmaine left, Michelle put a plastic cover over the dress and hung it near the machine. She wished one of her daughters still lived here, but she understood why they had left as soon as they could. Opportunities in a small town could not compare to those they would find in a metropolitan city. But why Dawn had become so much of a wanderer, never able to settle anywhere, worried her. What the girls had experienced would have had an impact. The expression on her daughters' faces when their father became rough and used filthy language was all she'd needed to convince her that she had to get them as far away from him as possible. He'd found them before she left Montreal and taken both girls to his car, screaming as he dragged them from the house. The neighbours heard something and called the police, but it was hours before they brought Elise and Dawn back.

Michelle felt her own parents had lived out a kind of grand love story, however sordid some of the details seemed at times. Although Maurice Dufresne was her mother's only love, she never learned his language. At first, they lived on mine property, where most of the other residents lived. Except the men in the bunkhouses whom they rarely saw dressed in anything other than miners' garb heading underground — the English, French and the DPs who came from Europe. Finns, Ukrainians, Poles, Russians. It was said that the Finns were the best shaft sinkers in the business. Some of them lived on the mine property. One had a sauna and after sitting in it, a bunch of naked Finns would jump out into the snow.

Now when she stood at her father's grave or kneeled in front of it, she would trace the letters of his name and whisper to him, telling him about his granddaughters, so young when he died that he'd scarcely known them. He was there for the ceremony when a street was named for him, but a year later he was gone.

Dear Michelle, I'm sorry for your loss and my heart is with you. Your father was a man of courage. He gave a lot to this town.

A note had come from Mrs. Allen, the wife of the stockbroker who was there in the early days, another from the daughter of one of the general practitioners, and oddly enough, one from Nick Petranovich. There was no letter from Libby Muir, but she hadn't expected one. If she'd known Libby's father had died, she wouldn't have written a note either. But the hope held for most of her life, that the feeling of being ostracized would go away, that she'd finally been accepted, never happened. To the mine engineer and his daughter, to everyone in that family, Michelle was always her father's daughter. *And yes, I was my father's daughter. But if he were a high-grader, I didn't have anything to do with it.*

8.

NICK LAY ON the bed in the former bunkhouse, more recently converted into a bed and breakfast, on the main street of what had been Bourlamaque, now absorbed into Ile d'Or. The other mine was just beyond the houses, close enough to Alpha that he wondered if long ago there had been competing claims. He was conscious of history surrounding him, a history that included him. Ile d'Or was a frontier town when he was a child, Bourlamaque where the two mines were and the houses on company property. He supposed that the miners who slept where he now lay must have used a nearby path that went through the bush to the entrance of the mine. He hadn't walked that way yet. An image of the house in Lawrence Park, a solid brick structure overlooking a ravine on an affluent tree-lined street in north Toronto, where he'd lived with Marie and his daughter, flitted through his mind. A stack of dirty laundry and an unmade bed awaited him there. What good was that house to him now? Maybe he should sell it.

His belongings could go in a locker and he would store whatever furniture he wanted to keep. Maybe he'd move into a hotel room or a flat until he decided whether he wanted to buy a condominium or rent something. For a long time, he'd wanted to go to India and follow the Ganges up to its source in the mountains. He wouldn't have time to go there now, but he could start to plan such a trip. He would bathe in the Ganges. Maybe write a book about it, although someone had probably already done that. And why would he want to write a book? The few articles he'd written had taken more time than he wanted to spend. As well as more concentration and isolation than he enjoyed. Dealing with individual patients in his practise already required enough of that. But the idea of both the trip and a book wouldn't go away.

What about a novel about this town? He could remember his father, sitting at the table in the kitchen. Sometimes he'd talk about gold, saying he knew that some men stole it. All he needed was to end up in a jail somewhere, Roman Petranovich had told his family. He was an honest man and Nick respected that about him, but he still bore the wounds of the thick strap his father's strong right arm had wielded. Not the red marks and bruises of his childhood, but the wounds that were still burned into his psyche.

But the book wouldn't be about that, rather something to do with high-grading. He could give some of Roman's characteristics to this high-grader, a tough man, probably not a French man like Maurice Dufresne. He wouldn't tell Michelle. She might be offended, thinking that he was basing a character on her father even so. To remove any doubt, he'd make him a DP who came from Russia or Poland. A displaced person. That's what he himself was called as a child. Either that or an *Hinglish Polack*. His character would be clever, able to fool both the bosses and the police. He wouldn't get caught. Even when security became more ingenious, he would get enough gold out of the mine to do something that made him stand out. It would be something fancy. Not a dive with hookers like the Purple Pig. In the early days, the man who managed the mill owned the Purple Pig, the local whore house. On payday, he met his men there and that was where they spent their money. It was on the main street of Ile d'Or next to Archie's, the dry cleaners, not far away from a slight rise in the centre of town where St. Luc's, the Roman Catholic church, towered over everything. When the first traffic lights were put in, one was installed in front of the rectory. The local priest never thought the red light was for him and after looking both ways, he drove right through it. No, the establishment in Nick's novel wouldn't resemble the Purple Pig and it would be even more substantial than The Flamingo. A hotel perhaps. With a dance hall. A dining room. Chandeliers.

The high-grader might have accomplices on surface. After he left the cage that brought him up from underground and before he reached "the dry" where he changed his clothes, he would need someone to pick up what he left beside the path cached in small rock piles. Before that became necessary, he would sometimes hide the contraband on his person, somewhere no one would think to look. Or he might throw it over the fence and retrieve it later. That way he would receive his cut from the big guys in New York and wouldn't have to worry about anyone else.

There were various middlemen involved who would reimburse the miners for a fraction of the gold price. Everyone took his cut on the way to the ultimate buyer.

At some stage, "the dry" was split into two parts — the first an area where miners took off their street clothes and stored them in lockers. After taking showers, they donned clothes that they wore only underground and at quitting time they did the reverse. The work clothes were wet and dirty when the men came up to surface and were hung on a basket and raised high above to dry. Then the miners would walk naked through the security and shower area to where they would don their street clothes again. He'd heard that the rate of thievery fell then.

Nick had heard a lot about "the dry" because every time his father went on or off shift, he went through it. It was from him that Nick knew the revamped "dry" had made it more difficult for anyone to steal anything. How did Maurice get away with it? Nick wondered. It had been rumoured, and believed by many, that his high-grading was what helped him open The Flamingo.

Laundering the miners' clothing was sometimes lucrative when contracted out because some dense gold dust might have settled in pant cuffs and pockets. Nick wasn't sure how the laundry staff got rid of it to earn their profit, but he supposed that those who sought buyers knew the men who would take the fine dust. A bit like the townspeople knew the local stockbroker and some of them bet on penny mines trying to strike it rich. Some of them did, too. As far as he knew, all of that was legal.

The sound of blasting rumbled underneath him and Nick felt his bed move ever so slightly. Falling asleep soon after, he dreamed of the subway running only a block away from the first apartment he and Marie had rented near Bloor Street. Marie was standing at the door, peering in at him. She had no clothes on above her waist. He leaned against the wall and looked at her breasts, one of them dripping gold. A river of gold.

"Want some?" she asked.

He tried to catch the gold in a plastic bottle, but she kept dancing around so he couldn't.

"You're useless," she said.

He wanted to kill her. As he struggled to breathe, he woke up, afraid he'd hurt her. Then he remembered that she was in Texas. This was another dream, worse even than the ones he'd dreamed about his father for so many years. He didn't know why those stopped because they went on for a long time after his father died. Then one day he realized it had been months, even years, since he'd had any.

Looking at the red light on the clock radio beside him, he saw that it was almost six. It wasn't too early to go to the cookery. No one there would recognize him any longer; he wouldn't be able to go in and eat a huge breakfast of eggs and bacon, toast, marmalade, coffee just because he was Roman Petranovich's son. Porridge if he wanted it. Sometimes he'd eaten there with his father when Roman was in a good mood, expansive, showing off his son who would soon be old enough to go underground and work in the mine. But Nick had other plans. He would go to New York and study photography. He did, too. But after a matter of weeks, he decided that he wanted to be a doctor. It took forever, but he had been determined. Now he wondered if he would have been happier if he'd stuck with photography.

By the time he showered, shaved, and dressed, it was eight o'clock. He went out and headed toward a small restaurant on the main street. He liked going there because there were photographs on the walls of the early town site, of scrubby trees and houses in bleak landscapes, of mine shafts. Roads of gravel and wooden sidewalks on the commercial streets. It wasn't the only place he'd walked by where he'd seen such photographs through the front window, but he'd tried this one and would likely keep coming back to it. As he walked, the boy from the other day, who had peered at him over the rock, suddenly jumped out from the dark corner of a building and stood directly in front of him.

"Hello," the boy said, as if they were old acquaintances by now. His lightweight jacket had ragged edges and he wore no mitts or gloves.

Get lost, Nick thought. He shrugged, buried his ears in his collar and pushed his scarf up over his chin. It bothered him to have to pull out French phrases from the recesses of his past. He'd be glad to have the language come back to him, but he didn't want to be forced into it by unexpected intrusions.

"Cold?" the boy asked, putting his hands up his sleeves. *Froid?*

Now he'd likely offer to show him some coffee shop. But Nick beat him to it. "Hey," Nick said. "Come with me and I'll buy your breakfast. Where do you live anyway?"

"Je ne comprends pas."

Oh, well, polish up your fractured French, Nick thought, talking to himself. It wasn't hard for him to imagine what life this boy had stepped out of, one where the father drank or maybe the mother, where the dishes were strewn around the kitchen and in the sink, unwashed for days, perhaps weeks. Empty bottles, broken glasses, dirty bathtub, towels on the floor, hairs in the sink, a yellowed bowl in the toilet, a cracked toilet seat, broken windows. It had to be something like that. Maybe Michelle would know.

Nick soon made himself understood and the boy ended up sitting across from him at one of the tables, gobbling up fried eggs and sausages. He looked almost gaunt, with dark circles under his eyes. The town must not be doing as well as it appeared on the surface. Nick couldn't understand what the kid was doing wandering the streets on his own and how he had come to attach himself to a man who was to him a stranger.

"What's your name?" Nick asked.

"Marcel."

"Who's your father?"

"Don't have one."

That's where questions would get you, Nick thought. He'd trapped himself in one line of inquiry and didn't know how to recoup. *Pretty stupid for a shrink.*

"Okay, kid," he said. "Do you have a last name?"

"Blouin."

That was the name of the lake where Nick had gone to swim with Guy Dion and Paul Paquin when they were the age of this vagabond boy. A gravel road ran out of town and crossed the railroad tracks until it passed a one-lane road down to a spot on Blouin Lake where small bush planes took off and landed. He, Guy, and Paul rode their bicycles down to Hall's Landing where they sat and watched the single engine planes glide in above the trees. They landed on floats on the water, rocking from side to side as the pilot steadied the aircraft, leaving a long trough of waves behind as they pulled into the dock.

He wondered about Guy. His name hadn't come up yet in conversation, but he'd noticed a headstone in the cemetery. Dead for a year now? He would have been a young man when he died, probably around the time of his own fictitious obituary, Nick thought. How could he have forgotten to ask Michelle? He remembered when Guy and Libby Muir had seemed so entangled with each other; Guy enamoured for sure, although he'd never been able to tell with Libby. He'd certainly seen them together often enough, back then when they'd all known each other. Even though he was older, as was Lucien, their lives had been intertwined because they all lived either in company houses that belonged to Alpha or not far away from them. He'd forgotten how much that sense of being part of something had mattered to him. When he saw Michelle, he would ask her about Guy, and about Libby.

"*Merci,*" the boy said, wiping his arm across his face.

Nick was so deep in thought that he had momentarily forgotten Marcel's presence. He nodded at the boy, then chuckled softly as he noticed that Marcel's plate was so clean he might have picked it up and licked it.

"Do you want anything else?" he asked.

The boy's eyes lit up. "*Chocolat,*" he said.

"A croissant?"

Marcel shook his head as if only an imbecile would ask such a stupid question. "*Non,*" he said. "*Chocolat chaud.*"

Of course, Nick thought. Just what a tough kid who knew all about hookers would ask for. How was he supposed to know? Well, he'd order another coffee for himself at the same time. Or maybe he'd have a hot chocolate, too. Hot milk mixed with chocolate, topped with whipped cream. He looked around for the waiter, thinking that once they'd had their drinks he wanted to get rid of the boy. He hoped he could do so easily.

9.

AFTER LUCIEN RETURNED to the pharmacy, Libby remained seated in the restaurant under a black and white photograph of a mine shaft, set down in rocky terrain. She studied it for a long time. Did she remember the bare land where trees had been cut down or was she just remembering the many photographs her father had kept in albums and of stories she'd heard?

She stood up to examine the other photographs that were hung around the room. Log cabins surrounded by birch. Lac Leboeuf, seen from the rise at the end of town. Scrubby trees everywhere. The houses for the miners, the lakes and rivers used as the primary means of transportation at first. Images from her childhood that were so familiar had become a historical record.

A colour photograph of a sky as wide as over the prairies, a thin strip of pink on the horizon with the head-frame of a mine etched against it as the town's sentinel caught her attention. Looking at these photographs, even a stranger would be able to tell that mine shafts were the centre of everything. Much like the Eiffel Tower was the symbol of Paris, she thought. In linking the two, she wondered how she might paint them together, their surrounding landscapes nonetheless so disparate. She tried to remember the mine where she'd worked in the assay lab during summers while at university, out a few miles from town, off the highway. They tested for lead, zinc, and copper in the lab, not gold. Yvette, the woman who had taught her how to measure the samples and mix them with hydrochloric acid, spoke only French. Libby began to dream in French that summer. But when Yvette wasn't there, the rest of the women all spoke English.

Libby was seventeen her first summer at the mine. She knew about the man who owned the whore house and what whores were, but she didn't know much about sex yet, hadn't paid much attention to her mother's awkward attempt to explain what she called "the birds and the bees."

That seemed preposterous now, but that summer had changed things. When the women in the lab started to talk, her eyes widened.

"Seven inches," said the tall blonde with greasy hair.

"You're kidding," laughed the redhead.

"No, it's true. Big and hard and at least seven fucking inches."

Did they ever wonder what she thought? Talking as if the daughter of the engineer at Alpha would understand whatever it was they knew. Maybe not caring if she did. Whatever their reasons, she was careful not to let them know what they talked about confused and shocked her.

Libby smiled at this recollection of a time when she was still so incredibly young and naïve. As the waitress poured more coffee into her cup, she returned this smile. Almost as if they shared some secret knowledge.

"You're English, aren't you?" the waitress asked, looking pleased with herself.

Nodding, Libby was surprised at the intensity of the other woman's scrutiny, as if she were trying to figure out not only who Libby was but also why she was here. As if she prided herself on keeping up with everything in town and would be able to pass this on as some nugget to her friends and family later. *This English woman came into the restaurant with Monsieur Dion.* Libby could hear the gossip that would emerge. At least it would have when she was a child or teenager and some stranger had appeared in Ile d'Or. Well, she didn't intend to tell the other woman that she'd lived here, nor about the two children she'd just described to Lucien. Her daughter, Rosemary; her son, Paul. The waitress probably knew the three Dion children, grown up and working in other parts of the province. And that was enough, Libby thought. It was other names and faces she began to think about now. Guy's, in particular. His mischievous grin and his dark eyes darting everywhere. He never missed a thing.

When she finished her coffee, she left the restaurant and walked until she found the playground beside the path to the mine. A barren lot where once there'd been a slide, swings, and a set of teeter-totters. She could almost hear the voices of children playing "Truth or Consequences." *Libby, kiss Guy Dion.* That was the consequence, but Guy ran off into the bush.

After wandering from the playground to the rocks across from the fence outside the mine and down a path to a trail that led out of town to the ski hill, she was tired. Stopping on her way back to the hotel only long enough to buy a newspaper, all she wanted was to put her feet up. Spreading the newsprint pages across her bed, she lay down on her stomach with her head raised and her hair falling over her forehead. As she skimmed through the pages, names jumped out at her. *Paquin, Dion, Frechette, Charlebois.* No English ones any more. Finally she fell asleep, sprawled across the pages. A horse neighed in the distance and she ran toward it. Coming suddenly over a rise in the land, she saw it sinking into mud. Susan was crying. And there were other voices. *Calice. Tabernacle.* She awoke sweating, jumped up and went into the bathroom where she drank a glass of cold water. The horse. The horse. Always there, creeping up on her unexpectedly. Riding through her life. Sinking into quicksand.

The telephone rang. When she reached for it, she had no idea how long she'd been asleep or what time it was.

"What about dinner?" Lucien asked. "I can't leave such an old friend of Guy's back in town to have dinner alone. Please join me."

His voice aroused vague fears in her and she found it momentarily hard to remember the man on the other end of the line was not a stranger.

"Will you meet me downstairs in the lobby?" Lucien asked. "I'm just about to close the pharmacy."

Still feeling anxious, she nonetheless agreed. It could be anything she was afraid of, the noises from underground. The thought of those dark recesses where only men could go. It seemed foolish now to have come here. When she looked in the small, cracked mirror over the wash basin, she saw tiny lines fanning out from the corners of her eyes, lines that would deepen as she became older until her face became her mother's lined face. Maybe it was old age creeping up ready to snare her that frightened her. She backed away and took her purse from the bed. A strip of light from the hall filtered in along the edge of the door, onto the faded orange carpet peppered with cigarette burns. It was a mining town, after all! Libby had to remind herself.

Downstairs, Lucien leaned against the receptionist's desk. He took a drag on a cigarette and blew smoke out into the room. His face softened when he saw her. The receptionist looked surprised.

Like the waitress, Libby thought. At some level, it amused her. At another, she felt almost spied upon. Everyone would know something without really understanding anything. But maybe that was true of her also. She thought she knew a lot, but what did she actually know?

"My car is parked over there," Lucien said as they stepped out onto the sidewalk.

"Can we walk a while?" she asked.

"*Bien sur.* "

A block away, they stopped in front of the Second World War monument in the middle of the boulevard that led to the mine. Libby read the names listed under the dates, 1939-1945. *Tremblay, Hawryluk, Kalliomaki, Martin, McDougall, Dufresne, Paquin, Paquin, Paquin.* Three names from one family. Twenty-seven men from Ile d'Or killed in that war. Yet the town had barely been born.

"Do you remember when the war ended?" she asked.

Her father had written from overseas that soon he would be coming back. The Muir family had lined up in front of their white house for the cameras to snap photographs of the Union Jack raised on the lawn with the neighbourhood children gathered around. The end of the war meant the dangers they'd heard about regularly over the radio were over, but to the Muir children it mainly signified their father would soon be coming home. It was a few more weeks before Walter Muir actually arrived on the steps of the house on rue Champlain and practically as soon as he'd had a chance to sit down, Libby ran to the shelves to find a book for him to read. Her father, who had gone overseas to protect Britain and because of something he talked about called democracy, was finally back. Nor had she understood what it meant that as a Captain and an engineer, he was called upon to train young soldiers who would go to the front. That assignment meant he did not manage to go overseas himself until the last year of the war and never saw battle, something that had disappointed him. But he'd come back to Bourlamaque, unlike those men whose names were listed on the monument.

"Sheila scarcely remembered him and Wally thought this man at the dinner table who slept in the same room as Mum was an intruder," Libby said. "Wally was only a month old when he left. As the eldest, I guess I was the only one who really knew him, he was gone so long. Before he left, I sat in the green armchair in the living room nestled in the crook of his arm while he read about Rikki-Tikki-Tave and Shere Khan. And some book called *Jock and the Bushveld* which he brought from South Africa." The books he read to her had opened other worlds. Outside snow might be falling on the northern bush, but she was in the jungle. In India. Or in Africa. *Don't stop, Daddy!*

"When I found a book and asked him to read it to me, he said he had to go to the mine."

To see McNab, the mine manager. Her mother had frequently asked Cathy McNab to come home for dinner after church on Sunday. But when Cathy came she and Libby fought over something trivial. And Cathy, a year younger, with the authority she was able to exert by fearlessly making her own decisions, would stay only as long as she had to.

"And he didn't say he would read to me later. I was so disappointed," she said. "He just went out the door and started down the road. I waited and waited and waited. When he finally came home, it was after supper and dark already and his words were slurred. There was someone else with him. I looked out my bedroom window and saw Black Steve." He was called that because of his dark curly hair. The other Steve in Ile d'Or, who was blonde, was called White Steve.

"Oh, Walter," her mother had said when he came home later. "For heaven's sakes." Surely he hadn't gone away to join the army to come home a drunkard.

"Of cors'h not," her father had replied, leaning against the wall to keep himself steady.

It was after that war, the one known as the Second World War, that Walter Muir became a serious drinker. That night was just the beginning. On weekdays, her father would go to the white stucco hotel on the main street, to the bar in the basement where the men from the mine went to drink. They called it the sump. It was in the Alpha Hotel, the hotel where Libby was now staying. Whenever she'd see her father head in that direction as she watched for him from the back window, her stomach would churn. She knew his place at the head of the oak table would be empty and they would eat their meal in uneasy silence punctuated by their mother's occasional comments. Trying to read the signs of what to expect next, her mother's forced cheerful tone left Libby even more apprehensive.

When she heard the door slam late in the night, she'd listen for her father's unsteady gait in the hall. She'd count how many times she heard caps come off bottles of beer in the kitchen. He should have been grateful he didn't die in the war. Instead he did this stupid drinking thing that made him stagger home and fall downstairs. *Please Daddy. Won't you stop?* She wracked her brain for something she could say that would make him stop. *Crash.* Once he fell down the basement stairs and landed in a heap at the bottom. Libby thought he was dead that time. When he rose slowly, his eyes befuddled, blood dripped down his forehead. She'd cried softly as she watched him lurch toward the bedroom, a dirty handkerchief pressed against his forehead.

"Not again, Walter. Not again," her mother said plaintively. "You promised. You heard your father, Libby?"

"Umhn," she'd nodded, but Libby had ceased to believe him. Oh, sometimes his resolve lasted a week, a month, but never longer and she imagined herself part of some other family who lived far away. Sitting on the far side of the rock across from their house, she forgot her mother had sent her out to pick blueberries. Or that her father had gone to the sump again. Instead, she studied the contours of rocks and the shapes of trees. And one day she took a scribbler with her and began to sketch the trees in the margins, small white spring flowers, the clouds, and the swings in the playground in the distance. When she did this, she forgot time altogether. She forgot everything.

Lucien put his hand on her shoulder. "Are you hungry?" he asked.

She read the names on the monument once more. *Tremblay, Hawryluk, Kalliomaki, Martin, McDougall, Dufresne, Paquin, Paquin, Paquin.* Then she counted them again. Twenty-seven.

"What happened to Guy?" she asked quietly.

Lucien's hand dropped to his side and he cleared his throat. "He drank himself to death," he said. "They found his body in the Leduc Hotel. But they didn't find him until the smell got bad. Until you couldn't even recognize him. They called me in to do the I.D. I've never seen anything like it. He'd burst in the heat. We didn't let Maman see him."

There was a green Export cigarette package on the ground next to the monument. Her parents, Charlotte and Walter Muir, had smoked Sweet Caporals and Guy's Maman, Buckinghams. Libby didn't want to think about her father's drinking or about Guy Dion splattered on the walls of a hotel room. It was easier to remember the twenty-seven men killed on the battlefield.

Lucien picked up the empty Export package and crushed it in his hand. "Let's go and eat," he said.

10.

MICHELLE SORTED THROUGH the fall merchandise, deciding what she would put on sale as the Christmas season approached. It didn't take her full concentration and she found thoughts of Nick Petranovich breaking into her awareness. His presence had brought memories to the fore in a way she hadn't faced in a long time. Right back to her earliest childhood when they were all newcomers. Not many knew about the areas around Amos and Senneterre that were settled earlier, that the reason it was possible to get to Ile d'Or by water then was the river that ran from these early settlements to the newest gold find. It was a means of transport that drew prospectors, miners, money. And new towns were born almost overnight with roads built of cordwood and hastily constructed houses.

Michelle had her first drink in a bar when she was just fifteen. When Duplessis was in power, no one was ever stopped for drinking under age. No one ever seemed to be arrested for putting moose meat into the hamburger in the local restaurants either. Everyone knew in October or November when the season began and the hunters drove into town with a moose strapped to the roofs of their cars, the darkened hamburger would appear soon after.

There was a tap on the glass and Michelle looked up to see a shadow on the other side of the door. It was dark now and she had already locked up, but she went to see who was there. It was Marcel Blouin.

"What is it, Marcel?" she asked, thinking he likely wanted something to eat. The boy scavenged and often prevailed upon the town's residents for food. Everyone knew that his mother drank too much and that his father had taken off long ago.

"There's a man in town from Toronto."

"Yes, I know." It had been a couple of days since she'd seen Nick. He'd said he would call, ask her to dinner. She was surprised by the sense of disappointment she felt that he hadn't yet.

"Did you know him from before?" Marcel persisted.

"Yes." She'd known him as a child, she told the boy. Why did he want to know? Marcel always asked so many questions. He was a bright kid, probably bright enough to go to college, but odds were he'd never get there. Maybe he was looking for a father; maybe that was why he attached himself so easily to strangers.

"I'm hungry," he said. *J'ai faim.*

If she were at home, she would make him a peanut butter and jam sandwich and watch him eat it hungrily. As it was, she decided to give him enough money to buy a hamburger. He'd like the dark red meat more than something she could cook for him. She always gave him either food or money. At the beginning, she did it for the company. Now it was because she saw he needed the food. She'd given him work to do to earn it: he helped her out in the store sometimes, taking out the garbage, running the vacuum over the floor. And cut her grass at home with the old push lawn mower. In the winter, he shoveled the sidewalk at both places.

"I don't know how long the man is going to stay," she said. "I don't suppose for long."

The boy nodded, his straight dark hair falling forward over his eyes. He brushed it away and turned to the door. He shrugged.

Michelle watched him cross the street and go into the hamburger joint, coming out a few minutes later with a brown paper package. Did he ever take food home for his mother, she wondered. She knew the public health nurse and the social worker had been in, but nothing seemed to change and the boy remained there. He probably protested loudly to anyone who even suggested he might be better off elsewhere, making up stories to cover his mother's negligence.

As soon as Marcel was out of sight, other thoughts preoccupied her. Nick had flirted with her once, long ago. He was older than her, but every so often they would meet at the teenage dances at the Rialto. All the kids went, even those who were not much more than children. That time, when he had asked her to dance, he had nuzzled her neck and later stolen a kiss when he followed her into the dark hallway that led to the washrooms. Even now she felt desire rise in her. The thought of someone's penis inside her, it could be Nick's, excited her. But she didn't care much whose it was at this moment as long as she could have an orgasm that she didn't cause herself, a long moaning release from the tension building in her since she had encountered Nick at the cemetery.

Moving toward the back where she kept a sewing machine for small alterations to her customers' purchases, out of sight of the window, she began to touch her breasts through the soft cloth of her blouse. Then her pubic area. Rubbing against the top of her clitoris through her slacks, she began to groan. Once she had let out a quiet gasp and the throbbing subsided, she knew to have sex with any man would be a disaster. She would get in over her head and not be able to see if things were going badly. She would need more than anyone could possibly offer. Since Dominic, there had been the occasional fling, but nothing lasting and it was ages since she'd even been on a date. She'd been unsure she would be able to differentiate between a truly caring man and one who wanted only to hurt her. With an intensity not felt in a long time, hatred for what her former husband had done to her welled up. Even more she hated that she might let someone else do the same thing.

She stared blindly at some bills on her desk. What was Nick really doing here? If she went out to dinner with him there would be an opportunity to figure him out a little. Not that it was of any consequence to her, she would say were anyone to ask. She was simply curious.

Returning to the front of the store, she moved some vests on a rack, marking down prices with a red marker. Not as low as she would make them in a month or so. Some winter jackets and coats. Slacks. The dressy outfits might still sell at full price, at least until most people had finished shopping for the season. When Michelle went to Montreal on buying trips, she always had particular customers in mind and called them when she returned. It was guesswork to some extent, but when she saw the fashions she knew the styles and fabrics that would appeal to different women. Since she also did the alterations, she could take in a tuck here or there and shorten skirts and slacks even if a size were slightly off.

When customers asked her to look for an outfit, for a cruise or party or wedding, it pleased her. Especially when it was the manager's wife. Or someone who worked in the office at the mine. They didn't know how their predecessors had spurned her family; that it had been Walter Muir who'd told his daughter, Libby, not to play with Michelle. Libby was a year older than her, but the town was small then, and anyone who lived nearby became a friend. It didn't matter that Libby met with her anyway for a while; she knew and felt some stigma attached. She felt it from the other kids, too, and soon even Libby stopped talking to her. Nick probably felt that way about being called a DP when he was growing up, although they hadn't talked about it. Maybe she would ask him.

She felt sure that she and Nick had many overlapping memories that would shape their conversation when they went out to dinner. Their fathers. Their mothers. What would happen when the gold ran out? She didn't like to think about that. When gold was still sold for thirty-five dollars an ounce, it took a ton of ore for seven dollars worth of gold. A ton of ore! But even in those days there was talk about the gold running out some day and Ile d'Or becoming a ghost town. No one believed it when it was still early times. Even though it meant long hours underground setting off dynamite in jagged rock walls where samplers had hammered away small bits of rock to be assayed for mineral content. And then the question of how long it would all last would loom again. Anyone in the business knew what could happen.

11.

L'ANGE BLEU SAT on an outcrop of rock on the highway to Montreal. A large sign on top in flashing blue lights could be seen for miles. Across from it, the head frame of an abandoned mine jutted out of the surrounding rock.

"They have good food," Lucien said. "Better than The Flamingo. Better than La Cabane."

"It's new, isn't it?" Libby asked.

"*Ah oui*, it's been around a few years, but new since your time, for sure."

Inside l'Ange Bleu the lights were dim. The tables looked full, but the waiter soon cleared a place for them. Lucien nodded and smiled at people who greeted him, but he didn't engage in conversation. The waiter knew his brand of beer and Libby asked for a gin and tonic.

"My wife's an Anglo," he said, amused by her surprised look. Had it been Guy who said it, Lucien suspected she wouldn't have been. Unlike him, Guy had associated freely with the Anglos.

"Someone I know?" she asked.

"*Mais, bien sur*, of course you do. Susan Lambert."

Lucien had tried to forget the events of the past year. Ile d'Or had been his home his entire life. For almost fifty years now. As he approached that milestone, he'd felt solid about everything. And he'd looked forward to spending time with Susan now that the children were no longer at home. They'd talked about travel as something to anticipate. Maybe to France. Or to one of the French-speaking islands. Haiti. Tahiti. Somewhere.

"Paris," Susan had said, eyes gleaming.

Then the owner of the Leduc Hotel had found Guy in one of his rooms. Not quite a year later, Susan left town. He hadn't known then that she'd followed the engineer who arrived that summer to do some work on the hoist at the mine.

"Susan?" Libby said. "Susan?" Her tone was perplexed and a frown crossed her forehead. Susan was the girl in her dream. Someone she thought would surely have left Ile d'Or. And certainly not someone she thought would have married and settled down in a mining town.

"Always up to something as a kid," Libby said. Never getting caught. "Remember when she stole chocolate bars and gum from Marcel's variety store." It was next to the dry cleaners, no longer called Archie's but still known by that name by the early residents. "I was mad at her, but Susan just laughed and passed a box of Chiclets to me. 'Come on,' she said, 'have some.' I couldn't say no." Susan was twelve then, a year older than Libby; Cathy McNab was a year younger. The three of them had been inseparable for a while. "She was always after the two of us to do something that would get us into trouble." She paused. "When did you get married? I thought she left Ile d'Or. The year before I went to university in Montreal, didn't she run off with the circus or something silly like that?"

"*Semble folle, je le sais,* but it was a way to get out of town. That's all. Maybe that's all it is now also," he said, then added, "She was pregnant. She came back."

"And you married her?"

"The child was mine." He didn't tell her that the summer Susan got pregnant was the same one Urho Tomi's dog wore kotex pads. That when Susan saw the spaniel with the pad, she'd already missed her period. When he forgot to bring the rubbers, at first she'd said no. It was the only time he ever forgot in all the times they went down behind the curling rink in his father's car to the shack by the railroad tracks. You would think after being careful for so long that just that once they might have been lucky.

"So you kept the baby?"

"No, she had an abortion in Montreal." He gripped his knife and fork so tightly that his knuckles were white. He cut into his steak.

She looked at the red trickle on his plate and was glad she'd ordered fish.

"More wine?" he asked.

"*J'en ai assez mainentant,*" she said. "For now anyway. This trout is great, by the way."

"*Bon.*" He began to talk about fishing down at the river. "Pickerel, pike," he said. "Bass, sometimes." The trout were in the small spring-fed lake out farther.

"I remember it," she said. "I learned to drive on the dirt road from Lac Leboeuf to Trout Lake. There was always a dark green canoe at the smaller lake." She and Guy had paddled over to the opposite shore to walk farther into the bush.

He was silent.

"What are you thinking about?" she asked.

"Oh, nothing," he said. "*Rien.* I was remembering that old blue Nash you drove around and around the block before you got your license."

As she listened to the familiar cadences of his voice, the same ones that had moved her when she'd heard Michel Tremblay and Roch Carrier, Libby could smell leaves burning. See the rocks across from the house on rue Champlain. He was quiet for a while, too.

"Tell me more about you," he said finally.

"Such as what?"

"Such as what you do *comme métier.*"

"I'm an artist."

"*Une artiste*," he said. "Little Elizabeth Muir an artist. *Mais, c'est merveilleux, n'est-ce pas?*"

"Thank you." She told him about exhibitions of her work in Toronto and Vancouver and the paintings in juried shows. "I frame most of my own paintings now." She'd worked late into the evenings before the show at the Moritz, the mattes carefully chosen, to get them ready.

Recently she'd sold a couple pieces to corporations. A painting and one large piece of sculpture. "I paint in a downtown studio I share with two other women. We visit galleries with slides and samples of our work and invite the owners to the studio. It's a tough business, although we're getting better at promoting ourselves. It seems to help that there are three of us. We encourage each other and sometimes we collaborate on something."

What she didn't tell him was that the horse haunting her dreams still, the horse from the past she shared with Susan, emerged unexpectedly on her canvas, a head breaking through mud. The dream had recurred off and on for as long as she could remember, always in black and white. She used to awaken to the thought that there would have been blood. Surely there would have been. On her canvas, the colours were vivid, bright reds, vermilion and the horse's eyes sometimes mainly yellow.

"What happened to your husband? Wasn't he a doctor? I always thought of you as a little housewife with your doctor husband."

"So did he," she said, laughing. "Yes, he was a doctor."

"It was big news when you married him," he said. "Now, *mon Dieu*, you've been married, divorced, and have grown-up children. You're an artist. The time she flies."

"I paint under my former husband's name." She held her arms tightly across her chest. She was thirty-five when they separated. That spring Barton had told her that their differences were irreconcilable because she wanted to have her tubes tied. It had astonished her so much she'd stepped backwards as if he'd struck her. They had two children already and didn't plan to have any others. It made no sense to her. Maybe it would have if she'd already seen him with the woman on the subway platform at the Rosedale station, but that didn't happen until later. Just after they were separated.

"Morley. Elizabeth Morley," she said.

"Why?" he asked.

"I don't know. Probably because I'd already begun to sell under that name. Anyway, the name Muir belongs to my childhood."

"I thought when we were kids you'd marry Guy."

"He asked me."

Lucien drew in a long breath and took a sip of wine. "Tell me, Elizabeth, isn't there a man in your life?"

"Nothing serious." She saw Dan's deep brown eyes, the blotches on his dark back, his muscular legs. "Until recently," she added. Would it surprise Lucien that Dan was black? Or was it her father who would have been surprised by that? Libby's earliest memories contained stories of her father as a small boy in a mining town in South Africa. He'd often told the one about the dog that saved him from a snake. A puff adder. Another about the gun his mother, a nurse, carried. Then there was the black nanny who cared for him until his family left South Africa when he was five. Libby recalled the first black person to come to Ile d'Or was a student who came north to work in the mine one summer. Before him there were no blacks at all, only one Jewish family who owned a jewellery store and the movie theatre. There were no old people either then. It was a frontier town and the early settlers were all young. It took a very long time for there to be old people, for the Chinese restaurant to open, for the main street to be paved and for cement sidewalks to replace the old wood ones.

"He enjoys art and going to galleries," she said. "We've been to the one in Buffalo and a lot of little ones in Toronto. To lots of movies. Occasionally, the theatre." The times in bed together she didn't mention, although it was then that they'd shared the most, talking as their arms and legs were interwoven, as they basked in the warmth of having made love again. "But that wasn't enough, I guess, because there's some other woman now as well. And things he never bothered to tell me." She didn't sound angry, but she felt it.

"Are you in love with him?" Lucien asked.

Libby didn't know how to answer that. Their last night together, only a few weeks ago, Dan had said he loved some woman called Daphne. He'd looked up at her from the tangled knot of the bed sheets. "It's just too soon for me. I need longer." Yet he also added, "You know I want to be with you."

"None of that makes any sense," she'd said angrily. Soon after he'd left and he hadn't called her since.

After reading the article in the magazine her son had given her, she was even more confused. What did she really know about Dan? Her relationships with men had left her skeptical, but she'd trusted something about him from what she'd read and seen of his public persona, as if his private life would be a reflection. As if he wouldn't have the same problems and complications as everyone else. She had fallen into the same trap as most people. Either public figures weren't to be trusted at all, or they were placed on pedestals. The dichotomy was as great as imagining some politician was tall only to be shocked by his or her actual diminutive stature. René Lévesque, Pierre Trudeau, David Crombie. But Dan was not small. He was more like a huge mountain lion, watching and pacing. When she met him on that night at the gallery, the idea that he might become her lover did not occur to her. Although a fleeting thought had brushed her heart gently, like the touch of a feather or an autumn leaf spiralling in a breeze.

"We were both lonely," she said.

A week or so after her show, Dan had called and they'd met for lunch. Three weeks after that, with another lunch or two in between, dinner and a movie, he came to see her house on Walken Avenue. For a long time, he'd looked at a photograph she'd framed of a yellow canoe heading out into unknown territory of water and tree covered hills. The paddler was shrouded in mist rising from a river, but the canoe's prow was moving out into the distance.

"Wonderful," he'd said, turning to her. Then, "You're beautiful," leaning slightly toward her.

Sensing he was about to kiss her, she could have moved away, but she'd wavered. He reached out simultaneously so that their lips came together in a long, slow kiss that left her tingling.

12

A FTER THEY LEFT the restaurant, Lucien drove Libby to the front door of the hotel and walked with her into the lobby. The room throbbed with loud music from the bar below and it felt almost as if the building itself were shaking.

"I hope you'll be able to sleep," he said.

Looking toward the door to the side of the reception desk, festooned with green twined ropes around the lattice at the sides, Libby was curious about who might be down there.

"Does it go on all night?" she asked, too tired to suggest exploring.

"Pretty late. I can go to the store and get some of those wax ear plugs the men use when they're blasting."

"I'll get them tomorrow." If the sound kept her awake, she would accept his offer. For the moment, she felt too tired to wait for him to get them.

"Drop by any time, Libby," he said. But his eyes were guarded and Libby wasn't sure what he might expect from her.

"I remember scooping out ice cream cones for a nickel," she said. "I think there were four flavours. Chocolate, vanilla, strawberry and Neapolitan. Your father let me eat all the ice cream I wanted."

"I'll let you do that," Lucien said with a hint of laughter in his voice. "I'd like to invite you to dinner again, too."

She smiled at him, "And I'll accept!"

As she walked across the lobby to the elevator, she heard the slow, creaking rumble of machinery and turned instead to the stairs.

"*Bonsoir,*" Lucien called.

Even four floors up, Libby could hear the music, the last strains of one of the songs in Plume Latraverse's album, *En Noir et Blanc,* with its loud, earthy lyrics. It appealed to her, but she realized it would keep her awake. Turning the key in the lock, she opened the door and closed

it firmly behind her. The sound was slightly muted and she hoped she
would drift off quickly.

As she turned down the blanket on the bed and put on her pyjamas,
Libby was thoughtful. What a day this had been. Susan of all people.
It was incredible. Susan, often in her dreams, had once told Libby
and Cathy McNab she rode a horse out by Lac Leboeuf. Libby had
pretended not to hear her. Dismayed that it still haunted her, Libby
hoped she wouldn't dream about the horse again. Or about her father
stumbling around after another bender. She didn't remember the music that played when she went to the sump to find him, just the lilting
sound of French surrounding her.

"It's Elizabet'," the man behind the bar said. "*Monsieur Muir. Votre
fille.*"

Her father would stare at her as if he'd never seen her before.

Libby wondered what Dan would say if she called him. Propelled
by a sudden strong urge, she dialled his number and listened to the
tone. There was no answer. When she replaced the receiver, she felt the
room tremble, like the rumble of the subway under the ground a block
away from her house in Toronto. But more than that, it was the same
sound she'd heard as a child, the sound of dynamite underground at
two every morning as regular as the mine whistles that blew during
the day to mark shift changes.

When she lay down and looked up at the ceiling, she could see long
cracks criss-crossing above her, and wondered if the plaster would begin
to fall. Maybe Guy had staggered out of the same bar as her father.
Time after time. Guy. The one person she'd wanted to see in Ile d'Or.
Noticing the books on the night table, *The Hockey Sweater and Other
Stories* and *The Fat Woman Next Door Is Pregnant*, which she bought
the same day she picked up her ticket from the Air Canada office on
Bloor Street, she thought of her father again.

"You'll never be lonely as long as you have a book to read," he'd
often said in sober moments, but she was lonely now. More lonely
than she'd felt in a long time. More lonely since Dan. Sometimes even
worse than after her marriage ended.

Why hadn't she gone to Paris? She was there once with Barton. And
once with her family. As a teenager, she stood under the Eiffel Tower
while the rest of her family saw the city from a vantage point high above
her. More interested in the young soldier she'd met while waiting for

them, in the concièrge in their small hotel on the left bank, with the elevator that moved slowly between the floors making strange noises, she had not wanted to be engulfed by her family. Savouring chocolate éclairs, *milles feuilles*, fruit and cream-laden tarts in the windows on the streets everywhere they walked, she'd imagined living there. She'd wanted to take a long trip to France ever since Barton left, but it hadn't happened. Instead she'd begun to dream more often about the horse sinking. There were always French voices in the background.

Finally she fell asleep only to toss and turn fitfully. Fragments of dreams flitted through her restlessness. Dan in his jockey shorts on a street in Toronto. Moving away from him to hail a taxi. Leaving him standing on the curb in front of The Flamingo where a pink bird landed on his shoulder. He reached for a bathrobe. She couldn't remember the name of the street she was looking for. "*Mais peut-être tu veux autre chose*," the driver said as she struggled to remember. There was something about a place where there was mud. A place where there was a horse sinking in mud. "*Mais il n'y a pas les rues comme ça ici maintenant.*" Stopping, he turned off the meter and began to touch her.

Light filtered in through the curtains and Libby woke up with her heart pounding. She lay there for a long while, before finally slipping out of bed and placing a white bath towel on the carpet. The name of the hotel, Alpha, was stitched in blue on the top edge. Stretching out on the floor she did some back rolls to warm up her spine, still conscious of the anxiety coursing through her. Then she did the cobra, the shoulder stand, and the camel. The yoga didn't seem to help. Would she always be lonely? Only Guy had broken through to share the silence with her. Barton hadn't and then resented time she tried to carve out for herself. Breathing deeply into her abdomen, she moved into a sitting position, letting her breath out with the sound of Om. When she was finished, it was just after seven. She dialled Dan's number again, but there was still no answer.

She reached for her suitcase, and drew out the packet of letters she had brought with her, the letters her father had written during the war. Her mother had given them to her some time ago, but she'd never read them. She thought that it would be fitting finally to read them on this visit back. The letters he'd sent to Libby when she was at university invariably had short notes scrawled at the end by her mother. She wished she'd kept them, but she guessed there was a time for discarding. As there had been for her mother who kept her husband's letters in a red chocolate box until she moved to Friendship Villa from the Toronto apartment she'd shared with him until his death.

As Libby opened the packet, the letters leapt out at her as if a spring had been released. The first one was from the troop ship that carried her father to England.

March 21/1945. At sea. The final move came very suddenly. I only learned on Tuesday in the afternoon that I would be leaving today, even then had no idea that I would be coming through without any stopovers. This letter may, or may not, give you some idea. I asked Newkirk, after a time lapse to allow for security, to drop you a line and let you know I was on my way.

Six of my roommates are French so I expect to be able to speak the language by the time the trip is over. They are a good crowd, but just a trifle too ebullient for me under the crowded conditions in which we live.

A long time since she'd read anything written by her father, his handwriting was instantly recognizable. She smiled at the letters so neatly and evenly formed and slanting to the right. Yet at first glance they were almost illegible.

The next letter had CENSORED printed on it. The return address was Capt. Walter Muir, No. 1, CERU, Canadian Army Overseas. The content was innocuous.

Here I am safe and sound in a northern British port. We passed through a number of places that were familiar from hearing Dad and Mother speak of them, particularly Berwick, the place where my Grandmother Muir spent her childhood. Some of those watercolours she did were of scenes in the area. I only wish I had the novelist's eye and pen to describe it all.

When Libby heard the mine whistle blow, she put the letters in her shoulder bag and went out. Walking until she came to a small diner, she went in and ordered pancakes and peameal bacon. As she sat over a cup of coffee, she flipped once again through the letters, soon engrossed by her father's remarks on politics. He was glad the Progressive Conservatives had received a clear majority in Ontario. *I hope it is some indication of the way the Dominion election will go, but I am afraid my friend Mac King will get in again.* In the next letter, he exclaimed on his wife's winnings at poker. *They are phenomenal. I suggest you try the market.*

Libby recalled the day she came home from school and asked what a strait was. It was something the teacher had talked about along with islands and peninsulas.

"It's a series of cards," her mother had said. "In numerical order."

She would have to remember to tell Lucien that story.

13.

NICK WANDERED DOWN the highway toward the mine. He
would ask at the gate to see if he could walk around on surface, to see the mine where his father had worked. Instead he
veered toward rocks on the side of the road and sat on a flat one across
from the main entrance. From this vantage point, he watched the men
as they emerged from the cage that came up from underground walk
toward the dry. As a child, he'd given no thought to the change area
for the underground miners. Or the name for it. Now he recognized
it as quite odd.

Bikadoroff seemed like a good name for this character, a Russian
name. Steve maybe. Steve Bikadoroff would have to go through life
as a miner. A DP like Nick. Although he didn't think Steve was a Russian name.

Serge? Boris?

Why did he think he could write a novel? His patients were enough
drama for him. Maybe it was because some of their confessions sounded
more like fiction than any reality he could have imagined. Maybe he
would have a priest hear a high-grader confess. Although not Bikadoroff. He never confessed to anyone and he never got caught either.
The priest could be the main character.

There would be a lot of research to do. Nick wanted to understand
mysteries of his childhood he'd taken as givens. As soon as he'd left
the town in his late teens, he confronted people who had no idea about
a mining town, about prospectors, underground, pyrite, the sounds
of blasting and whistles blowing, the gong at the cookery. About
high-grading and how the fence would get it to a runner. And then
to the mob connections in cities far away like Hamilton and Buffalo.
He'd begun to understand that he was different because of growing
up in Ile D'Or, not only because he was the child of immigrants. Sure,
that played a role, but as he garnered high marks in school he also

attracted the encouragement of teachers and the principal to further himself, to go to university. They had been disappointed when initially he went to take the course in photography, later congratulatory about the quality of his work. He thought they were pleased when he went into medicine, but that wasn't why he had. He'd always had many interests and maybe now his passion about psychiatry had also run out. Twenty years of practice was either the entry to some new level of wisdom and compassion or the endless stream of misery was more than a mortal could deal with any longer. Maybe he should have been a priest and listened to confession. At least he would have been able to grant some kind of absolution. Not the role of a shrink. Absolution. Nor was what he heard confession. Maybe a psychic would be a better healer. Well, he couldn't be either priest or psychic. For one he didn't have faith in some strange God with all the trappings, for the other he lacked prescience.

The whistle blew and men began to stream across the surface toward the dry. When they emerged, they headed toward the gate and the road to town. Not to the bunkhouses that were no longer in use. He sat with his chin in his hands, not sure what he was doing here. Ever since he'd gone into medicine, there'd been a route to follow. His career and his marriage had provided some structure around his life. Would he be able to reset his compass by returning here to a time that preceded that? What did he think he was going to find in this place that he had left so long ago? He remembered a colleague once remarking that a person sometimes needs to return to the last place where they were happy. Nick wasn't sure he'd been happy here, but life was simpler. He spat on the cold surface of the rock beside him that in summer would be covered with blueberries, and pulled his jacket and sweater tighter around him.

As Nick stood up, he looked up at the sky. It seemed to go on forever. In the city he missed it, as those who came from the prairies said they missed wide expanses of sky. And more sky. Yet Toronto was home to him now in a way he never could have dreamed would happen. Pockets of neighbourhoods that felt like small towns. Yorkville and the Annex. Bloor West Village. Greektown. The subway joining them. Little Italy along the streetcar tracks on College Street. The lake at the foot of the metropolis, the hub of transportation for the early settlers. Now blocked off with huge buildings and highways, seemingly lost to the inhabitants. The railroad was there from early times and could have been incorporated in some exciting vista of the future. Instead there was a crunch coming. Either his city would rise to assume some prominence or it would sink into mediocrity.

Walking down the side of the rock toward the highway and heading back to town, he didn't try to enter into the mine property. Enough to sit and watch and ponder, he thought, and now he would go back to the bed and breakfast and have a shower. Maybe call Michelle and ask her to join him for dinner.

When he arrived at the bunkhouse, the boy was waiting on the wood steps.

"*Bonjour Monsieur.*" Hello, Mister.

"Hello." Nick didn't ask what the boy was doing there as he went up to the front door and turned the knob.

The boy grabbed his arm.

"What do you want?" Nick was irritated. If he'd wanted this attention, he could have stayed in Toronto. He could have been seeing patients in his office in the building across from the art gallery. The ambience on nearby Queen Street West, and a few blocks where the strip was becoming increasingly arty, pleased him. What he was trying to escape was the feeling of being needed. Everyone needs someone, Marie would have said. She'd needed him, but so much of the time he'd been absent. "Oh, yes, you're here," she said. "But you might as well not be." *Who do you need, Nick? You won't admit it, but you do need affection and warmth. And people.*

But not this boy. This was his time, for himself.

Brushing past, he went inside to the hallway where there were envelopes on a table. He was relieved that he wouldn't receive any mail here because no one knew where he was. A patient sending him a note filled with protestations of love, something he would have to deal with at the next appointment. Transference. All that affection that wasn't real, that reflected someone's neuroses. The painful realities that would be hard to face in their forty-five minute appointments. It could take months. He saw people who had no insight and to whom he prescribed one drug or another to calm their demons. Maybe he needed a drug also to rid himself of a map with Dallas and Houston as the major cities that had taken over his thoughts. Marie's new husband, a French Canadian surgeon who had found a position in Texas, was on the staff of a hospital in Houston. Not in Montreal where she'd always said she wanted to live. It wouldn't have been so bad if Henri hadn't been a friend of Nick's. Not any longer.

I hate that fucking bonehead surgeon.

Here in Ile d'Or, he was running away from this new reality. That was the truth, he thought. And it kept chasing him. More fool he since more than anyone he should have known this would happen.

"I can get you fast chick," the boy said.

Oh, go away, Nick thought. "I don't want fast chick," he said. "Do you want to show me a good restaurant?" Maybe the boy was hungry. He remembered how he had hastily gobbled his breakfast the other morning and how conscious he'd been then of the fact that the boy didn't have regular meals, that maybe no one was looking after him. He would take the boy to lunch somewhere, feed him, and anyway, Nick was suddenly acutely aware he needed the company.

14.

THE DOOR OF the pharmacy was painted a deep red and through the glass you could see the soda fountain along the left side. High stools lined the counter where the original milkshake machine stood. Lucien was on the other side of the store, straightening out the magazine rack. No matter how often he did, it would be a mess again soon. A copy of *l'Actualité* would have been left on top of one of the newspapers, *La Presse* or *Le Devoir*. When he saw Libby come through the door, he waved.

"I came by to say thank you for dinner," she said.

"*Mon plaisir*," he said. "Did you sleep?"

"A little. It was noisy though."

Nodding sympathetically at the thought of the loud music, Lucien said, "I'll go get you those ear plugs." He walked behind the counter where he dispensed prescriptions and took a small plastic container from a shelf. He knew many of the miners ignored wearing the ear plugs, often suffering hearing loss later. When his children were at home, playing rock music, he'd used them himself.

Libby took out her wallet and started to reach inside the billfold.

"No," he said. "It's a welcome gift."

"Well, thanks then," she said. "I expect I'll make good use of them."

"May I pick you up at the same time for dinner?" Lucien asked, suddenly slightly unsure of himself. Maybe one evening had been enough for her.

The telephone rang as he handed the ear plugs to Libby. He spoke quickly. *Sore throat. Prescription. Ginger ale.* Someone would pick it up. When he hung up, he grimaced tiredly, dark circles under his eyes.

"Did *you* sleep?" she asked.

"Not much," he said. "A couple hours. It's been like this since Guy died. Worse since Susan left."

As she nodded with a worried frown in which he could see sympathy written, the door opened and a man in blue jeans came over to the counter.

"Export A," he said.

Libby waited until he left. "I'll see you later," she said.

As she moved through the door, Lucien watched her go out onto the sidewalk and stand near the pink flamingo in the window of the club next door. Across the street was St. Luc's, the Catholic church where Father Chicoine had been priest in the early days. One of the first settlers in Ile d'Or, he was at the parish until he died thirty-five years later. The thought of him leaning forward in the confession box with the purple satin sash bulging over his huge belly still made Lucien quiver. In those days, it was accepted that the priest made the rules for most of the town, how to vote and how to educate the children. Libby must have been glad she wasn't Catholic. Although he recalled Guy once told him she said it was difficult enough being told to go to church to make her mother happy, that if she'd had to confess to Father Chicoine, too, she would never have been able to stand it.

Lucien followed Libby out onto the sidewalk when he saw her looking across at the church.

She nodded at him. "Do you remember Father Chicoine?" she asked.

"How could anyone forget him?" Almost as if she knew what he was thinking.

"Francine…"

When Francine Dufresne was killed, almost everyone in town went to Marchand's funeral parlour to see her. The coffin was open and she lay there in a silver lamé dress. Susan had told him that Father Chicoine took a class from the Catholic school to show them what would happen to them if they drank too much. "You'll end up at Marchand's," he'd said.

"I wanted to drive Francine home that night, but she was already in another car," Lucien said. "She was only sixteen and the driver didn't look much older. It was just after her father built The Flamingo, you know. A lot of people weren't speaking to Francine or Michelle Dufresne then."

"Yes, Mr. McNab wouldn't let Cathy talk to them, I remember."

"You have a good memory, Elizabeth Muir. *Peut-être c'est l'artiste* in you. *Oui?* You know, when McNab was manager of the mine, any man seen talking to someone let go for high-grading was also fired. It was tough for the Dufresne girls. Michelle Dufresne moved back here a while ago, you know."

Libby didn't say anything and the silence stretched out between them. "So many memories," she murmured finally.

Lucien waited for Libby to say her father told her not to talk to Michelle also, but she didn't. Instead she thanked him again for dinner and said, "I'm going to wander about for a while, although I'm not sure where I'll go. And, yes, it would be nice to have dinner with you again."

Watching her walk away, Lucien observed the sway of a woman he wouldn't have imagined when they were children. A young freckled kid with pigtails down her back was now an attractive woman whose hips moved in a slight circular rhythm. Going to the cash register at the prescription counter, he took out some photographs from a drawer underneath. One of him and Susan with their children when the kids were teenagers. Another of Susan as a teenager herself, her dark eyes peering out at him. How defiant she was then. When he first noticed her, her father was up in the bush in some remote place where he slept in a tent. Where Jack Lambert went was always a secret; he would say only that he was looking for gold. No prospector wanted anyone else to get there first and stake a claim. Until he did this for the mine in the 1940s, Lambert went off prospecting on his own, looking for that one claim that would make him rich, the gleam of the golden metal driving more than one man to their deaths in the bush. But Jack Lambert knew what he was doing out there and he came back safely each time even though he never found gold. Maybe it was just a good reason to get away from his family; the four children always remained behind with their mother.

Mrs. Lambert didn't go to the sump in the basement of the Alpha Hotel like Libby's father, but when her husband was gone she drank at home. Then after a month or two or three, Jack would come back again. Often he would have to get something for the children to eat. When Susan's mother was sober, she would do a lot of cooking and put it in the icebox. Her father would get out the axe and chop off a chunk of casserole or stew to heat in a large pot on the stove. Or else they would have beans or something else from a can bought at Mulholland's, the general store where the butcher was at the back in his white apron with red smears on it. The rest of the food was on one side while the clothes, boots and other things like that were on the other. It was on one of these days he'd learned later, when her mother was too far-gone to notice, that Lucien caught Susan with something she'd stolen. He'd started to be aware of her before that; the little buds under her bathing suit the previous summer acted like a beacon.

"Hey, kid," he said. "What you got in your pocket?"

She started to run, but he caught up with her, put his hand on her shoulder and spun her around. "I know." *Je sais.*

"What?"

"You're a t'ief. *Un voleur.*"

"You're a liar."

Reaching out quickly before she could stop him, he pulled a chocolate bar from her pocket. "I saw you," he said. "If you don't meet me down at the mine gates after dark tonight, I'm going to tell Jutras."

Jutras was the town policeman. Suspecting she wasn't afraid of Jutras, he wasn't surprised when she shrugged her shoulders. "Tell him," she said. "Do you think he'll believe you?"

"*On va voir.* Maybe you'd better meet me, little girl."

She looked at him scornfully. "You can forget that," she said.

He shrugged. "We'll see." Something about her last glance and the way she tossed her hair told him she would come. Although when she got into his father's car with him, what she wanted to do was drive it.

"I've been watching you," he said.

"Yeah," Susan said.

When he tried to kiss her, down behind the bunkhouses near the shed by the railway track, she scratched his face and shoved him away. He laughed and leaned back on the other side.

"You're not a big girl after all."

"I bet you haven't ever stolen anything," she said. "I even stole a fishing rod once."

"Anyway, so what?" He took her arm. "Hold this." Guiding her hand toward his crotch, he could tell she was curious because she didn't resist. He told her to hang on.

"*Tabernacle,* don't let go now," he hollered when she started to, until he let out a loud cry. "Okay, Okay," he yelled. "Okay."

"I don't want to get pregnant," she said as she slid back on the seat, her hand on the door handle. She looked at his red face and watched his heavy breathing.

"You can't unless I put it in you." They could try that next time; he would bring a rubber.

"If you're lucky," she said.

Leaping out of the car, she started to walk back toward town. He hollered after her that she didn't have to walk, but she paid no attention. For all he knew, there wasn't going to be a next time. When he looked back now though, that night was how it started. What he didn't understand was how, so many years later, it ended. There was no warning. Or did he miss it? The last letter from Susan was written in English. She had always talked a mixture of French and English in their home, mainly French. Not any longer. *I've changed my address again,* she wrote. *Please forward any mail. I have a lawyer and she'll be in touch with you.* No word about what she was doing and she did not ask about him. Was she with the man? He knew nothing. Ripping the letter, he'd thrown the jagged pieces into a large wicker basket under the counter.

15.

RETRACING HER STEPS to the houses that had belonged to the company when she was a child, Libby stopped in front of the one where Michelle Dufresne had lived. As she moved slowly around it toward the lane, she noticed a stoop at the back with a tiny pointed roof that had not changed. From the Muir's backyard, across another garden and a lane, you could practically see into the Dufresne's kitchen. As a child, Libby had liked to prowl around the lanes, peeking into windows, trying to figure out what went on in other people's houses.

It was rumoured there were many men who carried small bits of gold out from underground at the end of their shifts. It had not been clear to Libby how they did that, although she imagined they'd hidden it in their pockets or in their black lunch pails. Sometimes in their mouths and even in their privates. What had been clear then was that Michelle's father was one of them. Everyone knew it. But when his house was searched, no trace of gold was ever found.

At some point when it was talked about in the Muir household, her father had again said, "I don't want to see you with the Dufresne girl."

Michelle was a year or so younger and Libby had been envious of her because she wore lipstick before any of the girls Libby knew and played first base on the mixed baseball team that gathered down on the diamond near the mine in the summer. Her flawless French and Gallic flair undoubtedly came from her father and from her mother a fluent facility with English.

One summer evening, Michelle came up to bat and the men who walked from the bunkhouses past the wire mesh fence around the mine stopped to watch. Libby could see their eyes linger on Michelle. All of thirteen or so, with budding breasts under her t-shirt and long legs that had taken on a more rounded shape, she stood out from the other girls. A little more than a year older, Libby was as tall as she was, but still gangly.

Maybe it was the evening Michelle walked home with her after a game that her father took her aside for what he'd called a little chat. He'd seen them come over the wooden bridge across what was no more than an indentation in the ground between the bush on one side and the houses on the other. Maybe he was waiting to see if they were together.

"I don't want you to associate with her, Miss Muir. If you do, there will be consequences," her father said when they were alone in the living room.

Only occasionally had he called her that. How old fashioned it sounded even then, but it made the point he wanted to make. And from whispered conversations the children were not supposed to hear, she knew the Dufresne house had been searched again. She also knew that there was extreme frustration at another fruitless hunt.

Studying the grave expression on his face, Libby quavered slightly as she felt how unjust his words were. "But she hasn't done anything," she pleaded.

"It doesn't matter," he said, his voice firm.

Suppose she dared suggest Michelle might be asked to stay away from her because of his drinking, Libby thought. Michelle's parents probably saw him stagger down the same gravel road she and Michelle had just taken. But she didn't. Nor did she ask what the consequences would be. Once she had defied him and he'd slapped her hard across the face, his red palm imprinted for hours on her cheek. That was the only time he ever hit her, but she never forgot it. Her mother was away in Toronto because their grandfather was ill and Sheila and Wally were staying with other families on the property. That night she slept in a car parked in the lane where she could hear a shrill female voice she recognized as Michelle's mother speaking in English.

"Don't come into my kitchen in those dirty work boots. I just washed the floor."

The male response, "*Sacre bleu. Tabernacle. Je travaille pour toi et...*" A slammed window. She thought Michelle must slink around harsh words sometimes just as she did.

After her father forbade her to see Michelle, Libby met her occasionally at the restaurant on the main street downtown where she figured her father would never see her. It was a place where all the kids went after school. It was called Splendid Sweets. There they ate French fried potato chips and gravy or chocolate sundaes and drank huge glasses of Coca Cola, picking out pieces of music on the juke box. "I was dancing with my darling to the Tennessee Waltz." Going down the list and then inserting their nickels.

"Your turn."

If a girl didn't like the boys who came to the table, she concentrated very hard on the titles on the song lists in the juke box. But if instead she liked one of them, she might ask him to sit down. She might let him pick the music. One June day when one of the older boys who played on the men's baseball team came in, he spied Michelle in the back booth and moved toward them. Libby watched Michelle's face turn from a pinkish hue to bright red as she put her head down slightly. A left-handed pitcher who put more runners out at first base than Libby knew until then was possible, his last name was Clark and everyone called him Knobby. He didn't live in the town. There were always older boys around over the summers who would leave in late August or early September. In their late teens or early twenties, sometimes they were future engineers or geologists who were there to earn money so they could continue with their education. Libby didn't know what Knobby Clark was doing there. From the rocks overlooking the mine and the baseball field that summer, she often watched him play. And what she knew was that he was handsome and she had a crush on him.

"Hi, Michelle," he said. "I haven't seen you down on the diamond for a while."

He doesn't even know I'm alive, Libby thought, surprised he knew Michelle's name. She'd told Michelle she thought he was cute and then she wished she hadn't said anything.

"No," Michelle said, brushing out of the way a strand of hair that had fallen over her forehead.

Libby hadn't objected when Michelle was taken aside and asked not to come to play on the team any longer. She knew it wasn't fair, that Michelle was their best player. She knew, but she was silent.

"You're a good player. They need you on the team," Knobby said. Michelle shrugged.

"Next game I'll look for you."

Libby waited for Michelle to tell him that she wouldn't be there, but she didn't. What would Michelle have said if she were alone? It was clear that he had eyes for her, but she didn't let on she noticed. He remained separate from the crowd who lived on the property, but toward the end of summer, Libby saw him on the main street holding hands with Michelle. By then she was no longer speaking to Michelle and thought that might be just as well.

Now she felt a flush rising over her face, embarrassed that she was almost spying. She moved away quickly from the house, wondering where Michelle lived now and what they would say to each other if they met. It could happen any time, on the street or in one of the stores. It crossed her mind that she could look up Michelle's name in the phone book, but she wasn't sure that seeing her was what she wanted.

16.

THE CEMETERY WAS empty except for the Chevy parked at the entrance. Someone driving by on the highway might wonder why Michelle's car was there again and then going around the next curve have already forgotten.

A breeze blew as Michelle walked through the dark grass carrying an assortment of branches and green leaves with a waxen texture that would stand the early wrath of winter. Stopping in front of Father Chicoine's grave, she frowned.

"You old bastard," she muttered.

Oh, there's that Dufresne girl again. The priest still speaking from beyond the grave. *Outlived all of us. Not like her sister, in that car accident. Sixteen and drinking too much already.*

A priest's grave set among those of his parishioners was more egalitarian than when they'd come into the confession box. They still sometimes stood there and cursed him. As if that could change anything. He'd listened to their sins; often petty, inconsequential things that nonetheless made them squirm. It was a bloody shame to have been relegated to this northern place with no easy way to get out and let off steam. He'd been stuck here. He couldn't go to the Purple Pig or The Flamingo. Nor could he drink except in the privacy of his quarters where he kept some whiskey in a purple and gold cloth bag in a drawer beneath his underwear.

He did what his place in the town required, gave advice, exhorted from the pulpit. The politicians left the priests alone as long as they were supported, the grand alliance between church and state, the arbiters of society. And the politicians came to confess also, often the most crooked of anyone who sat outside his window and said they'd sinned.

"My son," and then the requisite number of "Hail Marys."

Alors, Michelle, you can stop crying. Still, the high-grading was a messy business. He listened to the middle-men who went off to New

York or Montreal to sell what was passed on to them and then gambled there. He knew they solicited men who worked underground when they were all drinking in the bars. Not everyone was tempted, but there were always takers.

I didn't condone it, but it's not the kid's fault. Pauvre fille. "Your kid goes to school along that trail, no?"

One man threatening another. Nothing more needed to be said.

"Father Chicoine, you were a bloody hypocrite," Michelle muttered.

He was, too. Spouting off from the pulpit.

Oui, mon enfant.

17

S SHE WALKED along the main street toward the mine where her father had been the engineer, Libby came to a path that led over a rise to bunkhouses covered with green siding. She'd heard one had been turned into a bed and breakfast. Back then, the men who worked underground had lived there, at the edge of town. At the sound of the metal triangle ringing out like a chime echoing across the wilderness, the miners had streamed into the cookery for meals.

She recalled that in winter, when the path was narrow, the only adult who had ever moved aside so the children would not have to jump into deep snow had been Arthur White. The name, one she'd forgotten until that moment, sent shivers through her. She remembered the night she woke up to find her mother missing. It was during the war and her father was still overseas. She ran from room to room looking for her mother, even looking under her mother's bed and in her closet. When she finally came home, Libby was sitting on the bottom step of the staircase just inside the front door, huddled to one side, crying. The other children were still sleeping.

"I just went to the corner to get a pack of cigarettes," her mother said, somewhat sheepishly pulling out a white pack of Sweet Caporals. "I'm sorry. I was gone for less than ten minutes." She must have thought no one would wake up in the few minutes it would take.

A man's shape appeared in the door, looming up behind her like a large ghostly presence. "What is it, Charlotte?"

"It's all right, Arthur."

Libby was relieved that night to see Arthur White's face. He lived in a log cabin near the mine and, like a kindly relative with no children of his own, gave all the children on mine property the best chocolates and candies at Halloween and Christmas.

"All right, then," Mr. White said, closing the door gently behind him as he disappeared into the night. He didn't come to the house again, but once stopped Libby on the path to town to ask how her mother was doing.

"Will you say hello to her?" he asked. "Say hello to Charlotte."

"Oh, yes," her mother said when Libby told her. That was all.

"Why doesn't Mrs. White live with him?" Libby asked.

"She doesn't like it here," her mother said. "She lives in Montreal. You really can't blame her, but I'm sure he misses her." Her face was suddenly as red as her brightest lipstick.

Wally, who was the youngest of the three Muir children, started to cry. Her mother ducked her head and disappeared into his bedroom.

Libby veered off the path toward the small log cabin where Arthur had lived. It had also been the mine's guesthouse where visiting engineers and geologists had stayed. In this cabin she saw Arthur White hold up rocks with veins of gold in them and listened to him explain the difference between the real thing and pyrite. Fool's gold. Something every prospector needed to know. His voice came back to her, explaining how the veins had formed.

As she walked around to the back of the cabin, Libby was surprised to discover it was being dismantled log by log, that the entire rear wall had been demolished. She peered into the room where Arthur White taught her and her friends how to play cribbage. Even more, she recalled the chocolate fudge he gave them when they turned up on his doorstep on Halloween.

"Oh, what a beautiful princess you make, Elizabeth." Or witch. Or pirate. And then came the reward, the sticky, yummy fudge.

As she picked her way around the door of an old car and a pile of logs, Libby recalled what Sheila had once told her about Arthur White. About his arrival at their house on rue Champlain, on another day, in a dazed state.

"I wondered if Elizabeth and Sheila could take part in a bubble gum blowing contest," he said.

"Libby's gone away to school in the city," her father replied. "Sheila's shooting partridge. We had some for our supper." So maybe she was too old for the contest, he suggested. Sheila already knew how very proud of her he was and he'd called her Miss Muir as he told her. This is what she'd told Libby, gloating a little Libby had thought at the time. But she'd ignored that, wanting to hear the whole story. Sheila had been twelve that year and since she liked guns, she was the one their mother taught to shoot. The previous winter, their father had taught Sheila *you never point a gun at a person*, not even the old pistols her father had from some ancestor who was at the Battle of Waterloo. Then he showed Sheila how to clean and load the 410. It was funny about their father. He never went fishing or hunting, but he'd taught Charlotte how to shoot, and then Sheila, and their mother never missed a season.

"Oh," Arthur said. "I have lost track. What about Wally? Is he too old for bubble gum now, too?"

"Come in," their father said. "You can ask him yourself. We are just finishing dinner. I'm sure there's more to eat if you'd like something. Isn't there, Charlotte?"

According to Sheila, Charlotte had flushed deeply, and said of course there was. There was always enough for friends and visitors.

When he came inside, Sheila said she could smell whisky in the air. This was a surprise, as Mr. White was known never to touch a drop. Even in the bush.

"He's the quintessential gentleman," Mrs. McNab had said one day when their mother was having tea with the ladies in the living room.

As a child, what Libby had liked most about her mother was how she could do just about anything. In hunting season, she'd go out early to the single track dirt road that led to the lake where she stopped on a sandy stretch to shoot partridge. She also played a mean hand of poker at the dining room table with other women. On other occasions, there might be women around that table drinking tea from dainty cups and talking about the curling bonspiel. Or the bean supper at the church. She didn't like driving the car in town much and hadn't learned how until she was over forty. Still, she managed, although she could never back up as easily as go forward. If she overshot the mark when she was parking, she would drive around the block and try again.

"Thank you," Arthur said. "I've already eaten. But I would like to come in for a while."

They all sat in the sunroom with magazines spread out on the couch and a jigsaw puzzle on the coffee table. Her father turned down his military music.

"Sheila was marching," he said. She still stood at attention with the broom over her shoulder, their father's model soldier.

"I'm sorry I didn't have children," Mr. White said.

Her father looked bewildered, as if he didn't know what to say.

"Evelyn never wanted to come up here." Mr. White said. "She never wanted children either. Now she wants a divorce."

"Sheila," Charlotte said, gesturing toward the door. "Could you go and do the dishes?"

Sheila didn't want to leave the room. Here was a story she wanted to hear unfolding.

"Aw, Mum."

"Sheila," her father said sharply.

So she went into the kitchen and tried to listen through the sound of the running water and the splash of the dishes, but she couldn't make out much except this wasn't the Mr. White she'd known forever. This wasn't the man who always had answers for every child's question and was like an uncle who made up for all the times parents yelled at you by being calm and kind and, well, almost perfect.

When Sheila and Wally both went to the bubble gum blowing contest on the weekend, Arthur White gave her his cribbage board. His favourite rock went to Wally. There was something else for the McNab children and a small rock for Jeannie Petranovich. He seemed pleased at their squeals of excitement.

Their mother looked baffled when she saw their prizes. Sheila heard her tell her father she didn't like it, that it didn't make sense to her. A few nights later, in the midst of a party at a neighbour's house, Arthur left hurriedly. Only a few hours later, as Sheila listened to her parents talk in hushed voices, she overheard that Arthur was found lying inert on the floor beside the wood stove with a bullet hole in his head.

"His gun was lying beside him," Sheila had told Libby in a low voice, as if it were a secret.

Sheila said she'd had nightmares for years after that and at some point decided she didn't like guns after all.

As Libby walked away from the cabin and around a corner to a rise in the road where she could see a chain link fence around the mine, she was still baffled by Mr. White's suicide. He'd been so cheerful all the time, and generous. She remembered that Sheila had told her his wife, instead of joining him, had decided to divorce him. Libby thought he must have talked to some people about that, since it became part of the gossip that survived him. The death didn't seem to have affected her mother as much as Sheila, although how could any of Charlotte's children have known how she felt about it. All Libby knew was that her mother had continued to shoot partridge. And sometimes Sheila had still gone with her.

18.

S NOW FELL ON the cemetery.
    It covered Father Chicoine's grave like a soft white blanket.
    Arthur White confessed to me. Confessed to touching that woman. Mother of children who didn't come to the church. Worse than adultery. Raising Protestants.

His wife came to get him, travelled back on the train with the body. But it was lost at some junction, the wrong body turning up in Montreal at first. Not buried in the Ile d'Or graveyard, Arthur was buried somewhere on the side of the mountain.

I should have been buried there, not in this forlorn place where I didn't belong right from the start. Although better than being in a city where I would have been insignificant. Here everyone knew me, listened to me. Even now, they remember. They say they don't. But I still haunt them, all those who were here at the beginning of this town.

Across the highway, all the weeds were covered by the white flakes.

19.

THE DESK WAS stacked high with enough paper to discourage almost anyone from trying to find something. But Lucien was determined as he tried to ferret out the unpaid bills without disturbing the rest of the pile. No wonder his accountant was upset at how disorganized he'd become in the last months, he thought. The clutter he'd let accumulate here was almost hopeless to sort through, but he consoled himself that even though he was making a mess of things since Susan left, he still wasn't losing any customers. *They come in to buy soft drinks, toiletries, cigarettes and prescriptions. Sometimes they come just to talk. If they told their doctors some of the stories they tell me, some prescriptions would be unnecessary.* His interest in people was like his father's. Not like Guy who retreated into a world of his own at some point, although he was the gregarious one as a child. *Maman's favourite. The baby.*

"Monsieur Dion," Charmaine called from the cash register.

"Pardon?"

Lucien didn't hear what she asked him, only his name. *Monsieur Dion.* Like his father. Libby must have called his father *Monsieur Dion* when she'd worked in the store that summer long ago. His father liked to listen to the local gossip also, except when he became it. Lucien remembered when he and Guy fought over a lighter Guy had found under Libby's window. His father was out somewhere while his mother was visiting her sister in the Gaspé.

"I didn't know I lost it," Lucien said. "Where'd you find it?"

"Near a ladder," Guy said. He was angry.

Lucien took out a cigarette and lit it with a shrug, wondering how Guy knew about the ladder under Libby's bedroom window. "Keep your mouth shut, kid," he'd said. Buried in Lucien's tone were all the threats he'd ever made. *Remember the time I caught you in the bush with Libby.* Only five years old, peering at each other's genitals to see how they were different, they'd looked up at Lucien with frightened eyes when he found them. Up until then that was all it took to keep Guy quiet. This time Guy swung his arm and blood spurted in a jagged stream from Lucien's nose. Only when the back door opened and their father stumbled in did the fight stop.

"What the hell?" Papa said.

There was a large red mouth on his right cheek and lipstick smeared on his collar. When he saw the way they looked at him, he went over to the mirror. "*Oh, mon Dieu,*" he said, reaching for a cloth and starting to scrub at the red imprint of a woman's mouth. Then he noticed his collar and grabbed at the buttons, taking the shirt off and throwing it on the floor. Stomping over the tiles, he reached for a beer in the refrigerator.

"*Oh, mon Dieu,*" he said again. "What a mess. Please don't tell Maman."

"No," Guy said. "You can tell her."

All these years later, Lucien still didn't know if his mother had ever learned about his father's affair with the mine manager's secretary. Lucien didn't know who the woman was that night. It was only later he learned, mortified to overhear whispers that the woman was pregnant, that the child was his father's.

Papa sighed, his head in his hands. Pursing his lips and grimacing, almost as if he were about to cry, he gestured with his big hairy hand toward the chairs. Picking up a deck of cards they played poker with some nights after supper, he began to shuffle. He didn't say anything at all, just waited. Lucien sat down at the table, his eyes not daring to meet his father's. Guy moved slowly across the room and pulled out the chair across from Lucien. Their father made a fan of the cards, lips compressed, eyes alert. Guy's card was the king of spades. Then Lucien took one, jack of hearts. Then it was their father's turn. His was the ten of clubs.

"Your deal, Guy," their father said.

"What is it, Charmaine?" Lucien asked.

A roll in the cash register was creating a balloon of white paper rather than one bill at a time. She was having trouble getting the roll set up, so he did it for her and showed her how at the same time.

"I meant to ask you to order the cosmetics," he said. "You're good at knowing what we need. And you're good at selling them."

The smile that lit up her face extended right from her lips through her cheeks and around the edges of her eyes. All she needed to know was where to find the order forms and that was easy enough to show her. She nodded and started to turn away.

"Oh," she said, catching herself. "Doctor Cloutier called in a prescription for someone. He asked you to call his office."

When Lucien got Doctor Cloutier on the other end of the wire, he was surprised to hear that the prescription was for Michelle Dufresne. He hadn't seen her in the store for a while. When she'd first returned to town, young Jacques Paquin told him that her daughters had come with her. Paul Paquin had been Guy's best friend and Jacques, his son, continued to come into the store often even after his father and Guy had an ugly argument. The rift was still there when Guy died.

The telephone rang. It was his mother. She'd missed him the night before. And would he be coming for dinner? "I am making your favourite, Lucien," she said, her voice slightly plaintive.

"*Ah oui, maman*, but I didn't say I'd be there," he said, trying not to let his irritation show. He was wondering what Michelle would think about Libby being in town. Did she know that Libby was here?

"No, but you usually call," his mother said.

"I'm sorry. But do you know who's in Ile d'Or?" She would never guess.

"Nick Petranovich."

"Really?" Lucien was startled. "I didn't know that."

"Michelle told me. So, who else is here?"

"Oh, yes," he said. For a moment, he had forgotten. "Elizabeth Muir."

"Muir," Maman said. "Do you mean Libby? Charlotte's daughter?"

"Yes, that's who I mean."

"Well, invite her to dinner, too," his mother said, something that shouldn't have surprised him as much as it did. Although she was aging and hadn't been the same since Guy's death, his mother's hospitality was still legendary in the north.

"Not tonight," Lucien said. He wanted more time with Libby before he took her to his mother's house. "Before she leaves."

"This is so unusual. We don't get visitors in November. How long is she staying?"

Who would stay very long at the beginning of winter when the weather would only get colder? When the wind would blow down the streets carrying the snow into drifts and no matter how many sweaters and scarves you wore, would cut right through all the layers and make you shiver? Only someone who lived here would look forward to skiing and skating, to curling on the ice in the club down near the mine, to walking on the thick snow and hearing the crunching sound. Sometimes he even looked forward to it.

"I'm not sure. Sounds like it will only be for a few days."

20

A TALL CHAIN link fence separated the mine from the highway. From where she stood at the gate, Libby could see a blue and white fleur-de-lys at the top of the head frame. A young man in yellow hardhat and heavy work boots stood on the other side, just inside the fence.

"You can't come in here," he said. *Vous ne pouvez pas aller par ici.*

"My father worked here," Libby said. *Mon père a travaillé ici.* It hadn't dawned on her that the fence and the fleur-de-lys might be intended to exclude her.

"Oh, yes," he smiled slightly. "What did he do?"

"*Ingénieur.*"

"I'm the engineer now. My name's Jacques Paquin."

"Paul's son?" she asked. When her son was born, they'd called him Paul. She'd never said where the name came from when she suggested it as Barton had liked it right away, too.

Jacques nodded.

"Well, I'm Elizabeth Morley. My father was Walter Muir." That should gain entrance. How could someone so young deny her that?

"*Je ne m'en souviens pas,*" the young man said. I don't remember him.

It seemed inconceivable to Libby that her father had been so soon forgotten when his presence was writ large on every corner of this mine. The mill. The hoist house. The small cars that carried ore up from underground. The tracks that crisscrossed the surface. The assay lab. The men in their grimy clothes emerging from the cage that came up from the dark spaces under the earth. Noises, smells, memories of her father's work came back so sharply that she could not believe this man didn't share them.

"My father worked in that office." She pointed at a square building covered with large sheets of green asbestos.

"That's where I work," Jacques said.

"Is there anyone who can speak English anymore?"

"Yes, but everyone speaks French now."

Libby did not turn away as she thought he intended her to do. It felt to her as if they'd reached an impasse and she wondered if he would now ignore her.

Raising his hand to his hat, he straightened it. "Do you want to see the office?" he asked finally.

As she followed him up the incline toward the main building, Libby visualized the oak desk where she'd seen her father reach for a bottle of Seagram's V.O. in the lower drawer. Inside, she saw the white, porcelain fountain where she had stood on tiptoes for a sip of water. The secretary had worked on the payroll in the office next to the fountain and the same wooden stairs still led up to the floor where her father had sat at his slanted draughting table on a high seat like a bar stool. When the door behind them opened, Libby almost expected to see her father come through it with a slight whiff of alcohol on his breath. When he blew his nose, laced with thin purple veins, it would start to bleed.

"Miss Muir," he would say. "What are you doing here?" The reddish moustache above his lip would quiver. He would take her up to sit on his high stool where she would read his small, neat printing on the blueprints

"He's the best engineer in the north."

How many times had she heard that? Often, in the same breath, "It's too bad he drinks so much. His poor wife. Poor Charlotte!"

A man in a jacket and tie glanced at them. He stopped outside the manager's office. His hair, mostly grey, receded slightly at the temples as he stood there, seemingly waiting for an explanation.

"Her father worked here," Jacques said.

"Who was your father?" the man asked kindly. *Qui était votre père?*

"Walter Muir," Libby said.

A wide smile crossed his face. "*Ah, oui.* Walter Muir." Gesturing toward his office, he broke into English. "Come in." When they were inside, he pointed to a photograph on his wall among a series of black and white shots of men, some in shirts and ties, some in hard hats, all of them waiting for the photographer to capture them. "This is her father, Jacques. He and this man, John McNab, and these others, built this mine. They were here at the very beginning." He turned to Libby. "I worked here in summers as a young engineering student. Your father hired me. I'm Maurice Gauthier."

"I'm pleased to meet you," Libby said.

She watched Jacques nod almost imperceptibly, his lack of interest palpable. He ran his fingers over some rock samples while the manager asked about her family.

"I was sorry when your father died," he said. "How's your mother?"

"She's okay," Libby said. Her mother had arthritis that was often painful and these days was sometimes dizzy. Not too long ago she'd fallen. It was fortunate she hadn't broken anything. Libby supposed overall her mother wasn't doing too badly.

"I'm glad to hear it. Please give Charlotte my regards."

"Yes," she said. "I'll certainly do that. She'll be delighted, Monsieur Gauthier."

"Jacques, show Walter Muir's daughter whatever she wants to see," the manager said.

Nodding, Jacques headed quickly toward the door. Libby spun around to follow him up the stairs to his office, the same one that was once her father's. Her eyes were drawn to the bottom drawer of the oak desk. She thought of the child who had for the longest time imagined when the bottle was empty it would disappear and her world would be safe again. When her father was out of the room, she couldn't resist pulling out the drawer. Another brown paper bag was what she found and she fingered the edges of the paper and opened it carefully, still hoping it would be something other than the dreaded bottle.

Oh, Daddy.

Inside was always yet another Seagram's rye whisky.

Jacques cleared his throat noisily, leaning against the draughting table. His eyes were narrow slits as he watched her. He looked impatient, as if she were a strange animal who had wandered into his territory.

"Do you want to see anything else?" he asked.

Through the window, she could see the conveyor belt carrying crushed rock to the mill.

"Yes," she said. "I'd like to see the mill."

As she stood staring into the dark mass in the settling tank, she could hear her father's voice over the drone of the motors as he'd explained how the rock was drilled and blasted and brought to surface. Whenever he stopped, Libby asked another question.

"It has to be crushed until it's finer than sand before the gold can be extracted," he said.

Tons of crushed rock later, in shift after shift of sweating, groaning men, blast after blast shaking the town at regular intervals, after the rock was ground to fine sand, there was one small bar of solid gold. It took her such a long time to grasp this whole process, but now she wondered that so much work went into something the value of which she'd never understood. She'd asked her father many questions, which he'd answered thoughtfully, but she shied away from this one without knowing why. Yet it was why they lived there in spite of the danger lurking under the earth for the miners. And for the children who flew model airplanes on the waste that was trolleyed out to form a large pile of grey clay. No fence kept her and her friends from playing there, on a field of poison that was as large as a baseball diamond.

"What's it like underground?" she'd asked her father. "How can the men see?"

"When we get back to the office, I'll draw you some pictures."

Later her father had sketched a man setting up holes for dynamite on a rock face and told her how other men on another shift cleared away the debris blown out a few hours earlier. There were only two shifts so there was time in between to clear poisonous gases from the air. Then the rock was put in trolley cars and dragged over to the grizzly. Her father said the man who had to hammer the rock to break it into small enough pieces to go down through the ore pass had almost the worst job in the mine.

"What's the worst one?" Libby asked.

Her father blushed. "Honey man," he replied.

"What's that?" she asked, startled at his embarrassed demeanour.

"Well..." His voice was low and he turned his head slightly away.

"What's that?" she repeated.

When he started across the room toward his desk, she didn't ask the question again. She was afraid if she did he would open the bottom drawer and pull out the bottle.

Jacques began to move away from the tank and when Libby realized she was alone, she turned to follow. "Will you show me the gold?" she asked.

The door of the oven was open and she could see the flame where liquid gold streamed through a narrow opening into a mould. Amazed at the ingenuity that found a way to create this marvel from barren earth and sheer rock, Libby asked herself another question she'd never broached with her father. To what end? Did it have something to do with why he, Walter Muir, was so gentle one day and staggered home a day later from the bar in the hotel? Where was the good man from a fine family her mother had said he was?

Jacques leaned against the wall, reading a piece of paper tacked to it. "Did you know my father well?" he asked.

"He lived on the same street. We played together," she said. "Where is he now?"

"He went to work for the government in Quebec last year. He's an inspector. He goes around to mines to check on safety." Looking away, he took in a deep breath. "Did you know Guy Dion, too?"

"Yes," she nodded. "I knew Guy, too."

"You know he died?"

"I found out yesterday."

"My father still won't talk about it."

"They were good friends as kids."

"All their lives. Until about a year before Guy died." He paused. "I guess you know Lucien, too."

Libby nodded again. "I had dinner with him last night."

"Yes?" Jacques said, his voice warming into almost a welcome now. "When I talk to my father, I'll tell him I met you. It's Muir, isn't it?"

"That's it. Elizabeth. He might remember me better as Libby."

Jacques walked with her back to the gate near the office. "Where do you live now?" he asked.

"Toronto."

"*Mais maudit, c'est une grande ville là, n'est ce pas?*"

It was a large city. Not like New York or Tokyo, but it was large. Ile d'Or and Toronto were different in far more ways than just size. Even with the cosmopolitan population of Toronto, there was a vibrant undercurrent that flowed throughout French Canadian society. Despite the communities that had enlivened Toronto over the years, the undercurrent there felt to her nonetheless muted. Warmth emanated from the lilt of the spoken language here, from expressive faces and gestures, from an enthusiasm that was immediate and embracing. Jacques hadn't been like that when she encountered him at the gate, but she understood he'd been cool then to an Anglo in his midst who was also a stranger.

"Yes," she said. "It's a large city."

She crossed the highway and waved at him as she started back past the rocks, toward the town.

21.

NICK WATCHED THE boy slather his hamburger with ketchup and mustard. It looked tempting, so he put some on his own, along with a dill pickle and some sliced onion. What would Michelle have to say about the kid? Would she be at home now making something fast to eat? Or had she become a gourmet cook? She'd said she would make time to have dinner with him, but he found himself nervous at the thought of asking her, of eating across from her. It had been a couple of days and he hadn't yet phoned her. It was ridiculous, he thought, someone he'd known briefly in his teens, kissed once, awkwardly. How could that prove to be anything but a relaxed opportunity to reminisce? They had so much they could talk about.

"Hey, mister," the boy said.

"Yes."

"Can I go back to Toronto with you?"

"I hardly think so," Nick said. "Why would you want to do that?"

The boy grimaced. "Not much here for me."

"You'd need to speak English."

"You think I can't learn. I want to. Then I can make a lot of money."

"What would you do with it?" Nick asked, fascinated by the boy's ongoing ability to surprise him.

"Buy a motorcycle."

He supposed the boy wasn't so different from him, caught up in dreams. And with more reason than he had, living an impoverished existence, foraging for food. All Nick could think of was escaping to some remote country to hunt for big game or take photographs. Or writing a novel that would immerse him in a different reality. He wanted to blot out all his memories of Marie living in Texas having a good time with Henri Tremblay. His friend. His friend no longer.

And he still didn't want to go back to his practice. His patients had become a burden.

"So?" the kid said.

"No," Nick said. He'd already raised a daughter, what did he need with a vagabond boy?

"Hey, Mister, I know which whores do blow jobs."

"C'mon. It's time for you to go home. Don't talk like that." Nick turned to look at the couple in the next booth. They didn't seem to be listening and he wondered why he felt he'd be embarrassed if he'd found they had.

"What do you want?" the boy asked.

Nick sighed. Not anything the boy could offer. It made him sad to see the desperation in Marcel Blouin's eyes, but how could he take that away? "Tell you what," he said. "I'll go talk to your mother. Maybe we can work out some kind of arrangement for you."

"You want to sleep with my mother?"

"No," Nick said, shocked at the speed at which the boy had jumped to that conclusion. "I'm worried about you."

The boy grimaced and shoved his chair back. He swore under his breath. Turning toward the door, he disappeared through it. Nick wasn't sure what he'd said or done to make the boy so upset, but he felt relieved to be on his own again.

The waiter brought coffee. Nick asked for the bill, and then drank the hot coffee slowly. A sequence of blurred images flowed across his vision. His father coming in from the mine, reaching for the belt if Nick said anything. Especially if Roman was already angry. Nick could never read his mood right away. He wasn't alone in having an unpredictable parent. Libby's father sometimes staggered down the lane when he'd been drinking, wandering into whatever house had a door open. Susan's mother had often come to the front door and shouted in a loud voice, her words slurred. Yet he knew that the boy's experience was worse than all of that. Many of Nick's contemporaries were separated or divorced now, had been through stuff that had left its mark, but they still had opportunities if they looked for them. He wasn't sure what his own were, but he knew he would uncover them when he was ready

The waiter poured more coffee into his cup.

"Half," Nick said. *Merci.*

Reaching into his pocket for his wallet, he put his credit card on top of the bill. He wasn't sure where he would go from here or how long he would stay in Ile d'Or. Maybe he would drive out of town by the other route through Mont Laurier and the Laurentians and stop in Montreal on his way back to Toronto. That highway went through a long stretch of forest, mile after mile of mind-numbing sameness, before it reached Mont Laurier. The drive was broken by one very large park with hunting and fishing. From the highway, he recalled seeing cabins and canoes, a restaurant of some kind, men with tackle or guns.

On the street, Nick looked up at the sky and noticed clouds forming on the horizon. "Dreamer," Marie had called him. "Star gazer. Even when you're at home, you might as well not be." She'd wondered if it were something about people who came from the north. Who knew? he thought, musing that her criticisms often seemed more a pretext for something deeper. But he could never fathom what that was.

He walked through town toward the former bunkhouse where his room was on the second floor. All the rooms were small, no more than cubicles, and while he couldn't imagine how men had lived there day after day, there was a certain charm to the place now. And who was he to judge what would have been perceived as adequate for miners who went underground, he with a veneer that had grown over his years of lucrative practice? To the men in those days, these rooms likely had all they needed. Even though the frame building had been a fire trap, and who knew how many men smoked and drank in their beds? The conscience that sometimes surged up demanded to be heard, the voice of his father. Who would have taken the needs of miners into account? Before unions especially? Some distant managers in Toronto or New York were probably responsible. How could they know about the men who slept in their underwear like his father had, so angry all the time that if Nick so much as made a sound the belt came out. Roman Petranovich wasn't like that when Nick was very young, but after he saw a man killed underground he changed.

Walking the familiar streets, Nick peered into store windows. It was a distraction to try to figure out which ones were there when he was growing up and what might have disappeared. Woolworth's was gone. Or was it Kresge's? The dairy had been turned into a hardware store, the pharmacy was familiar, *Pharmacie Dion*. He'd have to go in before he left and see who the owner was now. Maybe whoever it was would also remember that fearful night when the sirens had gone off and everyone on the property had heard the news of an accident underground. Gradually people had gathered at the mine gates for the cage to come up, hoping to find a husband or father or brother emerging safe from the deep chill of the earth. Nick hadn't really understood much, except that his mother cried when she saw his father come down the path.

"Oh, Mollie," he said.

Later Nick heard sounds through the thin walls of their log cabin. The groans of his mother and father making love. He wondered where the boy lived, then felt irritated that even when his recollections were most intense and focused on what he'd needed to come here to face, he couldn't stop thinking about Marcel Blouin.

22.

AS HE COUNTED out pills and scraped them into a small plastic container, Lucien's mind wandered. He wondered if Michelle knew Susan had left him. It seemed that everyone in town knew so she likely did. After he put a top on the bottle, he slipped it into a bag on a tray among an array of other small, white bags arranged in rows in alphabetical order. On his way for lunch, he would deliver it although he knew he should probably visit his mother. Madame Dion, as she was known in the community, still lived in the house he had grown up in. It was on rue Champlain down the street from what had been the Muir's house, close to the war memorial.

"Monsieur Dion," Charmaine said.

She had the order form already filled out for the cosmetics. He'd have to remember to give her a raise soon, he thought. Before she decided to leave and go to Montreal like so many of the young girls did. He hoped she would find a reason to stay. He thought Jacques Paquin had been in and out of the pharmacy so often lately that it was likely to see Charmaine, although neither of them gave any sign anything was going on. If they had started to see each other, he expected he would have heard about it.

"Thanks, Charmaine. You do good work."

A smile lit up her entire face, the bright pink lipstick on her mouth glistening.

"What time do you want to go for lunch today?" he asked.

"One o'clock?"

"I'm going to deliver a prescription. I'll be back before that."

The address Dr. Cloutier had given was at the end of town and he recalled Michelle lived in Paradis du Nord, the permanent mobile home area. He should be able to drive there, drop it off, and still have time to pick up a hamburger. He slipped on his jacket and tucked the white bag into his pocket.

At the door to Michelle's place, Lucien hesitated. Some Christmas decorations already hung in the window, gold and red streamers crossing in the middle and a red cardboard poinsettia with a gold ribbon stuck to the glass. What would he say to Michelle about bringing the medication himself? Although they ran into each other on the street or in the pharmacy from time to time, he had never really gotten to know her all that well. Susan used to go to Chic Choc and afterwards had told him how well the shop was doing, that Michelle had given it a new vitality. They'd all known each other as children, but Michelle had gone to a different school than he and Guy had, a Catholic one like theirs, but hers was English. And she hung out with a different crowd on the property, the ones Guy's age. She had left town just when those kinds of age differences were ceasing to matter. Hanging between them had also always been the knowledge that if he'd driven Francine home that night, she might still be alive.

When Lucien rang the bell, there was no sound of footsteps or a knob being turned from the inside. He remembered that her two daughters had both left Ile d'Or. He rang again. Pulling the prescription from his pocket, he studied the address. There was no mistake; he was in the right place. Then he remembered that Dr. Cloutier had said Michelle would pick up the pills the first chance she had. She was probably in her store. He could just as easily have gone there. Why had he come rushing out to her home? He hardly understood his own reactions these days, so often did they arise from a sudden impulse that later struck him as verging on desperation.

Alors, Michelle. He would see her in the pharmacy. He would have to go right back to the store in case she came during her lunch hour. These pills were sedatives or tranquillizers that he assumed meant she must be having a hard time, too. Maybe that was why he'd acted so quickly, aware of his long hours awake in the night, the endless tossing and turning, sleep elusive.

"That was quick," Charmaine said.

A glance at the clock told him he had been gone only about fifteen minutes. Nodding at Charmaine, he placed the prescription in the tray under D and hung up his jacket. Rather than engage in conversation, he headed for the back where he started to look again at the accounts and unpaid bills and at his bank statement, at the confusion that had crept in since Susan's departure. He despaired of ever being able to sort out the mess on his desk, like a garden that had become so over-grown that even a large scythe would have difficulty carving through it. Maybe he would drop in on Maman after all. No, there wasn't time for that now. He could go after work if he called Libby to let her know he would pick her up a little later. A memory rose to the surface of seeing Wally Muir on an airplane from Los Angeles to Chicago when he'd been out to California for a convention. Susan hadn't come to that one. On the way back, he'd asked the steward about the score of a hockey game, one between the Habs and the Leafs. The man looked at him strangely, obviously baffled. But next thing he knew the pilot was standing beside him.

"The Habs won. Three to one," he said. "I knew you had to be Ca-nadian. But someone from Ile d'Or? I can't believe it. Do you remember me? I'm Wally Muir."

"You're the pilot?" Lucien said. Wally was younger than Libby, so considerably younger than he himself was. Too young, he felt uneasily, to be at the controls of the airplane.

"I dreamed about flying ever since I was a little kid," Wally said. "Mum always had some kind of thing about airplanes, too. Do you remember when she was a volunteer spotter for the government and counted planes for the Distant Early Warning Line. So did Mrs. Du-fresne. You know she came from England?" He didn't wait for Lucien to answer any of his questions. "I used to go out with Mum to spot. She pointed out C-46's, the whole shebang. I used to shout whenever I saw one. It seems bizarre now, but it's a good memory."

"She was probably counting Canadian and American planes," Lucien agreed. In those days, a Russian bomber would have run out of fuel long before it got that far.

It surprised him that he hadn't thought of this encounter with Wally before as it would have been natural to tell Libby about it. *I saw a Muir not all that long ago. I saw Wally.* "Oh, yes," Libby would have said. "My brother, the pilot." Or something like that. So much had happened in the intervening three or four years that Lucien had for-gotten until now. At the time, it had been an isolated incident, one of those unexpected meetings of two people that makes a good story for a couple of weeks. Now it connected to everything else about the Muir family and the white house on rue Champlain, just up the street from the Dion bungalow. It was around the curve and past the house on the corner where Jeannie Petranovich had lived. Until he told Susan about seeing Wally that time, he hadn't remembered that Jeannie had married Wally. Susan had then told him that they lived in southern California. Now he remembered when Wally had thrown a rock at the scarecrow in the Petranovich's garden. The rock had hit Jeannie hard in the face and Mrs. Petranovich had rushed out onto the street and marched toward the Muir's house. All she could say when she got there was "Wally, Wally, Baloney, Baloney." Madame Muir took both Jeannie and her mother to the hospital, then spent a day in Mrs. Petranovich's kitchen a week or so later learning to make cabbage rolls. The story filtered out in bits and pieces until just about everyone knew about it. Even if the two women hadn't said anything, as they probably hadn't, it was a story that gradually became legendary.

"I'm going now," Charmaine said.

Surprised at the sound of her voice, Lucien looked up at the clock. It was one already. Reaching into his pocket and taking out his wallet, he asked if she would buy him a hamburger. He would take a coke from the cooler in the pharmacy.

"*Avec frites?*" she asked. With fries?

23.

THE DARK SHADOWS of tree branches moved against the wall of the bedroom as Michelle took a container of pills out of the cupboard in the bathroom. The night felt eerie and it seemed to close in on her. Tired of her migraines and not sleeping very well, she had managed to forget to pick up her new prescription at the pharmacy. She hoped when she did the pills would make a difference. Sometimes when the sound of the blasting woke her up around two in the morning, she lay there for over an hour with her mind racing. Perhaps it was as long as two hours. Tonight it was almost midnight and she hadn't yet gone to bed.

She let the water run and filled a glass, then flipped one of the small white tablets into her mouth. The doctor had agreed to order the others, although he didn't want her to become too used to them. Still, he was concerned that she wasn't getting enough sleep.

The telephone rang, startling her. She had no idea who it might be at this hour other than a wrong number.

"Hi," Nick said. "I hope I'm not disturbing you."

"It's all right," she said, puzzled, waiting to hear why he'd called. She watched the shadows move on the wall.

"Could I come over to your place?" he asked.

He slurred a word. He's been drinking, she thought.

"What?" she asked, guarded now.

"You can say no."

"Of course I can say no. I know that." What did he take her for?

"I'll call again," he said.

Michelle noticed that he hadn't mentioned dinner. It was too late tonight, but he could have invited her for another day. Did he drink a lot on an ongoing basis? Anything was possible since she really didn't know him.

"That kid asked me to take him to Toronto," Nick said.

"What kid?"

"You know, the one I told you about who seems to be shadowing me around this place."

"Oh, you mean Marcel Blouin," she sighed. This could have waited until morning. "Well, he's harmless."

"I suppose. But he's also a nuisance."

"Depends on how you happen to view it. Maybe he's just hungry."

"I bought him something to eat again," he said in a defensive tone. "It didn't end there. He keeps on trying to find a prostitute for me."

What did he expect her to say? Nick didn't sound drunk now, but she knew he'd had something, his voice a little louder than it needed to be.

"So what did you say?" Michelle asked.

"What kind of man do you think I am?"

"I actually don't know," she said. "Someone who's ready to rush off to Africa and find some trophies."

"You think I'm a spoiled rich guy, don't you?"

"Well, I would if I didn't know you from way back."

"Can I come over?" he asked again. He sounded like an adolescent who wanted to see someone but couldn't figure out why himself.

"Didn't we go through this already?" Michelle tried to think of a way to end the conversation short of hanging up on him. She was afraid if she didn't that she might actually agree to let him come over and she knew that was a bad idea at the moment.

"I've started to meditate," he said. "I could show you how."

"You didn't ask if I already know how. But that's beside the point. Why would I ask you to come around to meditate at almost midnight? You can tell me about it when we go out to dinner." She heard a beep on the line. "I have another call," she said, surprised someone else was also calling at this hour. "I'm going to take it."

"Oh well," he said. "Good night."

Michelle pressed a button and said hello. It could be Elise in early labour. It could be anyone. All she knew was that she rarely received calls this late unless there was a crisis somewhere.

"Mom, are you there?" Dawn's voice asked.

"Dawn? My goodness, *chérie*," Michelle said, her spirit rising at the sound of the familiar voice she hadn't heard in such a long time. Then she began to worry that this call had been prompted by some calamity. "Are you all right? Where are you?"

"Yes, I'm all right," Dawn said. "I'm in Montreal."

"Are you staying with Elise?"

"I haven't called her yet. I just got here today. I'm at the Y. Could I come to see you?"

Michelle breathed in deeply at the wistful, almost frightened, voice that came over the wires. Maybe she did need to learn how to meditate. "Of course," she said. She'd been longing for Dawn's return for what seemed like ages now. She didn't understand why her daughter had become such a rebel. While Elise was immersed in a banking career and expecting her first child, Dawn had been angry for years and Michelle had never been able to break through that. At first, Dawn had left because she wanted to make contact with her father's family. The man who abused them. The man they'd escaped from.

"Well if you want to, go ahead," Michelle had said warily. "I don't think it's wise, but it's your life."

Dawn had decided it was her mother's fault that the girls hadn't known their father. Michelle hadn't so much tried to prevent the girls from knowing him as she'd tried to protect them, the need for which there was surely enough evidence. The man had once kidnapped the girls and on another occasion had taken a knife and threatened to kill them and their mother.

"I found my father," Dawn said finally, her voice gruff.

"Oh," Michelle said, alert for an attack that seemed bound to follow.

"You were right," her daughter said. "He's an asshole."

Michelle gripped the receiver. In the silence that followed, she could feel relief flow over her. Finally it seemed there was an opening.

"I'm so glad to hear from you, Dawn," she said.

"I really am sorry," her daughter said.

"I know," Michelle said, hearing the remorse in her daughter's tone. All that mattered was that she was there now, at the other end of a telephone line, no longer running. "When did you say you'd like to come to see me?"

"Soon. After the weekend."

Only a mother would understand the relief, the anticipation, the joy she now felt, Michelle thought. Her own mother would have understood. She had also worried about Dawn in those last months before she died, even though Michelle had protected her as much as she could. Pretending sometimes she knew where Dawn was, that Dawn would be coming home soon. It was all she could do for her frail and failing mother who had loved both Elise and Dawn with that special care of a grandmother who had a sense of continuity because of them.

"I'll come on Tuesday. I'll take the bus," Dawn said. "I'll go and see Elise first. Maybe she'll let me stay there for a couple of nights."

They'd been close as children, with the ordinary bickering of two sisters not far apart in age. The fabric of a family the three of them had built together was something she had seen Elise suffer at losing also. After a while, Elise had stopped asking about Dawn, had not wanted to talk about her at all. Michelle imagined that she would be surprised, and she hoped happy, to find Dawn reaching out to her. She supposed Elise might also be very angry, but Michelle hoped her relief would outweigh everything else.

On the other end of the line, there was silence, the daughter who had not made contact in over two years seemed to wait for her mother to continue.

"Do you want to tell me what happened?" Michelle asked.

"Some time, maybe," Dawn said. "For now, I just want to apologize to you." She'd seen her father soon after she left home, she said, and knew then that he was a loser who didn't give a damn about her. And then she'd started running, as she put it. "You were right, but I guess I had to find out for myself."

There was nothing Michelle could add to that, her own mind racing.

"It was all worth doing," Dawn continued. "All the travelling. You learn so much. And gather stories as you go. But it took me a lot longer than it needed to."

Years, Michelle thought. It had taken years for this moment to arrive, times when she'd worried, cried, and spent nights awake. Anxious. Panic in the pit of her stomach, her body rigid. Not knowing where her child was, if she were safe. Or on a street somewhere. Hungry. This had been the hardest circumstance of her life, to have one of her children estranged from her and not be able to do anything about it. When she received an address, it was all she could do not to reserve a flight to wherever Dawn was. Once she had, and after flying to Paris had taken a train to a city in Provence. Dawn had been furious and refused to speak to her. Except to say if Michelle ever did anything like that again, she would never speak to her again. Never.

"I look forward to seeing you," Michelle said. She could scarcely wait now that she knew it was about to happen, but she was afraid to say so. She couldn't bear the thought that Dawn might change her mind.

24.

LIBBY FOLLOWED THE path past the playground to a small wooden bridge. She expected to see the houses next to the bush loom into view, the first, the one at the end of rue Champlain that the Muir family had moved into just before Sheila was born. Before that they had lived in a semi while the house that awaited them on rue Champlain was being built by a contractor for the mine. As she drew closer, Libby saw new wrought iron numbers on the front porch and bright blue shutters against the familiar white asbestos shingles. In spite of the numbers and new coat of paint, the house still looked much the same. She could imagine the oak dining room table and could almost hear her father saying grace — *Benedictus, Benedicat* — and her mother asking nervously, "Is everybody happy?"

Libby imagined that she would find the oak table just as it had always been and the same blue cupboards in the kitchen. The photograph of a small boy in a white sailor suit with his black nanny would be hanging on her bedroom wall. A vision of running eagerly to the shelf near the fireplace to find the book with gold letters on the spine, *Jock and the Bushveld,* to give to her father when he returned from overseas. But when her father came back from the mine that day, it was late.

"Okay, Captain," Black Steve said under her bedroom window. "Good you come back."

Her father fumbled with the doorknob.

"See you at the sump," Black Steve called as he started to sing into the night. "Onward Captain soldier, marching off to war."

Libby turned away. Maybe it was not the gold that had made him drink. Maybe it was the war. Even though he never saw battle and had ultimately been overseas for only a few months, it was after he came back that he had become preoccupied in odd ways. It was also when the drinking began to become a problem. He must have seen things she could scarcely imagine, injuries and blackouts, younger men who did not return from the front. Although her mother had once told her that even in university he was a quiet man who drank a little more than was good for him. She had not known him until later, so she must have heard that from someone.

It was hard to imagine the life her parents would have from the wedding photograph of the handsome couple on the bureau in her mother's room. Her mother had worn a wide brimmed white hat and long dress, her head slanted in a mixture of shyness and saucy awareness. In her right arm, she held a large bouquet of daisies. Her other hand held her new husband's arm. His face was proud and hopeful, his eyes nonetheless cast down toward the ground. In his left hand, he held a hat and a pair of gloves and his dark shoes were highly polished. Since the photograph was in black and white, Libby had to guess at the colours of everything, including the ribbons on the flowers and the tie her father was wearing.

Whenever she saw this photograph, Libby stopped to contemplate it. It was the kind of portrayal that elicited hope that the young couple would find what they wished for, that their lives would be happy. From this photograph, no one would ever guess the treacherous nature of the waters they would encounter.

Libby walked across the street to a narrow laneway and what was once a shortcut to the town's small Anglican church. It wasn't long before she found St. Andrew's, still standing in front of a clump of pine trees and an outcrop of rocks. As a child, she'd squirmed through both Sunday school and regular services. But Charlotte, her mother, had insisted on it. It was the church where she and Barton had married. Guy had not been at the wedding. She hadn't invited him. Not long before that day, she'd seen him on the street.

"Bonjour," he'd said and kept on walking. He never said more than that in those days, as if it were only yesterday that she'd broken off with him when it was almost two years by then. She wondered if she should have let him know herself that she was getting married. And if he would have offered good wishes had she done so.

Over dinner the other evening, Lucien told her that Guy had gone to the cabin and stayed there until she left town after the wedding. As she thought about her ceremony, she couldn't recall any French people there. As if the Paquins, the Dions and all the French families she had known as a child ceased to exist when she married Barton.

She reminded herself that it had been a small wedding, but surely she could have invited the Dions and the Paquins. And Michelle Dufresne. Why not Michelle? Surely by then her father wouldn't have objected. Lucien had also told her that Guy had eventually married, but it didn't last long.

On the main street, Libby saw a *dépanneur* where she could buy a few apples, a banana, a container of yoghurt and probably some crackers. Back in the hotel room, she would sit at the window with her purple spiral-bound sketchbook. When she did, she wrote, *The Name of the Town is Ile d'Or* on the cover. Perhaps it would be the title for an exhibition. *They Called Us the English Polacks.* She had heard Lucien use that term about kids playing on the street, her sister, her brother and Jeannie Petranovich, when she was in the warm kitchen of the Dion house with Guy. Did Lucien remember? She would remind Sheila some day. It was more likely something her sister would use as a title for one of her short stories. She reached for *Vox*, the magazine her son had given her just before she left. This time as she flipped the pages she found a review of her latest exhibition with a colour photograph of one of the acrylics. Although the reviewer liked it, she realized it no longer made a difference to her, knowing as she now did that these paintings had been a diversion. The theme of guns and violence that had led her to paint a man stalking a woman along the Seine had been assumed for just such an urbane reviewer.

She crossed the room and lay down on the bed. The mattress was so thin she could feel the springs and she could see a hole in the ceiling. A spider crawled across the floor toward the radiator and disappeared into the shadows of the baseboard. She picked up the telephone and called Dan's office number, but only an answering machine greeted her. Without leaving a message, she put the receiver back in the cradle.

Libby was assailed by a jumble of images that kept on colliding. The mine-shaft dark against a starlit sky. Dan in a bed somewhere with another woman. Her father taking the brown paper bag out of the drawer of his desk at the office.

She decided to go out and swung her legs over the side of the bed and reached for her coat. When she got to the lobby, through the window she spotted a cab idling at the curb with AL'S TAXI written on it in large, yellow letters. She went outside to speak to the driver.

"I'd like to drive around a bit," she said.

"All right," he said. "You have anything in mind?"

"I'll leave it up to you."

"Okay. *Pourquoi pas?*"

They drove along the main street past a new cinema called La Victoire where *Bonheur d'Occasion* was playing. Libby thought she would likely miss some of the action in the movie without any subtitles. A hardware store with a skidoo in the window made her shudder with the thought of the noisy machines roaring through the quiet trails of her past. As they passed the drug store, the driver glanced at her in the rear view mirror.

"Pharmacie Dion. Hasn't changed much over the years. You been in, *n'est-ce pas?* You know Lucien."

Libby was startled. Now that Ile d'Or had over thirty thousand inhabitants, she had not expected news to travel as if it were still a small town.

"He's a good man," the driver said. "It was a tragedy about his brother."

"Yes, I know. It was a shame."

They drove through a residential district with ranch style bungalows and two-storey Georgian houses, which, aside from the bleak surroundings, could have been any affluent Toronto suburb.

"Guy's kids went with the former wife," the driver said. "Both he and his girlfriend were heavy drinkers, so it's a good thing. Her mother, the girlfriend's, spoke only Polish. When her father was fixing the chimney one day, he fell off the roof." His voice droned on and on. "Once Guy called me from somewhere on the St. Lawrence. He asked me to drive to Montreal, to bring his girlfriend and a twenty-four-ounce bottle of scotch with me.

"'Do you know how far that is, Guy?' I asked him. "He knew. Five hundred kilometres."

The cabbie made the trip, but he could not find Guy in the club on St. Denis where he'd said he would be.

"'Al, he's found a whore,' his girlfriend said. "So we drove all the way back. When Guy got in a day later, he called and asked for the twenty-four ounces. He told me to go get his girlfriend." He had come in another taxi and had to pay for both of them.

Libby wished the driver would stop talking, but she perked up when he mentioned Lucien.

"His wife left him for an engineer from Montreal who was living at the hotel where you're staying," he said, glancing over his shoulder at her. "Some looker, Susan Dion. That dark hair and those eyes. I remember when they were married. She hasn't changed."

"I left Ile d'Or not long before that," she said, aware he'd mentioned a man Susan was involved with and wondered if Lucien knew.

"You mean you used to live here?" the driver asked, eyebrows rising and the lines over his nose scrunched together as he turned to glance at her again.

"Um. Yes," she said. "I did."

"Well, I'll be damned. I guess I came here from Chibougamau just after you left. I'm Al Desjardins."

"Elizabeth Muir."

"Muir?" he said, his voice rising. "Muir? I remember your father. I used to bring him home in the taxi."

Libby could imagine her father staggering out to the curb in front of the Alpha, managing to find the door to the cab and slumping into the back seat. When they passed a vacant lot with a rusted car at the far end of it, she was distracted. "There used to be a greasy spoon restaurant there," she mused. "With a pool hall behind it." Guy had taught her how to hold the cue there, how to aim. The first time, she'd almost ripped the green felt when she scratched, but after a while she played so well she sometimes beat him. "I used to play pool with Guy."

"*Moi aussi*," Al said. "Guy was the best until the drinking got him."

"When was that?"

"It must've been getting worse for a long time. I didn't know until his wife left him." He pointed to a bank with large windows. "When I came here, that was a beauty parlour."

"I had my hair cut there when I was a kid. The sidewalks were made of wood then and the streets were all gravel."

"I met your father after he dried out in that place in Toronto," he said. "He gave me a couple of bottles. He said he wouldn't need them any more."

When he dropped her off in front of the glass doors of the hotel an hour later, he would not take any money.

25.

A MAN STOOD at the front desk of the hotel, talking to the receptionist. The pigeon holes behind the receptionist contained keys for the rooms and Libby could see hers in one of them sitting on top of a piece of yellow paper. There was a message for her. When the man moved away, he left his suitcase with a bellhop who took it and accompanied him down the hall toward the new part of the building. As he left, the receptionist reached for the keys in Libby's slot. Handing them to Libby, she also gestured toward the slip of paper that said Lucien had called.

"Thanks," Libby said, thinking that she would go up to her room and call him from there. She wished she'd had the foresight to stay where she would not be depressed by the aura of decrepitude her room evoked.

"I'll be half an hour late," Lucien said when she reached him at the pharmacy. "I'll call from downstairs when I get there, unless you're already in the lobby."

"I'll use the time to draw," she said. The house on rue Champlain. The mine. A sketch of Jacques Paquin in his yellow hardhat. He must look like his mother. Libby would never have mistaken him for Paul. Perhaps she'd do a sketch of the taxi driver. She could not draw Guy. The young boy she had once played with in a pile of leaves, his fingers the first to touch her budding breasts, could not be the same man who had taken those wild taxi rides Al Desjardins had described. Instead she lay down and rolled over on the bed. The springs creaked. Lucien was coming soon. He had never been more than Guy's older brother and a familiar face, but now the thought of his naked shoulders moving toward her was like a wave rushing over a bather at the water's edge. As her mind descended over the hair spreading downwards in an inverted triangle, her throat felt constricted.

Jumping up abruptly, she went to the closet where she brushed her fingers over a bright fuchsia blouse with wide shoulders and long sleeves that she had bought before she left Toronto. There was also an ivory sweater with purple and green woven through it. She almost never wore skirts, but she had brought one. She slipped the sweater on over her blouse, and then cinched the dark skirt at her waist with a wide belt. Next she pulled on a pair of knee high boots. Her coat and purse were over her arm as she went down to the lobby. She would wait for him there.

She was still thinking in English, although occasionally an entire French phrase emerged spontaneously as she spoke to the receptionist. Only as a teenager had it occurred to Libby how odd it was that her parents did not speak French. As a child, she'd tried so hard to learn — stuttering, stammering, longing to know the language that surrounded her. But the children she played with proudly spoke their heavily-accented English. Not until she was working in the drugstore, later in the assay lab at the mine off the highway, did she find people who spoke to her only in French. Once she had asked her parents why they had never learned the language.

"I spoke some French with Thérèse," her mother had said. "But she soon learned English." Thérèse had been with them when Wally was born. On Queen Victoria's birthday, what's more, her father had said, as if the birthday of some old, dead queen mattered. He had left soon after to go overseas. "Libby, will you get some onions from the basement, from the fruit cellar?" Thérèse had asked.

Libby came up from the basement with her hands empty. "I got the onions. See, Thérèse!"

"Oh, you *petite* rascal," Thérèse laughed. "You just have to go back down again."

Libby was so engrossed when Lucien arrived that she was startled when he greeted her. Smiling broadly, he handed her a small box of Black Magic chocolates. "Would you like to try a different restaurant tonight?" he asked as she tried to thank him.

"Sure," she said. "Though l'Ange Bleu was very nice."

"*Oui, mais* … you might as well see as much as you can while you're here." He took her arm as they walked down the steps to the sidewalk. "What about La Cabane?" he asked. "We'll save The Flamingo for dancing. You can't come back to Ile d'Or without going dancing at The Flamingo."

"Do you remember the Rialto?" she asked, recalling the club the Ukrainians or the Poles had started where she and Guy had danced on Saturday nights.

"It burned down years ago." He put his hand on her shoulder. "My car's over there."

Driving down the main street, he headed toward the centre of town.

There was a large map of the surrounding area on the wall of the restaurant. The head of a moose was mounted over the door to the washrooms. She remembered pick-up trucks carrying headless moose that appeared on the main street in the fall. The hunters must already have removed the head and antlers, although sometimes there would be a moose still with its head intact on one of the trucks. When she said something about darker hamburger in hunting season, Lucien laughed.

"Hasn't changed much," he said.

The waitress brought two menus, placing them on the table. "Anything from the bar?" she asked, scratching down their order without lifting her face to look at them.

In the next booth, two women with heavy makeup and false teeth talked in quick staccato. They tapped their fingers to Beau Dommage, playing on the jukebox.

Lucien fiddled with his napkin. "This man you told me about, what's he like, Elizabeth?"

"Oh, you mean Dan," she said. "Well, he likes people. Art and music. Rides a bicycle. A good sense of humour."

"Qu'est-ce qu'il fait?" What's he do?

"He's a lawyer. *Un avocat.* He got drawn into civic politics. Now he's an alderman." She had brought with her an article Dan had given her to read with his name in large letters on a yellow band across the cover along with the magazine her son had given her, her father's letters, her sketch pad, and the books by Roch Carrier and Michel Tremblay.

"Does he have time left for you?"

"I don't know," she grimaced, surprised at his insight. "He may have more time for someone else, someone called Daphne." Studying her face in the mirror that hung on the wall behind Lucien, she observed dark shadows in half-moons under her eyes and her mouth drawn tightly. Once she had heard a man talking about her in a bar.

"When I met her, she'd been separated from her husband for a year. She was still sleeping on her side of the bed," he had said. "The mattress sagged in the middle and the springs were broken." When he turned around and saw her, his face turned crimson. Would she one day turn Dan into an anecdote? He was careless about details, she would say. There were always cracker crumbs on the sofa, dirty coffee cups on window ledges. No, Dan loomed too large in her life for that. If it were over between them, he was nonetheless interwoven into who she was now. She wanted to hold onto some richness he had given her. Would her father have come to understand his own pervasive racism if he had lived long enough? If he had met Dan? It could be so subtle, something she wished she'd been able to confront, but when her father was still alive she hadn't understood it well enough to have words rather than inarticulate anger around what he said. It was his generation, where he had come from, all of that, because when she could articulate an argument about anything, he tried to comprehend it. He had changed his mind about women in subtle ways over the years. Yet her mother, who had wanted so much to understand, was more of a problem for Libby as she unexpectedly came out with the most surprising statements. Confused from taking too many pills one night, taken to emergency, she had sat up on the hospital bed.

"Make sure there are a lot of black people at my funeral," she had said.

"What are you doing, Mum?" Libby asked.

"I'm very busy dying, dear."

The next morning, she talked again about her funeral, naming specific people, some of them friends of Libby's, who were black.

"I don't think you're going to die this time, Mum," Libby said.

Lucien scanned the menu. "I feel like onion soup. And maybe steak again. What about you?"

"The soup," she said. "With a salad."

After he had ordered, Lucien looked at the booths around them. "*Qu'est-ce que tu as fait aujourd'hui?*"

"Walked around. When I got tired, I took a cab. Al Desjardins' taxi. He already knew I knew you."

"Oh, *mon Dieu*," Lucien said. "Sometimes I think that man knows everything. And what a raconteur, eh? But Elizabeth, you don't need to take a cab. I don't need my car when I'm in the store." He pushed a strand of hair off his forehead. "You can come in and pick up the keys any time."

"That's very kind." Then, "What about you? How was your day?"

"Flu season," he said. "Antibiotics. Cough drops. Not much call for ice cream in November."

"I used to like chocolate best. After that, strawberry."

"And now?"

"Oh, German chocolate cake, jamoca almond fudge, strawberry shortcake. If they'd all been around when I worked for your father, I'd have weighed a ton by the end of the summer." She laughed with her head thrown back slightly and her eyes sparkling. "I enjoyed that summer so much."

"I saw your brother a few years ago," he said.

"Wally?"

"*Oui.*" He proceeded to tell the story. Wally had invited him up to the cockpit where he had seen the light change as they had flown across the continent, from day on the west coast to brilliant rose over the mountains, then to darkness somewhere over the midwestern states. Lucien had changed planes in Chicago.

"Tell me, Elizabeth," he said then. "Were you a happy child?"

"What a question."

"You always looked as if you were."

"Were you?"

"Not very. I think Guy was Maman's favourite. Papa was too busy with McNab's secretary."

Her eyes widened and Libby took a while to reply. "I didn't know you knew," she said finally.

"Everyone knew." His voice was low, his lips a thin line.

Smoke from the next booth wafted in a spiral over them. The music from the jukebox stopped. The two women looked at them curiously, and then went on talking.

"Like my father's drinking," Libby said.

Looking at her hands, she saw a small bump in the finger that had once held her wedding band. She hoped it was not the beginning of the arthritis that had plagued her mother. As Lucien drank a second cup of coffee, he leaned against the back of the booth, and draped his arm over the ledge behind him. When Libby glanced up, she saw his eyes were on her. She was surprised at how easy it would be to smile at him, gaze steady, to let him know what was on her mind, the softening she felt that wanted him to touch her. If she did, would his body move with hers later until the dam broke inside her, until she began to moan? She saw Dan's face, the tilt of his head, the frown that formed on his forehead, the lines on his cheeks that became deep funnels above his beard. His loping, restless stride stopped and his large dark hands with the pale palms reached for her. But in that moment, it was Lucien's voice that caressed her.

"Elizabeth," Lucien said softly, eyeing her thoughtfully.

"Did Susan ever tell you about the horse?" she asked.

"Susan loved horses." Lucien said. "She groomed the harness horses out at the track for years hoping to get a chance to drive them."

"Once we stole a horse."

"*C'est vrai?*" Is that true?

He looked doubtful, but he waited expectantly.

"Susan took Cathy and me to that field on the other side of the railroad tracks. She used to ride the horse there."

As they'd walked downtown past St. Luc's and the movie theatre, Susan gave away chocolate bars and gum she had stolen to younger children they met along the way. Looking away, Cathy had pretended nothing was happening. I was mad at her, Libby thought, but she'd already told him about that. And she had chewed some of the Chiclets anyway. Then felt guilty. As usual.

The traffic light in front of the church, the one Father Chicoine had ignored, was new then. On the other side of the street was the A&P store, built around the time the light went in. On the hill at the edge of town, the water tower was visible for miles. The sun glinted off the letters of Ile d'Or and a lake glimmered in the distance. Between the railway tracks at the edge of town and the lake were a few open fields, land carved from the unrelenting bush, dotted with granite.

"Sounds like Susan."

"I was afraid. I didn't want to ride it."

"I would've been afraid, too," he said. "I sometimes think Susan wasn't afraid of anything."

"When we got to the field, there was an old, grey horse grazing on..."

"Tell me another time," he said, his voice a caress.

She looked down at the table, feeling as she had that day when she realized that Susan really thought she, Libby, would ride that horse.

"Elizabeth," Lucien said. "You're a beautiful woman."

She shook her head, glanced at the purse on her lap.

"So beautiful."

Please. She could already hear him telling her he liked her breasts. *Please stop.* She was like a tinder box ready to burst into flames, afraid she would begin to rock in her chair to the rhythm of the throbbing inside her.

"Let's get out of here," he said. "I'll go pay the bill." When he returned, he held her coat for her.

"Thank you," she said.

Lucien put a dark scarf around his neck, pulled on his coat, and guided her gently toward the door. On the steps, he looked up at the sky and inhaled deeply. Above them the northern lights shone through the smoke from his cigarette that curled upward in the dark. When he wheeled out of the parking lot, she leaned back and watched the swaying tops of trees against the stars and the pink streaks of the northern night sky.

"I remember driving along this road with Guy," she said. "I was supposed to get home before midnight. Mum would lie awake until I came in. She'd ask what time it was the moment I stepped in the house. Even before I could start to creep up the stairs. I'd say, 'Oh, it's just a little after midnight,' and she'd say, 'That's funny. I thought I heard the blasting.'"

"'Oh, I don't think so,' I'd say. 'It can't be that late.'"

"'We'll talk about it in the morning, Elizabeth,' she'd say."

Her mother's voice was firm, with an edge, and when she said Elizabeth, Libby knew she was in trouble, that she really had heard the blasting. You could hear it all over town. It came from so far down that the house acted like an echo chamber. You could almost set your clock by it. Twice a day. The blasts were all set for the same time. You could hear it walking home from school in the afternoon. You would sense a shudder and hear something. And again at night, at precisely two in the morning, you could not miss it, the dull thudding louder when everything was quiet.

"*Ah oui.*" He smiled. "The sound of the dynamite underground was the curfew for all the girls. And with good reason, *n'est-ce pas?*"

They were driving away from Ile d'Or. "Where are we going?" she asked.

"I thought I'd show you the lake. *Qu'est-ce-que tu penses?*"

"It's late."

"We're almost there."

The moon and stars glistened on Lac Leboeuf as Lucien parked the car beside a small log cabin. As he turned off the engine, he leaned forward and rested his arms on the wheel.

"Susan loved it here," he said.

"I can see why."

There was a rustle in the bush and Libby saw eyes in the dark, peering at them. A fox, she thought, but there was no way of knowing. Then the eyes vanished.

"Maybe Susan will come back," she said.

"She'd be like a wild animal caught in a trap. I think she only stayed as long as she did because of the children." He pushed against the door, came around the car and helped her out onto the rocky ground. "Come down to the water."

On the beach, he stood with his hands in his pockets. She listened to the sound of the waves against the shore. When she shivered, he put his arm around her.

"Would you be angry if I asked you to stay with me tonight?" he asked softly.

"No," she said. "But I'm not sure…" Her voice drifted off as she thought of all the things she could say now. There was Dan. But then there was also Daphne, wasn't there? What about having been Lucien's brother's girlfriend? It made this sudden attraction feel strange to her. "Guy," she said. "What about Guy?"

"Guy," Lucien sighed. "I can't see how that matters now." He looked tired as he removed his arm from her shoulder. "I'd like you to stay, Elizabeth," he said. "But if you want to go back to town, I'll take you." He walked up the slope to the cabin and opened the door. He turned a light on, and then turned it off again. "*Allons-y.*"

"I remember the time you ran into my sister in Montreal," she said.

"Years ago."

"Sheila told me you wouldn't speak to her in English. When you saw me the other day, you did though." She did not add that during the referendum, she had felt almost as if she wore a banner, "*Mon non est Québecois*," even in Toronto, the vote she would have marked on her ballot in the referendum had she still lived there.

"Oh, maybe. It probably has to do with Susan leaving. I feel as if my life's been wasted. And I turn fifty next month."

Fifty still felt a bit remote to her, even though she knew it was the next major milestone she'd have to face also.

"Lucien, I'd like to stay," Libby said, walking toward him.

"It's all right. I shouldn't have asked. It just seemed like..."

"I'd like to stay."

26.

A S SHE PULLED down the duvet on her bed that night, Michelle felt peaceful in a way she could scarcely remember having experienced before. Underneath the fluffed up pillow, she'd left a light flannel nightgown, embroidered at the collar. Memories of Dawn at various ages flooded her mind. The toddler on the handlebars of a tricycle Elise was sitting on, the two faces uplifted toward the camera. Dawn playing with little, brightly-coloured cars and trucks in a sandbox. In her first skirt and blouse for school, carrying a tiny backpack, trying to keep up with Elise.

Sighing contentedly, she crawled under the duvet and reached to turn off the lamp on the night table. She would sleep through this night without the shroud of angst that had troubled her for so long. But no sooner did she drift off when she was awakened by the telephone ringing. This is astounding, she thought, this series of unexpected calls, but then she noticed it was morning and the hands of the clock were moving toward seven. It was early, but she'd slept.

"Well, what about dinner?" Nick asked. "What about tonight?"

"Well, why not," Michelle said. "But why call so early?"

"What time is it?" he asked.

When she told him, he was momentarily quiet. "I apologize," he said then. "And for calling so late last night, too. Profusely."

"Okay."

"Think of where you'd like to go."

"I'll be celebrating," she said. "I heard last night from my wandering daughter."

"Then we'll make it a special dinner."

When she hung up, Michelle picked up a photo of her two daughters and looked at it intently. She could hear Nick saying, "The younger one looks like you."

"She does. And the older like Francine, a bit. Don't you think?"

"I don't remember her that well really."

Why did she need an imaginary conversation to think about her sister? It was still so difficult. Dawn's absence had often reminded her of that earlier loss. The night Francine was killed, Michelle had been sleeping. A loud knock at the door awakened her and she heard whispers in the downstairs hall, then her mother's agonized cry. Michelle could tell something terrible was going on and thought of the mine. But her father wasn't working underground any more; he'd left the mine to run The Flamingo. She'd crept to the top of the stairs and watched Jutras touch her mother's shoulder as he spoke quietly to her. What could a policeman, even one who knew the family well, have done to alleviate the pain her mother felt?

"Maman," she'd called, but only Jutras had looked up to see her.

For days her parents' eyes were veiled or filled with tears and Michelle moved around them feeling she was invisible. For a long time, her mother retreated into silence. Later Michelle became the focus of all their expectations. At times she hadn't been able to bear it. No one understood how her whole world was reshaped forever by that accident. When the car her sister was in, on the way home from a party, crashed into a tree out on the highway. The road had become icy in the few hours since the party began and clearly the car had been going too fast. Francine and the boy were both under the influence of too much booze. Lucien had gone to that party to pick up his brother and drive him home. He could have brought Francine home too, but he hadn't. Michelle couldn't blame him. Francine had already crawled into the car ahead of him, although he knew she'd seen him. She had waved him away. Or so Lucien had told the policeman when he stopped at the accident, moments after it happened, because he recognized the car. Losing Francine was devastating, Michelle thought. Losing her only sister, her older sister, who had always been there — she couldn't imagine anything worse. Until Dawn disappeared.

She looked out at the deck beyond the kitchen window to see if the *Montreal Gazette* was there, the newspaper her mother had read regularly. Sometimes the teenager from across the street who delivered it was late. Or even forgot. She put the Fair Trade coffee Elise had given her in the pot and plugged it in. Dawn would be here in a matter of days. That thought was enough to submerge memories about her sister and Michelle started to hum a few lines from the *Hallelujah Chorus*.

27.

ONLY THE STARS and moon lit the path to the cottage. From the porch, Lucien beckoned to Libby to follow him inside. She could hear a dog barking and as she entered a golden retriever leapt toward her.

"Down," Lucien said sharply. Patting the dog with one hand, he reached with the other to plug in a small space heater. A couch with a red blanket thrown over it faced the window and he motioned toward it, inviting Libby to sit down. Before he joined her, he let the dog outside, noticing the tops of trees waving in the wind.

"It looks like we may be getting a storm," he said.

Libby nodded. "What's the dog's name?" she asked.

"Figaro."

"What made you think of that name?"

He shrugged. "Susan chose it."

The dog scratched to come in again and circled the room, sniffing.

"Lie down, Figaro," Lucien said in a low, firm voice. But the dog followed him as Lucien poured dry food into a large bowl on the floor. He picked up another bowl and took it over to the sink where he filled it with water.

"*En voilà, chien.*" He brought a bottle of wine over to the couch and sat down beside Libby.

"Tell me the rest of that story now," he said as he handed a glass to her.

Taking a sip, she put it on the wooden table in front of her. "When we got to the field, Susan said we'd ride bareback," she said.

"Trust Susan."

Libby was quiet, but Lucien could feel her eyes on him. This hardly seemed like the time to kiss another woman, but he wanted to. He wanted to put his arms around her and press her breasts against him. He reached toward her and his whiskers scratched against her cheek.

"Libby," he murmured.

She didn't resist and as his tongue twisted around hers, he moaned. When he unzipped her sweater, she helped him ease it up over her shoulders. As he undid her bra, she moved so that her breasts tipped up to meet his lips. His mouth on her left breast, he groaned again as she pulled at his belt. Soon their clothes were flung around the room and he lifted her gently and guided her to the bedroom, stopping just long enough to turn off the lights.

Afterward, when his semen dripped out of her onto the sleeping bag that covered the bed, he turned away. Since marrying Susan, he had not been with another woman. He was embarrassed.

"Lucien," Libby said, touching him lightly with her fingers. His body heaved and she stroked his face and shoulders until the sobbing subsided. He turned and held onto her as if she were a life jacket and his existence depended on it.

After a while, she pulled her leg out from under his and drew the sleeping bag over their bodies. He could see the dog, lying on the floor at the end of the bed, raise his nose to sniff at Libby's feet. When Figaro growled, Lucien knew it was because these were not the feet he was looking for. Rain began to fall on the roof with a hollow sound as the drops splattered on the shingles. Finally he fell asleep.

When he awakened in the morning, Libby was on her side with a blanket around her shoulders. She did not stir. Slipping out of the bed, trying not to make a sound, Lucien dressed in the bathroom. Figaro watched him, tail wagging.

As Lucien pulled on his coat and boots and opened the door, the dog leapt out. Sniffing at the snow that fell overnight, he trotted toward the bush and lifted his leg to emit a yellow stream. The temperature had dropped and the rain that had fallen during the evening had changed to snow and ice. The boughs of trees were covered with white flakes. Lucien watched the sun rise over the opposite shore of the lake. The colour of the sky changed from pink to yellow to a hazy blue. He never tired of watching the sky here, especially in winter. People who never came north did not know the power of the sky at dawn, and at sunset.

Walking slowly to the edge of the water with the dog circling him, Lucien threw a stick along the beach. Figaro leapt for it, bringing it to him with head stretched out as if to make it easier for Lucien.

Snowshoes leaned against a tree at the side of the cabin where he'd left them. Soon there would be enough snow, he thought, but not yet. As he followed the trail next to the lake, basking in the silence and the pure white of snow on pine, on poplar and birch trees, he could feel tears ready to fall.

"*Mon dieu,*" he whispered. "*Où est ma femme? Où est Susan?*"

The head frame of the old MacNac mine was visible in the distance. One of the first stakes in the area, it was on an island that could be reached only by water at first. At some point, a causeway was built to connect it to the mainland. Susan's father had made one of the early claims there, then sold it to some company from Toronto. Or maybe it had been New York money. He was not sure any more, except that sometimes he had blamed Susan for the entire situation of the French in Canada.

"I'm part of Quebec and its history," she had said. "All the time my father worked in Ile d'Or, he knew who the real oppressor was."

"Who?" he had taunted her.

"Maurice Duplessis."

"Oh, come on, Susan," he said. "*Les financiers anglais lui graissent les pattes et il devient leur concièrge. Just like his predecessors.*" The English financiers greased palms and...

"What about the Catholic church?"

Father Chicoine, for sure.

It was an argument that never had any resolution. Except sometimes between them there had been some softening. On one point, there was no difference. Neither of them believed in violence. They had both objected to the tactics of the FLQ.

Lucien turned back toward the cabin. The dog had disappeared, not finding a playful companion this morning. Some days Figaro stayed outside. Maybe he knew he would soon be locked up otherwise. Lucien wondered what he would say to Libby. Almost fifty and he still did not know what he was doing. When he climbed back up the slope, he saw his car parked where he had left it the night before. As he opened the door of the cabin, sun streamed in through a window over the sink. Libby stood at the mirror there. She stretched her arms.

"Hi," he said. "*Bonjour.* Did you sleep well?"

"Yes," she said.

That made him smile. How could she have slept? But that was the point surely, that she should have and that he ought to be glad she wasn't as tortured now as he was. Added to his longing for Susan, now also discomfort that he had slept with the woman his brother had never gotten over.

"Do you want to go for a walk before we go into town?" He watched her put on her coat, step outside and look around. When she started toward the water, he followed her.

"What are you thinking about?" Lucien asked

She sighed. "The light," she said. "How to paint it. See how it glistens on the snow. The sky. The trees, bare branches outstretched against blue. The mine shaft with the blue and white flag on it. That, too. Or against a grey, cloudy sky, wind blowing." She paused "I could use water colours," she mused. "Or maybe pastels. I'll do some pencil sketches while I'm here and take some photographs. Maybe acrylic. I like that medium and how quickly you can work with it to get something dramatic." She sighed and added, "The north is as it has always been – spectacular."

"You didn't finish telling me about the horse," he said. She seemed to have drifted off into another world, so he was surprised when she answered him straight away.

"I wished I hadn't followed Susan that day," she said. "If I rode the horse and my parents ever found out, I knew I'd really be in trouble. But if I didn't, I'd lose face. Susan rushed across the stream with the horse, jumping from rock to rock. When there were no more rocks, she waded through the water without taking off her running shoes. Cathy and I followed, climbing out on the opposite bank. We were covered in mud. Susan rode with her braids flying behind her. The horse trotted around the field. You could tell she'd been on that horse before. Once she slipped forward and put her arms around his neck. When she slid down from his back, she looked at me. I didn't meet her eyes, but she pulled the horse toward the fence where I was sitting.

"'Your turn,' she said. It was so quiet all I could hear were the bees buzzing around the raspberry bushes. I turned to see where Cathy was, thinking that maybe she'd ride. But she sat on the ground, watching me. She looked almost desperate. Oh, Jesus. I didn't care what Susan thought any more. I didn't care if she thought I was chicken. When I shook my head, she muttered, 'Sissy,' and veered toward the stream. I just sat there and let her go. Cathy stood up then and followed after

Susan. After a while, I heard them yelling. Yelling and screaming."

Lucien watched her face, animated by her story. He did not want to hear more now, but he did not know how to say so without offending her. A mine whistle blew in the distance and he looked at his watch.

"Libby, will you stay longer?" he asked.

"I can't," she said.

"You can stay here at the lake. I'm at the store all day."

"If there were a cabin I could rent out on MacNac Island, I might."

"I guess we'd better get going," he said and she started toward the car.

"There's Guy's cabin," he said when he slid into the driver's seat next to her. "No one's using it."

"I didn't know he had a cabin."

"It was Papa's."

"*Bien sur*. Your father used it for fishing."

"It's still pretty much of a shack, but there's a propane heater now. You wouldn't have to use the wood stove if you don't want to. It's not far from my place. You could have my car whenever you wanted. If you drove me into town, you could pick me up later. I almost never use it during the day." He hoped she didn't think he was pleading, but it felt to him as if she couldn't help but hear his cry for help. *If you stay a while, maybe I won't drown.*

"I'll think about it," she said.

28

LIBBY WATCHED THE side of the gravel road as Lucien drove toward the highway. The earth was covered with a carpet of tiny, glistening crystals.

"The horse was struggling in mud on the opposite bank of the stream," she said quietly. "Susan pleaded with him, tears running down her face. It must have been some kind of quicksand because the more the horse tossed his head and heaved forward, the more he sank in the mud. I dream about it. Over and over. The horse keeps sinking. The farmer screams at him and then begins to beat him. I want him to stop. He swears *Tabernacle. Sacre bleu*,' in a terrible, high-pitched voice. Then he takes out a gun." As she spoke, Libby thought about her nightmare. When she awakened from it, she never connected it with these memories even though it clearly was connected. What the nightmare meant and why she dreamed about the horse repeatedly was still a mystery.

"A gun?" Lucien said. "Are you sure?" As if she hadn't been there.

Sometimes she had thought she had dreamed the story about the horse, dreamed that the farmer shot him. Like the story about Arthur White that Sheila had told her. Although maybe something had happened between him and their mother on that long ago evening when Libby had awakened to find her mother missing. But there was a gun, the farmer had had a gun, she was certain of that.

"I didn't think…"

"I was there," she said. "He shot his horse." Who else would believe her? She didn't know anyone else here but Lucien any more. When he was quiet, seemingly doubtful at her version of the story, she said so.

"You know my mother. You knew my brother," Lucien said. "They'd both believe the story. And as for not knowing people here now, you've met Al Desjardins who must know everybody."

"That's true." *C'est vrai.* But somehow she didn't see herself telling Madame Dion about the horse.

"Maman hopes to see you."

"Yes, of course," she said. "I'd like that."

They drove then without speaking until they reached the store. Libby followed Lucien inside and sat at the counter where he brought her a mug of coffee with the pharmacy's name on it.

"I was born in a mining camp that's no longer there," Lucien said, leaning against the counter. "What about you?"

"Out of town."

"One of those," he said. "A first-born."

"Sheila was born out of town, too." There had not been enough hospital beds for anything but mine emergencies until Wally came along. The doctor had come to the house where her brother had been born in the bed with the maple frame in her parents' bedroom.

"So your mother flew back in with you in a bush plane?"

"I think she left Toronto on the train." She told him about the last part of the journey on the plane that landed on an isolated lake en route. It was there a policeman brought two handcuffed men aboard. They'd been arrested for smuggling bits of gold from underground in cigarette lighters and lunch pails.

"Or so my mother told me."

Lucien nodded as she told him. "High-graders," he said.

"After Wally was born, Thérèse came running to the yard across the street to tell us." She waved her arms over her head. "Libby," she called. "Sheila. Your mother had a little boy."

Libby had wondered if her mother's belly was flat again, if she would be allowed to crawl in bed with her now that there was another baby.

"Do you remember Thérèse?" Libby asked.

"I don't think so."

"I thought you would. She worked at our house when I was a kid, helping Mum with the new baby. I think I resented Wally when he was born. When Sheila came along after me, I wasn't very old and I don't remember how I felt. Was it hard for you when Guy was born?"

"I suppose so," Lucien said.

A woman who had been browsing through the cosmetics drew closer. She could have walked in from downtown Montreal in her trim black dress and jacket, magenta silk scarf at the neck. Her hair, brushed back behind her ears, had a few streaks of grey in it. Libby could feel her scrutiny and sensed something familiar about her. She was uncomfortable with the hostility that seemed to emanate from the woman.

"Libby Muir?" the woman asked.

"Yes." Libby wanted to recognize her in turn, but couldn't. Then it dawned on her. She was talking to the daughter of the man who had built The Flamingo. This woman had once been a friend. Until her father forbade it.

"Michelle Dufresne?"

The woman nodded before turning to Lucien and breaking into French.

"*Bien sur*." He moved to the counter at the far end of the store to find her prescription.

Michelle turned back to Libby, still regarding her with suspicion. Libby felt as if there were an invisible electric current in the air. After all these years, she was shocked to think her presence warranted this treatment.

"How are your parents?" she asked finally.

"They're both dead," Michelle said. "My father died years ago and my mother in the spring."

"I'm sorry."

They both seemed at a loss for words then.

"So you stayed?" Libby said.

"Let's just say I came back," Michelle said. "I took over the dress shop."

Libby wondered what would have become of her had she stayed in Ile d'Or. Very few of her generation who were English had. Other than Susan, Lucien's wife, she knew of no one. Did Susan now speak with the trace of a French accent?

"I didn't expect to find anyone who would speak English to me any more," Libby said.

"Oh, the French are starting to speak to the Anglos in English again," Michelle said. "René's on the way out. Anyway, I'm not a separatist. Neither was my father. Everyone went to The Flamingo when he owned it. Except Monsieur McNab." She paused. "And your father." Her lips were tightly pursed, and then she added, "When McNab left, the next manager, he came to the club. On any given night you'd see the guys from underground, the kids from school, the couples out for a night on the town, the business girls who followed the miners around and knew when it was pay day."

"The prostitutes?"

"Yes," Michelle said. "Everyone came."

To Libby's ear there was still a note of hostility in the words. "I get the feeling that you still resent my father," she said. "He was wrong to try to influence my friendship with you, but he was doing what he believed in. And I was too young to know any better."

"Well, it's over, isn't it? My parents are both dead," Michelle shrugged "And the Flamingo is still here and everyone still goes to it."

"Why did you come back?" Libby asked, aware that nothing she said was going to change what had happened long ago, that maybe they would get beyond it and maybe they wouldn't. There was no point in trying to defend her father's view that high-grade gold stolen from the mine in even the smallest specks was not the ethical basis on which to build anything. It was a crime, her father had said, wanting Libby to understand that. But he'd been wrong to punish Michelle for something he'd only suspected of her father back then, something that had never been proved.

"I moved to Montreal and got married there," Michelle said. "I came back when I left my husband."

Lucien handed Michelle a small, white paper bag with a bill stapled to it. As she unzipped her purse and stuffed it inside, Libby saw him look at Michelle as if he were seeing her for the first time. Libby recalled the button Paul had bought for his father a few months after they had separated. *Just Passing Through.* She knew suddenly how Barton might have felt when he saw it.

"I'm sorry about your marriage," Libby said.

"Don't be. It was a good thing to leave it," Michelle said. "He was a bully and a con man." She looked at Libby's hands. "What about you?"

"Divorced." When she refused Guy, he'd found a new girlfriend within weeks. By the time she came home from university, he'd found someone else again. He wouldn't speak to Libby at all. Avoided her when she passed him on the street. If she had not refused him, she might have spent her life in Ile d'Or. Instead she had married Barton and had two children. "I have two kids," Libby said. "One of each."

She visualized Paul sprawled on the floor with a bowl of chocolate ice cream, his books strewn across the worn grey rug. His frayed denim jacket and the jeans with threads dangling from the holes on the knees. The reddish hair that fell into his eyes as he played with the ginger tabby cat that slept on his bed or on the clothes he left scattered on the floor. Her daughter, Rosemary, was an outgoing child, quick to smile, from the time she was a toddler. Until recently, Paul had been quieter, although always more determined. She would have to call her son when she got to her hotel room to tell him she would not be home for a while longer. She suddenly realized she was in no hurry to leave and that surprised her.

"I have two daughters," Michelle said.

Libby smiled. What would life have been like had she never married Barton and had her children? Would she have gone to Vancouver and found a job there? And then on to Australia, as she'd dreamed of doing? She might have if she'd had any idea how artists could make a living.

"What do you do?" Michelle asked.

"I paint." Only now had it all come together for her — the teaching, selling a few paintings here and there, the occasional grant or prize. Open to possibility, one way and another, she managed. The settlement when she was divorced had been helpful, too, although she was never again able to spend money without counting as she had for a while when she was married. After Barton finished his residency and started his surgical practice, even with all the debts they carried at the beginning, for a time she had not worried.

"My sister's buried out there." Michelle pointed toward the end of town. "You remember Francine?"

"Of course. That was a terrible tragedy." A vision of the silver lamé dress flashed across her mind. And she'd heard about Father Chicoine's words at the funeral home, when he took his class there. She hadn't gone to the funeral service itself. No one in her family had.

"I'm going out to take a wreath. Would you like to come?"

Libby struggled to hide her surprise at the unexpected invitation. But she accepted. And Michelle, at last, seemed to soften.

29

LUCIEN LISTENED AS Libby agreed to accompany Michelle to the cemetery. Was Libby just curious, or did she really care about what went on here? Michelle, too, had lived in a city for a long time. Now that her children were gone, maybe she would sell the store and return to Montreal. Only Susan had been able to live in Ile d'Or. She loved the north. Loved the life. When she'd felt like doing something different for a while, she'd set traps in the woods, skinned rabbits and scaled logs for a season somewhere on the way to Rouyn. That was Susan. Unpredictable. As the eldest daughter who went along on some of her father's shorter trips once she had left home, she'd learned a lot.

"See you later," Libby said.

Michelle looked back at him as she took out her car keys. "How is Madame Dion?" she asked.

"*Pas pire.*" Not bad. Considering.

As the door shut behind the women, Lucien slumped onto the stool behind the counter to drink his coffee. Charmaine did not come in until ten most days and nor did most of the customers. It gave him a chance to go through the newspapers from Montreal, set up the coffee pots, and do whatever tasks he had left from the night before. Sometimes he was so tired by the time he locked up that he left cups unwashed and crumbs on the counter. Susan would have made sure everything was in shape for business the following day, but he had stopped following much of a routine. Everything was slightly askew except when Charmaine worked evenings. He liked being behind the counter after she was there, knowing it would be as neat and clean as Susan would have left it.

A gust of cold air burst into the store with the arrival of one of the local policemen. Gustave headed toward the counter, his glasses clouding over like windows in winter. Sitting on a stool, he put the glasses on the counter in front of him and gradually the fog began to clear.

"*Café au lait*," Lucien said. "Coming up." Gustave liked his coffee around this time every day.

"*Alors, mon ami*," the policeman said, his moustache still white at the edges. He ran his fingers over his red cheeks and screwed up his lined face in a broad smile. He must have been here for fifteen years now. Jutras had left long ago and might be dead, for all Lucien knew. Soon the priest would likely come in also. He and Gustave would talk about the hockey game in Montreal the night before. Nothing had changed much, except these men were less colourful than Jutras and Father Chicoine had been. Nor did they curse as much. Even younger than he was, at least ten years younger, neither of them had been here since the beginning of the town. This thought suddenly made Lucien feel old. The day would come when there would be a premier who was younger. A pope, maybe. Although he supposed the latter was unlikely for a long time.

"What do you hear from Susan?" Gustave asked, never hesitating to say right out what everyone else was thinking.

Lucien was still surprised. "Got a lawyer," he murmured.

Everyone thought Susan would get tired of Montreal, even Lucien, although he had not let on to Libby how much he hoped that would happen. It was not as if she had never gone off before. There was the time she went over to the sawmill for a couple of months, the children all somewhere else that summer, working at jobs or camping. Everyone knew that Susan was a woman who often needed some new challenge and that Lucien had married her because she was like that. She was not like him, she was more like Guy. Except without the drinking, without the anger.

"*Merde*," the cop said, his face reddening as he saw Charmaine come in. Not far behind her was the priest, Father Jean. The three men watched Charmaine rub the palms of her gloves together and bend her fingers before taking them off. Putting them in the pockets of her white parka, she unzipped her coat and hung it on a hook. Before going behind the counter, she straightened out the newspapers as if Lucien had not already done so. The priest leaned over and took a copy of *Le Devoir*. After all, the editor was from Abitibi, a few miles away in Rouyn. A separatist, too. He was not, for practical reasons. It might mean the parishioners would not have enough money for the church so he did not preach that even though he thought that the French should be *maîtres chez nous*. It was one of the paradoxes he faced daily, like the women who talked about pills and condoms. He turned his head the other way then. The pope did not have to raise eight children in shacks in the bush. Putting some change on the counter before going out the door, he could feel that Gustave was not far behind.

Lucien went into his office and sat at his desk, surprised to see an envelope he had missed the day before. It had the name of some firm in Montreal on it. Maybe it was from the lawyer. Instead he found a letter from Susan inside. *I don't want a divorce,* she wrote. She wanted to talk about money and how to divide it. Could he come to Montreal to meet her? *It might be all right now*, she wrote, *but I don't want to get into a situation where later you might change your mind and not want to send as much.* She wanted it settled.

Lucien put the letter down. It sounded like divorce to him. As if she had forgotten how their lives had overlapped almost since they were children. As if she had forgotten everything that mattered. His sweat on her body, the wetness under the dark thatch of hair on her pubic bone that was the semen flowing from him, the hairs on the edge of her dark nipples which lay flattened from the touch of his tongue.

The front door of the shop opened and he heard Charmaine speaking with Madame Robichaud, his mother's next-door neighbour. He knew that his mother and Madame Robichaud often talked about moving into apartments, hopefully in the same building.

"*Bonjour, Lucien,*" the older woman called out to him.

"*Bonjour, Madame Robichaud.*"

Leaving his office, he walked over to her, knowing she would tell him about all her grandchildren. Two in Shawinigan, one in Quebec City, two in Chibougamau, three in the Gaspé. Lucien had stopped counting. Her husband had been the butcher at Mulholland's until it closed after the first big supermarket opened. Many of the smaller stores had also shut down then, except for a few *dépanneurs* that stayed open for longer hours.

"And Juliette?" he asked. The youngest, the daughter who had come years after all the others and had never done what you would have expected.

"Working in a small French restaurant on Yonge Street," Madame Robichaud said. "She says Toronto's a friendly city. She likes it there." She looked bemused.

Lucien was glad at least that Susan had not gone to Toronto. He knew she could probably manage anywhere, but the thought of her in Montreal gave him some hope still for their marriage. Odd as that might seem were he to articulate it to anyone, he thought. Yet if she'd opted for Toronto, still the bastion of WASP commerce, he felt he would have given up all hope by now.

30.

FROM THE RISE at the far end of Ile d'Or, the main street stretched out until it disappeared over another hill in the distance. The street was typical of towns of that era in Abitibi, lined with more bars and hotels than anything else. The Purple Pig was long gone, but there were other places men could find hookers without anyone noticing. Archie's was still a dry cleaning store, but now in the hands of a French man who had never bothered to change the name hanging over the window. The Flamingo had been there so long that it seemed likely to last as long as the town did.

Beyond the rise, the car passed the mine where both Libby and Michelle's fathers had worked. A mile or so after that were the two graveyards. In the Catholic one, neat lines of head stones bore a sea of French names interspersed with occasional English, Polish, Ukrainian, or German ones. Across the road in a smaller cemetery, grass long, the Protestants, mainly English, were buried under tombstones that stood in uneven lines. Michelle turned into the Catholic cemetery and parked just inside the gates. They walked quietly between the rows until Michelle stopped.

"This is Francine's grave," she said, pointing at a tombstone with a picture of her sister and the keys from the car in which she'd been killed encased behind a clear cover underneath a black and white cross. Watching Libby as she gazed at the photograph, Michelle turned away and moved a little ahead, toward another tombstone.

"This is Father Chicoine's," she said with a tinge of bitterness in her voice. "Right next to my sister's. In the end, the same thing happens to priests as to teenagers who drink too much." *The bastard liked to drink, too.*

Oui, oui, but don't be too hard on me, a breeze seemed to murmur.

Michelle reached for strands of hair loosened by the wind. "You weren't at the funeral so you didn't hear old Chicoine then. Nothing he said did anything to alleviate the suffering of my family. Nothing to lessen mine for sure." It was probably what had hastened her departure from the church, she added after a brief pause.

Libby was silent. She didn't know what to say. Finally, "I'm sorry."

"Guy's over there," Michelle said.

Walking slowly along the next row until she reached a grey stone monument with Guy François Dion inscribed on it, and the dates, 1937-1982, Libby struggled to hold back tears. She tried to remember the year Guy had come to Montreal to visit her.

She had been lying on the bed in his hotel room on Sherbrooke Street, a block from her residence at the university, her bra tangled in the sleeve of her sweater. Looking into his eyes, she was about to push him away when he put his hand under the woollen sweater and stroked her nipples. Her body had started to throb and she'd liked the feel of his fingers. So afraid someone might know what they were doing, her body had nonetheless stiffened. When he pulled her to him, she'd felt something hard move against her stomach.

"We'd better not, Guy."

He pushed his tongue between her teeth, exploring the inside of her mouth with it.

"Don't Guy." She tried to stop him.

Reaching down between her legs, he rubbed his hand against the outside of her pants. Frightened by the knowledge that the one thing a girl must never do was to get pregnant, she had shivered.

"Touch me," Guy whispered.

When she reached tentatively toward the hard thing against her stomach, he moaned and there was a sudden wetness in her hand. She drew away, pulled her sweater down and huddled in the corner.

"We'll get married," Guy said. "Please marry me, Libby."

"I can't, Guy," she said.

"Why?"

Libby had not known what to say. Slipping her hands up her back under her sweater to fasten her bra, she swivelled around to reach for her shoes on the floor beside the bed.

"Is it because you don't love me?" Guy asked plaintively.

"No." Not able to imagine life without him, Libby couldn't figure out how he fit into her future either.

"Is it because I'm French?" Guy then asked, starting to sound angry. "Is it because I work at the mine?"

"No," she said. "Of course not."

As far as she was concerned, it had nothing to do with either. Or maybe it did. It certainly influenced her parents, but for her it was because of the places she wanted to go. And even more, the vivid flashes of colour that came in visions. She felt she had to remain open to something that would encourage that. And she sensed that marrying Guy would prevent her from ever discovering what these yearnings were all about. But only two years later she'd married Barton Morley, still not knowing quite what to do either with those vivid flashes or her longing for something more.

Michelle came to stand beside her. "Are you okay?" she asked.

Libby was startled as she looked up to meet the gaze of the other woman. "What happened to Guy?" she asked.

"I don't know," Michelle said. "All I heard were bits of gossip. He drank a lot. He turned up at Paul Paquin's house one night really drunk. He and Paul had a fight and after that Paul never spoke to him again."

They were quiet as they headed back toward the Chevy. Libby slipped in and leaned against the headrest. Michelle's hands gripped the wheel, her knuckles almost white with the pressure, as they drove out of the cemetery. When they turned away from town, Libby was about to ask where they were going. Something made her hesitate and she didn't say anything, curious to see where Michelle would take her. When they stopped near a beach not far from Lucien's cabin, she was surprised to see the water covered with gulls.

"If they don't head south soon, they'll get stuck in the ice," Libby said.

"Some do sometimes," Michelle said. "They die unless someone chops it away." She turned off the ignition. "I'm stuck here," she said, turning toward Libby with what seemed like resignation.

"I thought you wanted to come back."

"I couldn't think of anything else to do," Michelle said. As she stepped out of the car and slammed the door, the gulls, startled by the noise, rose from the water and headed across the lake in a large V-formation.

Coloured balloons had surrounded the swim area at this beach during summers of long ago and boys had paraded across the sand in their tight trunks with the bumps in front. Sometimes one of them looked at the girls, who pretended not to notice. Even Jutras was there in his bathing suit and Libby discovered then that he was not that much older than she was. When her father went to his house later to get a dog for her birthday, he must only have been in his early twenties.

"I only stay because it's familiar," Michelle said. "It's a tough town under the surface. It always was." She pointed toward a field at the far end of the beach. "The horse sank over there," she said.

"The horse," Libby murmured. "What horse?"

"The one Susan used to ride," Michelle said. "You know she left Lucien? She's gone to Montreal. I don't think she's coming back."

Michelle knew. How?

Libby listened to the throbbing of the mill across the silent stretch of pine trees. The vacuum pumps at the mine had mufflers on them made out of forty-five gallon oil drums that created a constant thumping, twenty-four hours a day, seven days a week. If it was quiet at night, you could hear them pulsing in the background. Anywhere within a one-mile radius of the mill, you could hear the pumps. Along with the French language, it was the background noise of her childhood, interspersed with the mine whistles at shift change. And the blasting.

Did she stay in Toronto because it had become familiar? As she'd stayed too long in her marriage? In neither case had she intended to. Barton, who had read poetry to her, who had seemed interested in everything about her, had objected when she'd started to paint when Rosemary was a baby. Utterly baffled, she'd continued clandestinely, hiding her canvasses in the closet in the baby's room, a place she knew was safe from Barton's scrutiny. Only years later did she understand that her images frightened him. There was so much about her that had bothered him. Like conversations with a man next door who kept a motorcycle on the lawn, the man who reminded her of Guy although she never said so. One day Barton came along the street and, having seen them talking, strode into the house without speaking, his anger palpable. When she entered the kitchen, he'd banged a cupboard door. "I don't want you talking to him," he'd said, the vein above his right eye bulging.

"Good God, Barton."

"He's violent," Barton said, his voice tight.

The vein moved like a snake across the part of his head where the hair had begun to recede. A stark blue under seemingly transparent skin, that vein seemed to have a life of its own. It became for her an unwelcome barometer. Wary when it began to throb, she listened to his voice rising in tandem. Perhaps he was the violent one. All she'd ever talked to the neighbour about was art. Now she thought she also might be as stuck as the gulls were. Every time she visited Sheila in Vancouver, she considered moving there. Once she took Paul with her to see if he would like it. For the first four days, the city was shrouded in fog and even when it lifted, Paul said he would prefer to live in Toronto. Soon he would be gone and she would be alone in the house on Walken Avenue. Then she could move anywhere she wanted.

"Did you know I was there when the horse sank in the quicksand?" Libby asked. "I saw the farmer shoot him." She could still hear the sound of the gun and see the horse's head suddenly thrust back as the bullet went through his skull. Maybe what she needed to absolve her feeling of guilt around this misadventure was for Michelle to say there was no gun and that the farmer had not shot the horse. She visualized the words, *Je me souviens*, on the license plate of Michelle's car. To remember let all the debris emerge from under the surface.

"I don't think it was quicksand," Michelle said. "A bog maybe."

"Maybe."

Even the unravelling of her marriage might have been for reasons she still understood only vaguely, Libby thought. Barton must have met the woman he later married before he moved out on that cold February day, before he left the rotting fence posts for her to deal with in the spring. Maybe her art was always just an excuse for what he would eventually do.

"In my dreams, it's always quicksand," she added.

31.

SAINT SAUVEUR, A pale yellow brick building, once the French Catholic school run by nuns, was on the main street of Ile d'Or above the stretch where the hotels and bars were, beyond The Flamingo. Beside it was the house where the sisters had lived, next to it was St. Luc's Catholic Church, and beside the church, the priest's residence. As Nick walked past, he thought about how much influence the priest and the nuns had on the town when he'd lived here. So much had changed. Or had it? he wondered.

A sign for the film, *Bonheur d'Occasion,* hung just ahead over the entrance to the local cinema. He'd liked Gabrielle Roy's novel although he didn't read much fiction. When Marie found a book that excited her, she'd passed it on to him with comments about the characters or the plot or what she observed most keenly, lyrical language.

"Most thrilling when the novelist is also a poet," she'd said. Her favourite writers were often from Quebec and had not been translated, so she awaited eagerly the English versions so she could share them.

Crossing the street, he looked in the window of the drugstore. The sign still said Pharmacie Dion, but he knew new owners could have kept the name, depending on the good will associated with it, to keep and attract customers. Looking up, he saw the flamingo still in the window of the club next door, although he thought the sign was new. Painted perhaps, with the same lettering. Many were the times he'd had a beer there and watched one of the acts brought in to entertain the locals. High quality, too: a jazz musician from America, Oscar Peterson from Canada. Others who became famous later.

Condoms, he thought as he looked in the pharmacy window. It seemed strange to think of them when he hadn't considered he would need any for a long time. Not that he thought anything would happen with Michelle, but since encountering her in the cemetery, he'd been aware of how much he missed Marie. And of a glimmer of anticipation when he thought of Michelle.

So he pushed open the door and went into the store where he walked up and down the aisles until he found a display of different brands. Trojan. Marie had had her tubes tied so he hadn't used these very often. On one or two occasions since their separation it had been useful to have a pack in his pocket. Once he'd met someone at a dance and found himself suggesting coffee, then accepting an invitation to go back to her apartment for a drink.

There was a display on the end of the unit and as he reached to retrieve one yellow package from the top, the whole pile came tumbling down into the aisle. Eyes behind him seemed to burn into his back and he felt his face turn a vibrant red.

"I'm sorry," he muttered, embarrassed. Even though only Michelle knew he was in town, now everyone in Ile d'Or would know what he was up to.

"I'll take care of it," a voice said. "*C'est rien.*"

Turning to see the man who had spoken, Nick shuddered. "A Dion for sure," he said.

"And you are?" the man asked.

"Nick Petranovich."

"I'm Lucien Dion." He put out his hand and Nick shook it, saying again that he was sorry.

"Don't worry."

"I remember you," Nick said. "Hockey."

They'd played on opposing teams in high school, he for the English Protestant school's team and Lucien for the French Catholic one. Lucien's team usually won, an unusual experience for Nick the first time it happened as up until then he'd always been on the victorious squad.

"You married Susan Lambert, didn't you?" Nick asked.

He was curious about what kind of woman Susan had become. He remembered her as spunky and recalled an incident at school when the principal had brought Susan from her Grade Five classroom to his Grade Nine one. In the early days, students of all ages and grade levels were combined in one building as they awaited construction of a high school. When Nick was growing up, there still wasn't a regular one anywhere in the area and the children who had reached higher levels earlier had gone to board with someone in Kirkland Lake. He thought the French children had gone to Rouyn or Noranda. He'd stayed in Ile d'Or though as by then the building for the elementary school was big enough to house all the grades by combining some classes, and the high school was almost finished.

"I remember when Susan's teacher made her stand in the hall because she was chewing gum," he said.

There she was when he'd returned from the washroom. He'd asked her what happened. So she told him when the teacher caught her chewing gum, she grabbed Susan by the arm and marched her out into the hall. When Nick was about to go back to his classroom, Mr. Hall, the principal, came along and also asked why she was there. Sheepishly, she told him.

"Do you have any gum left?" Mr. Hall asked.

Susan took out two sticks from the almost empty Wrigley's package.

"I want you to come with me," he said to Susan. "You, too, Nick."

They both followed the principal into Nick's classroom. Nick was surprised when Mr. Hall led Susan to a spot in front of the teacher's desk. Nick's teacher was leaning against the blackboard, watching them.

Blushing, her head down, Susan twisted one braid in her fingers while she waited for the principal to say something.

"I want you to stand right here," Mr. Hall said. He moved aside as she moved onto the exact spot he'd indicated. "Now teach these students how to chew gum."

Susan took the package out of her pocket, looking baffled. She slipped a stick into her mouth and her cheeks swelled as she started to chew. Nick could imagine the peppermint flavour slowly disappearing. With a red face and beads of sweat running down her cheeks, she chewed methodically, determined despite her humiliation.

Finally the principal told her to stop. "You did a good job," he said.

Nick would bet she never chewed gum in school again. Whenever she ran into students from his grade, she would rush by with her head down. Except him. When she saw him, she would give him a lopsided smile and then he'd wink at her. That fall when the high school opened its doors with a full range of classrooms, he went there with all the older kids and Susan and the gum-chewing incident fell off his radar.

Lucien nodded, his eyes sliding away to the left. "That was her younger sister though," Lucien said. "Susan told me about it."

Nick didn't think so, but said nothing. He was thinking how unreliable memory was. And maybe Lucien was right.

"What happened to her sister?" Nick asked.

"She dropped out of school early and went to Chibougamau to work as a hairdresser," Lucien said.

"Susan's gone now, too," he said. "She left me, not long ago." He stepped backwards.

"I'm sorry," Nick said, feeling as if he should offer something. "My wife left me, too," he blurted out.

They stood in silence, as if pondering this shared reality.

It was Lucien who broke the stillness. "It's very strange that you're here," he said. "Why did you come?"

"I don't know, to tell the truth," Nick said. "Probably something to do with the break up. I haven't figured out why about a lot of things."

"Libby Muir's in town, too. Did you know? But you would know, wouldn't you? She's almost family for you."

"You'd think," Nick said. "But I've only seen her once since I left here. It was after Jeannie and Wally were married. They told everyone after they'd tied the knot and then had a party in Montreal afterwards so everyone could celebrate. I don't think they came back east very often after that and Wally's flights are mostly in the U.S. You know how it is with northerners, spread out all over the place. They live in California. Where does Libby live now?"

"Toronto. What about you?"

"That really is strange. I live in Toronto, too, but I've never seen her there. It's a big city though and I suppose there could be a lot of northerners living there."

"It would be unusual at any time of year for two 'old-timers' to turn up here at the same time," Lucien said. "But in November? What are the chances of that?"

"You have a point," Nick said, with a chuckle. "And so, why is Libby here?"

"I don't know. Maybe for the same reasons you are."

32

MICHELLE DROVE THE Chevy through town with Libby beside her. From the top of the rise, the water tower, inscribed with the letters Ile d'Or, gleamed like highly polished metal in the bright sunlight. The women looked toward the valley that stretched out for miles. You could see the head frame of a mine at the other end of town, one that had been closed down for a while and now was open to visitors for underground tours, something unheard of until recently. Even women could go down, the taboo finally broken when the mine was no longer in operation. You could see the early log cabins set in rows around it. Between the water tower and the cabins were two suburban areas as well as the new industrial park with Beaver Lumber and Cimente Laberge employing many from the town.

They drove along the main street of taverns, restaurants, shops, the Catholic church, and a hall where service groups met. Halfway along they passed Pharmacie Dion and The Flamingo on one side and two blocks later, Chic Choc across from the Alpha Hotel. Both Libby and Michelle had lived close to the mine at the far end of town. Jutras, the town's only policeman then, had lived near the water tower.

"You should have a dog, Libby," her father had said unexpectedly one day.

Libby went with him to the policeman's house because he had heard Jutras had a pup to give away. They stood on the porch, under a clothesline, white sheets and long grey underwear pinned to it with wooden pegs, billowing upward in the breeze.

"We want a dog for Elizabeth, Monsieur Jutras," her father said. He was pleased with himself. "Steve said you have a beagle. You know, Black Steve."

Jutras did not open the screen door. "I don't know." He shook his head. "*Je ne sais pas.*" The pup wound its body around his ankles. "I think he should live with a French family."

"Really?" Walter Muir said, his tone bemused.

Libby could tell this was beyond him. He had had dogs all his life, from the time he was a small boy in South Africa. If anyone knew how to take care of dogs, her father did. There were photographs of him with a small, white terrier in old albums and on the walls of the house on rue Champlain.

Michelle stopped the car in front of Chic Choc. "Come and see my store," she said.

"Do you remember Jutras?" Libby asked.

"Pierre Jutras. I was going to marry him. But when I went to Montreal to study, I met Dominic. That was the end of that. Pierre left to go and work somewhere else. I never heard from him again."

Libby remembered standing nervously on his porch, twisting one of her pigtails. She was nine years old and her father was back for the first birthday she'd had since he went off to join the army; since he had been to that overseas place. Her mother said he'd gone to fight for king and country. He was not the only one who went. On the monument on the boulevard, where the names were recorded of men who were killed in the Second World War, most of the names were French. They were not men who joined because of England, unlike her father. She had also often heard her mother say that her father went because of some man called Churchill, not because of anything the Prime Minister said. Charlotte, who came north to Timmins to teach, where she'd met Walter Muir, had not cared as much about England as Libby's father had. Not with her Irish and French ancestors.

"It's for Elizabeth's birthday," her father said. "I brought her so she could see the puppy."

"*Peut-être*," Jutras said. "I'll have to think about it." He opened the door slightly and beckoned for Libby to slip inside, leaving her father on the steps.

Libby hadn't known that Jutras had been interested in Michelle, but maybe he hadn't known about her English mother.

"He was the one my father asked for a puppy for my ninth birthday," she said now. "After my father came back from overseas."

The pup sniffed around her feet, then raised his black nose and dark eyes. Libby knelt down and began to pat him gently, to croon over him. The two men were talking at the door, but she did not pay any attention. She wanted this puppy. When her father said it was time to go, she left reluctantly.

"Can we have him?" Libby asked.

She followed her father along the sidewalk, past St. Luc's, to the small green Austin parked in front of the nightclub on the other side of the street. She did not pay attention to the flamingo in the window or the cars on the street or anything else. Her mind was focused on one thing, that puppy. "Please, Dad."

"I remember that dog," Michelle said. "He ran away, didn't he?"

"He was a wanderer, for sure," Libby said. "Dad would get phone calls that he was sitting on the steps of St. Luc's again." She thought he probably got quite fed up at all the phone calls and all the taxis. But on the way home that day after seeing the dog for the first time, her father had seemed as pleased as she was.

"Miss Muir, this is going to be one grand birthday," he said. "A fine pup for a fine daughter."

On the day of her birthday party, Libby waited anxiously for her father to arrive. She was worried that Monsieur Jutras might change his mind about leaving the puppy with her if her father showed up plastered.

"I'll drop by to see your shop when I get settled," Libby said. "I'm moving out to Guy's cabin."

Monsieur Dion was a regular patron in the sump also. Guy once went with her when she had to bring her father home and they found the two men sitting together.

"Eh, Dion," her father said. "I wasn't at Dieppe, but I got as far as England."

"*Oui, Monsieur Muir,*" Monsieur Dion said. "*La guerre. Le désastre de Dieppe.*" He had not gone. He'd stayed home to look after his family and run the pharmacy, but the younger brothers of some of his friends were among the dead. "*Service obligatoire outre-mer.*"

The two men reeked of alcohol and their voices were slurred.

"Papa," Guy said.

The men looked up with glazed eyes and gestured with arms flailing at Guy and Libby to get out of the tavern.

"*Oui, mais Maman veut que tu viens chez nous,*" Guy said. Libby echoed him in English. "Mum wants you to come home."

The two men almost fell over getting to their feet, swearing, and followed Guy and Libby out onto the main street where they staggered up Fifth Avenue behind their children toward the war memorial and rue Champlain.

"Guy's cabin?" Michelle looked baffled.

"Lucien offered it to me. I think I'm going to stay around for a couple of weeks. Longer than I intended."

Michelle reached for her purse. "I remember Lucien watching you when you were a kid. At the beach," she said. "Do you remember that yellow bathing suit you used to wear? He couldn't keep his eyes off you."

"Susan had the yellow bathing suit," Libby said. She remembered Lucien's eyes following Susan at the beach. "What did the honey man do underground?" she asked, changing the subject abruptly.

"The men used empty dynamite powder boxes for toilets. When the boxes were full, someone had to nail their tops down and take them up in the cage to surface. That was the honey man's job."

"My father told me it was almost the worst job in the mine. Now I know why."

"It was my father's job."

"I never knew that," Libby said, embarrassed. "I never would have asked about it. I…"

"Ça fait rien," Michelle interrupted. "It's all right. At least that job wasn't dangerous. Not like everything else he had to do underground."

When Libby reached the hotel, she dialled her Toronto number to tell Paul she was going to stay on longer. The first time she got her answering machine. Half an hour later, when she tried again, her son answered.

"Dan Robinson called this morning before I went to school," he said. "I told him you'd be back on Thursday."

"That's why I'm calling," she said. "I won't be back on Thursday if that's all right with you. I'd like to stay a while longer."

"Okay," Paul said, sounding almost pleased.

"There's lots of food in the freezer." She knew he would go through it quickly, especially the hamburgers, ice cream, and apple juice. "When you need more, if you have to spend any of your own money, I'll pay you back later."

"Gee, that's great," Paul said.

"So you really miss me," Libby said, chuckling.

"Well, I do," he said. "But this is neat."

"I sort of figured. But don't throw any wild parties."

He snorted.

"Let me give you a number," Libby said. She looked up the one for Lucien's store. "If you leave a message with Lucien Dion, he'll let me know."

"Who's he?"

"He owns the drug store. He lived down the street when I was a kid. I'm going to stay at his brother's cabin. There's no phone there."

When she hung up, her mouth was dry. What would she say to Dan? At the thought, she felt nauseous. Was she supposed to have ignored his comment about Daphne? She fluffed up the pillows and lay down, too tired to take her shoes off, even to untie the laces. Her suitcase was on the floor under the window, brought in by taxi from the airport when it had arrived on the next flight, the green pompon intact. After tossing restlessly for a few minutes, she put it on the bed to pack the slacks and sweaters she had hung in the closet. She took her blue flannel nightgown from the hook on the back of the door in the bathroom and her toothbrush and paste from the ledge over the sink. When she was finished, she went down to the receptionist's desk.

"Are you leaving?" the woman asked.

"I'm going to stay out at Lac Leboeuf for a while." She paid the bill with her credit card, not mentioning that her wedding rehearsal dinner had been held in this hotel. Nor that her father used to drink in the bar in the basement. She told the woman she had spent summers at Lac Leboeuf as a child. "My family had a place there."

"That's how you know Lucien," the woman said, sounding pleased with her shrewd observation.

33.

WHEN NICK ARRIVED at Michelle's home the evening he was taking her out for dinner, he had a lit cigarette in his hand.

"Do you smoke?" she asked.

"Sure," he said. "What do you expect a DP kid from a mining town to do?"

Michelle laughed. "Well, you'll have to put it out because there's no smoking in this house."

"All right." He twisted the end off and put the butt in the saucer she handed to him. They stood awkwardly just inside the kitchen until she opened the refrigerator and offered him a beer.

"What about tea instead?" he said.

"I suppose that would go better with meditation," she said.

"It's cold in here. Can you turn the heat up?"

"Is that what happens when you move to the big city?" she asked, her tone scornful. "You get so you can't stand the cold any more. I like it like this."

He shrugged. "I meditate in the nude."

He had no idea why he said this. He couldn't blame her if she asked him to leave.

"Imagine that," she said. "You really are full of surprises. Let's just go and eat."

"Did you take lessons from Marcel Blouin?" he asked curtly.

Why was he so angry? Michelle wasn't sure anymore if she wanted him there. "Why? Do you think maybe I should?"

"No, I don't think so," Nick said, his voice softening and then rising again as he continued. "Listen, maybe I shouldn't be here. The truth is my wife left me and married some jerk from Texas. Or at least that's where they live now. A friend of mine, to boot. And I'm a screwed up psychiatrist who doesn't know what he wants and is still in love with the bitch." *There. At least I've told her.*

She eyed him thoughtfully. His fists were held tightly at his side and his face was contorted. Was there any way to turn this into a pleasant evening, she wondered. "Let's have our tea now and then catch up over dinner," she said.

Smiling to encourage him, she added, "We're old friends. That's what we are. We can decide to talk as much or as little as we want. I could tell you about my violent ex, but I'd rather tell you my long-lost daughter Dawn is coming to stay with me for a while. I don't know for how long. She had to go and look for her father first. She had to travel around on two or three continents. A ray of hope … she's decided that Dominic is as bad as I said he was and I only said so to protect her, so she wouldn't get hurt." She, too, had now blurted out her story.

"The kettle's boiling," he said, as they both became aware of the whistle from the kettle. He followed her into the kitchen where she motioned him to take a seat at the small pine table by the window. A crystal vase filled with yellow chrysanthemums stood next to a bowl filled with grapes and apples.

Michelle pulled out the plug and poured the hot water into a tea-pot decorated with tiny flowers like forget-me-nots that her mother had brought long ago from England. There were also matching cups, but she chose instead two large mugs from the cupboard. She hadn't anticipated the uncertainty of this man. Of course, she didn't know him anymore, but she carried a memory of someone with a gentle confidence. Not like he was now at all. She knew he'd thought momentarily the previous night that she'd make a good lay, a convenient one. Whatever had deterred her wasn't prudery or fear of the consequences. She had steeled herself against feeling anything around a man for a long time. If she chose to, she could as easily carve notches on a belt as any man could. She was surprised that she didn't even want to. What they shared was something deeper, she thought, a history of living in this place, of knowing each other's families. And she didn't want to jeopardize that.

As they carried their mugs back into the living room and sat across from each other, there was a long silence.

"I'm so glad about your daughter," Nick said quietly. His long frame seemed awkward in the plush Queen Anne armchair that had been her mother's.

"Thanks." She'd been frantic about Dawn for such a long time, never sleeping soundly. As a mother listens for her newborn in the dark of night, she'd felt if awake she could almost hear Dawn, wherever she was.

"If you don't mind me asking, what happened with your husband?"

"It's not something I want to talk about much," she sighed. "He was abusive, dangerous, and I had to escape with the children. It's been a long time and perhaps he's given up on hurting me, especially since I gather he has a woman he lives with now, but I'm still afraid sometimes that he might find me, hurt me again." She didn't say he'd found another victim, although she hoped Dominic might have changed enough so as not to threaten another woman. She wished her no ill.

"I imagine there's a lot more to tell than that."

"Yes," she said. "Of course there is. There always is."

"I'm not probing," he said. "I'd just like you to know that if you want to talk, I'll listen."

"Thanks," she said. "But we have lots to talk about without that. Or without me listening to you talk about your separation. Although I'd be willing to."

"That's kind of you," he said. "But I agree with you." He picked up the photo of Michelle with her two daughters that she'd imagined him commenting on and examined it thoughtfully. He didn't say anything.

"Do you think the older one looks like Francine?"

"Yes," Nick said. "She does a bit."

He put the photograph back on the end table. "Any suggestions for dinner?"

"Why not The Flamingo?" she asked. "It isn't the best food in town; I don't suppose it ever was. But it's full of local colour."

"That would be fine," he said. "Although could we save it for another evening when we also want to dance? Or perhaps go for the entertainment?"

"All right then," she said. "I'd like a quiet dinner, too. A quiet celebration. I know a good place."

34

EVERY DAY FOR three years, Michelle had hoped for the return of her younger daughter. The weekend finally over, she could hardly believe she would at long last see her again. On Tuesday evening, when she finally heard a rapid knock on the door, Michelle caught her breath slightly. She opened it to find a young woman standing on the porch, her long, tawny hair in dreadnoughts halfway down her back. She wore black tights under a denim skirt and a dark jacket with a rip in the front pocket and a large patch on one elbow.

"Ma," Dawn said, suddenly in tears. Her patterned backpack also had a tear in it that didn't go through, but made it look as if it were about to rip open.

"I'm so glad to see you, *chérie*." Michelle said, wrapping her arms around her daughter as the relief of seeing her shot through her body, and then backing inside to leave room for Dawn to walk in and peer around.

"It looks so wonderful," Dawn said. "It was my home, too, for such a long time."

"It still is."

"Thanks, Ma. Although not in the same way ever again. Something about growing up and leaving," she said. "And I don't suppose Ile d'Or is a place with much opportunity for employment anyway."

Michelle plugged in the kettle. "You can put your pack in the back room," she said. "There are towels on the bed. Relax. Have a shower. There'll be time to talk."

What had once been the girls' bedroom was now a den with a sewing machine on a small table. In one corner, Michelle designed clothes for herself at a draughting table and beside it was a female mannequin with her measurements. There was also a futon where Dawn could stretch out and sleep.

"*Merci*, Ma."

Michelle was relieved to feel no animosity from Dawn, recalling how she had bristled the last time they'd seen each other. She would wait until her daughter chose to talk. It had been a shock when Dawn decided she wanted to find her father again. As far as Michelle was concerned, he was a dead beat who had almost killed her and then continued to haunt her after she'd escaped from him. But if that search had brought her daughter home with new understanding, she was glad.

"I saw Elise," Dawn said. "She's doing fine. Big as an elephant." She laughed. "It's exciting," she added. "And Aunt *Moi* wants to be around more. I might even look for work in Montreal."

Turning then, she went toward the bedroom and the next thing Michelle heard was water running in the shower. As she looked in the refrigerator for the steaks she'd bought on the weekend, she hummed. Something she hadn't done for a long time.

"Oh what a beautiful day!"

Any mother would want to celebrate, she thought, surprised that she hadn't heard from Elise who usually telephoned at least once a week and would, she hoped, be exultant about seeing her sister. Michelle had seen the hurt on her older daughter's face when Dawn had sent a letter back unopened. It was a letter Elise said she'd struggled over and thought would elicit an answer. It had happened to Michelle, too, but she had persevered. Perhaps mothers couldn't give up. She could remember each daughter lying across her stomach right after the blood was wiped off, eyes closed, and head only slightly misshapen after descending through her vagina. Nursing at her engorged breasts, sucking and gurgling.

She set the table with the best cutlery, silver her mother had brought from the old country along with the china set acquired when she married Maurice Dufresne. Immersed in French Canadian custom and artifacts, Elaine Dufresne had managed at the same time not to have her English side submerged by her French Canadian husband.

"Ah," Maurice would say. "She's happier here than she ever was in England."

"Yes, of course," Elaine would say. "How can I help but be delighted with unpaved roads, dark outhouses, and pink flamingos?"

"We got rid of the outhouse," Maurice said. "I made sure we got the best toilet in town."

But the flamingos were never replaced, Michelle thought. One silly bird still graced the downtown club inviting passersby to enter. Moving back and forth in the kitchen, she didn't hear her daughter come back into the room.

"What are you designing, Ma?" Dawn asked. "Interesting hemline on that outfit on the mannequin."

Dawn sat down on a chair at the table, across from the counter in the kitchen, and put her bare feet up on another chair. She had changed into a light robe. It felt to Michelle like nothing had happened since the last time they'd been in this room together, Elise already working in Montreal, the two of them mulling over the day's events. Or perhaps playing cards. Even having an argument about something trivial. They'd had more of those after Elise left and only then had Michelle realized the extent to which her elder daughter had acted as a buffer.

"Would you like a drink?" Michelle asked. "Wine perhaps."

"Is there any beer?"

"Help yourself."

Dawn went to the refrigerator and took out a bottle, opened it and sat back down again.

"Tastes good," she said, sipping.

Michelle smiled, content to see Dawn again. Why now? she wondered. Did it matter?

"I really am sorry, Ma," Dawn said. "I wanted so badly to have a Dad, so I went looking for one. And when I found him, it was a disaster. He had no interest in me at all. He couldn't be a Dad to a cockroach even though that lousy imitation of a man is a cockroach himself. It must have been hell for you. I should have let you know then, but I couldn't. I had to keep moving. So I travelled and travelled. It didn't dawn on me how much time was passing and then one day it was suddenly three years since I'd seen you. And what I wanted most was just that. To see you. I wanted to come home."

Michelle reached out to hug her daughter. She didn't ask how Dawn had been able to afford to keep on moving, knew her daughter had always been resourceful and could live on very little. Perhaps she didn't want to know even though at times she'd feared that Dawn might be living on the streets somewhere, that she might be hungry. Elise had always said that was one thing she didn't think they had to worry about, that Dawn would always find ways to earn enough at least for food and shelter. Michelle was relieved to see that Dawn was not at all gaunt. If anything, she was slightly heavier.

"I'm not here for long, but before I start looking for a job I wanted to come and see you."

"Thank you, *chérie*," Michelle said, not saying anything about how hard these years had been. "I am just so happy to see you."

Scratching noises outside the door attracted their attention. There was the sound of footsteps and then a knock, but because the blind over the door was pulled shut neither of them could see who was there. Dawn jumped up and opened it.

"Who are you?" she asked.

Michelle looked around Dawn to see Marcel Blouin standing just out of range of the light. She flicked a switch and the porch was suddenly illuminated.

"What is it, Marcel?" she asked.

"Who's she?" he asked, gesturing at Dawn.

"Marcel, this is Dawn. She's my daughter."

He turned away, snorting like an annoyed horse. This was more than she wanted to deal with, to have to salve the boy's threatened ego. Maybe Nick was right, Marcel was becoming a nuisance.

"And who is he?" Dawn asked, but her question seemed more amused than annoyed. "This boy who seems to think he belongs here."

"From the town," Michelle said. "Marcel helps me out, don't you, Marcel?"

He shuffled his feet and wouldn't look at the women.

"At the store," Michelle said. "Sometimes here. You know, cuts the grass, shovels snow. Runs errands. He's good at that." She could see Marcel bite his lip to keep from smiling, but slowly he turned to face them.

"I need money," he said.

"Do I owe you some?" Michelle asked.

For a moment, he looked tempted to say she did. Then he shook his head.

"Is it food you need?" she asked. "Is that it, Marcel?"

"I need to get some pills for my mother."

"I see." She thought Lucien would be as likely as she was to pay for any prescription his mother needed if it wasn't already covered. "Is she ill?"

Marcel turned away, a shadow crossing his face. It was the first time she'd ever seen him look frightened.

"Do you have a prescription from the doctor?"

He shook his head, but handed her a piece of paper and she read the names of two drugs on it. A painkiller. And something else she didn't recognize. If she called Lucien, they might be able to figure out something.

"Can I help, Ma?" Dawn asked. "I have a little money."

"It's okay, Dawn. Thanks, *chérie*. I think I'll phone the pharmacist. You remember Lucien Dion, don't you?"

When Dawn nodded, she went to the kitchen and picked up the receiver. The pharmacy number was on a list on the refrigerator and she thought about dialing it, but then put the receiver back again to turn to look at the tableau at the door. Dawn was eyeing Marcel suspiciously, while Marcel stared at the floor. Everything felt fragile to Michelle, as if she could do or say the wrong thing and her daughter would vanish. Like a ghost. Or a genie. After three years, she had convinced herself that she must have done something terrible, something she wasn't aware of that made Dawn leave, and although Dawn's assertions about Dominic reassured her, she thought it would take a while to sink in.

"I thought you were going to phone about the pills," Dawn said.

"That's right, I was." She was annoyed at Marcel for interrupting her first hour with Dawn, as well as the increasing frequency of the boy's visits. Still, she wouldn't send him away without something so she reached for a pad of paper and wrote a note to Lucien.

"Here, Marcel," she said. "If you give this to Monsieur Dion, he'll figure out what to do about the pills."

When he was gone, she turned on the broiler.

"Let's make something to eat," she said.

"I am hungry," Dawn conceded. "And to have something you cook!" After such a long time was left implied.

"A toast to your safe return, *chérie*."

35

"LUCIEN," A RASPY voice said from across the counter. "I need something for my throat."

He turned to see Al Desjardins. "Been to see the doctor?" Lucien asked.

"I don't have time for that." Al leaned his elbow on the ledge between them. "You met the Muir woman, *non?*" he said in a low voice. "I knew her father. Used to bring him home in the cab. When I first met Jutras, he told me that dog was always running away. Monsieur Muir told me he spent more money on cab fare for that dog than for anyone else in the family."

Lucien laughed, but he was embarrassed. How much did Al know about his evening with Libby? Did anyone know? He hoped not. It was none of their business. But you could not keep anything from Al for long. He probably did not even have a sore throat; he was probably fishing. All the same, in spite of all the stories he told, he never seemed to gossip maliciously.

Lucien took some lozenges from a shelf. "Tried these?" he asked.

"Won't hurt, I guess," Al said.

"I knew all of the family, *tu sais,*" Lucien said. "We lived just a few doors away from them on rue Champlain."

After Al left, he found it impossible to concentrate.

"I'm going out for a while," he said.

Charmaine nodded, continuing to arrange lipstick tubes in a display case. The eye shadow was all neatly lined up, the testers in the front row. A mirror a woman could use to see her face as she tried out the colours hung just above the display.

On the sidewalk, against a car angle-parked on the wide street, Lucien stood with his jacket up around his neck and lit a cigarette. Across the roadway, the priest walked from the rectory down to the side door of the church. Both buildings, perched on a slight rise where they looked out over the town, were still among the most substantial in the area. This priest, Father Jean, was a small, unimposing man, not one given to oratory as Father Chicoine had been. Lucien had not been to confession for a long time, or to church. Susan had, though. Not French, she had surprised him by converting to Catholicism before their children were born. And until recently, when she left him without warning, she had done all the things the mother of a good French Canadian Catholic family was supposed to do. Except for the abortion and he did not know what the priest had said when she'd confessed. Or even if she had confessed. He had never asked her.

A car honked. He turned to see Michelle in her Chevy. He exhaled slowly, watching as the car drove past. It was the local gossip that Maurice DuFresne, Michelle's father, had amassed quite a fortune by the time he died, but how would anyone know for sure? Unless Michelle's lifestyle had changed dramatically after her mother died also. And it hadn't or he would have heard about it or noticed. She continued to live in the mobile home she had moved into soon after she returned to Ile d'Or. At the most, he supposed she might have used her inheritance to pay off the mortgage.

When he had settled back into his chair, in his office, he noticed Madame Frechette at the cash register, holding a bottle of shampoo. Even from his office, Lucien could see that it was one to get rid of dandruff. While Charmaine rang in the purchase, he looked over an order for one of the large drug companies. Nearly everyone who came into the store called out a greeting to him. Madame Frechette had already smiled in his direction. Lisette Charlebois, Jacques Paquin, Hélène from the hairdresser's, René from the bank.

"*Bonjour, Lucien.*"

As they waved, their gestures flickering across his vision, he nodded and smiled in return. Usually he would have gone out to speak to them, but so far today he had done so only with Madame Robichaud. She wore her fur coat already, fitting tightly across her hips like the skin of a moose. She was still standing at the magazine rack, trying to decide what she wanted. Or perhaps she was just reading the covers. There was a white streak down the part of her dyed red hair and her lipstick was smeared at the edges of her lips. If he hadn't spoken to her, she would have said something to his mother. Then Maman would ask if he were worried about Susan and if he had heard from her. It was enough that he dreamed about Susan, saying to him plaintively that she was tired of the city and wanted to come back. In the dream, he found a way to ask her to return without either of them losing face.

"Such a good idea you have my love, to arrange a party for our son's birthday. Everyone will come."

Then he woke up, disappointed to find nothing had changed. He knew if he suggested she return, it would make her furious. Quite probably she would never speak to him again. Then he drifted off into another dream that he couldn't fathom. There were divots of grass all along the walk beside his house in Ile d'Or, as if someone was going to replace his front lawn. As he awakened, he was baffled that at the same time as he hoped desperately that Susan would return, he was angry with her for making a fool of him. And with Guy for leaving him alone to take care of their mother when he would never be good enough for Maman. His mother had never said so, but he knew it. Since he was old enough to know, Guy had always done everything better as far as his mother was concerned. Guy had even played with the Muir kids and Jeannie Petranovich. He had heard Madame Muir tell his mother she wanted Libby to learn French.

"Oh, *non*," Maman said. "It's for Guy a chance to speak English."

"The Hinglish Polacks," Lucien sneered under his breath. He'd wanted his mother to hear him, but was nervous that she might have.

Libby must have overheard though. She'd said as much when he babysat the Muir children. And had told him the story again when they'd been recalling events that bound their histories together. This time her story had not been laced with a sense of triumph as it had been when he was the babysitter. Then she'd enjoyed telling him about the time his father stumbled into the Muir's house. Apparently he sat down at the kitchen table as if he were in a restaurant.

"A sandwich," he said to Madame Muir, thinking she was a waitress. "Roast beef." Usually they referred to each other politely as Madame Muir and Monsieur Dion.

"He was too drunk even for that," Libby said. "He ate the sandwich, then stumbled out again. 'Taxi,' he said. '*Je veux un taxi.*'"

Lucien had glared at her when she'd told him for the first time, his face twisted into an angry knot, a pink flush across his cheeks. "You stupid English bitch," he whispered. "*Tête carrée.*"

He waited for her to call him a Frog, but she didn't.

"I'll tell my mother," she said.

"What?" he asked quietly. "What will you tell her?" Pursing his lips, he went to the refrigerator and took out a beer. He sat on the stool at the kitchen counter and flipped off the cap, startled to hear the back door open. Before he could even get up, Walter Muir came stumbling in. He headed toward the door to the basement where he went down two steps and stopped abruptly. Another step, more tentatively. Then a sudden loud crash, followed by a yell as he hit the bottom.

Libby raced down the stairs. Lucien was right behind her. Walter Muir was lying on his face on the floor, like an animal hit by a car on the highway.

"Lucien," she screamed.

A gash on her father's forehead was oozing blood that ran down his cheek. He did not move.

"Call the doctor," Lucien said.

"You call." Her voice was low and shaky.

Lucien went to the phone in the kitchen and dialled the hospital number. When he explained what had happened and that Monsieur Muir was still lying on the floor, the nurse said the doctor would come right over. When he arrived, Dr. Pierrefonds helped Walter Muir come to his feet, then draped one arm over his shoulder. Together they moved slowly and awkwardly upstairs. Everything was quiet overhead for a while. When the doctor left, he said Monsieur Muir would sleep through the night and in the morning he might be quite sore. "But there doesn't seem to be a concussion and nothing broken either." Dr. Pierrefonds left Lucien and Libby sitting at the kitchen table. Libby stared straight ahead.

"Do you want to play ping pong?" Lucien asked, knowing she would likely beat him.

"Okay."

When they went down into the basement, there was still blood where Libby's father had fallen. Libby walked carefully around it, and then threw up on the floor. He still marvelled that Sheila and Wally had slept through everything. Or maybe they were just too frightened to come out to see what was happening.

"Yoo-hoo," Charlotte Muir's voice called from the front door. "Where is everybody? Are you still up, Libby?"

"She's down here," Lucien said.

"Everybody happy?" the voice sang out.

Lucien had found Libby was still very solemn when she'd told him the story again, but she'd been somewhat amused about Charlotte.

"That was what Mum always wanted, no matter what," Libby had said thoughtfully. And then laughing, she added, "She always wanted everybody to be happy."

Lucien thought their overlapping histories created an interesting tapestry that hadn't previously occurred to him in this way. If he raised some of these memories again with Libby, he would do so more delicately than he might have previously with an Anglo. Even with Susan, for that matter.

36.

THE LOBBY OF the hotel was quiet in the early afternoon, especially now that tourist season was over. An occasional hunter still came through, but most came earlier in the season, before the onset of winter. They came to shoot moose and to take home their trophies, the antlers and a trunk full of the meat packed in ice.

Sun shone through a window beside the front desk and turned the receptionist's dark hair auburn. Libby sat in an armchair off to the side, waiting for her taxi. She listened to the woman's telephone conversation about a homework assignment in algebra. At the same time, through the window she saw Al Desjardins park and get out of his cab. As he came through the front door, he was puffing. A paunch around his middle defined his shape and tiny red veins laced his nose and his chin.

"*Bonjour, Elizabet'*," he said. "I hear you'll be staying at Guy's cabin." He picked up her bag and carried it out to the street.

"How do you know?" Libby asked, surprised. She had not given her destination when she phoned for the taxi. It felt as if the entire town was wired.

"Oh, it's easy," he said. "People say things around me all the time as if I'm not even there. I heard Lucien make a phone call about turning on the hydro for Guy's cabin. He said a friend from Toronto was going to use it. Things like that. But I don't gossip. Don't worry."

"Sounds like it's too late to worry," Libby said, her smile wary.

Al opened the trunk and put her suitcase in next to the spare tire. There was a case of Molson's on the other side.

"I'd like to go to the pharmacy," Libby said. "I was going to drive out with Lucien later."

"I can take you," Al said. "Flat rate. Not expensive."

"Thanks," Libby said. "Still I'd like to let Lucien know."

"*Pas de problème*," Al said.

When Libby arrived at the pharmacy, Lucien was in the back. When he saw her, he came and stood next to her at the end of the aisle with cough medicine and headache remedies lined up on the shelves. There was a nasal spray in green and white packages beside them.

"My suitcase is in Al's taxi," she said. "He said he could take me to the lake, but I'd rather go to Guy's cabin with you."

"Go to my place with Al if you want. I'll meet you there when I leave the store to show you how things work in the cabin. I have some propane in the car for the heater and I already turned on the water. The place is clean. There are sheets and a couple of sleeping bags."

"I'll pick up food at the supermarket."

"Don't worry about tonight. You can have my car tomorrow to shop. You'll know by then what you need."

Al was at the curb when she went outside. "After I drop you off, I'll go to the airport for the last flight from Montreal," he said.

As they started toward the road to the airport, Al pointed out the house he lived in, one of the original log cabins near the mine site. The door was now painted orange.

"They started selling them a few years ago," he said. "So we bought ours. What you can do is limited. The town wants to retain the original log cabins as much as possible so they can promote Ile d'Or as a historical village. But they let you paint the trim."

His wife, Blanche, usually had coffee for him at this time of day, he told Libby. If he didn't have a fare, he would drop by.

"Gives me a chance to stretch," he said.

"You must need it, sitting behind the wheel so much."

"My wife tells me that her sister worked for a Madame Muir when she came here as a teenager. Probably your mother."

"What's her name?"

"Thérèse Drouin,"

"Thérèse," Libby said. "That's amazing. I always wondered what happened to her."

"She's in Montreal now," Al said. "She was seventeen when she worked in Ile d'Or. She worked for your mother after the last baby was born. She said a few weeks later your father left to join the army."

"Yes," Libby said. "A month later." After Wally's birth, her father was gone for three years. Thérèse stayed for a few months and then she left to get married. Libby did not remember the names of any of the girls who came after her, not even the one who accompanied them to Petawawa before her father went overseas. The young girl had opened a drawer in the Welsh dresser and taken out a silver spoon, which she then put in her pocket. Libby, watching her from behind an armchair, sneezed and the girl whirled around.

"Sneak," she said, moving toward Libby and slapping her.

Running out of the room, Libby headed to the kitchen where her mother was making grilled cheese sandwiches.

"You have such an imagination," her mother sighed. "Please don't make up stories. When something really happens, no one will believe you."

Libby was furious and stomped down the hall. Her mother never believed her, not even when the minister with grey hair and thin, sallow cheeks under his horn-rimmed glasses had reached under her smocked dress to stroke her leg and the edge of one cheek of her bottom. She was sandwiched between him and another girl as they stood learning about confirmation one afternoon after school, preparing for the ceremony that lay only a few weeks ahead of them. When she felt something touching her, Libby was so surprised she froze for a moment, then reached back as if she were going to slap a mosquito. The minister removed his fingers quickly. It all took place so fast that she wondered later if it had really happened.

"How is Thérèse?" Libby asked.

"Very well. Still married with three grown children. Grandchildren, too. She'll be interested to hear about you."

"She called me Libby."

37.

THE STREET IN front of the bed and breakfast, the former mine bunkhouse, was quiet, only in Nick's imagination filled with the sounds of young men living there as in the days when the mine was in operation. He parked his car, his mind preoccupied with the thought that he was no longer a young man. He was forty-eight, getting close to the big five-oh. It surprised him that he suddenly felt nervous about taking Michelle out to dinner again. He'd behaved outlandishly the past couple of days, he thought, not used to being single.

For many months after the separation and divorce, after Marie's remarriage, he'd put all his energy into his practice. This trip was probably just another way of running away, but it was turning into something else as well. Until he'd met up again with Michelle, he hadn't thought of himself as a "spoiled rich guy." That's what Michelle thought of him. Maybe she was right. Encountering people from his past, in this town where he grew up, caused him to come up against himself in unexpected ways.

The woman who owned the bed and breakfast stood inside the door. Younger than he was, quite pretty with her light hair pulled back behind her ears, he already knew she spoke no English. A remarkable change from when he'd lived here when most people tried to speak English even if they had thick accents and couldn't find the right words to describe something.

"*Pour vous*," she said, handing him a message.

He thanked her and went to his room before looking at the slip of paper she'd given him. Only his daughter knew where he was so he wasn't surprised to find Diana was the one who had called. He'd get back to her as soon as he'd made a few notes in his journal.

Sometimes the only way he could clarify his thoughts was to write them down. If they seemed inclined at all, it was what he sometimes suggested to patients. "Keep a record for a while. You'll be surprised at how helpful it can be."

He'd resisted keeping a journal himself for a long time. "But writers do that, don't they?" he murmured, resist writing. One patient had described writer's block as a blank page that would confront him whenever he sat down. "It's almost like a conspiracy that prevents me writing at all some days."

Nick went upstairs and lay down on his bed, his hands resting behind his head. He was troubled by his inability to move on. His imagination had often saved him, his sense of potential where others saw only impossible challenge. Thinking he could reverse Marie's decision even after she'd married Henri was getting in his way. Imagining an affair with Michelle perhaps suggested he was ready to finally get beyond Marie, but something deeper would be possible if he let go of the impossible hope that Marie might return.

After a while, he stood up and went to the small writing table under the window, turned on the lamp and sat down. He'd left his notebook there and opened it now, but when he tried to think of what to write all he could do was note the weather. So plebian, he thought. Then he started to scrawl the first words that came into his head.

Serge Bikadoroff came from Russia in the 1940s and found work in the mines of Abitibi.

He didn't find that sentence boring, but he hardly imagined one sentence would get him much closer to writing a novel. It would be a full-time job; he knew that. He thought about the old joke where the surgeon tells the writer that he too would write a novel if he had the time. The writer responds by saying, "Yes, and when I retire, I'll become a surgeon!" He didn't know why he was suddenly so interested in writing this book. He knew his character flaws, at least as they had been pointed out numerous times by Marie, and arrogance was not one of them. He knew it was ridiculous to think he could write a novel. He was under no illusions about his ability to do so. Maybe he just needed to write about his past. To understand the present. Diana had suggested that he might follow some of the advice he gave his own clients.

"I forgot to call Diana," he said to himself out loud, suddenly remembering the message he had just been given.

When he reached her, Diana told him about the lasagna she'd cooked for dinner the previous night. "You would have loved it," she said. "Full of vegetables like eggplant and zucchini and three kinds of cheese."

Then she asked him when he would be coming back to Toronto. "Any time soon, Dad?" It was partly because she needed to borrow some money. C'mon kid, I'll give it to you. "And I'm sorry, Dad. I didn't mean to say mean things about you. You're a great Dad."

"Yeah, well," he said. "Some of the time I'm preoccupied. You were right about that."

"So, when are you coming back?" she asked again. "I miss our dinners together. I miss running ideas by you. All of that."

"Thanks, Diana. I miss you, too," he said. "You'll be the first to know, but I haven't decided yet."

"Are you going to get back into your practice?"

"Of course," he said. "But I need more time away from it. At the very least, I'm going to go to Montreal when I leave here and look around. I'm not finished with whatever I came here to do and see yet though. I have to be back to Toronto for sure in a couple of weeks because I didn't make arrangements for any longer."

It occurred to him that it was time to change in some significant way. It bothered him to know this and not to know what this meant. Or how to achieve it.

"Why haven't I ever been to see the town where you grew up?" she asked.

"That's a good question," he said. "It's so far from everything for one thing, and the drive gets tedious. You go through so much bush that all looks the same."

"Are you taking photographs?"

"I will," he said. "Listen, Diana, I want to ask you something."

"What's that?" she asked.

"I've been thinking of writing a novel. What do you think of that idea?"

"Oh, Dad, you can probably do anything you want to do," she said, her tone slightly exasperated. Then added a question he hadn't even considered. "But is that where your passion lies?"

Nick felt thrown off track, as if an unexpected arrow had pierced his armour. He didn't try to answer her because it seemed irrelevant.

"Thanks, Diana," he said.

When they both hung up, he lay down again. What was his passion? It had always been people, understanding what made them who they were, helping them to achieve some kind of balance. It was natural to be attracted to writing a novel, he supposed. A writer would have that same interest in people, but maybe writing wouldn't sustain him in the way he imagined right now. Photography had not in the way he had once hoped, but it still interested him.

He wondered if Gabrielle Roy had seen the movie adapted from her novel before she died a few months earlier. Perhaps if he went to see it, he would be inspired. He needed inspiration to come from somewhere, but tired and dejected, Nick knew this wasn't a night when he wanted to sit at a desk and write. Nor to think of what he might still do with a camera. For now, one sentence with whatever images it conjured up would have to suffice.

38

THE PIZZA ON the front seat beside Lucien had his favourite toppings on it — mushrooms, pepperoni, onion. He hoped Libby would like them too. When he drove up to the cabin, she was standing at the edge of the lake. After slipping the box in the oven, he walked down to join her. The centre of Lac LeBoeuf had begun to freeze and a layer of ice around the shore had started to form, although it was so thin it was barely perceptible. Libby shivered and did up the top button of her coat.

"Look at the sky," she said. The stars had already begun to come out. "It's so wide here and the stars are so bright. In the city, everything gets lost behind tall buildings and the shine of street lights."

He squeezed her slightly. "Gets dark early now," he said.

She leaned down and picked up a stick and threw it into the lake. It landed a few feet out on top of the ice. "It's thicker than I thought," she said.

"I brought some pizza," he said.

"Al told me Thérèse is Blanche's sister," she said as they walked back up the slope and stepped gingerly over large roots and rocks in the path. "She used to work for us for a little while. Do you remember her?"

"You think you don't know anybody here any more! Already you've met Jacques Paquin, Al Desjardins. What was Blanche's sister's last name?"

"Drouin."

"*Non, je ne me rappelle pas.*" No, I don't remember.

"She left when I was just over five. So, you would've been nine or ten."

"Oh," he said. "I know who you mean. She used to come and have coffee with Maman after mass on Sunday. *Elle était si belle.* She was so beautiful. I was just a little kid to her."

As they took off their coats back at the cabin, Lucien reminded Libby his mother would like to see her. "I don't want to pressure you," he said. "But, I told Maman I'd be sure to invite you. She is excited that you're here and that you can bring her news."

Lucien reached for two plates with green borders and he placed them on the pine table in the kitchen. There was lemon yellow linoleum on the floor and the curtains in the window were bright orange. In the summer, they billowed inwards when a breeze blew off the lake. Opening the oven door, he reached for the pizza and set it down in the centre of the table.

"I'll get a bottle of wine," he said.

When he had filled two glasses, he handed her a slice with the mozzarella cheese still bubbling from the oven. She thought she could detect the smell of the pepperoni and waited only long enough so that she wouldn't burn her mouth before taking a bite.

"Tell me more about yourself," he said, his eyes studying her face with genuine interest. "What happened to your marriage?"

Libby shrugged and swallowed her first mouthful. If only there were simple answers. Barton grew up in Montreal. She had thought that was like growing up in Ile d'Or, but it was not. What he had loved about her when he met her later made him angry. Her warmth, her spontaneity. He was all big city and all English. Maybe she should have known. He'd spent his first few years in Toronto. But what she said to Lucien was, "He didn't like it when I talked to strangers." Nor had he wanted her to draw or paint. Although he never quite said that out loud to her, he'd made it apparent. She didn't tell Lucien this. She didn't know why. Except that she knew now it was time for her to sit down again and see what happened when she confronted a blank canvas. And it was something she couldn't really talk about to anyone. What images would surface? She wanted to deal with the horse somehow, to go right to the centre of the nightmare and get beyond it. When she looked up, she saw that Lucien was studying her with a curious, almost expectant, frown.

"Why?" he asked.

"You'd have to ask him. I never understood it."

Fumbling with a knife, he turned to look out the window. When he turned back, he had regained an unhurried expression.

"Do you like music?" he asked.

"Yes," she said. "I love music."

"We'll go dancing soon, *n'est-ce pas?*"

"I like that idea."

"*Bon.*" He took a bite of the pizza and spoke around the food in his mouth, rolling it about so it was not overly apparent. "Once I made Susan throw out all the kids' clothes with English on them," he said. "We spoke only French at home."

"Did she mind?"

"I don't think so. *Pour la plupart.* She always loved the French language and people. But I didn't ever ask."

Libby took a large bite of pizza. "Do your kids speak English?" She sipped on her wine.

"Not very well. When they were really small they just talked, they didn't know the difference." He divided the last two slices and gave her one. "Why didn't you marry Guy?" he asked.

"I was seventeen!" Her voice rose. From the time she was a toddler, Guy was her buddy. And yes, he was her boyfriend, her first boyfriend. But did that mean she should have married him?

"All the same," Lucien said. "*C'est dommage.*" It's too bad.

He started to run hot water and squeezed some liquid soap from a yellow plastic bottle into the sink. Libby put on her coat and stood fingering the buttons. When he looked at her, his face was slightly red.

"I don't know what happened," he said. "It's just been so long. And..." Taking a package of cigarettes from his pocket, he opened the crisp silver paper.

"It's all right," she said.

"I dreamed about Susan," he said, pointing at the sofa. "If you want to sleep here tonight, you could have the bed. *Moi, je peux dormir là.* I'll take the sofa."

"How far is Guy's cabin?"

"Five minutes."

"I'd kind of like to get settled."

"*Je comprends.* I was just thinking you might like to go when the sun is up."

The leaves and branches on the path were stiff with a light frost when they walked down the trail beside the lake, the trees black against the glow of the moon and stars. As they arrived, Libby noticed there was a huge gash in the screen around the veranda. Under that porch, she and Guy drank beer they had taken from the cooler while the adults were at some party. Only twelve that summer, they'd sung *Alouette* loudly, directing their voices at the moon.

Lucien pointed to a large red oval container underneath one side of the cabin. "The propane for the heater."

After he opened the door, he handed her the key. Inside he turned on a lamp with a glass chimney, one that had been converted to electricity. Then the heater. From a chest, he lifted out a heavy blanket with black stripes on one end as well as two lighter grey ones, sheets and a large pillow he threw toward a bed at the far end of the room. Last a sleeping bag with a plaid lining.

Libby felt queasy at the thought that Guy would have slept here. Guy Dion. Skin and bones in a coffin, pieces that did not fit together, pieces no one could have put back to resemble anyone she had ever known. A picture of him hanging on the cabin wall with two small children caught her eye.

"Where are they now?" she asked,

"Chicoutimi and Montreal."

Beside it was another photograph, an old one of Guy with a fish he had caught, which Libby thought she remembered. How proud he was of that trout from the spring-fed lake down the road where they'd fished together as teenagers.

"Funny," she mused. "We had a cabin down the trail from you and your house was just down the street in town, but I don't think my parents really knew what good friends Guy and I were."

"They knew," Lucien said.

"Well, maybe they did."

"There's no telephone," Lucien said. "You can use the one at my place if you need to."

The arrangements made before he left were for her to drive him into the drugstore in the morning so she could have the car. He leaned over to hug her.

"You miss Susan, don't you?" she said.

"*Bien sur*," he said. "But last night, it was *merveilleux*, Libby."

As he continued to hold her gently, she massaged the back of his neck below the hairline, then up toward the bony part of his skull.

"Feels good," he murmured, then broke away to stand at the door. "What about Dan?" he asked.

"I don't know, Lucien."

39.

AS LIBBY WATCHED Lucien disappear into the trees, the ice on the lake glowed in the silver light of the moon. It made her think of photographs she'd seen taken from outer space. Her thoughts drifted to Dan. He had touched her in ways that awakened her senses again and made her feel glad to be a woman. It surprised her that he'd kept on calling. Adept at not showing when she was angry or saying anything about love or her hopes or expectations, he probably had no idea what she felt about him. Had she become too adept? Able to remove herself from the most intense encounters, she could watch as if two other people were making love. Only later did the full awareness of their passion flood over her. She continued to stare out at the landscape long after Lucien had disappeared into the night and the trees. What would it be like not to be afraid of love? she wondered.

When a tree branch cracked overhead, she jumped slightly. An old angst arose, a memory of a day when a sudden onslaught of rain and wind had appeared from nowhere. Everyone had run from the beach on Lac Leboeuf to the small green Austin with the yellow turn flickers embedded in its sides. She, nine years old, lagged behind the others. Without warning, there was a loud crash as lightening struck the tree just behind her, the sound of thunder and the crash of the tree occurring simultaneously. Yelling, she ran to catch up with the others as they all piled hurriedly into the car, none of them aware of how close she had come to being hit.

When she returned to Toronto, the house would feel like a storm had struck there. Paul, typical teenager that he was, would not even notice. Holes in his socks. Dirty dishes. Clothes strewn everywhere.

After a while, when the only sound was from a slight breeze blowing through the trees outside, she put on a pair of long johns and a heavy sweater. She lit a candle on the table where she arranged her sketchpad, pencils, and books. As she did, a blue notebook with a spiral binding lying on a shelf beside her caught her attention. She hadn't noticed it before and now opened it at random to see the familiar slant and curve of the letters. Guy's handwriting. Looking more closely, she read descriptions of the lake, of dark thunderclouds coming in from the west, of a bear eating blueberries on the path to the outhouse.

Il n'y a pas assez des bleuets pour les ours cette année, she read. Not enough blueberries for the bears this year.

No one else of her acquaintance knew the outdoors as Guy had. She'd watched him shoot partridge on a dirt road beyond the mine, track animals, cut enough wood for a fire, name trees and plants and birds. She wanted to read more, but began to feel as if she were spying. Anyway, right now she was too tired and, putting it back on the shelf, she blew out the candle and let the sound of the wind rustling through the trees soothe her. Once Barton had come to Ile d'Or with her early in their relationship, intrigued by the idea of bush and a small town. She'd wondered before that what it would be like to have him visit her home town. She'd found out quickly it wasn't a place he could fit into easily. When they went out into the bush, he spent his time looking over his shoulder for bears and smacking at mosquitoes. He couldn't relax either out at the lake or in town, wasn't used to having so many people know who he was before he was introduced or to the way the English, French, and immigrants seemed to mix with each other. So engrossed was he in protecting his urban Anglo identity that the subtle interplay of class and language and the prevalence of gossip was of little concern for him. He quickly lost interest in living in a smaller place. Like his sense of who she was that led to their marriage, his interest seemed to have been built on illusions.

A scurrying sound underneath the cabin made Libby's heart beat harder and she pulled the blankets tightly around her. It was probably just a small animal seeking shelter, but she was sure she would never fall asleep. Wrapping herself in one of the grey blankets, she climbed out of the bed and made her way to the window. She could see nothing in the dark outside. Sometimes she found it difficult to be alone in the city when both children were with Barton, but this was worse. Without even a telephone, if something happened she would be stranded. The animal she'd heard earlier began to move through the bushes beside the cabin. She imagined that she would lie awake all night, listening for and keeping track of all the sounds. Surprised to see the yellow beam of a flashlight shining on the path that came out of the bush, she heard Lucien's voice.

"Libby," he called. "Libby."

When she opened the door, Lucien was standing there with a nervous frown on his face. "I was worried about you," he said.

Standing aside to let him in, she realized how relieved she felt and began to shudder. As he pulled her to him, Libby felt warmth start to flow back and forth between them and she let her body curl into his arms.

"*Un moment,*" he said, hanging his jacket over a chair.

She backed away toward the sofa. "Want a coffee?" she asked.

"No," he said. "I just wanted to make sure you were all right."

She sighed. "I'm glad to see you."

"Shall I stay?"

She nodded.

Crawling into the large bed where she'd thrown the sleeping bag and blankets, he slipped off his shirt and trousers. Then he held her head in both hands, gradually running his fingers over her nose and lips, down to her breasts. She drew back slightly and with her fingers traced a long scar on his belly.

"What's that?"

"Appendix."

"What about this one?" She touched a line down the outside of his right arm, below his elbow.

"Hockey," he said.

Dan told her he'd played football, a sport that was not popular in Ile d'Or when she was growing up. His high school teachers assumed he would go to some university in the States on a sports scholarship. No one asked what he wanted.

"What are you thinking?" Lucien asked.

"Nothing."

He traced the lines on her cheeks, his finger running over them, then her breasts, moaning as he held her tightly. She did not want to know if he was thinking about Susan.

40.

LIGHT FROM A full moon shone through the window onto the foot of the futon, illuminating the geometric pattern on the duvet under which Dawn tossed and turned. Michelle could see the dark shape from where she sat in the living room with the radio playing in the background. She enjoyed listening to music in the evening, but she wasn't really paying attention now. She was thinking about her daughter. Dawn had said she remembered her mother lost in jazz or a symphony and not responding even if they were in the same room. It didn't seem to bother Dawn now, but the feeling of not being noticed then must have been hard to tolerate. So many little things Michelle could blame herself for, but she didn't any more. It was futile. And besides, Dawn was finally with her again, if only for a brief visit.

"I'll call Elise tomorrow," Dawn had said before she fell exhausted into the bed. "I'll wait 'til you come in from the shop in the evening so both of us can talk to her."

What surprised Michelle most was that she could accept Dawn's story of her long absence. Not even angry anymore that Dawn had found her father. What a bastard he was, trying to enlist his daughter to convince some new woman he was a decent father. He also couldn't resist dumping on her, telling Dawn that it was because of her mother that he had left. Elise had stayed away; she had no use for him either.

The next morning when Michelle awakened, Dawn was still sleeping so she left a note on the table beside a fresh baguette. She propped it against a glass dish with raspberry jam in it — *Call when you wake up, chérie.*

Dawn had said that as a child she was continuously trying to figure out what was going on when she'd overheard conversations her mother had on the telephone with friends. Sometimes when Dominic — she refused to call him her father any longer — was out at work or having a beer with his buddies, she would hear her mother talk about escaping.

Escape was a word Dawn didn't understand then; it was something captured princesses did, not her mother.

"What about me?" she'd asked her mother once, visualizing being left behind. She said something about a castle where she was afraid she would be left and Elise, listening to them, told her they lived in a house like all their friends and that castles only existed in books.

"Except in England and France," Elise had added knowingly, although she was only six or seven at the time and only knew about castles in places where they had ancestors.

"We lived in an apartment then, not a house or a castle anyway," Dawn had said when she was older.

It must have been terrifying for her, Michelle thought.

Michelle moved a rack out to the front of the store where the large "sale" sign on it could be seen from the street. The policeman, Gustave, waved at her as he headed toward the pharmacy. Michelle waved back, recalling that when she'd arrived in Ile d'Or he'd been kind to her. Her mother had known him and he'd come to call, with the promise of whatever police protection he could make available. When later he wanted to date her, she'd allowed some distance to develop in their relationship.

"Gustave is a good man," her mother had said. Obviously disappointed. For Michelle who did not want a man in her life at that time, it was awkward for a while. He was not only kind to her, but rather handsome. Although his nose looked as if it had been broken at some point. Maybe in a fight. Now Gustave was married and that made ongoing conversation easier.

The telephone rang and Michelle jumped to answer it. Dawn, she thought, but it wasn't her daughter. Instead it was information about stock that would arrive later that morning. She was disappointed not to have heard yet from Dawn. Surely she wasn't still sleeping. Not wanting to appear demanding, Michelle decided to wait a bit longer to call her daughter. There was always plenty to do in the store.

"I wanted to take a long run before phoning," Dawn said half an hour later.

Michelle knew how annoying Dawn had found her in her teen years. Often she would retreat to the room she and Elise shared. There she would bang her pillow against her bed, in the top bunk above Elise's lair. Or she'd put on a parka and head outside to hurl snowballs at signs and trees. As a teenager she'd often made sharp comments to her mother, and to her sister.

"I had a call from Elise asking if I can go back to Montreal for an interview on Monday. A woman phoned in response to my résumé," Dawn said. "She's looking for someone fluent in French, English and Italian."

"I didn't know you spoke Italian." There was so much she didn't know about this daughter, so much that must have occurred during her three years of absence. It felt as if she'd lost that time entirely, but now that Dawn was back she hoped they would be able to share more.

"I'll tell you about it some other time," Dawn said. "I need to think about this interview. I do know I'd like to start working soon."

Later she told Michelle she'd managed to stay footloose for quite a long time with her knowledge of three languages, the Italian acquired in Siena where she'd spent a few months taking a course and sitting in small cafés. In one café across from the square, she'd met a man called Rocco. It took her longer than she would have liked to recognize his bravado concealed the same arrogance as her father's did. But a few weeks later, she'd figured it out, left him and moved on.

In the end, a mother can protect her daughter for only so long, Michelle thought. But, it seemed as though Dawn had learned a lot during this time.

"I'll confirm that appointment for next week," Dawn said. "No matter what happens, I won't go off again without warning. Elise made me promise I'd leave forwarding addresses if there's a next time."

"And?"

"I promised. What else? You know, I'm anxious to see Elise, but I don't understand her. Moving up the ladder at the bank is one thing. And being married suits her. But, why would anyone want to bring a child into the world now? The threat of the Soviet Union. War in the Middle East. Pollution getting worse every day."

She sat back on the small sofa Michelle had in the back of the store. When Michelle was tired, she could sit and close her eyes for a moment, still aware if anyone came in the front door.

"Elise sure let me know how worried both of you were, not warming up at all until she had a chance to say so. She knows that won't happen again now and we did talk about how good it would be for both of us if Aunt *Moi* could live not too far away in Montreal."

"I could babysit," Dawn said. "Elise was pleased when I suggested that. And have a mailbox downstairs in the lobby of some apartment building near Elise where I pull out letters addressed to Dawn St. Cyr. There'll be stamps from far-flung places that I'll save for the baby's collection. I'll even start a stamp book for the kid. Oh, and when I go out to work in the mornings, I'll wear an outfit from Chic Choc."

Michelle laughed.

Dawn hadn't met Elise's husband, Yves, as her sister had begun to date him after she went incommunicado. Michelle was glad to hear that they had invited Dawn to stay with them when she returned to Montreal. If she'd kept in touch, she would have been her sister's attendant and witness. It was a very small wedding, Elise had said, expressing disappointment that Dawn had missed it. Dawn hadn't even known about it until afterward.

"He likes you," Elise had said after she'd met him just before coming north. "It's a chance for you to get to know each other."

Nonetheless, Dawn had told Elise she wanted to find her own apartment quickly. Even though Elise said there was no hurry. "Even so, Mom, I want a place where I can hang my clothes in a closet and have my toothbrush and cosmetics in a bathroom that I don't have to share. A refrigerator where none of the food is labelled with the names of different people. Where I won't find something I bought has been eaten by a stranger."

"I'm going to close the shop and go down to help out when his or her majesty arrives," Michelle said. "This lucky baby will be surrounded by love."

"Wow," Dawn said. "How can you manage that with the store?"

"Oh, I'm sure I can close Chic Choc for a week, even two, at the end of January. I'll probably be able to do some shopping for the store when I'm there as well. There's a young woman who sometimes helps out and I can ask her to come in if I decide I want to keep it open."

"Are you doing some designing, too?" Dawn asked. "The mannequin looks quite elegant in that red chiffon and satin."

"I am," Michelle said.

"When I went for my run, the air felt so clean," Dawn said.

Michelle could visualize her leaning against the gatepost while she stretched out the muscles in her calves. At first she would have run slowly, building up speed gradually.

"I could almost smell the difference. No fumes. Nothing. I ran by Grandma's house. She would never have left it like that. Peeling paint. Then I ran down near the lake."

"You always liked that run."

"I'd like to come back in the summer and canoe here," Dawn said.

"Any time, *chérie*." As a teenager she'd rushed in to tell Michelle about the men in canoes heading toward James Bay on routes that had been used by early voyageurs and trappers. Probably before them by Native people.

"It would be bliss to live in solitude like that for a few days." She'd pitch a tent on a secluded rocky point and make a fire. After eating, she'd hang the bags of food on ropes from branches high enough to keep the bears out of it.

Michelle listened to her daughter talk, almost afraid she was asleep and would wake up to find she had been dreaming.

"When I was out on my run, that boy leapt out from the bushes at the side of the path and startled me. The one who came to the house." Dawn sighed. "He started to run alongside me, his short legs almost spinning so he could keep up. At first I ignored him, but he was like a shadow." She'd asked him why he wasn't in school. "He said it was none of my business."

"That's Marcel," Michelle said.

"What an arrogant brat. Why do you put up with him?"

Michelle smiled.

"I suppose he reminds you of me," Dawn said, a cheeky smile on her face.

"Not really," Michelle said. Although as a teenager Dawn had been as mercurial as the weather. Even on into her twenties when she'd graduated from CEGEP and felt she needed to contact her father.

They were startled by a loud noise overhead and, running to the window, were surprised to discover an airplane flying so low over the centre of the town that Michelle could almost see the Cree Air symbol painted on its side. Likely it was coming in from the area of the hydroelectric dam, she thought. Once Dawn had flown into Montreal with a plane being taken in for repairs by one of the pilots who flew that northern route. She'd met him on a bus up from the city. Michelle had objected, but Dawn said she would go anyway, that it would be safe. And that she was old enough and no one could do anything about it.

It was during one of Dawn's vacations from school. "Anyway, he probably won't call," she'd said. But on New Year's Day, the phone had rung. There was a plane he had to take south to the city, could she make it out to the airport in three hours? Dawn's eyes were bleary from a dance at The Flamingo the night before, but she'd drawn in a deep breath and said nonchalantly, "Sure, I could do that." Michelle had overheard her, starting to shiver with apprehension

When Dawn got off the telephone, she started to pack frantically. She didn't tell her mother about the repairs until after she'd landed in Montreal. It was enough for Michelle to absorb that she'd hitched a ride on an airplane. Later Dawn recounted tales of the flight, that on the trip south she'd sat in the cockpit behind the pilot. After it took four hours to get the plane started. Flying over snow-covered forest, sitting in the cockpit where she had the wide span of the pilot's view, was an adventure that ranked as high as later ones in Europe, she'd said. "Even more so than bazaars in North Africa and Turkey." Cold air had circulated through the plane, the heating system one of the broken things, and she was sure she would have frostbite before they landed.

"Marcel asked if he could come to Montreal with me." He was like a thorn picked up from a bush that was hard to extricate from one's clothing.

"I told him of course not," Dawn said "Where are his mother and father anyway?"

"No father. Mother drinks."

"Poor kid," Dawn said. She was thoughtful for a few moments, and then said she'd pick up something for their lunch. "I'll probably go down on Saturday or Sunday," she added. "Once I'm sure the interview is on Monday."

"That doesn't give us long," Michelle said. "We'll have to make good use of the time."

The smile on Dawn's face disappeared and she tightened her lips. But then she took in a long breath and let it out.

"*Je t'aime, Mama*." Dawn said quietly. "I'll come north again soon. And you'll be in Montreal in January."

"*Ah oui, mon enfant*," Michelle said, aware that something had shifted. "*Je t'aime aussi.*"

41.

WHEN LUCIEN WOKE up, he lay listening for a sound that would tell him where he was. It sometimes took him a few minutes to figure out he was not in town. In the summer he awakened early to the morning light and the sound of birds chirping was all it took to know he was at the lake. Now it was the whistle from the mine, which had a different sound from this distance, that told him it was also time to get up.

He turned to one side and was momentarily surprised to see Libby. Creeping quietly from the bed so as not to disturb her, he went to shave in front of the mirror in the small bathroom. He was shocked at the appearance of his face, so much older than he expected. Each morning, he was surprised at the proliferation of lines that mapped his face. And at the increasing grey hairs mixed in with the darker ones in his sideburns, and in the fuzz around his cheeks and chin.

He hoped Libby would wake up soon, that he would not have to make loud noises or shake her gently. He always felt better if he was up before the long jarring buzz of the alarm clock. If she wanted the car, she would have to drive him into town. He did not have to wait long to hear her yawn and roll over. Then, the light tap of stockings across the cold floor as she headed to the kitchen. Shortly after, he smelled coffee brewing on the propane stove.

"I'm going to let the dog out," Lucien said. "Let her run a while." Figaro. What a name for a retriever. Of course he would feed her. Susan had not had to say so. Didn't she remember what was good about their marriage? He could have complained when she had gone to scale logs. Even when she went camping in the bush, he had not minded that she had as usual not taken any of the children. She liked to canoe on silent lakes where the sound of loons awakened her, where an occasional plane flying high above over the northern route to Europe, over northern Quebec and the tip of Greenland, was the only reminder of civilization. He wondered what this vast barren land looked like from the moon.

"*Notre pays*," Susan would say. "*Québec*." But did she mean it? In an imagined conversation with her that continued an argument they had engaged in for the whole time they'd known each other, she would maintain there wasn't something called the rest of Canada.

"*Ah oui*," he'd mocked her. "In a city like Toronto, the language of the streets might as easily be Portuguese or Italian." It took generations for the French to find their voice. Even though the vote had been 'No' in the referendum, he knew that had not settled the aspirations of a whole people who saw themselves as a nation. Aspirations that were not understood in the rest of Canada. Whatever the rest of Canada was.

"*A la prochaine*," René had said.

It was certain there would be a next time.

"I'll get dressed and drive in with you," Libby said. "I could use the car today. I am going to drive around and take some photographs. Of the mine, of houses. Things I might draw and paint later. Get groceries."

"I'd like to see some of your work."

"I could show you sketches," she said. "And I have a magazine with an article in it my son gave me to read. It shows a painting. I'm after different images now, but I can show you the magazine later. I have this notion now of putting the Eiffel Tower in the same composition as a mine shaft. Something about the shapes of the two structures."

Lucien opened the door to let Figaro nudge past him and run across the snow toward the lake. Libby seemed oblivious.

"I remember teenage summers. One when I spent a few days in Paris, others when I went on the shift bus out to Manitou. I ran tests on samples to see whether the men underground were mining the right deposits. On the graveyard shift, I slept on the counter between the two sets of samples. A man brought them over from the mill in small brown paper bags, the first set around midnight, the other just after four in the morning."

"I'll be back soon," Lucien said, noticing Libby nod, lost in reverie. He did not think she would notice his absence. Almost thirty years separated them from the times they recalled in their conversations, thirty years of time when their lives had not overlapped at all. And now Susan was gone. His throat, head and stomach ached.

Figaro ran toward him and jumped up, almost knocking him over with his exuberance. Lucien tossed a stick and the dog bounded after it, bringing it back and dropping it a few inches from his feet, wagging its tail. They played for a while before Lucien returned to the cabin, leaving the dog outside to run.

Libby sat at the table, drinking coffee. There was jam and toast on a plate set down in the middle. Lucien took a cup of the steaming dark coffee, poured milk into it, and stood at the window.

"Do you remember the beach that joined the two islands at Mac-Nac?" he asked. "The grey sand was like clay. We parked on it. Or at least Susan and I did. You were part of the crowd from the mine site, too. The kids who lived near the highway."

"I suppose," she said. "Although I remember sitting alone in the bush and drawing pictures more than being part of any gang."

"Nicky Nicky Nine Doors!" Lucien exclaimed. "Knocking on doors and running away."

"Oh, that," she said.

"You and Guy and some of the other kids on rue Champlain did that," he said. "The next street over, too." He remembered Wally almost waddling along behind them, so young he could scarcely keep up. One time Jutras was called. All the older kids, including Libby and Guy, had vanished and Jutras had found little Wally, only three or four then, hidden under the porch of the Dufresne's house.

"Someone threw a rock at the roof," Madame Dufresne told the policeman.

"This little fellow couldn't have done that," Jutras said. "But maybe he knows something."

Wally cried, so Jutras took him home to the white house next to the bush.

Libby nodded. "*C'est vrai*." She conceded she had been there. "Poor Jutras. He never caught us, but we were much more careful after he caught Wally."

Lucien chuckled. "I'll warm up the car," he said.

When Libby got in, he told her he would stop just long enough to pick up some papers at his place. After that, they headed into town.

"How old were you when your father came back from *outre-mer*?" Lucien asked.

"Eight."

"Most of the guys who went were younger. And single." The names on the monument were brothers of men who were now fathers and grandfathers. Most of them had not been married.

"What a waste," Lucien said.

"My father didn't think so."

"Yeah, but your father was an Anglo."

42

WALTER MUIR'S LETTERS had started to mention *Japs* before the war in Europe ended, warning his family they were still some kind of danger. He wrote he might not get to Ile d'Or as soon as he had thought he would. What Libby knew was that people who came from a place somewhere far away had bombed Pearl Harbour before her father left to go overseas, a place out in the middle of an ocean, and that her father said maybe the ones in British Columbia were spies. In his letters, there was something about going to fight them in some theatre when the *Jerries* were all cleaned up. But he didn't have to and instead before too much longer he arrived back home.

Libby knew there was something not right about what he was saying about the people in the west who might be dangerous and so were moved away from the ocean into towns in the interior. It confused her. Weren't they all Canadians? But because she still thought her father knew just about everything, she couldn't figure it out for a long time. She did know when he talked about dividing things between his children some day that Wally getting half of everything because he was a boy did not make any sense. As if boys were better than girls somehow. But it was a lot longer before she figured out her father thought whites were better than anyone else in subtle ways also. The picture on her bedroom wall with the black nanny had made her squeamish. There was her father like a small prince sitting on his pillow beside her. Libby wondered as a child if this woman, known only as his nanny, was another grandmother. And when her father went overseas, she thought at first he might have gone back to Africa.

"Lots of changes," Lucien said. "Since your time."

"Still seems familiar."

Libby knew the route into town and the pharmacy as if it were embedded in her consciousness. They drove past the supermarket, Mulholland's long gone now, then a Sony dealer.

"Could I use the telephone in your office?" she asked as Lucien opened the car door.

"Of course." *Bien sur.*

She went to the back of the pharmacy where his desk was covered with papers. There was a photograph of Susan in a gold frame on one side. Surprised at Susan's greying hair and the lines around her mouth, only the dark eyes and knowing smile told her who the woman was. She supposed she would always think of Susan as somewhere between twelve and seventeen.

She picked up the receiver and started to dial Dan's number at City Hall. One digit escaped her and she decided to call his apartment instead. She noticed that the poster of a winter scene on the wall in front of her was a Krieghoff.

"This is Dan Robinson speaking," the familiar voice greeted her on Dan's answering machine.

Relieved not to have to speak to him, Libby left a message that she did not have a telephone and would call him when she returned to Toronto in a couple of weeks. When she stepped out of the office, Lucien watched her walk down the aisle where bottles of shampoo were lined up neatly on shelves on one side and tubes of toothpaste, dental floss, and mouthwash on the other.

"What time do you want me to pick you up?" she asked. Much to her own surprise, she was enjoying the time they spent together. As if Dan didn't exist, as if Lucien had accepted Susan would never return. Even thoughts of Guy couldn't make her feel guilty about the easy camaraderie that had developed with his older brother.

"Five. Six. Whenever you arrive is fine."

On the highway, she drove past the graveyard again, onto a road that led past deserted shacks to an old mine site. The ground was frozen and the buildings were all empty. The gold was gone. The copper and zinc, too. Some day the town would disappear. A willow tree leaned over the ice at the edge of a creek nearby, as if claiming the territory now that people had left it.

On the car radio, an announcer began to read the news and she tried to understand what was happening in the world beyond her. Israel and Lebanon were still at loggerheads. War in the Middle East seemed inevitable. She waited for the weather forecast. In November it was bound to prove she had been foolhardy to decide to stay in Guy's

cabin where the only heat came from a small propane heater she found
difficult to use or the wood stove that needed to be stoked and fed
constantly. She might have grown up in this place, but she lacked the
skills to survive in the outdoors any more. Were she really stranded,
she might not have enough wood to heat the cabin nor a man who
would come over and keep her from lying awake terrified that every
small noise meant imminent disaster.

Surveying the area, Libby remembered swimming with Guy in the
creek near the mine site. This was also where the Native people had
lived in shacks. She had never known any of them, had scarcely seen
them, except as shapes at the edge of this road, miles from town. As
a child, she had asked a lot of questions, but it was only recently that
she began to find out about the schools Native children were forced to
go where much worse things happened than anything she could have
imagined. She thought that was why there had been so few of them
hanging out in town when she was growing up.

A car horn honked and she looked up to see the driver's friendly
wave as he drove slowly by on the bumpy road. Although she might
have been nervous in the city, it did not cross her mind in daylight that
she might be in danger in this isolated place.

When she arrived back at the cabin, Libby looked for lard to make
some pastry. All she could find were tins of pork and beans and an
old package of spaghetti that looked as though mice had been at it.
Pacing around the room, her eyes were drawn to the wood chopped
and carefully piled in a box near the cabin's old stove, just like the
one they had used to heat hot chocolate as children. And the bright
blue, yellow and red enamel cups hung in a row on hooks over the
sink. She found a broom and began to sweep the floor and the brown
twisted braid rug with bits of twig and leaves embedded in it. Always
struggling to carve out time to paint, now that she'd found it she could
not figure out how to use it. Sketch a tree or mine shaft? It was so
easy to get side-tracked. Although when the images finally emerged,
and a painting gradually became just the one she wanted to paint, she
would know she was doing what it was she was meant to do. That
sense of purpose usually lasted only as long as the images took over
her life and it could wreak havoc with everything else for the duration.
To give up art was to give up the underlying river that linked her life,
tantamount to stopping breathing. Yet Barton had left her because of

it, because what else so clearly defined who she was? He had tried to suggest it had something to do with her wanting to get her tubes tied, but Libby knew he had been looking for an excuse for a long time. Until he found one, she just hadn't noticed.

Libby swept the bits of fluff, leaves and twigs into a yellow dustpan. When she opened the door to empty it outside, even this far away, she could hear the low rumbling sound from the mill that carried across town and water. Would she feel the earth tremble with the blasting underground in the middle of the night? She had not noticed when she had been with Lucien, but she might have missed it. How important those sounds had been through all her childhood, framing her sense of time and place. She might seem to be an urban creature now, but the appearance was deceiving. Just under the skin were all the memories. Of the night, for instance, when her mother finally locked the front door when her father did not come in even after the supper dishes were washed and put away and the table set for breakfast. When he did arrive, he pounded furiously.

"Why did you lock the damn door?" he shouted, his words slurred as he banged repeatedly on the wood and fumbled with the handle.

Her mother paced back and forth on the landing, her shoes loosening the grate in the floor where the warm air came up from the furnace. She wrung her hands, and muttered under her breath. "What am I to do?" was the only thing Libby had been able to make out.

"Open the damn door," he'd shouted. "Charlotte. CHARLOTTE!"

As Libby stood frozen at the top of the stairs, waiting for the door to break and her father to come flailing through it, her mother went to the closet in the hall. Tears were streaming down her face as she reached beyond the coats to the shelf above. When Libby's father's footsteps staggered across the porch, her mother turned to face the door, a gun in her hands.

Libby started to shake. She had heard her father say the gun was never loaded and she knew her mother only touched it when she went hunting partridge. She trembled at the thought of what might happen. What was her mother doing? There was a loud crash against the outside wall.

"Charlotte," the pounding began again.

Charlotte lifted the gun to her shoulder. "Don't you dare step inside," she shrieked, her hands shaking, her entire body shaking.

"Charlotte," Walter Muir almost sobbed. "I love you."

"How can I believe that?"

"Just let me in."

Gradually, the shouting subsided, the pounding stopped. Her mother's shoulders sagged as she put the gun back in the cupboard. "Oh, dear God," she'd sobbed, her body heaving. "Have mercy upon us. Lord, have mercy upon us." After a while, she continued. "The Lord is my shepherd." Finally when there was quiet and her father might even have fallen asleep, Charlotte opened the front door.

Libby moved away from the stairs, not wanting her mother to see her. She heard her father crash to the floor as he lurched through the door and later a familiar litany.

"It won't happen again."

"You've promised before, Walter."

"This time I mean it," he said. Then there was silence, followed by a loud belch. "Please believe me," he pleaded.

When the voices finally stopped, Libby heard the dull, steady throbbing from the vacuum pump at the mine and she wished her father had died in the war after all.

43

MICHELLE STOOD IN the kitchen, watching her daughter cut up greens, relishing the time they'd had together in the shop that afternoon, talking at last. About where Dawn learned Italian, the new designs for winter dresses that hung on hangers in the display area of the store, Dawn's interview the next week, Michelle's date with Nick for that evening. She'd felt the need to run it by Dawn again.

"I hope you don't mind that I'm going out to dinner," Michelle said. "Nick won't be here for much longer and since you and I had the time in the shop I thought when he called I'd see him again before he leaves."

"Of course it's fine," Dawn said. "I'm happy to have some alone time. Is there time to call Elise before he picks you up?"

Michelle longed to know more about the months and years Dawn had been travelling. There seemed an endless period of time that she knew nothing about, that Dawn did not seem to want her to know about. Even as they'd relaxed in the shop when no customers were there, when she'd asked once without thinking about her whereabouts in the last year or so, Dawn had bristled and changed the subject.

"Chérie, I'm not prying. I'm just interested," she'd said, wishing she hadn't asked.

Of course there was time to call Elise. "Nick won't be here for another half hour." She wore a dark skirt that came to a point just below her knees with an ivory blouse and a bronze vest made of a slightly shiny taffeta-like material.

"You look terrific, Ma," Dawn said.

Michelle smiled.

Dawn reached for the telephone. "You call, Ma," she said.

Michelle wasn't sure what Dawn expected. Maybe to create the small, happy family she'd always hoped for, something she knew was an unattainable dream for most people. But maybe with the new baby the glue that had been missing would make them all feel more connected.

They reached Elise just as she came in from work. Yves was starting dinner, she said, some fried potatoes with leftover cold beef. Yves enjoyed cooking. Michelle had bought a chef's apron for him and tucked it away in a drawer she kept for gifts. She thought if she didn't forget it was there, she would give it to him for his birthday or for Christmas. It was no more than a perfunctory conversation, but both Michelle and Dawn were pleased about it, their gestures and expressions calm in ways that were noticeable to each other.

Just after they hung up, there was a knock at the door and Nick's face appeared on the other side of the glass, lit up by the yellow beams of the porch lamp. When he saw Dawn standing next to Michelle, he shifted awkwardly from one foot to the other. When Michelle introduced them, he scrutinized the younger woman, taking her hand.

"Did you know your mother and I knew each other when we were younger than you are?"

"Well, not until an hour or so ago." Dawn's laugh was a trill of notes that rose and fell.

"Would you like to come to dinner with us?" Nick asked.

"Oh my goodness, no," Dawn said. "But thanks for the invitation." She looked relieved when Michelle reached for her jacket. Nick held it while she put her arms, first one, and then the other, into the sleeves.

"I won't keep her out too late," Nick said.

"I'm not a chaperone," Dawn said, but she was smiling.

Michelle was embarrassed. "C'mon, you two," she said. "That's enough." She stepped out through the door, into the evening, and waited for Nick to follow.

Outside, she arranged her scarf so it covered her neck and pulled her coat over it. "Take that road over there," she said. "To the left."

"Are you taking me by some new route?" he asked.

"I suppose this road wasn't here when you lived in town, but it's a shorter way to downtown than any you'd recognize."

"I'll just have to trust you," he said lightly, casting a glance as she smoothed her skirt over her knees and tucked her purse down beside her feet.

As soon as they were on the main street, Michelle knew he would be on familiar territory and find a spot to park near The Flamingo.

"So, the famous night club," he said.

"Ribs and wings," Michelle said. "It's a pretty limited menu. But for old time's sake."

When he reached the sidewalk on her side, she was already almost out of the car and he closed and locked the doors.

"Back in the old days, we never ate here, did we? I don't recall people eating here."

"No," she said. "We didn't. But it's still symbolic of our childhood, isn't it?" The outcome of underground labour. Although she wouldn't ever say that. "Everyone came here then. Mostly to have a drink. There weren't too many other choices. When did you have your first drink? Where did you have it?"

"You have a point," he said and laughed.

At a dimly lit table toward the back, Michelle and Nick studied the list of cocktails, chatting and laughing as they talked about which wine to order with their meal. Eventually Nick ordered a bottle. Beer would probably be more appropriate to the occasion, they agreed, but they preferred a red wine. As they toasted each other and he admired her splendid cheekbones, he averted his eyes as they strayed downwards to the outline of her breasts under her blouse. Had he put the condoms in his pocket? What good would they do though, now that her daughter had arrived and his room was hardly more than a closet with thin walls and a creaky floor? She would never go there with him.

"Let this be the beginning of the rest of our lives," he said.

"What does that mean?" she asked.

"It sounds good," he said. "I know I came here without a real sense of direction. I seem to have lost it. And I guess I must have thought that somehow I would find myself again by coming back. Now I'm trying to figure out when to go back to Toronto and what to do when I get there. I don't know really what I want. Some new start would be welcome."

"Don't you want to resume your practice?"

"Well, yes, of course. I'll be doing that. But for the last while I wasn't able to offer my patients as much as I would have liked," he said. "Maybe I'll be able to after this. I do feel less depressed and less angry. My daughter keeps asking me what my passion is and I've been looking for an answer. It used to be psychiatry. Now, I am not so sure anymore."

"Tell me about your daughter," Michelle said, smiling at him.

"Diana," he said. *Oh, Diana.* He could go on about the wonders of a young woman who never ceased to amaze him, but she wasn't why he was here in this town or, for that matter, in this nightclub. He told Michelle enough about Diana to satisfy her and then asked her about *her* passion. "Is it the shop?"

"Oh, I do love the shop," Michelle said. "But more than Chic Choc itself, I love fashion. I always have. It's such a delight to see a woman come in the door and contemplate what would make her look dazzling. Sometimes it's more than clothes, a new hairdo or something to do with cosmetics."

"How on earth do you get someone to change all of that?"

"Well, I usually don't. But if she trusts me, she might ask. Some do."

"Are you going to stay in Ile d'Or?" Nick asked,

"Probably," she said.

"Is that what you really want to do?"

"Well, now that my mother is gone, I'm not really sure anymore. Sometimes I feel kind of stuck," she said.

"Why?"

"Think about it," Michelle said, taking a sip of wine. "It's not so different from what you've been telling me. Perhaps complicated by knowing that I'm comfortable enough here. And how would I manage to start something like Chic Choc anywhere else? Where would I go? I've built a clientele who knows me. I make a living."

"Toronto," Nick said quietly, as if he'd just had an idea but hoped she wouldn't quite hear him.

She laughed. "That's not one that would ever cross my mind."

"It's a lot better place to live than it used to be."

She shrugged.

"Well, come and visit some time," he said, reaching across to touch her hand. "See for yourself."

"Oh sure." Her expression was pensive. "But what on earth would I do there?" She pulled her hand away gently.

"I don't know," he said. "There's a whole garment industry, I think. Not that I know much about it. Maybe you could find new fashions. New designers."

"Maybe," she said.

"If you do come for a visit, I'll show you around," Nick said. "I'll take you out on the town."

"Okay," she nodded. Michelle was smiling but she buried her head in the menu. He had made her uncomfortable. She looked up at him, her smile guarded now. "What are you going to order? Do you know?"

"You mean ribs or wings? I thought perhaps both."

Michelle shook her head. "Men," she said.

When the waitress approached their table, Nick told her it might take a bit longer for them to decide. But before the woman disappeared, Michelle said she'd have the wings and he smiled and ordered wings for both of them and ribs as well for him.

"What about taking a trip? Coming to Toronto for a visit," he asked. He didn't know why it was suddenly so important to him that she come to the city, be with him.

"It's hard to get away," she said, sipping her wine and avoiding his gaze.

He understood that; a small business that depended on a clientele would be similar to a medical practice, not something you could leave for long. It would be hard in a small town to find someone to take over even for a short period. He would ask her about that, but now he was wondering if she might be interested in going some place with him, even to India, and he didn't want to let the practicalities intrude yet.

"You remember that big game hunting idea?" he asked.

She smirked. "Of course."

"Well, how about if you come with me?"

"Now I know you're crazy."

"I'm being serious. I've wanted to go to India for a long time and..."

"Let's enjoy this moment," Michelle said, eyeing him thoughtfully. Reaching for his hand, she added, "It's really rather precious."

He supposed it was, a moment that he could not have imagined. Having dinner with someone he'd known as a teenager and feeling a certain comfort that he hadn't felt for years. A comfort that had grown over the few days he'd been here. It hadn't occurred to him that the reason for this trip might have been to recapture a time when there had been an extended family of northerners to which he still belonged. Once both his parents were dead, that thought had disappeared with them, and his trip here had been only a whim until it finally happened.

"Thanks, Michelle," he said, smiling at her. "Let's do that."

44

D ARK CAME EARLY in November, around five o'clock. The days felt uncomfortably truncated and it would remain like that until after the middle of February when they gradually became longer. The streetlights were on as were those in the shops. Noticing a line-up of customers in the pharmacy, Libby drove to rue Champlain once again and stopped near the white house next to the bush. A light over the front porch shed a glow over the path to the street. A man walked up the steps and a child ran to greet him. Through the curtains of what had once been the Muir's dining room, Libby could see a woman's face watching them.

An oak Welsh dresser with blue and white crown derby china on the shelves had stood against the wall that separated the dining room from the kitchen. In the middle had been a matching oak table and chairs. The chair with arms was at her father's end of the long table. Libby had studied the grain on those days when her father had barely been able to keep his head up. When he'd been drinking, he yelled no matter what she did.

"Mish Muir, stop that now!"

Once he spilled a glass of tomato juice and blamed it on her, shouting. Libby could not stand to look at him then. For years, all she had to do was to see oak to feel sick to her stomach, holding as it did the memories of too many family meals where she'd kept her head down so as not to witness her father's stumbling efforts with his fork. She had refused the dining table when her mother moved into Friendship Villa.

When she drove back to the pharmacy, Lucien was standing just outside the shop. He came over to the car, opened the door and slid into the seat on the passenger side.

"There was a call for you from Toronto," he said, looking at her curiously. "Dan Robinson." His eyes veered off to the side.

"Did he say anything?" Libby asked.

"He said he could come up here."

"*Merde*," she sighed. "Is the store still open? Can I call from there?" At first she had wanted Dan here, to show him everything. Now his presence was the last thing she needed. It would be like a shadow looming over her, obstructing her vision. What did he think he was doing, intruding now when she had waited and waited for him to call in Toronto? When she'd finally called him, he had been involved with another woman. Daphne.

"I'll unlock the door to the store," Lucien said. "*Pas de problème.*"

The first time Libby dialled, the line was busy. She was aware of Lucien pacing back and forth in front of the magazine rack as she dialled again. No one answered. Even Dan's answering machine did not come on. For all she knew, he might just turn up here. What on earth was he thinking? She began to work herself into a frenzy as she remembered again the time they had made love only to discover afterwards that he thought he was in love with Daphne. From the corner of her eye, she could see that Lucien had turned to watch her and she nodded at him. About to replace the receiver, she heard a gruff voice at the other end.

"Dan?"

"Libby." He'd been in the shower, he told her. "Did it ring many times?

"Probably a dozen."

"Well, I'm here now," he said. "I've been thinking. I have some time. I could come up and join you. See where you come from."

"I'd rather you didn't."

"Who's the man?" Dan asked. "And this Pharmacie Dion place?"

"His brother and I were pals when I was a kid," she said, but it wasn't any of his business and she resented the proprietary tone in his voice, as if it were his right to know. She could imagine his irritated reaction if she had asked questions about Daphne.

"When are you coming back?"

"I'm not sure. In a couple of weeks probably."

"You can call and reverse the charges," he said, his voice softer now. "Any time."

She knew that she would not, but she thanked him.

"You didn't tell me anything about the man who took the message."

"There's nothing to tell other than what I already said."

As she hung up, she felt a hand on her shoulder.

"*Alors, Libby, allons manger quelque chose en ville.*" Let's go and eat something.

"I think it's my turn to treat you."

"Oh," he said. "I have plenty of money. *Et les artistes sont souvent pauvres, n'est-ce pas?*"

"I have enough."

They left the car in front of the pharmacy and walked toward the centre of town. Libby looked in a store window with greeting cards in it. *Bonne Fête, Bonne Anniversaire, Joyeux Noël.* Beyond that was a shoe store with women's heels on one side and flat walking shoes and boots on the other. Then the hardware store with the ski-doo in the window where her brother, Wally, had worked one summer during high school. After that he quit school and went with the air force to wire power stations on the Distant Early Warning line. She remembered looking at a map to see where Thule was, thinking it looked as if it were at the end of the world. Wally scarcely wrote any letters and he told her later that when he did their mother sent the letters back with the grammar corrected.

"*Alors,*" Lucien said. "How about going to see my mother?"

"We should eat something first."

"Maman always has enough for at least a dozen extra people," he said. "Anyway, I told her I'd bring you one night. Tonight is as good as any other. She doesn't go out much any more and she always enjoys company."

"Okay," Libby said. "Nothing I'd like to do more than see Madame Dion." With the memory of the warm smell of dough rising in the Dion kitchen, she could almost taste the first slice of bread lathered with butter. And hot chocolate, too, her own never as good as Madame Dion's with the marshmallow melted in it.

When they headed back toward the car, Lucien slid in behind the wheel. Reaching over, he put his hand on her arm. "Did you have a good day?" he asked.

"I spent most of it thinking," she said.

He looked bemused. "Is that the life of an artist?" he asked.

"Sometimes. Often I draw or paint something, too," she said. "But I didn't get to that yet." She always forgot that thinking counted. And making notes and small drawings. Sometimes she developed the beginnings of a piece in her sketchbook, jotting down some descriptions that she would use later. At the time, it seemed like a way of communing with herself, of working things out, not like something special that went with painting.

"And you?" she asked. "Your day?"

"It went quickly," he said. He did not elaborate.

Libby focused on the houses as they drove up a street from a boulevard that joined what had once been Bourlamaque with Ile d'Or. She recognized a duplex with brown insulbrick covering its rectangular shape as one where she had played with a girl who had lived in town for only a year or two. She could remember the girl had brown eyes and light, tawny hair with waves in it. Good at math, she was the only one up until then to get a higher mark than Libby. It was a surprise to find that she, Libby, was not always the smartest. From then on, from time to time, someone new in her class would outdo her again. Once, a boy in Grade seven, whose family came from Russia.

There were two cars parked beside the house where the girl had lived and next to it was the turn to rue Champlain. Within a couple of minutes they would be in front of the small white bungalow where she had played with Guy, listening to the sounds of the Dion family. Loud, joyful sounds punctuated with the vibrant lilt of voices speaking a language she barely understood then. Aside from Lucien, the others had always welcomed her. Lucien had always seemed scornful then. She might ask him about that later.

"Maman," Lucien called from the front door and his mother's voice answered from somewhere inside.

A photograph on a white lace doily on a table next to the television set captured Libby's attention. Guy stood at a window, sunlight around his head like an aura. One hand rested on the sill and a lock of thick brown hair fell over his forehead. Beyond him were pine trees on the side of a hill. There was another of his profile with his head thrown back and mouth open in which he looked like a porpoise breaking out of the water. He'd been vain, Libby thought to herself, an attribute she'd forgotten.

"*Bonjour, Libby*," Madame Dion said from the door into the hall.

"*Quel plaisir.*" Her smile was genuine. She carried a tray with green and blue cups and a coffeepot to the table near the fireplace. Did Libby want cream? she asked. And *sucre?* How many lumps? "What a happy occasion to see little Elizabeth," she said. "You and Guy." Tears sprang to her eyes as her voice caught on her words. "*Mon pauvre Guy,*" she said quietly.

"I'm really sorry about Guy," Libby said. "It was a shock to arrive and find out." Almost like losing part of herself, almost like the limbs that went missing after Barton left her. Still, she was unprepared for the visible shudder that went through the older woman's body and she moved to hug her.

"*Je ne comprends pas,*" Madame Dion said. She would never understand. Guy destroyed his life with all the booze. Wrecked his marriage, neglected his children. Left his mother with a part of her dead that she would never recover.

"*Mais laissez-moi chercher quelque chose à manger,*" Madame Dion said, brushing away the tears as she retreated to the kitchen.

Libby glanced over at Lucien. "Some things you have to say," she said.

"You knew him," he said. "You loved him, too."

Libby bit her lip as she felt the tears well in her own eyes. She might not have come north, might have gone on living with the myth of this warm, loving family that was so much better than her own. The myth that Monsieur Dion's peccadilloes were the stuff of humour, that they did not hurt anyone. She would have remembered Guy asking her to marry him, his eyes pleading, and not ever have known what had become of him. She would have remembered him as the carefree teenager who had been her buddy, the one who shared the outdoors with her, who gradually awakened sexual yearnings. Had she married him, would the same thing have happened? Divorce. Alcoholism. Would it have been worse than the aftermath with Barton? Or would knowing each other from childhood have shielded her and Guy somehow? There were no answers to these questions. She wished Guy was still here to talk about it.

Madame Dion came back into the room, carrying a tray with sliced meats, bread, cheese, and butter. A bowl of pickles. Gesturing to Lucien to come to the table, she set the food down. Over the older woman's head, Libby spied photographs of Guy's two sons whom she recognized from similar photographs in the cabin. Another of Guy with his sons when they were teenagers. He looked happy. Proud.

"How is your mother?" Mme. Dion asked. "My old friend, Charlotte."

"Her arthritis bothers her," Libby said. "But, she's still active."

"We curled on the same team," Madame Dion said. "Charlotte was skip. A good one, too. We won the bonspiel, you know. More than once. Did Charlotte ever tell you that we spoke French together?" Madame Dion asked. "You know her grandmother, a Gravelle, *je pense*, Henriette, didn't speak English very well."

"I'd forgotten," Libby said. Her memory always appropriated everything French in the town and left the rest of her family in some English enclave. She also had a fleeting memory of a letter her father had written from overseas about helping translate for a soldier from Quebec who was struggling to learn English. "I never met my grandmother," Libby said. "She died before I was born. And we didn't have any aunts or uncles or cousins to tell us the stories our parents didn't. We had such a small family. Mostly we heard about dead people, buried in England, all Dad's ancestors."

"But you're a northerner," Madame Dion said. "That's a family." Her hand, crisscrossed with wispy blue veins and a sprinkling of brown spots, just like Charlotte Muir's hands, trembled slightly as she stroked Libby's arm. "It's Susan's family, too," she said. "I don't understand how she could leave here."

"Maman," Lucien said. "*Ne commence pas*." Standing up, he dangled his car keys in one hand and played with the change in his pocket with the other.

"*Eh bien*," Madame Dion sighed. She began to talk about the early days, the days before the railroad, before the highway, the days of the first settlers. "Lucien was born at another mine that closed just before we came here," she said. "Guy, out-of-town. In Noranda." She had an album of black and white photographs stuck to the pages with black triangular corners. Under each photograph were names and dates. Lucien went out to the kitchen and they heard the back door close as he stepped out onto the back porch.

"A cigarette," Madame Dion said.

Libby nodded.

"I thought of leaving Ile d'Or when Papa took up with the secretary,"

Madame Dion said.

Libby jerked in her chair and as her body bent forward, she put her cup on the table.

"Don't be embarrassed, *mon enfant*," said Madame Dion. "Of course, I knew." For a moment, she was quiet.

Libby was suddenly pensive. "Do you know what happened to Arthur White?" she asked. "Was there something between him and my…"

"*Je ne sais rien.*" The way she moved her head so that she was looking off into the distance, her cheeks slightly flushed, suggested that Mme. Dion knew more than she was saying.

45.

"SO SHEILA DID marry Brian Sloane?" Madame Dion asked. "I remember that when they were small children they were inseparable. Then when his family moved to Africa, I remember hearing that they wrote letters to each other. I thought they'd gone off in different directions after that."

"They did, but they crossed paths again later."

"And Wally and Jeannie?"

Lucien stepped inside, a sudden rush of cool air following him. His mother looked up as if she were checking to see if there was a storm brewing. He must have heard their conversation, Libby thought, and when he spoke it was apparent

"Only Libby married a stranger," he said, as Libby nodded in answer to Mme. Dion's question.

"The maverick in the family," Libby said with a wry smile. "Something I was always proud of until my life turned into a disaster."

"A disaster," Madame Dion said. "*Oh, non.* Or you wouldn't be here now. Looking for *les racines.* I think the English word is roots, isn't it? Finding people here after all these years who care about you."

"*La vie,*" Lucien said. "You never know."

"There's more coffee," Mme Dion said.

She reached for the coffee pot and poured the steaming brew into their cups, gesturing at the same time at a plate of brown sugar tarts made with nuts and currants. Lucien instead took a slice of chocolate cake from the edge of the plate.

It was almost eleven when they stopped talking. Every so often, Mme. Dion sighed and Libby bit her lip as she followed the older woman's eyes that would linger on a photograph of Guy or his trophy of antlers, something that reminded her of him and stopped her in mid-sentence.

When they said good night to Mme. Dion, they drove through town to the highway out to the lake. Lucien pointed toward a couple coming out of The Flamingo.

"Look," he said. "Michelle."

"Who's the man?" Libby asked, thinking he looked vaguely familiar.

"I think we talked about the coincidence of Nick Petranovich being in town at the same time as you, didn't we?"

"Oh, yes, Nick Petranovich. Practically a relative," she said. "Of course. Why don't we stop and say hello?"

As Lucien honked and waved at them, Michelle waved back. He rolled down his window and pulled up closer to the sidewalk. "Now, here's a strange thing," he said. "A reunion. Do you folks have time for a coffee? Or a drink?"

"Hey, Libby," Nick said as he leaned over and spoke across Lucien. "What a surprise! It's been a while. And you haven't changed a bit."

"Gee, thanks Nick," she said. "It's great to see you, too." It was strange that she hadn't seen him since his sister married her brother. Maybe he had as little contact with Jeannie as she had with Wally.

"Are you still living in Toronto?" Nick asked.

"Yes," she said. "I am. What about you?"

"That's still where I live, too. Crazy world that I never run into you there and here we are in Ile d'Or at the same time."

Michelle looked at her watch. "It's late. What about a rain check?" she asked.

"Michelle's daughter arrived in town more or less unexpectedly," Nick said. "I'm taking her home early so they can continue their visit."

Lucien took Nick's local number and said he'd plan something. "It will have to be before either you or Libby leave."

As Lucien headed out of town on the highway to the lake, he drove with one hand on the wheel, his other elbow resting on the windowsill. There were two bags of food on the back seat, bread his mother had baked along with the remaining cold meats, half a chocolate cake, a few tarts, and a bag of carrots.

"I drove out to that creek where Guy and I used to swim," Libby said. "You know the one down the road from an old mine site, near the shacks."

"You have to be careful, Libby. It's not like it used to be."

She wasn't sure what he might be referring to, but she didn't ask, not wanting to hear of men who might jump out of bushes or come along in rickety trucks and scoop up lone women wandering in the bush. When they arrived at the cabin, he fell asleep quickly while Libby sat at the window staring out at the trees and the sky. Mme. Dion had showered them with warmth and food at the same time as she was suffering Guy's descent into the booze and finally into taking his own life. She heard Lucien flailing in his sleep and then shout loudly. When she went to the door of the bedroom to check on him, he was punching his pillow hard.

"*Maudit*," he said. And something about a goddamned tramp. Who the hell did she think she was? He would kill her.

"Lucien," Libby said. "Lucien."

"*Q'est-qu'il y a*?" he said. What is it? He rolled over and stared at her. His eyes were wide open, but she could tell he was still asleep.

"Lucien," she murmured. "You're dreaming."

"Shut up," he said.

Libby shook his shoulders until he sat up and looked at her. "Who are you?" he asked.

"Lucien, I'm Libby. Elizabeth Muir. Don't you remember?" She was suddenly frightened.

Oh, yes, he remembered. "The one who was supposed to marry Guy and didn't. The bitch. I'd still have a brother if it hadn't been for you. It's all your fault," he said. "*Maudite anglaise*."

"What are you talking about?"

"Guy."

"What about Guy?"

"He went nuts later," he said. "He never would have if it hadn't been for you. He joined the FLQ. He went around flashing. He wasn't the same."

"It's not my fault what your brother did with his life," Libby shouted. "That's garbage. Sheer, utter garbage." Libby was stunned, and angry. What was happening to him?

Lucien shook his head. "What did I say?" he asked, his voice concerned. He was confused. He'd suddenly recognized where he was, in the cabin. Everything else had been part of his nightmare.

"Guy was in the FLQ. He..." Libby tried to explain. She was still shaking.

"I dreamed it," Lucien said. "There was some bitch with a gun to

Guy's head. They were going to bomb something. She wore yellow. She spoke English. Oh, *calice*. I can't stand many more of these dreams." He put his head in his hands. "I'm sorry," he said. "I've had a dream like this before. I'm sorry if I frightened you."

"It was a nightmare," Libby said. "I know about nightmares."

"*Oh mon Dieu*," he sighed. "What am I going to do?"

"I'll make some tea," she said. "No, I'll heat up some milk. That would be better."

"Guy was just a drunk in the end," he said. "He had no politics. No vision."

"I don't believe that."

"Whether you believe it or not, that's how it was," Lucien said.

An hour later, when he was snoring, Libby sat at the window watching the dark branches of trees and stars against the sky. It was almost dawn before she fell asleep on the couch.

When Lucien woke up, he could scarcely look at her. "I'm sorry about last night," he said.

"It was a dream," she said. "Dreams happen."

"I'm still sorry."

"Okay," she sighed. "It was pretty scary. Do you mind if I ask you not to stay here tonight?"

"*Je comprends*," he said.

"If I want to say hello, I'll come over. But I may not until tomorrow," Libby added. The prospect of listening to the noises of animals in the dark no longer bothered her.

"Do you want the car?" he asked.

"I'm not going anywhere today," she said. "Maybe tomorrow. Or the next day."

"*Comme tu veux*." As you wish.

46

WHEN THE NOISE of the car engine faded, Libby lay down on the couch and fell asleep. It was noon when she woke up feeling peckish. After eating some of the leftovers from the previous evening's bounty, she went outside for the first time that day. Walking along a trail in front of the cabins, she threw some pebbles out onto the ice. Then stopped to look at some of the places that were shut for the winter. She listened to the crunch of her boots on the frozen ground and watched her breath turn white. She was glad she had come. The geography of the north was so ingrained in her that she'd needed to satisfy the hunger to return.

Libby wondered what it was that also bound her to Toronto. It was *une grande ville*, no doubt about that, but she had never planned to live her life out in a city. As she came around a bend in the path, she almost ran into a tall man in a red jacket. His back to her, he stood looking out over the lake. When he heard her gasp, he turned around.

"*Bonjour*," he said. It was Jacques Paquin. "I took the day off," he said. "And I had a call from my father. I was going to come and see you, but I thought I might be intruding."

"Well, here I am," Libby said.

"I told Papa you were here, that you're staying in Guy's cabin. He said he has to come up this way to look over one of the mines. It's out near the river on the way to the Ontario border. He asked me to see if you'd have dinner with him."

"I'd like to."

"Can I pick you up when he's here, next Monday, after work? He won't want to come to the cabin."

The thought that her time might be entirely filled sometimes made Libby feel claustrophobic. It might interfere with the work she needed to do while in this place. Drawings and paintings that would recapture something she'd lost. But she'd learned that one of the baffling aspects of making art was that everything that appeared to be in the way later became essential. This invitation was like that, she thought. Not that there had been any doubt about her accepting it, just the sense of time collapsing on her again, not leaving space for reverie. Yet, she felt that in seeing Paul there might be something she would understand that could lead to new beginnings. Sometimes, that new inspiration took a long time to come. She'd thought that when she was finished with her Paris series, some new clarity would emerge. It hadn't.

"Of course," she said. *Bien sur.*

"So," Jacques said. "That's settled. Six o'clock?" He turned toward a cabin she had not noticed as she came upon him on the path. "Our family's place."

"*Je me souviens.*" Yes, she remembered well a loose screen on the Paquin cabin's front porch. She'd removed it once to crawl through and step down onto a bench underneath the window. She had not known what she was looking for or whether she was doing it simply because she knew she should not. There was no one at the lake that day except herself and Guy, and Guy had gone off to fish in the river. He was annoyed that she had not wanted to go with him.

"Paul would have come," he said disparagingly as he paddled away from the shore.

"He's not here," she said. "I don't feel like it, Guy. Not today."

So there she was, in the Paquin's cabin. But aside from a room filled with bright colours that her mother probably would not even have imagined using together, there was nothing else remarkable. She left hurriedly by the same window when she realized what she was doing. She had walked into someone's cabin as if it belonged to her. Not a thief, but the closest thing to it.

When Guy came back, he showed her the trout he had caught before he started to clean and fillet it. Libby could not stand the sight of blood and had even fainted once when she watched the doctor give Wally a needle. When Guy came inside, he said he would light the wood stove and cook the fish before her father came to take her back to town.

"It'll be my mother," she said.

They were fifteen by then and often lay down together, but they never took their clothes off.

"You want to come in," Jacques said now.

"Thanks," she said. "I just woke up. I need to get some exercise. *Je vais te voir lundi prochâine, n'est-ce pas?"* I'll see you next Monday, won't I?

"*Mais oui.*"

Continuing along the shore just above the rocks at the edge of the water, she stopped from time to time to look at the frozen lake, scrunching up her eyes as she tried to figure out how to paint the vibrant mauves and yellows of winter ice and snow. The greys and blues. The miracle of what shone through what appeared on first sight to be pure white. When she returned an hour later, Jacques was gone, the silence broken only by branches shifting and cracking in a slight breeze.

Inside the cabin, she spread her pencils out on a table at the window and looked through her sketchbook. As she began to sketch, she was unaware of anything but the lines on the paper and the images appearing as she drew. When she finally glanced at her watch, it was almost dark. On the page in front of her was an almost finished drawing of a horse, emerging from earth and water. The juxtaposition of a horse bursting forth in what had begun as a landscape painting of the cabin and the lake in the colours of winter seemed incongruous. Yet at the same time it felt just right to her. In her imagination, all these images belonged together. She could as easily incorporate the Eiffel Tower. A mine shaft. The fleur-de-lys. Maybe even the Union Jack. It had flown on the flagpole in their front yard when her father returned from overseas. It had no place anywhere in Canada now except as a relic.

Libby stood up, hips and legs aching, and started to do some stretches. With her body at an angle, she noticed again the notebook where she had found some of Guy's notes. Opening it at random, she noticed that for the most part it had been written in years earlier. But there was one entry dated the previous year, one entry that must have been written not long before Guy died. He wrote about how lonely he was, that he had ruined his life, that he should have been a better father. He was sorry about the drinking. About the fight with Paul. He wanted to apologize to everyone he'd hurt. He hadn't meant anyone any harm. Especially not his children. His handwriting was difficult to decipher and she had to translate the French into English. Toward the end he wrote that he was going to a hotel room where he would spend his last night.

So he knew, Libby thought. He planned it.

But he didn't know when someone would find him. He didn't know it would take a while and that he would no longer be recognizable.

47.

A S NICK WALKED out of the converted bunkhouse, he shivered in the chill air. Everything was transformed sooner or later in these mining towns, he thought, ultimately falling into disrepair when the resource ran out. Searching for something he recognized in the clear starlit sky, the Big Dipper, the North star, he pulled up the zipper of his jacket, pulling the collar up around his neck.

Surprised to find the main street empty, he looked at his watch. It was well past midnight. What did he expect? If no sounds disturbed the silence, soon enough the blasting would do that. In this moment, he was pleased not to hear the screech of a distant siren or streetcar. Or the throbbing drone of cars and trucks on the 401 in the distance from his house in Toronto. It didn't matter that he lived on a ravine miles from the highway. At night, lying in bed, he could always hear the underlying hum of traffic.

He found a bar that was open just beyond St. Luc's. It was almost empty except for two men at a table in the corner, a woman slouched precariously on a stool at the end of the bar, and the bartender with his sleeves rolled up so that the dark hair on his arms showed.

"A beer," Nick said, leaning on the counter. "Draft."

He was aware of the woman at the other end of the bar making a gurgling sound and he turned to look at her. Her dyed reddish hair looked greasy and unkempt. Turning away, he took out a ten-dollar bill from the recesses of his wallet. One beer and he would return to his room and fall into bed, ready to sleep for a few hours. What he was doing back in Ile D'Or was still a mystery to him. He felt as though he were following a script that he might understand later. He had never imagined that he would come here and meet people he'd known in his childhood. He hadn't considered the possibility that anyone he knew would still be here. Even when a mining town survived, you wouldn't necessarily expect that. People went to other jobs in other mines and their children followed opportunities across the continent. Even in other countries. Meeting Michelle, and Lucien, then Libby, gave him a chance to do something more than just reclaim a sense of that earlier community. He hoped Lucien would arrange a get-together.

A party at The Flamingo, Nick thought. Coincidence, fate, or whatever it was that had created these unlikely circumstances, ought to be honoured. *Michelle, Libby, Lucien.* It seemed incredible. A girl he'd kissed at a dance once. The hockey player he had tried hardest to beat in scrimmages on the ice. The daughter of the woman who had been consistently kind to him as a youngster. His sister married her brother. And Libby had moved to Toronto, too. It was odd that he hadn't run into her there long before, that he would have to come to Ile d'Or to see her again.

His motives might be questionable. Perhaps he wanted to see what would happen when all these people were in the same room with whatever raw edges still survived. Maybe he was just gathering fodder for his novel, doing what he'd seen patients who were artists do, steal material, use people ruthlessly. And he'd encouraged them.

"That's the role of an artist or writer," he'd said.

To take what he or she needs for purposes of creation, to develop images and symbols for a society. For a culture. How arrogant he was after all. But this was an opportunity that his practise didn't afford him. He couldn't use any of that material, which had client privilege, and he a professional with a grave responsibility. It was too much sometimes. He would explode if he had to contain everything. Or was it only his own life he couldn't deal with? Texas. Imagine. The woman who had always maintained her love of Montreal, living in a place like Texas. What a hypocrite Marie was. Or was he, Nick, the hypocrite, still trying to come to terms with what had eventually happened to his father? Roman's lungs coated with silicone dust. His painful death when Nick was in his early twenties. Why hadn't some doctor diagnosed Roman's condition and told him to stop working underground? Or recommended him for compensation? He began to feel there was no moral high ground in this town. Or maybe his father who had worked blasting out the gold underground, knowing too well the dangers, could claim it. The father who had been exploited, the father who had beaten his son. Each of the people he'd encountered in Ile d'Or had a different experience of growing up on this frontier and likely a differing perspective. Maybe all they could do as children of this place was to go on trying to deal with the paradoxes. But he really didn't think he wanted to write a novel about it.

At that moment, a dark head popped up next to him.

"What the hell are you doing out so late?" Nick asked.

It was probably illegal for the kid to be in the bar, but the waiter ignored him.

Marcel acted as if he didn't understand which was likely since Nick had spoken in English. But his eyes showed he understood the tone, one of surprise, of condemnation. No welcome in that greeting. Shrugging, he slipped down onto the wooden floor and walked over to the woman, whose head was now resting on the counter, her arms loose at her sides. He shook her arm and she groaned, her head falling backward and coming to rest in the beam of one bright light above her. He was saying something to her, but she only looked at him through slits in her eyes, then rolled her head away from him.

Marcel shrugged and then pushed open the back door of the bar, disappearing into the darkness of the night.

"He lives behind here, off the alley," the waiter said. "He was looking for his mother." He glanced at the drunken woman.

Nick sighed, and looked at her more closely. It didn't appear as if she were going to wake up any time soon. He wondered if he could still catch up to the boy, but then he didn't know what he would do. Take him home to his lodgings? He could get arrested for child abduction. Why did he feel it was up to him to fix this? He who ought to know better than anyone that it wasn't possible, even that any attempt on his part might make the situation worse. When he left town, the boy would latch onto some other unsuspecting person.

Instead of feeling better, Nick felt guilty. Here he was contemplating a party for those who had grown up here and done well. Even if he felt he was a failure after the breakdown of his marriage, he knew that he was privileged. A psychiatrist. He'd fulfilled a dream and also made a lot of money. Not to mention that it was something he'd enjoyed doing, at least until recently.

"Who takes care of the boy?" he asked the bartender.

The other man, younger than Nick by twenty years, shrugged. "Dunno," he said. *Je ne sais pas*. There were probably others like Marcel Blouin this man knew about. But for Nick, this boy, Marcel, had become a symbol of sorts. A challenge perhaps to his own sense of futility that paled beside the situation the boy lived in. Even as a child in an immigrant family, sometimes scrambling for enough food until his father was established at the mine, Nick had never felt unloved or alone. Even when his father had taken off his belt and left red welts on his buttocks, Nick had known that Roman was frustrated at something other than his son. He'd known that he would not be left alone or hungry. How he had known the difference wasn't quite clear to him, but he had. Although he supposed he'd ended up in psychiatry to resolve whatever residual demons dwelled in him. In spite of that, he realized Ile d'Or still represented a time and place when he'd experienced a measure of happiness.

Nick picked up his glass and drained it.

"Good night," he said and walked out onto the main street again.

Glancing to his right and his left, he spotted an alley leading off into the darkness. He wondered if the boy would still be somewhere around the bar. A big grey and black cat walked across his path and into a doorway where it sat and watched Nick, twisting and pushing its body against the wooden stoop. Further up the alley, there was a light shining in a window and he stood quietly, waiting to see if there were any movement there. After a while he began to feel foolish and headed for the street again.

On a whim, he returned to the bar. The man with the rolled up sleeves looked at him with his dark eyebrows raised as if to say, so now what? The woman had moved to one of the tables and now had what appeared to be a cup of black coffee in front of her. Her eyes looked glassy and every so often her body swayed a little.

"Who looks after the boy?" Nick asked again, in a low voice.

The bar tender shrugged.

"How does she get home?"

Again the man showed little interest. "Sometimes the kid comes back," he said.

When Nick left, he didn't feel any the wiser.

48.

THE DOG BARKED at Lucien with the exuberance of an animal that has been confined too long. Stepping inside his cabin, Lucien let him pass and run down to the lake. Straining to see through the bare branches to the clearing beyond, there was no sign of life from Guy's place next door where Libby was staying. As soon as he dropped a bag with some bread and corn flakes on the floor beside the refrigerator, he walked down to the water with Figaro, gathering a few sticks for the dog to fetch. It was at least fifteen minutes before he returned to the cabin.

The food he'd brought home from his mother's the previous night was stacked haphazardly inside the refrigerator. He took out some ham from the top package wrapped in aluminium foil and reached for a beer. Some vegetables from the freezer. He placed a pot of water on the stove, and dropped in some frozen peas, carrots and corn. If not for these leftovers, he would probably heat up a frozen dinner every night, Lucien thought. Or open a tin of spaghetti or pork and beans. He did not mind what he ate, but he missed eating with Susan. She was a good cook who had never felt too proud to ask his mother for recipes. Sometimes that she could cut his mother off when they had grown so close baffled him as much as her rejection of him. She was as stubborn as her father had been when she made a decision.

As the water in the pot swirled into small white bubbles and almost reached the top, Lucien turned the heat down. He thought again of that day when he had caught Susan stealing. Apparently she'd crept out the back door and had gone down the lane toward rue Champlain. She'd arrived in time to see the milk wagon in front of the Muir's house, the horse's head drooping. It was so cold there were icicles in the horse's whiskers and the milk had pushed the cardboard lids on the bottles up into ice towers. Susan ducked down where the milkman would not see her, whispering to the horse as she waited for the driver to come back. When he drove off, she was crouched down on one runner of the sleigh, holding onto the back of the wagon so just her red wool mitts were visible if the driver looked around. When they reached the main street, she jumped off and went into Mulholland's.

After they were married, Lucien learned that Susan found the time when she made her decision about what to steal later the best part of her day. It might be a chocolate bar in purple and white paper. Or Chiclets in a yellow package. Cookies from the grocery shelves. A new pair of mitts. As soon as she made her selection, she'd figure out how to take it without anyone seeing her. And how to get out of the store as if she had just been browsing. That day when Lucien caught her, it had been so easy to take the Jersey milk chocolate bar that if she'd had the money she would have paid for it. She liked stealing better when it was a challenge. Sometimes people commented that she was like her father — stubborn, shrewd, and determined.

Out on the street, Susan had wondered if she could wait until spring to go down to the farm on the other side of town. That September she'd discovered a horse and had started to ride him. Lucien knew about the horse, but had not wanted to tell Libby. He was not sure why. He didn't want her to know he'd followed Susan and that was how he knew, but it was more than that. Maybe because it was after Susan left him in the car that first night, after he'd caught her stealing, she acted as if nothing had happened. Head held high. That was Susan. She did not tell him until a long time later that she had liked being with him, just turned her head in the other direction whenever they bumped into each other after that. Until she decided to taunt him on the road out past the mine when she came across him one day several months later lying near the railroad tracks, getting a tan on his legs and his belly.

"So," she said. "Maybe now we can try it."

Oh God, he thought. He did not have a rubber. And then he remembered that there was one stuck in the bottom of his pocket. They went off into the bush where he cleared a spot to lie down in the underbrush. She was a little hesitant as he touched her carefully, not wanting to hurt her. He was surprised that once they got into it, she'd moaned and hung onto him, her legs wrapped tightly around his back. The thought now of some other man touching her enraged him. There must be someone or she'd still be here. Always before this he'd felt confident he was the only one.

His telephone rang. He just stared at it. Sometimes he did not feel like talking to anyone, then afterwards he would wonder if it were Susan. Finally, he picked up the receiver to hear a man's voice he did not immediately recognize.

"It's Paul Paquin speaking." *C'est Paul Paquin qui parle.* Calling from Quebec City. "I'm coming up on business," the familiar voice said. "Could we get together for a beer one night?"

Lucien agreed readily, although as soon as he hung up he began to feel uneasy.

"You have to move on, Lucien," his mother had said recently. "I don't mean forget."

How could he forget? It was all there so clearly at times that it obliterated the present. Guy. Blood on the wall. Darkening already. The smell. He would never forget the pungent odour, yet he could not describe it. A body already decomposing. If there had been flies, they would have been all over Guy. Or what remained of Guy.

"You've been a good son, Lucien," his mother had said. "You are a good son."

Lucien almost cried then and he could feel tears in his eyes now. He knew better. He had been a poor son, envying Guy. A poor husband, maybe even a dubious father. He went into the bathroom and peed in the toilet, leaving the seat up. Susan was not here to admonish him. Susan. He missed her. He put the seat down. Would he ever stop missing her? When he came out again, he heard the dog scratch at the door. When he turned on the television, he let Figaro lie down on the couch beside him. The news came on first, then something mindless during which he drifted off to sleep with his clothes still on. In the morning, he woke up cold and dishevelled.

"Oh, *mon Dieu*," he groaned. His children called long distance, but they did not need him now. "What do I have to live for?" He no longer knew.

49

O UR REAL LIFE *was on the skating rink*, Roch Carrier wrote. In the red, white and black sweaters of the Montreal *Candiens*. Libby had dreamed of playing hockey like Maurice Richard, too. If she had received a blue and white sweater ordered from Eaton's catalogue, it would have been as much a tragedy for her as for the character in the story. It did not matter that Nanny and Gramps had lived in Toronto, her heart was with the *Canadiens*. Even as an Anglo, she would not have been insulted if Roch Carrier's character had sent his sweater back to Monsieur Eaton, but she knew his mother had been right, that Monsieur Eaton would have been.

Libby fell asleep with images of Montreal after the *Canadiens* had won the Stanley Cup, seeing Jean Beliveau in the parade. Montreal had captured her heart in her youth in a way no other city had until much later, and when she and Barton moved to Toronto, she'd hated it at first. It took a long time to think of Toronto as anything but a place where she lived because she had to. Both she and the city she now called home had changed a lot in the interim.

When she awakened at six the next morning, she lay listening to the crackling of branches. If she could catch Lucien before he left, she would drive with him into the pharmacy. She had not seen him the evening before; instead she had curled up in her sleeping bag with the book by Roch Carrier.

Finally she slipped out into the cold room and turned on the heater. When she had drunk a cup of coffee and eaten some toast, she wrapped herself up in her coat and followed the snowy trail to Lucien's cabin.

"Did you sleep better?" Lucien asked as they drove toward town.

"Yes. Although I read something by Guy yesterday I found pretty disturbing. I feel as if perhaps I shouldn't have, as if I were snooping. But the notebook's on a shelf with old magazines and a photograph album. I'm sorry, I feel embarrassed."

"What did you read?"

"A note apologizing for all his mistakes. Regrets about just about everything."

"Doesn't sound like Guy. He was a mean bastard in the last years."

"Lucien, it sounds like he killed himself."

"Well, he did. All that drinking."

"I mean he went into that hotel room knowing that he wouldn't come out again." He had written that he would die quickly, not go on with the misery any longer, the misery of knowing what a mess he had made of everything.

"Guy wouldn't."

"It's there on paper," Libby said. She watched the road, almost afraid to see what his face revealed.

Lucien swerved the car onto a side road and backed out onto the highway again. This time he headed in the direction from which they had just come, driving straight to Guy's cabin. He slammed on the brakes and jumped out of the car. When he went up to the door, Libby waited, hoping the storm her words had unleashed would subside when Lucien read the entry in his brother's journal. A few minutes later when he still had not emerged, she went inside tentatively and discovered him sitting in an armchair with his head in his hands. The notebook was open on his lap. When he finally looked up at Libby, there were tears on his face and he started to mumble.

"You were right," he said, his voice flat. He didn't move.

She went over and put her hands on his shoulders, wondering nonetheless if her touch could offer any comfort to this man who seemed so familiar and then could quickly become a stranger.

"I don't know when he started to go over the edge," Lucien said. "Or why."

"It wasn't your fault."

"No, but he was my brother. My life is beginning to look like his, except I'm older than he was when he separated from Nicole. I can understand some of what he was feeling now. I didn't understand when he started drinking. I didn't understand any of it. Now that I'm starting to comprehend how he must have felt, it's too late for Guy. Maybe for me, too," he said. "I get so frightened sometimes, *tu comprends.* I go into the pharmacy every day where I do the same things over and over. I'm tired of it. At night, I wake up in a panic. I don't know why. There's nothing to be afraid of. I just lie there and..." He stood up abruptly. "I shouldn't be telling you this."

"It's okay," she said. "I'm here because of Guy, too."

"*C'est vrai?*" Is that true?

"There was some part of me I left behind when I married Barton. I guess I'm trying to find it."

"I don't understand."

"I don't either." Maybe it was the part of her that had still believed her dreams were possible that she hoped to find here. Not that she was dissatisfied with her life, but she felt sometimes clothed in a thin veil of cynicism she detested.

"Shall we go now?"

At the store, Lucien stepped out of the car slowly and when he disappeared inside, Libby slid across the seat and drove to the centre of town to park in front of a small coffee shop. Inside, she found a newspaper and sat with the steam rising from a cup of hot chocolate, not wanting to go back to either the store or the cabin. When she went out onto the street, she noticed two mannequins in the window of Chic Choc, one dressed in a black suit, the other in a deep blue dress with gold buttons down the sleeves. It was a dress Libby could imagine wearing and she found herself moving toward the door of Michelle Dufresne's shop.

"*Bonjour,*" Michelle said. "I'm glad to see you."

There were racks of dresses down both sides of the shop with slacks, blouses and skirts in the middle. Bright coloured casual sweaters, two-piece outfits, ski wear. Tags were attached discreetly with sizes and prices.

"It's the nicest store in town," Libby said as she stood next to Michelle, trying to get her bearings.

"Thanks," Michelle said.

"The dress in the window," Libby said. "The blue one. With the gold buttons on the sleeves."

Michelle found her size and handed it to Libby who smiled as she held it up in front of the mirror, imagining how she might look wearing it rather than her usual slacks.

"Try it on," Michelle said, smiling also.

"I think I will." Libby went into a cubicle and pulled the curtain across the opening.

When she stood in front of the mirror again, Michelle drew her breath in. "*C'est merveilleux,*" she whispered. "It's made for you." Libby knew it was not a sales pitch, that she really thought so. When she took the dress off, she handed it to Michelle and said, "I'll take it."

Michelle folded the dress and wrapped it carefully in white tissue paper before placing it in a large yellow bag. On the bill she lay on the counter, Libby noticed she had taken fifteen percent off the price.

"Maybe I'll wear it here," Libby said. "To The Flamingo. Lucien asked me to go dancing."

"Would you come round to my place before you leave?" Michelle asked. "I live at the far end of town. My daughter is visiting for a few days, but soon she'll be gone again."

"*Les enfants,*" Libby said. That was surely something they had in common as well as having known each other as children. Her father had made a mistake. Well, maybe not about the high-grading, but about forbidding her to see or talk to Michelle. What choice had he had though?

"Thanks," Libby said.

"You'll come then," Michelle said. There was a slight question in her voice.

50.

THE SUN SHIMMERED on the snow by the side of the road. A few clouds in long narrow gossamer streaked across the sky. Lucien supposed many would find it a bleak landscape, but he found it beautiful. A boy on skis headed off into the bush at the junction where Lucien turned from the lake road onto the highway. Libby, who had come over to meet him for the drive into town and was sitting beside him in the front seat of the car, rummaged through her bag.

"What are you looking for?" he asked, his words piercing the silence that was unbroken since they'd set out. After he'd read Guy's notes the previous day, they'd returned to their separate cabins, he to an unexpected phone call from Susan and Libby had said she wanted to draw.

"My camera," she said. "I think I'll take some pictures and draw the scenes later. Before painting them. The mine. The main street. Even the graveyard."

"Susan wants me to go to Montreal to see her," he said quietly.

"Are you going?"

"*Peut-être*," he said. "I need more time first."

Why he wasn't running there was a mystery to him. He wanted desperately for Susan to come back, but he sensed she wouldn't stay long even if she did. Not with a man on the verge of fifty. All he did was work now. There was not much else he was interested in. Shooting moose in the fall. Listening to some of the local singers. He liked Richard Desjardins, but he had not been out to a club in ages. It was only Libby's arrival that had made life seem appealing again, sparking memories that might have remained buried. And another woman's body. She had wonderful breasts, still high and firm with such large nipples. Susan's did not respond as much to his touch as they once had. Knowing what he would find as his fingers traced Libby's body, but the mystery nonetheless of how another woman might respond to him, had intrigued him. Now that he knew, what was he left with? Guilt, he supposed, even as he knew that was ridiculous. Fear, perhaps, that Susan might find out. But so what if she did? He and Libby were old friends whose paths had crossed unexpectedly. But it was Guy Libby had come to see. Always it was Guy in the end, dead or alive, who marked out territory that excluded Lucien. Except with Susan. Lucien had never felt he came anything but first there. Until after Guy died and this other man turned up in town. Susan left not long after, just as abruptly as she had when she went off with the circus to get that abortion all those years ago. She came back then, but this time she had not intended to and she was a woman with a mind of her own. Oh God, he missed her. She never hesitated to light into him if he came in sloshed or had not helped with the children. Or said something that annoyed her. Whether it was about politics, religion, sex, or just some inane comment about the weather. It did not matter that they were part of that generation marred by all the unrealistic expectations of the fifties. Susan was tough. She stood her ground on everything. What had happened to them?

Libby said something and he had to ask her to repeat it. He hoped she hadn't noticed that he hadn't been listening.

"Sorry," he said as he pulled up in front of Pharmacie Dion.

"It doesn't matter," she said. "I'll see you later."

When he got out of the car, she slipped into the driver's seat. As he turned the lock of the pharmacy door and picked up some papers just inside on the floor, he could hear the rumble of the car as she accelerated. It seemed as if he knew what was ahead of him and that everything was predictable. But how could he say that? He shook his head slightly, as though he were talking to someone not there. For the last year, nothing had been predictable. From Guy's death to Susan's departure to Libby's arrival. About what might happen next, he had no idea. He could drop dead of a heart attack. Putting the bundle of mail and newspapers he was carrying on the counter, he hung his coat on a hook in his office. When he picked up the newspaper again, he spotted an advertisement for a holiday in California. On the trip to the conference there, he hadn't had a chance to go wine tasting in the Napa Valley. If he went to Montreal to see Susan, he could suggest that trip to her. He was enveloped by a vision of him and Susan watching the sun go down over the

Pacific and eating fresh citrus fruit, oranges and lemons that hung from branches outside a window.

Libby drove as if she had known all along she was going to go to St. Andrew's, the small wooden Anglican church, covered with yellow asbestos shingles where she had unwillingly spent so much time in her childhood. If she didn't go regularly, her mother had said she would be very unhappy. Libby had felt as a child that the church and religion were some kind of torture her parents had invented. It was not until she became enamoured of the old stone churches and cathedrals in England that it became clear to her that the practise of going to some church had not started with her mother and father. Even the monuments in the graveyard of her father's ancestors, who were vicars at the small church in Titchfield, were from another century.

She parked the car beside the road and sat looking at the church where the minister had pinched her bottom, where she had once acted the part of Joseph. When she'd looked across at Cathy McNab, dressed as the pregnant Virgin Mary, they'd both burst out laughing. Libby's mother was mortified when the two girls went on giggling and weren't able to carry on with the pageant. Libby might have been six then. She could not remember. But there had been happy church-related moments, too. All the pork and bean suppers with booths where you fished with a rod, wondering what surprise was in store behind the large piece of cardboard over which your line dangled. It was exciting, never knowing what you might hook. The church was as much a centre of the community as the mine. She was married there. A whole album was filled with pictures, one of her going up the wooden steps with her dress flying in the wind, her father walking beside her. Her parents had approved of Barton. When the wedding party arrived back at the house on rue Champlain for the reception, one of the neighbours asked if her father had to sell the family's furniture so Libby could get married. The extra chairs and tables were in the basement so the guests could move and dance freely. But Libby knew that her father would have sold all of it if that had been necessary. Marriage was important to both her parents; their daughters had to marry well so he and their mother would not have to worry. Although, they genuinely liked Barton. He and her father could sit and talk for hours and no one realized for a long time that he was as ill prepared as Libby was for marriage.

There were good times in the early years of that marriage. A honeymoon on the eastern seaboard, then to their first home, a townhouse at the end of a crescent where interns from all across North America, from as far afield as California and Texas, came for a year before going elsewhere for speciality training or to start a general practise. The only newlyweds, Libby and Barton came straight from the jubilant wedding in Ile d'Or to watermelon on the lawn of a colonial house in Williamsburg, Virginia to the complex of white coats and townhouses in the mid-western American car manufacturing city.

A train whistle from the tracks across the road left Libby sitting bolt upright in the middle of many nights. Especially when Barton was either at the hospital or sleeping soundly after his long hours. She sometimes studied the strange creature she awakened beside. *He's my husband,* she thought. *Barton Morley is my husband.* During sleepless hours that year, she was baffled that she had done anything as irrevocable as linking her life with a man's before she fully understood what she was doing. Watching the cars stream by as she waited for him to walk along the crescent with his stethoscope dangling on his chest like a necklace, she swung from delight to terror.

A scene flashed across her mind, Barton flat on his stomach, one arm over the edge of the bed. His white intern's jacket was flung on a chair nearby and his shoes looked as if he'd dropped them as he fell across the bed. A ray of light crept through a broken slat in the Venetian blinds and across his legs. The sheet had fallen to the floor. As she watched, his arms flailed and he yelled for forceps. Told someone to stop. *Please stop.*

"STOP," he finally screamed. "I'm not ready."

She turned off the engine, opened the door and stood beside the car. The church seemed almost vacant now. When she got nearer and could read the sign, she noticed that it was no longer only an Anglican church, but was shared by other denominations. No doubt as the air force base closed a few years earlier and the English population dwindled, there were no longer enough people to support an Anglican parish. Nonetheless, St. Andrew's was the place where she was christened, where she took her first communion. Odd that these landmarks should have pleased her mother so much when she had actually spent her own life in such doubt, something Libby wasn't aware of until she was an adult. It came as a surprise when her mother told her recently that she thought Jesus was a very good man, but she was not sure what else she believed.

"What do you think, dear?"

As if Libby, who had not gone to church now for almost three decades, held some answers.

The sun was behind her now. Taking out her camera, Libby held it up to frame the church against pine trees in the background, against a rock that separated it from a path to the street where the general store and the movie theatre had stood. Clicking the button, she moved to take another from a different angle. She did not want to paint this, but wanted some kind of record, something that would fit into an album that she could look at that would evoke memories that might lead to the unexpected. You never knew how things would fit together. Who would have imagined that she would come back here to find Guy dead and Lucien married to Susan? She wondered what happened to Cathy. She supposed her sister might know. The last Libby had heard most of the McNabs were living on the west coast. If she were to take a tour across the country, she would probably find someone from Ile d'Or in almost every major town or city.

A car honked behind her and she turned to see Al's taxi. He leaned out the window to holler at her. She waved and he honked again. When she looked puzzled, he turned off the ignition and came over to her.

"Lights on in the car," he said. "Kills the battery."

"*Oh mon Dieu.*" She went to turn them off. "Thanks, Al."

"Hear you're having dinner with Michelle."

"I don't believe it." She shook her head. "You know everything."

"Keeps me going." He did not gossip, he assured her again. "Not Al Desjardins," he added. "So, how's it going at the cabin?"

Libby was not sure what he wanted to know, but she simply shrugged. "It's a change from the city." It was a change from having a teenager around, also. "Do you remember?" she asked. "They create a storm around them." Paul moved through her life like a hurricane. Rosemary used to, in her own way, although by the time she reached her teen years she was quieter than Paul by any measure. It was certainly different now that her daughter was out in her own flat with a roommate and her room had become Libby's studio. Her conversations with Rosemary moved around another axis, not one where Libby had to take on more than she was asked to. She was glad to have children, one outcome of matrimony she was pleased about. What would she have done in Australia when she was nineteen or twenty? She had not been any more ready for that than she had been for marriage.

51.

AS DAWN PACKED, occasional loud sighs emanated from the back room. She was going out to dinner in town, but she had hesitated about saying who her companion for the evening would be. It wasn't something Michelle felt she could ask. Her daughter was a grown woman and if she chose to pick up strangers, she must know all the risks by now. When Dawn had told Michelle, it had freed up her evening to invite Libby over. It would be the first time either had been in the other's home, she thought.

Leaning over, Michelle put a bottle of wine she'd bought in the bottom rack of the refrigerator. There was a red in the wine rack, one from France. She still liked the French wines best, although sometimes she would buy a German Riesling for a change. Not sure what she wanted to cook for dinner, she'd bought an assortment of vegetables and she considered what she would take out of the freezer. Dessert she wasn't worried about since she always had ice cream on hand.

The telephone rang and a stranger's voice spoke to her in a muffled voice.

"You have the wrong number," Michelle said.

"I don't think so," the voice said.

Michelle couldn't tell if it was a man or a woman.

"Did you know Dominic St. Cyr?"

Michelle gasped. "Why?"

"I'm calling to let you know he was killed in a car accident. Your number was in his notebook."

Michelle breathed in a deep sigh, knowing that for years she had longed for just such a call, heralding an existence in which she and the girls would not have to worry about their safety any longer. It frightened her to think her phone number had been in Dominic's possession and she wondered how recently he'd obtained that information. And where he'd gotten it. Maybe he'd only just found it out.

Dawn came into the room and stared at her, sensing something was unusual about the call. For many families, even divorced ones, it would have been the worst news possible. There would have been tears flowing down Michelle's face and soon down her daughter's as well.

"What is it, Ma?" Dawn asked as she hung up.

"There was a car accident last night," Michelle said. "Dominic was killed."

Silence filled the room, like lava from a volcano finding all the nooks and crannies. It was an uneasy quiet, one into which Michelle did not know what words to offer. She didn't like to jump up and down in jubilation, but that was how she had always thought she would feel at the advent of such news. Now it scarcely mattered. Although she'd still have to confess to a feeling of relief.

"You know what, Ma. He only did us harm. I'm glad it happened after I'd found him though because it cleared up so much for me. And it allowed me finally to come back here and have a real relationship with my mother."

Michelle's eyes filled. She would accept this gift with a prayer for Dominic's soul. May he find peace, she thought. Somewhere.

"We'd better call Elise," Dawn said.

"Do you want to?"

"Sure, Ma. You can speak to her, too."

When they'd put down the receiver after talking with Elise, they sat quietly for a while. "Would you like me to stick around?" Dawn asked. "I'm not meeting anyone actually. I was just going to wander around and see who in town I might still know. I visited Grandma and Grandpère's graves earlier. So odd to have them in different cemeteries. Although I suppose it's just as it was when they were alive and going to different churches."

"Thanks, Dawn," Michelle said. "Libby is coming for dinner. Do you want to stay and meet her?"

"Do you still want her to come?"

"How do you feel about it?"

"It's up to you, Ma."

Michelle said she would call Libby, and then remembered there was no telephone at the cabin.

52.

IN THE PART of town where Michelle had settled, the houses were all new since Libby had lived in Ile d'Or. The streets were also unfamiliar, new ones carved out to create the area. Most of the houses, permanent mobile homes, were mainly white, set down on neatly divided small lots. Shutters in different hues distinguished some of the dwellings. There were rock gardens, occasional picket fences, and paved or pebbled driveways. Nothing except the rugged outcrops of rock suggested to Libby the town she had known so well. She had followed a short cut Lucien suggested to get there. Some time she would draw a large map with small diagrams to highlight specific sites. Obvious ones like the mine and St. Luc's. The cabins on Lac Leboeuf. The Flamingo. The water tower.

Michelle opened the door.

Libby, seeing beyond her to a young woman in the kitchen, recalled the arrival of the daughter Michelle had told her about.

"Hello, Dawn," Libby said as introductions followed greetings.

"Hi," the young woman said. "I gather you're one of the originals."

"You could say," Libby said. "Even before the railroad. Or roads, for that matter. Almost prehistoric."

"Well, I didn't mean that."

Libby smiled, amused by the repartee, nonetheless noticed the other two women glance at each other as if unsure what to do.

"Libby," Michelle said. "We had some shocking news just an hour ago and we're still trying to absorb it. There was a phone call that my ex was killed in a car accident and…"

"Oh my goodness, would you rather I didn't stay now?" Libby asked. "I don't want to intrude. We can do this some other time."

"Well, you're here now."

Libby backed toward the door.

"I don't want this news to spoil anything for Dawn and me and her sister. I wish I could feel badly about it, but it's the first time I've felt entirely safe in over twenty-five years. If it didn't sound so strange, I'd say tonight could be a celebration."

The sound of a radio rose in the background as they spoke. Libby couldn't tell who the singer was, a clear contralto. She thought of the Dufresne home across the lane at the other end of town and how she'd wondered as a child what it might be like. She recalled a picture in an album buried somewhere in the basement in Toronto taken on the hill beside the Muir's house with both her and Michelle sitting on a toboggan. Although she'd gone swimming and tobogganing with Michelle, both knew without words that the other's house was off limits.

"Well, all right," she said. "If at any point it feels you'd rather be alone together..." She left the sentence dangling.

Michelle opened a bottle of sauvignon and poured some into three wine glasses. Libby wondered if it would amount to sacrilege to propose a toast, then thought she could likely do so without mentioning the death that was causing some kind of subtle euphoria.

"To being together again," Michelle said, relieved that there was no more to fear from a dangerous man. Most of all this toast was for her daughter and her own release from an abyss of uncertainty. "And to friendship."

"Yes," Libby said.

They sipped quietly, Dawn watching the two older women for a while before going to the kitchen. "Tell me what needs doing, Ma," she called.

Michelle poured more wine. It was as if this would be the one chance she would get to set some record straight for posterity. It was like that here. You waited to get your clearance to go underground and then wondered why it ever struck you that was something you wanted to do.

"My father never got over Francine's death."

"I can understand that," Libby said. "I would imagine it's impossible to get over something like that."

"He lost money gambling. He almost had to sell The Flamingo. They said he had other women. Then my mother had a breast removed and he thought she was going to die. Maybe he thought it was his fault."

"Did he talk about it?" Libby asked.

"Not that generation. Men didn't talk." Michelle stood up and went to a counter between the living room and the long narrow kitchen. "Need any help?" she asked her daughter.

"Everything is ready to go," Dawn said. "I think I'll go for a walk. I'll be back soon." She carried a plate with crackers, cheese, pâté and black olives into the room before she put on her jacket and tied a bright red scarf around her neck.

Libby spread pâté on one cracker and brie on another, the second cracker shattering on her napkin. She smiled as she tasted the pâté. When the telephone rang, Michelle answered. Trying not to listen, Libby wandered over to the shelves beside the stereo where she found a copy of *Kamouraska* and then a fashion magazine with a woman in a tight black outfit and gold earrings on the cover. She was startled when Michelle spoke to her.

"Blanche says Paul Paquin is coming to town."

Oh yes, Libby recalled. Al's, the taxi driver's, wife. Sister of Thérèse, who had worked for Libby's mother. It was like everything else that had happened, everyone in town seemed to know. "Yes, his son told me he was coming," she said, not adding that she was going to have dinner with Paul, although it seemed clear that it was something people would soon hear about.

"Blanche is going to have some people over. She asked me to invite you. And Nick, too."

Long strands of philodendron woven through a lattice on the door-frame between the living area and the kitchen created the effect of an arbour. After a half hour of nibbling and chatting, Michelle beckoned Libby to the table. She took another bottle of wine and poured it into glasses on the place mats.

"*Un Beaujolais*," she said. Her hand shook a little. "Help yourself to crudités."

Sliced carrots and mushrooms were arranged on a leaf of endive with some slivers of white turnip. The vinaigrette was smooth, with just the right amount of Dijon and black pepper. When the telephone rang again, Michelle sighed as she leaned backward to reach for the receiver on the set on the wall.

"*Oui, bonjour.*" Her head jerked as she heard the voice on the other end. "*Non, il n'est pas ici.*" He isn't here. She talked in monosyllables and when she hung up, her eyes kept sliding away from Libby.

"That was Susan," she said finally. "Calling from Montreal. She asked me to give you a message. She said to stay away from Lucien."

"I don't think there's anyone who doesn't know I'm here," Libby said. "But how does she know I'm at your place?"

"She doesn't."

"I didn't come here to see Lucien," Libby said. "But I found a lonely man whose wife had left him. A man trying to find out what his life means. If Susan doesn't want anyone else to know about that, she should be here with him." She had to hide her discomfort, an old feeling that if Susan told her what to do, she might have to do it.

"All she asked was that I give you the message. I suppose I could have said I wouldn't, but I likely would have told you about it anyway."

Eyes fixed on a crucifix with Jesus in a white gown on a gold background hanging on the wall above the kitchen door, Michelle breathed in and out slowly

"If Susan has any other messages for me, tell her to leave a number and I'll call her," Libby said.

"I don't want to get in the middle." Michelle paused, and then changed the subject. "I remember I could see the window of your room from our back porch. I used to go with some of the kids who played Nicky Nicky Nine Doors. Do you remember that, knocking on doors and disappearing before anyone answered? Once when I got home, after all the other kids had gone, I sat on the back steps. There was someone on a ladder looking in your window and I crept as close as I could to see who it was. When I saw it was Lucien, I figured you weren't in any danger."

"Lucien?" Libby said. "You mean the peeping tom I thought might have been one of the guys from the bunkhouses was Lucien? Why?"

"I don't know. I'm just telling you."

"All the nightmares I had about that. I wonder if Guy knew. When I saw someone out there, I called him. I was terrified. He was very quiet after he saw the ladder. I thought he was worried about me, but maybe it was the Dion's ladder. No, it wasn't. I remember it as one Dad kept to climb up to fix windows. Although he almost never did it himself. Mum had to phone the mine for someone to come. Lucien? I mean, I can't understand that. Why would he want to spy on me?"

The door opened and Dawn came in again, her hair tousled, her eyes teary. "I'm sorry," she said. "I guess I need to be with people who love me."

Michelle hung her daughter's coat up, reaching out to Dawn.

Libby got up and moved toward the door.

"But you've scarcely eaten."

"You two need to be alone together."

53

THE ROAD HAD a thin cover of new snow on it that had fallen
since Libby went out earlier. When she passed Lucien's cabin,
all the lights were off. A deer on the side of the road appeared
in the beam of her headlights and she stopped the car while it disappeared into the bush. Then she drove on to park beside a sign with
DION on it in red letters painted at an angle as if by someone who was
intoxicated. She stood for a moment on the porch, looking for the Big
Dipper. Across the lake, the wind rose and the tops of trees swayed in
the moonlight, suggesting a storm before morning

Inside she turned on lights, the radio, and the heater before sitting
down at a table with a plastic cover she'd wiped off carefully after
each meal so she could set out either her art supplies or cutlery and
dishes. Now she lit a candle and turned off the light to stare at the
flame. When she crawled into her sleeping bag, it was as if she were
a teenager once more in her room on the main floor, terrified that
someone might try to get in. She got up and pulled a blanket around
her, breathing deeply. "I'm forty-six years old," she whispered. "I'm in
a cabin at Lac Leboeuf. Rosemary and Paul are in Toronto." She was
frightened, but she was also angry. How dare Lucien have done that?
When she finally zipped up the sleeping bag again, she knew that in
the morning she would confront him.

As she sat on the couch in Lucien's cabin after sleeping fitfully all
night, watching him take eggs out of the refrigerator, she could no
longer restrain her anger.

"I can't believe that you would have put a ladder to my window
when I was a teenager and climbed it to look in on me," she blurted
out. "The nerve. The gall." She continued to tell him all that she'd
been told. But she didn't mention Susan's call to Michelle.

"Couldn't have been me," he said, flipping the eggs as if he didn't
have any worries.

"Michelle didn't make it up," she said. "C'mon, Lucien. She saw you." Libby eyed him curiously. He obviously was not going to admit to it.

On a shelf up above the snowshoes, she noticed a gun she had not seen before. It looked like her mother's old 410; the one Charlotte Muir had used to shoot partridge. She stood up, took it down and checked to make sure it was not loaded. It felt as if her father were watching. His approval seemed to permeate the room; after all good soldiers ought to know, her father would have said. It was the same kind of gun her mother had taken down from the front hall cupboard while her father pounded on the door, garbling his words, shouting to be let in.

"What are you doing?" Lucien asked. *Qu'est-ce que tu fait?*

"Will you teach me to shoot?"

"You know how."

"That was Sheila. She was the one who went hunting with Mum. I was away at school by then."

"Why do you want to learn now?"

"Because I don't know how." And if she couldn't trust even Lucien, who could she trust?

He took her mug and rinsed it under the tap to wash the dark coffee grounds down the drain. Reaching up to put the 410 back on the shelf, she swore softly. "*Maudit.*" Why couldn't Lucien comprehend that an unknown person in the shadows at her bedroom window all those years ago had been terrifying? It could even be why, so many years later, she still remembered the incident. Instead he poured orange juice into two glasses with red stripes around the tops and started to lift the eggs onto a large plate.

"I'll show you how to shoot tin cans off tree stumps," he said finally.

She shrugged. That would do, but she didn't say so.

"I hear you're having dinner with Paul Paquin."

"No secrets in this place," she said. "Yes, I am. He's coming to town."

"You know, one night Guy went to his door in a raincoat. Paul's wife was sitting in a rocking chair near the fireplace, likely watching *Les Plouffes* on television. Colette liked that program. Guy went inside and stood by the fire, dripping water on the floor. He opened his coat. It was all he was wearing. When Colette shrieked, Paul came into the room. He punched Guy on the nose and told him never to come back to their house. He chased him down the street with a rifle. Of course, Guy was drunk. But they never spoke again."

"I kept trying to figure out why they weren't speaking," Libby said. "I thought it might have something to do with politics. You know, Paul the civil servant and Guy the radical separatist."

"It's Paul who's the separatist. Guy didn't care about politics. That bit about the FLQ — that was a dream, it never happened."

After breakfast, he handed her the keys to the car. He had to get to the pharmacy. "You drive," he said. When she got in behind the wheel, he sat down on the passenger side and turned on the radio to a newscast. "To hear the weather," he said.

Libby backed away from the side of the cabin onto the road that led out to the highway.

"I do remember putting a ladder under your bedroom window," he said. "I should have confessed to that a long time ago. I'm sorry. It was against your fence. The light was on in your room so I carried it around and peeked in. It wasn't a big deal. I wasn't going to hurt you. Or do anything at all. I just wanted to see what you were doing."

"Do you have any idea how much you frightened me? And it stays with you, too, you know. That fear."

"I was a kid. A boy curious about a girl," he said. "I'm sorry."

"And I could have been naked."

"I thought about that, too." He smiled before he continued. "Actually I hoped you were. But I was disappointed. And you must have known someone was there because you slipped out of your room. I couldn't figure out where you were. Then Guy came. I guess you phoned him. Later he told me he'd found my lighter underneath the ladder. He almost killed me that night. If Papa hadn't come in with lipstick on his collar, he might have."

"Guy knew?" she asked, dismayed. It had never dawned on her that he could have known. She wondered why he'd never told her.

"He figured it out."

Libby didn't ask him how Guy had done that. Or why he never told her. Maybe Lucien didn't know anyway. Instead she remembered the message from Susan to stay away from Lucien. As if it all might be connected.

"Guy was smart, wasn't he? Like Susan. She called Michelle when I was there."

"Why didn't you tell me this before?"

"I don't know," Libby said. She still felt embarrassed about sleeping with him, as if she'd had an affair with a married man. And that man happened to be married to Susan who was, unexpectedly, still her nemesis. "I'm telling you now. And she must still care for you. She sent me a message to stay away from you. Maybe that's why I didn't tell you."

"*Mon Dieu*," he said "What do I do now?"

"I have no idea." Of course she didn't, Libby thought. And had she, it would have been tactful of her not to mention it.

54.

THERE WAS A note on the floor inside his room when Nick arrived at the bunkhouse. He was surprised to see it was a message from Michelle, carefully printed. *Al and Blanche Desjardins are going to have a party. They've asked me to invite you.* He was glad he hadn't gone beyond creating lists in his head for a gathering at The Flamingo, knowing it was a conceit on his part to think he could plan it and anticipate people he hadn't seen in years would turn up. He was relieved at the prospect of Al and Blanche creating the atmosphere. There would be gaiety and laughter. He would offer to bring some of the booze.

As he turned back the quilt, he thought it wasn't quite so bad here as sleeping alone in the large bed in Toronto where he still felt so acutely the vast emptiness on the left side where Marie had slept. Her indentation was still there in the mattress, not as deep as his own on the other side, but still unmistakable. Here the bed was narrow and it wasn't one in which he imagined anyone else with him. He threw his clothes on a chair in the corner and crawled under the sheet and quilt, intending to read for a while. But after a few minutes he turned out the light and rolled onto his stomach, one hand down the side and the other up over his head. His feet dangled over the end, something he could avoid in a larger bed by sleeping crosswise at an angle.

It was in this position that he began to think once more of eventually going back to Toronto. He couldn't simply pack a suitcase and vanish; he had a well-established life in the metropolis. Nor would he want to. There was Diana. He longed to see his slim and worldly-wise daughter, to hear her delighted laughter. Not that long ago, he'd rung her doorbell with a package of sushi to share and he could almost hear the timbre of her warm response still. Diana never let him get away with much and he liked that about her also.

"Dad," she would say. "What are you? A troglodyte?"

Well, maybe he was on the verge of becoming some kind of prehistoric cave dweller at times, but Diana wouldn't let that happen. She was the one who had suggested he take up dancing.

"You must be crazy," he said.

"Well, Mum said you were a good dancer in university."

"Why were you talking to your mother about me and dancing?"

"I wasn't talking about you, Dad. I just remember that she often said that."

"Well, forget it," he said.

But he hadn't. Maybe he would try swing again. There must be a place for doing that in Toronto. Maybe he'd dust off his foxtrot, even take some lessons. He couldn't imagine appearing at some dance and asking a woman to go out onto the floor with him until he knew a few steps reasonably well. The waltz was another he thought he might be able to pick up again. Would there be enough room for dancing at the Desjardins' party? When he was a teenager, they did the polka at the Rialto, which must have been one of the dances he'd had with Michelle. As he drifted off to sleep, he thought he would ask her.

55

LIBBY WALKED ALONG the frozen lake, lifting each foot and planting it down carefully in steps that would disappear in falling snow almost before she walked back to the cabin. Once inside, she settled down in a wicker chair with her sketchpad and dark pencils, sketching the lake and overhanging branches and jotting down ideas about colour and perspective. Soon there were pages spread across the table, filled with her scribbles.

You could see so many colours in snow when the sun was shining, she thought. Some paintings by the Group of Seven still amazed her because of the pink, blue, and purple shades shimmering in the snow. Gradually she had also learned how to capture some of the luminous quality that made winter a season with its own hues and textures.

She thought that Lucien might find the road still open when he returned from the drugstore, but it might well be covered by morning. What did he do when that happened? she wondered. And how would she get into town for dinner with Paul Paquin who had left a message for her the previous day confirming that Jacques would drive out to pick her up? It seemed increasingly likely that might prove impossible. She picked up one of her pencils to draw the white fluff building up on the branches and lying in soft drifts against the cabin. She thought of going outside and lying down on the ground and raising her arms in large circles to make angel's wings as she had as a child. Once Arthur White had counted all the angels in the snow.

"Remarkable, Elizabeth," he'd said. "But then, you are an angel."

If he had ever tried it, there would still have been angels. Only bigger. But she had not said so. She had never wanted to say anything to hurt Mr. White. Too kind for anyone to want to be mean to him, it still baffled her that he had become so despondent that he'd shot himself. Unlike Guy, he'd left no clues that she could recall, except the gifts he'd given away to the neighbourhood children.

As she looked across the large room at an old grey wool hat hanging on a hook beside the stove, she thought of making a snowman. It would not be as cold as it would be lying on the ground to make snow angels. As a child, her snowsuit had always ended up wet from top to bottom and there had usually been bits of ice inside her boots, too, by the time she was finished.

Moving around the room, she hunted through shelves, in drawers and cupboards, and found buttons to use for eyes and a carrot for a nose. A red scarf hung near some old fishing rods. Soon she was in her jacket, pulling on her boots, rushing out to roll that first big ball for the stomach. She would need more buttons for the front of the coat, but she was having so much fun that she started to roll a second ball for the chest.

"*Bonjour*," a man's voice disturbed the silence.

Startled, Libby looked up to see a stranger in a navy coat buttoned up to the neck, a large stomach straining to break through. The man wore dark earmuffs. When she stared at him without speaking, he smiled.

"Paul Paquin," he said.

"*Ah mais, c'est un plaisir de te voir Paul*," she said. "I'm so glad to see you. I thought Jacques was going to pick me up."

"He was," he said. "That was the plan. But I thought there might be too much snow later for anyone to drive out to get you."

"I'm building a snowman," she said, a little sheepishly. She must be a sight, a grown woman rolling big balls of snow.

"I see that," he said with a delighted smile. He moved toward her and lifted the second ball of snow onto the first. Then, as she watched him, he began to roll a smaller one for the head. When she turned to put the hat on the head and the scarf around the neck of their creation, he winced.

"Guy's," he said, turning away from her and taking a few steps.

Libby watched him, wondering if this was all too much for him. What she had understood was that he would find it difficult to come out here, if not impossible. But he came back with a stick he set against the snowman, making him look like a man with a cane. Or a walking stick.

"Do you want to come in?" she asked. "There's coffee."

He followed her inside and sat down with his coat on, continuing to hold his earmuffs in one hand that twitched at intervals as if he had the beginnings of some condition like Parkinson's. He seemed oblivious to the movement. "Later there might be so much snow that I wouldn't be able to drive you back here either," he said.

"I was beginning to wonder." His hand gradually stopped twitching and she thought he may have just been nervous.

"So I came. There'll be too many people at Blanche and Al's to talk much tomorrow."

She nodded.

"After all this time, I would have recognized you anywhere," he said.

"So did Lucien. So did Michelle." She was getting used to the fact that in this place of long ago these people still recognized her.

"I think it's because you look like your mother."

Usually people thought she looked more like her father's side of the family, but maybe as she grew older there was more resemblance to how her mother had looked when they lived here. She shrugged slightly.

"Michelle came back, didn't she?" Paul said. "And Susan left. So much change."

"I hear you're still married, working for the government." He seemed to be the only one she knew of their crowd from the early days who was still with his first spouse.

"And you're divorced?"

She swung around to turn on the small propane stove to heat the coffeepot. "Yes," she sighed. "Who would have predicted any of this? Did you know that there's a diary Guy kept in which he apologizes for how he hurt everyone? He went to the hotel intending to die. It doesn't say how that would happen, but it's clear that he meant to. I don't know if there was an autopsy."

"I don't think so. There wasn't enough left of him to figure much out," Paul said.

"How did the two of you grow so far apart?" She sat down across from him.

Paul shook his head. "I don't know," he said. "I wish I did. In spite of our political differences, we were friends. I guess the rift really occurred when he started shouting at me in the street when he was drunk. 'Just because there are all those Paquins on the war memorial, you think you have a reason to be a separatist.' That's what he said," Paul said. "Conscription," he hissed. "They shouldn't have had to go to war for England. It's not the only reason I'm a separatist, but it's a good enough one. Do you think Mackenzie King gave a damn about Quebec? Or even about France?"

Libby was startled by his sudden vehemence. "I don't know," she said. "I just know going to war and going overseas was the highlight of my father's life. For him, it was tied to England where he lived for a while as a child. But didn't you care about what Germany was doing then?"

"*Bien sur.*"

She could tell he was offended as he stood up to look out the window, his back to her.

"Paul," she said. "Listen, I'm sorry. I came here to see Guy. I came here because I needed to explore where I came from. I have a son named Paul. He's named after you."

"So does Guy."

It sounded as if he were saying 'Big deal. So what?' she thought.

"You married a lawyer, *non?*" he continued.

"That's Sheila." She went over to the window and looked out to find the snow falling harder and she could not see the lake through it. "She married Brian Sloane. You know, the boy who lived in the green house on the corner near Mulholland's. They live in Vancouver."

"Where do you live?"

"Toronto," she said, suspecting that now she would hear what a terrible place she'd chosen. And the recurrent question, the one she still sometimes asked herself. Why hadn't she stayed in Montreal after university?

"I don't like Toronto," he said. "Where all the money is. Bay Street. Well, I guess you know by now this place isn't controlled by the English any more."

"That's for sure," she sighed. "But you know what? I think that's a good thing. No one in Canada who doesn't live in Toronto likes it, do they?" she asked. "Even I took a long time. After thirty years, I still cheer for the *Canadiens*. Anyway, Toronto's changing. People come there and they stay. They may not be passionate about it at first, but there's something that draws you in and over time it's where you want to be. Have you ever been there?"

"Conferences," he said. "It's not like Montreal or Quebec City."

Libby poured coffee into a mug for him. "Would you want it to be?"

"No, of course not," he said. "But they want us to be like them. They don't want to recognize our different culture. *Merde*, Libby, we have different laws. A different history. Two nations."

"Were you part of the FLQ?" she asked, not sure if this question would annoy him. But she felt she needed to know.

"No," he said, his face reddening as his voice rose. "I have no sympathy for killing. That's not the way to get anywhere. Laporte and Cross should never have been killed. But some awful things happened under the War Measures Act. I suppose if I'd been in Montreal, I might have been one of the ones thrown in jail. People were taken away in the night, people who had nothing to do with the FLQ, people where there was no evidence, no proof. I have a cousin in Montreal who's an artist and singer who was in jail and was later proven not to have had any involvement at all. None at all."

"I know that happened to a lot of people," she sighed. "It was a sorry time for all of us. Still..."

"The politicians panicked. They already had enough laws to arrest anyone they wanted. I know two people were killed, but they didn't need..."

"Yeah," she sighed. "Yeah."

"I need a cigarette," he said. "I'll go outside."

Libby looked over at the shelf at Guy's diary. "Do you want to read what Guy wrote before he died?"

"*Je ne sais pas*." I don't know.

"It's here," she said, placing it on the end table near the couch.

"After a smoke."

He went out, closed the door behind him and through the window she could just make out his figure hunched over to light his cigarette. Then he walked over to the snowman and seemed to adjust the scarf. When he came back inside, he took off his coat before sitting down in a large wooden rocking chair with a red cushion on it.

Libby passed him the diary and watched surreptitiously as he flipped to the back right away. His expression changed as he read the part that was more a letter to everyone than a journal entry. When he was finished, he sat staring straight ahead.

"It used to make me angry that he was wasting his life, that he had no interest in politics at all," he said quietly. "But we were still friends until he started making passes at my wife." He put the diary on the table beside his chair. "I suppose it was a cry for help. He did it to make me see him, to make me hear him. But how could I have known?"

"I don't think anyone likely would have. It sounds as if he did everything to drive people away."

"How long are you staying?" Paul asked.

"Not much longer," she said. It felt at this moment as though he actually saw her for the first time, and that now he wanted to spend more time with her. But they would both be gone in a matter of days. "The time's flying by so quickly. I'm planning to fly out on Thursday." She was surprised at the wave of panic she felt at the prospect of leaving. So quickly had she come to count on morning or evening coffee with Lucien, that visit to Michelle's dress shop that she intended to repeat, these small things she had built into her days without effort even though at first they had all seemed like distractions.

"What do you think?" he asked. "Do you want to risk going into town for dinner?"

"I have enough for us to eat something here."

"You know," he said. "I thought you'd marry Guy."

"You, too," she said. "I've thought a lot about that since coming here. I don't think it would have worked out. I wasn't ready to marry anyone then. I don't think he was either. I think he'd started drinking already, too, although he didn't think I'd noticed."

"He started early, for sure."

"Your son doesn't look like you. He showed me around the mine, you know."

"He looks like Colette. *Ma femme*."

"I thought so. But he has his father's politics and pride."

"Sure. Quebecois should be proud. Not like Guy."

"He was proud. There are a lot of stories about what people saw, but that diary tells another side of it."

"Did you read it all?"

"No, but I read enough. All it takes to know that is a few pages."

"Did he ask you to marry him?"

"Yes," she said softly. "He asked me. On the road to the mine at Manitou where I worked in the summer. We were only seventeen years old. Again in Montreal, later that same year."

"I wanted to see you because you loved him, too," Paul said.

56

"I'D BETTER GET going," Paul said when he looked out the window into the storm. "Before all of this snow prevents me from getting back to town."

Libby followed him outside to his car and, using her mitt, started to brush at the snow that was burying the wipers on the windshield. He opened the car door to reach for a long brush with dark bristles on the back seat.

"Lucky the rental agency remembered this." He'd noticed it when he picked up the Firebird, he said. "Guy would have liked these rental cars I choose to drive when I'm on business trips. I try out new models," Paul continued. "This Firebird was just brought out earlier this year, Guy would have particularly liked it, especially this red one. I drove Pontiacs for a long time. My first one was also red, but with long white panels." He and Guy used to drive around town in it, both married by then, their wives often in the back seat while they cruised, honking at people they knew on the sidewalk.

Paul tramped through new snow around the car, sweeping more of the white stuff off the top as he did. "I don't understand it," he muttered.

"What?" Libby asked.

"What he must have been thinking to kill himself. The despair. The anger." Their friendship had been so strained, he told her, that the care he still felt surprised him. "Colette forgave Guy. She said he wasn't himself, that he didn't know what he was doing. I figured the booze was just an excuse Guy used for his erratic behaviour. Maybe it was. But if I'd tried to find out what was underneath it all, things might have turned out differently."

"Don't be too hard on yourself," Libby said.

"No," he said. "You're right. I need to concentrate on getting back to my room at the Alpha before there's so much snow I get stuck in it."

"I wish you could give me a call to let me know you've arrived safely," Libby said.

Paul nodded. "You know, I'm used to driving in winter conditions. I'm not too worried." Nonetheless, he didn't linger and as he drove out toward the highway, she saw him hit a patch of hidden ice and slide precariously close to the ditch before managing to let the car ease slowly into a bank. When he moved onto the road again, he drove even more cautiously.

After a certain amount of time, Libby imagined he must have reached his destination. It would have taken him much longer than usual, but he would have arrived without incident.

Earlier, he'd told her if she'd married Guy, he imagined that Guy would be alive still, but he didn't think their marriage would have survived. "Who's to know," she'd said, not wanting to engage further in that conversation.

She imagined that he'd walked through the lobby, picking up his key at the registration desk. The receptionist would have smiled at him sleepily.

"*Bonsoir, Monsieur.*"

"*Bonsoir.*"

The woman would have turned to reach for a message and handed it to him, looking embarrassed that she'd forgotten. Noticing it was from Colette, he would have moved a little faster toward the elevator. When he reached his room, in the new part of the hotel, he would take off his shoes, sit on the edge of the bed and turn on the television. Flipping channels with the remote, turning the sound to mute, that would have been the moment when he remembered to call his wife.

He'd reach for a drink and then place a call to his home number. When his wife answered, he would tell her about dinner. About Guy's words in his journal.

"*C'est dommage,*" Colette would say.

Libby wondered if in those few words, or similar ones, Colette would have summarized what he felt. His wife, who sounded like a sensitive woman, would surely know his feelings would be deep and painful. And would also listen if he wanted to talk. Would he imagine her there beside him in a nightgown he'd bought for her birthday, black satin cut low in the front, with spaghetti straps at the shoulders? Imagine kissing the skin on her shoulder and moving onto the cleft in her breasts revealed so stunningly by the new gown.

"*Je t'aime, chérie*," he would say.

"*Je t'aime aussi, mon petit lapin*." Her little rabbit.

Likely Paul would say none of this and would have fallen asleep as he fell into bed, exhausted.

57

A S HE ROUNDED the curve near the cabin, the car's engine hummed. More than once, Lucien had felt hidden ice under the tires. It was more treacherous than he had anticipated, but a few minutes later he arrived at the lake. Leaving the car a bit higher up on the road, he shovelled a path before going to Libby's door to knock. When she answered, he could feel his shape illuminated by the beam from the lights inside.

"Quite a snow storm," he said.

"Paul was just here. He left before it got this heavy."

"The roads are bad, but it'll all be cleared before morning."

"It doesn't look as if it's going to stop." She moved aside, gesturing for him to come in.

Stamping his feet so the snow and ice would fall away outside, his cheeks red, his dark hair and eyebrows glistening with melted snow, Lucien stepped inside. There was something he wanted to say, but he wasn't sure how to say it. He took off his coat and hung it on a hook on the back of the door.

"I shovelled the path," he said. "So you can come across when you want to."

"I think Guy's snowshoes are over there." She gestured toward the fishing rods and skis piled up in one corner. Above them on the wall were two pairs of snowshoes. "If it keeps on like this, how will we get to Blanche and Al's party tomorrow night?"

"The plough will come."

"I'm so used to living in a city," she said. "The whole place collapses under snowflakes. Everything is paralysed. People can't get to work or to school. The cars slip and slide around, sometimes even the subway doesn't work. I'd forgotten that here we always got where we were going because of skis and snowshoes and everything. All the same, it's a few miles to town from here."

"Don't worry," he said. About to sit down, he saw the pile of papers, sketchpads and pencils that had been moved to the side of the table to make room for the plates that were still out from her supper with Paul. "You've been working," he said.

"A little. Thinking at least."

"Paul gave up on Guy, too, you know."

"Guy didn't leave much room for anyone who might have wanted to do something. I mean, from all I've heard he was doing some pretty strange things. He says so, too, in the diary. I think he'd gone so far he had no idea how to get back. Like swimming out into an ocean. He was drowning."

"Drowning," Lucien said. "*Oui.*" He knew almost how that might have felt. He was quiet. After a while, he turned on the radio to the local station. The announcer talked about the weather and said the snow would continue.

"Since you came, I feel better," Lucien said. "Not about Guy. About me. I was hungry for a body in my bed, somebody warm to cling to, but it wouldn't have worked if it had been just anyone. I never thought I'd say anything like this. Sex for a man is different, *tu comprends*. But I guess it wasn't only sex I needed. You came here at just the right time. If it hadn't been you, I might be out drinking. I might have ended up out at the cemetery next to Guy." He went on talking until he realized what he was doing. "I'm sorry," he said.

"We both did what we wanted to do," she said. "And it helped both of us."

He had a beer, and then they made arrangements for the party the next evening.

"Blanche said to come early," he said. "There'll be lots of food. She's one of the best cooks, for big crowds, too. She could have taken over at the cookery for White Steve when he died, but she didn't want to."

"I don't blame her. A party's one thing, but doing it every day?"

"What did Paul have to say?"

"A lot of things. He read the end of Guy's diary. I hope you don't mind."

"Of course not."

"We talked about Guy a lot. That's really why he wanted to see me."

Lucien stood up and took his blue and gold beer can over to a plastic pail under the sink where he stared out the window. "Poor Guy," he said. "We were beginning to get along when he started the heavy drinking." He buttoned up his jacket, put on his boots and headed out the door.

"Good night," he said. "I'll leave the store early tomorrow and pick you up then."

She said she would use either skis or snowshoes to explore a bit more of the area around the lake and she might also do some more sketching.

"How did Michelle know about the horse?" Libby asked.

Lucien was in the open doorway by then. He had wondered if she would ask. When she'd told the story, it was as if it were part of a dream, which for her it likely was by now.

"Probably because the farmer was a friend of her father's." Old Boisvert had poker games in the kitchen at the farm on long cold winter evenings. Michelle's father won a lot of money, gambling in his blood, gambling a way of life for the early miners.

"It's odd," Libby said. "As far as I know, none of us told anyone about it or mentioned it to each other ever again and when no one else said anything, after a while it was as if it had never happened."

58.

NICK WALKED ALONG the sidewalk past the log bungalows toward a small restaurant on the main street. He'd told the owner of his lodgings the night before that he would go out for breakfast again. No, nothing wrong, he assured her. He'd been to drink coffee quite often and had sat with a newspaper at the place he now entered. He was glad not to have to follow routine. He should have done this sooner. Just wandered out into the town, deciding to eat where and when he felt like it.

"*Bonjour*," the young waitress said as he sat down at what had quickly become his customary booth.

"How are you today?" he asked, glad she was working.

She put a cup of steaming black coffee with a small jug of cream in front of him, knowing by now not to offer sugar. When he ordered pancakes, crisp bacon and maple syrup, he waited for her comment. When she raised her eyebrows and smiled approvingly, as if to say she was pleased he was finally ordering a full breakfast, he grinned. A newspaper, *Le Devoir*, left on the windowsill, caught his eye and he reached for it. There was a photo of a young boy on the front that reminded him of Marcel Blouin. Maybe he could figure out something that would make a difference in the boy's life rather than presuming he could do nothing. But if Marcel wouldn't even go to school, what could Nick possibly do? Suppose he were to talk to Michelle about depositing money into an account for Marcel. Not something that would fall into the hands of his mother and get spent on alcohol or cigarettes.

After eating the pancakes and flipping through all the sections of the newspaper, reading a few articles, he took out his wallet.

The waitress brought him the bill. Had he enjoyed the pancakes? she asked. *Bien sur*. Would he be staying in town long? *Non*. She looked disappointed, reminding him of his daughter. He would come back again, he assured her, not sure he ever would. Her face relaxed then.

He decided he wanted to talk to Michelle about the boy and headed toward her shop as soon as he stepped out of the restaurant. From the entrance, he could see her dark head bent over a sewing machine at the back. Hearing the bell, she looked up and smiled when she saw him at the threshold.

"I didn't expect to see you here," she said. "Welcome."

"Would you like me to get some coffee for you?" he asked.

"I have a pot," she said. "I can pour a cup for you."

He sat down on a bench across from her. "I had this idea," he said. "One of those light bulb things."

She waited expectantly, leaning back in her chair now, holding the fold of the shimmering material in one hand with her knee resting gently against a bar that controlled the old Singer.

"It's about the boy," he said. "If you agree to give him money for specific things, you know, things like toothpaste, socks, school books, healthy snacks, I'll leave enough."

"I don't understand," she said. "How would you do that?"

"I haven't figured out the logistics," he said. "But there must be a way. And you could see that he has what he needs on a regular basis."

Michelle heaved a large sigh and scrunched up her eyes so that her face became that of someone much older. "Has it crossed your mind that he might refuse anything you tried to give him?"

"He doesn't have to know it's me."

"You or anyone. He's so proud. And besides, there's his mother. What if she objects? Or more likely, takes the money?"

"I guess I'll have to go and talk to her."

"Good luck," Michelle said. "She'll never be sober enough to understand what you're saying."

"I can try." Surely there was some way of communicating with his mother.

"There's something I'd like to tell you. It has nothing to do with all of this. It's another topic entirely."

"What's that?" he asked.

"My ex was killed in a car accident."

The words were so unexpected that it felt as if he'd been hit in the stomach. "I'm so sorry," he said.

"I'm not," Michelle said. "It's a relief. It would have been a relief whenever it happened."

"Well, thanks for telling me," he said. It was just the kind of comment that would have upset him recently had it been one of his patients, but he didn't hear any trace of malice in her tone. And under the circumstances, she deserved to be relieved. "I guess you must feel secure now in a way you haven't been able to for years."

She nodded. "For sure." And changed the subject again as if that were all the time it warranted.

He certainly wouldn't be happy if he learned Marie were dead, but he might be if it were Henri who was smashed up in a car or plane crash. What a shocking person he was, he thought, but after all not particularly unusual. He would never try to harm anyone, even a man he perceived now as his greatest rival. But he could wish him ill if he chose to. It was time for him to acknowledge these angry feelings were quite human, he thought, but also probably time to let go of them.

"Anyway," she said. "Why don't we see what Lucien thinks of your scheme? He might have some good ideas."

"How do you suggest I approach him?"

"Just go and talk to him at the pharmacy and we, and anyone else who might be interested, can talk at the party later."

"Oh, that's right," Nick said. "The party. I meant to tell you I've decided to leave the day after. There are some other things I want to do before I go back to Toronto. Maybe take some photographs in the Laurentians and wander around in Montreal with my camera. I think photography is more my thing than writing. If I ever go to India, I'm more apt to want photographs than to write a book." He paused. "And anyway a novel isn't something for a dilettante to take on. Most of all, I'd like to see my daughter soon and maybe she'll come to Montreal for a weekend to visit my old haunts with me. Then I need to get on with things."

"That would be tomorrow?" Michelle said, her tone surprised. Perhaps disappointed also.

A woman came through the front entrance and began to go through a rack of blouses in petite sizes. Pulling out a red one, she brushed one hand down the front as if savouring the sensation. The way women shopped had always astounded Nick. Marie had been able to spend hours just looking at one item after another. Trying on dresses for an occasion, how does this black one look? she would ask. Or the one with the short skirt and the high bodice? He had only rarely accompanied her on shopping trips, but she always wanted his opinion as soon as she'd bought something. Michelle turned to watch the woman who was now moving on to the long dresses. She stood up and started to move toward the racks of clothes.

"I'd like to buy something for my daughter," Nick said, putting his cup down on the edge of the table where the sewing machine sat. "What would you suggest? I don't know her size except that she's slim. Average height."

Michelle stopped, appearing thoughtful. "Some accessories," she said. "I'll get out some things and you can look at them after you talk to Lucien."

"Thanks," he said, watching her approach the woman, listening to her friendly greeting.

He nodded at Michelle as he went out through the door again and walked up the street. The pharmacy looked fairly busy so early in the morning. He made his way carefully past the magazine racks, the cough medicines, the pain medications, and then the condoms, on the other side of the aisle. He was glad to find Lucien alone in his office. All the customers were being dealt with by the young woman at the counter. How would he broach with Lucien that he also wanted to get permission for Marcel Blouin to visit Toronto and that he hoped Michelle would accompany the boy on that trip? He was afraid that Lucien would assume he had ulterior motives, especially after the episode with the condoms. Maybe he didn't have to speak with him. He could go and see the boy's mother before he left and see if she were sober enough to talk with him. There wouldn't be much time if he were leaving the following day, but in the morning when he checked out of his lodgings might be as good a time as any. Perhaps the Blouin woman would be less inebriated then, recovering from the night before. She might even be lucid.

59

WHEN THE GUESTS stepped into the living room of Blanche and Al's home, they could see a large table at the opposite end covered with a red cloth. At the centre was a sleigh full of boughs and red and green ribbons. Libby remembered that in the north, the festive season began early in December and went on for two or three weeks. This year it would start a bit earlier.

By six o'clock, there were more than forty people crowded into the living room and kitchen. Jacques Paquin opened a beer and leaned back near the old wood stove, his arm around Charmaine. She leaned against his shoulder. Jacques smiled at Libby and gestured for her to join them. If their relationship had been a secret before, it wasn't any longer. As Libby spoke to them in halting French, they nodded as if to encourage her.

"What a feast," she said, sure if she sampled everything she would burst the buttons of her skirt. Salads, casseroles, loaves of garlic bread and rolls were spread around the sleigh. Tourtière, spiced beef, Oka cheese, cheddar, brie, green grapes. On a smaller table in the corner were bottles of wine, Scotch, VO, cold beer, ginger ale and tonic, with glasses along one side. In the kitchen, the counter was covered with desserts — tarts, a maple sugar pie and a huge chocolate cake.

"Imagine Paul, Libby and Nick back in town at the same time," a deep voice intoned.

Hearing his name, Paul drifted over from the crowd that now surrounded the table and Michelle followed him. Blanche also appeared, carrying out a tray of hors d'oevres from the kitchen with an apron flung over her shoulder.

"The hostess never gets to talk to anyone for very long," Blanche said. "Everyone can wait a little while we chat."

She welcomed Libby back to Ile d'Or. She seemed to have forgotten Nick. Then she saw him, taking bottles of wine and beer from a large cardboard box and adding them to the table.

"Thanks Nick," she said. "Please come join us."

Michelle nodded. For a while, they all seemed to talk at the same time, until they burst out laughing.

"There's something I'd like to bring up while we're all here," Nick said.

They waited expectantly.

"What is it, Nick?" Blanche asked.

"I think you all know Marcel Blouin," he began. "I have an idea and I'm wondering how we might get together on it."

He explained what he, Michelle, and then later Lucien, had discussed earlier and suggested they might all want to contribute some small amount. "Lucien will be in charge of the money," he said. "Of doling it out when Marcel needs things." He said Michelle was willing to make the trip to Toronto with Marcel next spring, something he'd thought about since the boy had asked him to go there.

"It sounds like a good idea," Al said. "But when it comes down to it, Marcel will refuse. Not the money for food, but the trip. I know the kid. We'll have to struggle to get him to go to school, but that part might happen."

"Why wouldn't he come to Toronto?" Nick asked. "He's been asking me for just that ever since I met him."

"It may sound ridiculous," Al said. "But he'll feel he has to look after his mother."

Nick shook his head. "Of course," he said. "He puts on a tough guy act, but he's really looking out for her, isn't he?"

A lot of head shaking, but the outcome was that the others were also willing to pursue the plan. Nick said when he returned to the city, he would set up some kind of transfer to the fund from his bank account. He didn't say so, but if Marcel wouldn't come down to visit him he'd come back in the spring to see how the boy was doing.

"You're leaving tomorrow?" Blanche said. "Well let's have a good time now and make the most of the party."

They all started to speak at once, and then stopped to let Blanche tell stories about some of the adventures she and Al had experienced since moving to Ile d'Or.

"That dog," Al said, laughing. "You know, the Muir dog."

He didn't have to go any further to have those around him in gales of laughter. They had all seen him in the taxi with the dog sitting on the front seat beside him as he drove away from St. Luc's toward the houses on mine property.

"How's your brother?" Michelle asked finally.

"Oh, Pierre," Blanche said. "He lives north of Toronto."

"I didn't know that," Libby said. "But then I didn't know about you either until I arrived here. Just about Thérèse and she disappeared from my world when I was still a child. I remember she missed her brothers and sisters, but I had no sense of them."

"Well, Pierre's the oldest in our family," Blanche said. "When he brought Carol back to Timmins at the end of the war, he said, 'You've heard of one-horse towns. Well, this is a half-horse town.' She never learned French. 'I don't care,' he said. 'It's her loss.' But I think he cared. They lived at MacNac after we came here. She was quite sick for a while, so they moved south. He said he had to live near Yonge Street because he needed to feel as if he could escape any time. The road to the north, you understand. He said she took a man from the north and expected him to live in an apartment. He wouldn't go that far. So they live in a house in Aurora. Now she's the one who talks of moving to North Bay. I guess all those years up there had an impact."

"Oh, yes," Paul said. "We end up in strange places for strange reasons, *n'est ce pas*? Do you know if he was drafted into the forces?"

"He was up north already," Blanche said. "I don't know for sure. He could have been. He wanted to leave the mines, so maybe not."

Al started to sing loudly. *Alouette*. After that, some other song. Then he put on a tape, Beau Dommage.

"This is a party," Al hollered. "Not much room to dance. But eat, drink and sing." He said it in both languages, although Libby and Nick were the only ones whose first language was English and Nick's might well have been Ukrainian. Someone touched Blanche's elbow and she turned away reluctantly. Lucien put his hand on Paul's shoulder.

"I'm glad you came back just now," he said.

Libby stood beside them, listening quietly as they began to talk about hunting for moose. It took a while before either of them mentioned Guy. The picture that emerged from their conversation was of a man who even as a teenager started to be known as the best shot in the north. Never missed a partridge or a moose. Later took the young kids camping. All of this before he drank too much. He knew every canoe route for miles around, once took his sons up to James Bay. Damn good miner, too. A shame he did not get to engineering school. He used to talk about Walter Muir designing the hoist and what Arthur White knew about rocks. Susan's father must have told him about prospecting because for a while he went off looking for gold with him. Later he went alone.

"I don't understand what the point of no return was for him," Libby said. "When did that happen?"

The two men looked startled, so lost were they in their own memories.

"It happened gradually," Paul sighed. "I think I knew when he was lost, but I didn't know when he started to move that way. Except he always had a streak of something that made you wonder how he'd end up."

"That was what made him Maman's favourite," Lucien said.

"What about Susan?" Paul said. "I'm sorry to bring it up, but I can't just ignore it."

"She phones every so often," Lucien said. "It's not easy in Montreal, but she says she's okay. She has some kind of job in an office supply store. And a room. I think the guy from out of town who was staying at the Alpha has disappeared, but if I bring it up and talk about her coming back, she's furious."

"Why do you suppose she told Michelle to tell me to stay away from you?" Libby asked.

"I don't know. I haven't figured that out, but it does make me hopeful." Lucien's face brightened, and then his eyebrows met in the middle of his forehead in a deep frown. "Probably doesn't mean a thing."

"What about the pharmacy?" Paul asked. "How's business?"

As Lucien replied, Libby drifted off toward the table where she poured herself a glass of red wine and took a piece of tourtière.

"Thank you for coming back," Madame Dion said. "You must keep in touch with us."

"Mum would be so happy to see you," Libby said. "Would you ever think of coming to Toronto for a visit?"

"I think maybe I'm too old now," Madame Dion said. "But you must give Charlotte my best love and tell her all the stories I remember."

"And the new ones," Al interjected, half filling his glass with scotch and water. "She's seen more of this town in two weeks than the rest of us see in a year."

When Lucien drove her back to the cabin, he started to talk about underground tunnels he had built with one of the McNabs and Paul

Paquin's older brother. "Down behind the manager's house. The one the McNabs lived in at the time."

"I don't have any memories of that at all," Libby said. "Only images from photographs I saw later."

"Are we going to go dancing tomorrow night?" he asked, glancing at her. "That's about the only thing you haven't done here."

"I don't know," she said.

"I'd like it if you would."

"Even if Susan heard?"

"Yes," he said. "Even if…"

"I'd like to drop by to say good-bye to your mother," she said. "Maybe we could go there on my last night, and then go dancing for a couple hours."

"Why not?" *Pourquoi pas?*

60

NICK PARKED OUTSIDE the cemetery where the Protestants and everyone else except the Catholics were buried. Snow was falling, but he figured he could take photos of his parents' graves. He'd intended to come back to visit them after that first day when he'd encountered Michelle on the other side of the highway, but it hadn't seemed important as he'd started to uncover his history and to make connections with people in Ile d'Or.

He walked through the snow that hadn't been cleared to stand beside the place where his parents were buried. There was one headstone, the dates of their deaths within a year of each other, in the late 1960s. His father had died first. He wondered if his mother's life had been shortened by that loss, but he hadn't been around enough to know what she'd felt. He had driven over from Haileybury when he and Marie had first moved there, to visit his parents. Disappointed that Marie wasn't particularly interested in repeating such a visit, he'd let the intention of going back slip himself. And he'd been incredibly busy as a young general practitioner in an area with a shortage of doctors.

Maybe Jeannie could answer some of his questions. They'd fallen apart over the years, but suddenly he longed to see his sister. He would send her photographs of the grave as well as ones he'd taken of the house where they'd grown up. Maybe he would even go and visit her in California, drive down the coast to Big Sur. Then further south. Why he hadn't done this before was a mystery now. He hoped she would want to see him.

When he left the cemetery, he put his camera in the car. Ready to start on his trip south to Montreal, he thought he would like to visit the Catholic cemetery one more time also. He didn't know why, not visualizing any particular grave, but closed the door of the car and walked to the edge of the highway. After checking for cars going in either direction, he crossed to the other side.

Inside the gates, he walked slowly. Ah, this was where he'd seen Michelle.

Another one from those days when this was little more than a dinky frontier camp. At least his father was honest. He was never lured into high-grading. Even though not Catholic, I heard about him. Saw him on the streets. Better man than most. Maybe even than me.

Nick was oblivious to more than a breeze lifting snowflakes around him. Maybe it was speaking to him, he wasn't sure, but he recalled what Michelle had said about talking with her parents. She even had the sense they answered.

How I would like to go with you now, young man. If I'd had a chance, maybe I would have gone to the head of the Ganges, too.

There was a loud crack near Nick, as if a branch had snapped and was about to fall. He looked around and saw nothing, thought maybe it sounded like someone laughing. But there was no one there. Only the grave of that big-bellied priest who had been there in the early days. Chicoine. That was his name. Father Chicoine.

61.

LIBBY SAT AT the window overlooking Lac Leboeuf, her arms cradling her knees and a blanket around her shoulders. She felt peaceful, as if she'd come home again. It didn't matter that nothing had been as she'd expected. After the news of Guy's death and the dinner with Michelle, the party had surprised her most of all with the pulse of northern community she'd almost forgotten.

After a while, she got up to look for her father's letters. He would be surprised at the face of the world as it existed now, the ongoing saga of Canada. As well as at the saga of his own family. In one letter, he'd written that it was perhaps too early to decide who should have the tea service, the trays, the salt and pepper shakers. As the last descendant of a family that had gradually become smaller and smaller, these artefacts had found their way to the house on rue Champlain. And it never dawned on him that the silver should not be divided, that it would not have a place in the future of all his children.

Libby remembered watching her mother polish this silver with deft strokes, Charlotte's absorption in making each piece shine. It had seemed to matter to her, but when Dad died she could not get rid of it fast enough. As if in polishing it all those years, she had somehow held the family together. Maybe she had. Perhaps the myth that had saved them from the utter ignominy of alcoholism was that her father was a gentleman. A polite man. Yes. That was what people had said. Libby could still hear them.

"Such a fine man."

"A gentleman."

"Enough," she murmured, thinking of the proud, angular lines of his face, his narrow nostrils. "Enough."

In a letter dated 13th July, 1945 that began *Darling Charlotte*, what followed was typical of what she had seen thus far. He missed her mother, it was clear, commenting on her last letters, on what she had written about the children. Libby, Sheila and Wally. The last paragraph was about coming home soon. *The consensus of opinion seems to be that the only way repatriation will be speeded up is for public opinion at home to force the Canadian government to throw its weight around a bit and get a larger share of the shipping available. Unfortunately, in spite of the government's propaganda to the contrary, I don't believe Canada packs as much weight in United Nations councils as they would like us to believe. The early rush of repatriation, since considerably slowed, seems to most of us to have had political implications. Now the election is over, we can stew.*

After that he wrote that he loved them all and signed it, *Your loving husband, Walter.*

Before he returned from overseas, the world had already begun to change in ways he considered unfortunate. *July, 25, 1945: The election results are coming out here today and are quite a surprise. I never thought that Labour would get in although I thought they would cut down the Conservative margin by quite a bit. I feel sorry for Churchill. He did such a good job that I thought the people might have shown more gratitude. I guess he thinks Roosevelt was lucky to die when he did. I can't see anyone of the Labour Party filling his shoes adequately at the Big Three Conference, or arousing the confidence of the rest of the world.*

The next letter began: *Sweetheart, I seem to have so much to say, but the words simply will not flow. I love you. I miss you. I miss the children.* Libby had never heard her father talk like that and felt reassured. There was a p.s. that ended *Charlie Roger Out* that reminded her of those times she, Sheila and Wally had marched, brooms over their shoulders, to the resounding rhythms of military music. In another letter, her father described a convoy he had seen during the ocean passage. He commented that he was reading *Barometer Rising. All my love, darling,* he ended a letter from England. *There is nothing to worry about. In fact, with the way the news is, I am safer than I was working at the mine.*

After she put the letters away, Libby doodled for a while on a piece of paper. Then she began to draw a mine shaft with the flag flying atop it, a tiny emblem, but unmistakably the fleur-de-lys. Soon she was so engrossed, she had completely forgotten her surroundings. As a child, she had found similar comfort walking on paths through the bush, kicking pine needles in one season and breaking trail on skis she put on as she left the house in another. Not lying in bed where she could hear lurching footsteps and angry voices. Not in churches. When she got up to undress for bed, her legs were so stiff she could scarcely move.

When Lucien arrived on her last evening, Libby had been working on her sketches and drawings for most of two days and her smock was smudged with bits of colour. These working drawings dabbed with some pigment could one day be part of an exhibition, the background that showed where the finished works had come from.

"Chow mein," Lucien said. He had offered to bring her some food before they went in to see Madame Dion again, before dancing at The Flamingo. Seeing that she was still preoccupied, he went over to the counter where he took a bottle of wine from a brown paper bag and opened it with a corkscrew.

"I have a letter for you," he said, handing her an envelope.

"Where did this come from?"

"It was delivered to the store."

Peering at the handwriting, Libby cringed when she saw it belonged to Dan. She threw it toward the counter where it landed upside down. Not until later, after they had visited with Lucien's mother and gone dancing, did she want to read it.

"I'm going to change," Lucien said. "Shall we go to the dance early? About nine?"

62

THE SMOKE FROM Lucien's cigarette wafted across his reflection in the mirror. He was unsure if the dark trousers and pale shirt he'd changed into were appropriate for the occasion. Or, if they weren't, if he would find any other decent clothes out here at the cabin that were clean enough. He hunted on a rack to find a tie that would liven up his outfit.

Sometimes he really did suspect it was someone else's life he was living. Looking at his heavy grey socks, he decided to change them for a pair in the drawer with navy and blue triangles on the sides. He and Susan had always been good on the dance floor, gliding with the music, with others sometimes lining up on the side to watch them. Tango. Waltz. Swing. Susan's dark hair had flown then, her bright skirt or dress swirling around her. He took down a photograph from the bookshelf beside his bed, one of her in the canoe at the dock. She was wearing his plaid shirt, waving with a paddle.

"*Mon dieu,*" he sighed. Would it never get easier? He put on dark shoes, then a heavy pair of boots over them before trudging across the path to Guy's cabin.

"*Allo,*" he called out to warn Libby that he was approaching. He swung the flashlight so the light beamed on the stoop of the cabin.

Libby opened the door to let him in. "It's dark so early," she said.

"Beautiful," he said as he looked at her dress. Although he had been aware of her as a woman, in her slacks and casual sweaters or blouses the impact had been more subdued. He felt almost mesmerized by the way the bodice emphasized her breasts and the slim waist below them.

"It's the dress I bought at Michelle's store."

"*C'est toi qui est belle,*" he said, shaking his head in wonder. She looked much younger than either of them could possibly be. It took him back to the Rialto, watching her spin around the floor with Guy.

There had been watchful eyes then, too, the same ones that had watched him and Susan, all their feet moving to the rhythm of the band in from Rouyn for that Saturday. Everyone knew they had been a twosome, he and Susan. And Guy and Libby, too. What a big surprise it was when Guy married a girl from the mine office, even though by then Libby had refused him. No one thought Guy would get over Libby and Lucien thought now that maybe he never had.

Once again they drove the road to town, the surface now a thick layer of hard-packed snow. Lucien parked across from the club and they went inside past the bar and found a table near the dance floor. There was a candle in the centre and a glass with pink swizzle sticks with little flamingos at the top beside it. It was not long before Libby slipped one of the sticks into her purse.

"A souvenir," she said.

Feeling almost as if he were in a time warp, Lucien nodded. Here he was on the verge of turning fifty, living with memories of being a teenager, with a woman he had not seen since then and his own wife off in the city. He could scarcely visualize Susan as other than a teenager at this moment either.

"What would you like to drink?" he asked.

"My treat," she said.

"*Mais non*. It's mine."

She must have heard the edge in his voice because she dropped it, just told him she would like a beer. Maybe something else later.

"You used to like those mixed drinks, didn't you?"

"That's right," she said. "Haven't had one in years though. There was a pink one, I think. Another with lime and gin in it. I prefer beer now. Or wine."

A fast tune roused him, "Let's dance," he said. He stood and sashayed to the music as he took her hand. So easily did they move together to the rhythm that it felt as if they had been partners on the dance floor for a long time.

"You're good," she said. "Guy was, too."

As the music slowed, he pulled her to him. He felt a stab of loneliness at the thought of her departure. *You're so warm and beautiful, Libby Muir*, he thought, but he did not say so. They went on dancing until an intermission at around ten, when he'd suggested they drop in on his mother.

Madame Dion was sitting in her breakfast nook, the aroma of coffee wafting through the room. The pot of coffee was always on, Lucien said.

"I remember," Libby said. "Everyone felt welcome in your mother's kitchen." There were always people dropping in and she would give them coffee or hot chocolate.

Inside they sat at the table while Madame Dion filled their cups. She gave Libby the cream and sugar, a plate of cookies and a croissant with chocolate on it.

"Tell me about your mother again," she said.

"She'll want to know everything about this trip. It will give her enormous pleasure to hear that I saw you. Do you know that I still have the old milkshake machine from the pharmacy? When you were going to get rid of it, Monsieur Dion said I'd made the best ones, that I should have it."

"Your father loaned him money when he started the store. When we came here, my husband was working underground. He wanted to get out. Even though your father said the mine was losing one of its best workers, he helped him. We never forgot that. Especially my husband."

Lucien picked up his mug, sipped from it, watching his mother and Libby talk. He had not heard this story before and he wondered why. Although neither could he imagine why anyone should have told him. It was just that the pharmacy was his life now and without knowing it, he had been unaware of an important bit of history.

"But that's really something," he said. "That's really something. Why would he do that?"

"He did it, that's all, Lucien. Walter Muir was a kind man. He did things that helped people, but he never made noise about it. There are lots of people still in this town who could tell you a story or two. They might not, or they might not want to remember, but they should. He deserves that."

Lucien didn't say anything because his thoughts were too complicated. He thought perhaps he'd maligned the Anglos and then instead that his father might have been patronized. Maybe it was neither, just two men who respected each other. He didn't ask if his father had ever paid Walter Muir back, but he assumed so.

Libby took the croissant and licked at the chocolate.

"Oh, *mon Dieu*," Madame Dion said. "You haven't changed one bit. I remember when you licked some of the chocolate brownies your mother made when you were just a toddler."

Libby smiled as she bit into the croissant. When she'd finished it, Lucien stood up to get their coats. He smoked in the hall, inhaling deeply. Tomorrow Libby would be gone. It wasn't that he could imagine her taking Susan's place, or living with her, but during her time here he'd found it easier to confront his life. If he could live through this he might even be able to accept the thought of being fifty. It was a huge leap to think that there was nothing other than to go through it, but that was what he was about to do. He took Libby's coat back into the kitchen and held it for her as she stood talking to his mother. As the two women hugged each other, there were tears on both their faces. He knew they were thinking about Guy, about all the ways in which all their lives could have been different.

"The dancing will have begun again," he said. "Let's go back for one last dance."

"Let's," Libby said. "He's a good dancer, you know, Madame Dion. As good as Guy was."

"He's a good son," Madame Dion said. "I try to tell him, but you know, Libby, he doesn't believe me. He never has. Now you can be my witness. Guy was my baby, but this one was always the one I could count on. Papa, too. Papa wasn't very good at saying so. He thought it though. He told me. 'That Lucien, quite a guy.'"

Lucien dropped his head, and then leaned over to hug his mother. "*Merci, Maman*," he said. "I guess I know that. Sometimes it's all so hard. I know you miss Guy and he was always your special boy. But I know you love both of us."

"I was glad to see Paul," she said.

"*Oui, moi aussi.*" Me, too.

"Thank you for your visit, Libby. It's meant a lot to me," she said, her face moving through the sadness in her eyes to a smile. "Have a safe trip back to Toronto."

Lucien touched Libby's shoulder, afraid she might burst into tears.

"Get on back to your dance," Maman said.

"Odd, isn't it," he said. "Me and Libby."

"No," she said. "Not odd at all. We're all northerners."

63

THE LIGHTS WERE turned low, a strobe light circling overhead at the centre of the dance floor. Tables bordered the room with a long bar down the left side and curtains were pulled back that could be draped across the stage before a performance. Rock stars, dancers, singers had graced that stage over the years, young actors and musicians traveling the province as they struggled to open doors in the cities. On many nights, the club became a dance venue.

Seated at a table on one side of the floor close to the bar, Libby watched the dancers. She noticed Michelle with a man she didn't recognize. When the music stopped between numbers, Michelle came and sat at their table.

"Want a beer?" Lucien asked.

"Sure."

He went over to the bar, leaving the two women alone.

"You look wonderful," Michelle said. "The dress suits you so well, the colour, the lines, everything. I'm glad to see you. I thought perhaps you'd decided not to come."

"We were here for a while and then went to visit Lucien's mother. We just got back. It's still the old Flamingo, isn't it?" Libby said. "Updated, of course. But it brings back all the old nostalgia."

"I didn't know you'd ever come here."

"Of course I did. I came for a drink with one of those out of town engineering students when I was barely seventeen."

"Your parents must have loved that."

They both chuckled.

"My mother didn't, but my father told her he figured I'd likely be taking a drink when I went to Montreal that fall to university and why not have the first one in Ile d'Or."

The noise of the band had become almost deafening and when Libby leaned over and tried to say something more, it was apparent by her grimace that Michelle couldn't hear her.

"Do you feel like going for a walk?" Michelle asked, almost shouting.

"Well, we just got back. Maybe after a couple of dances."

So later, after she had danced a few numbers with Lucien and he had begun to talk and dance with others, the two women found their jackets. Wending their way through the now crowded tables, Michelle stopped occasionally to say a brief hello until they reached a door at the back and stepped out onto a porch above a lane. It was what they might have done as teenagers had it not been for their fathers.

"I wish Nick had stayed another couple of days," she said.

"Do you think you'll hear from him?" Libby asked, trying not to sound too curious. She knew Susan was the only woman for Lucien. And that although he was now buried in the cemetery, the one she'd come to find out about here had been Guy. She didn't know how she would feel about Dan when she saw him and wondered why he kept contacting her if Daphne was the one he loved.

"I think so. About Marcel, at the very least," Michelle said as she pulled a bright scarf higher around her neck. "When are you leaving?"

"Tomorrow."

"The time has gone quickly."

"It has, hasn't it? I thought at first I'd stay only a couple of days. I wish you and I had had a chance to talk long ago."

"It is too bad," Michelle said.

Libby was quiet, waiting to see what more Michelle would say.

"My father was a proud man," Michelle said. "Maybe you didn't know that."

"I guess I never thought very much about it. To me, he was just your father." How simply she had been able to define everything in those long ago days. Now that naiveté astounded her.

"Like yours to me."

"Not a falling down…"

"No" Michelle interrupted.

"I think mine was a proud man, too." Of course, Libby knew that. Not an arrogant or egotistic man, but proud nonetheless. She didn't know how to tell Michelle that she was sorry for what had happened to their friendship, for the part played by their fathers. But maybe she didn't have to say anything. Here they were now in spite of their history and it felt as if that made words unnecessary.

"My father was respected in later life when The Flamingo became such a part of the community. And then someone started to talk about him, about the early days and spread rumours again about the high-grading, that he bought the nightclub with stolen gold. Then the gossip started all over again. That's when he started drinking heavily."

"*Oh, mon Dieu.*"

Someone opened the door behind them and the strains of a waltz drifted out. They were quiet until the door closed again. Whoever it was hadn't come out, perhaps deterred by their presence.

"He could hold a lot," Michelle continued. "But it released a deluge of talk. About his earlier life. His childhood. His mother. About how terrible it was to work underground. About starting to steal the gold. He talked and talked. Whenever he drank. And then one day, my mother didn't hear him. Or see him. And thought he'd gone off on a bender. But he was in a room upstairs above the nightclub where he used to go to listen to the radio. She found him hanging from a rafter."

It was a few moments before Libby caught her breath enough to speak again. How was it that she'd never heard this story? Then it dawned on her that she'd been offered a secret that wasn't shared in the community. For some reason, Michelle seemed to want her to know that her father had suffered.

"You have his determination and pride," Libby said. "Although I just thought of him as your father, I thought he was quite something."

Michelle's eyes glazed over. Maybe there were tears that did not fall. "Yes, I loved my father." And then she smiled. "I remember some of my mother's comments when your father came back from overseas," she said. "I guess because she came from England, she always thought it was special that he'd gone when he already had a family."

Libby recalled the photos that were taken next to that Union Jack flying from the fence pole in front of the Muir house on the day the war ended. Michelle was one of the children from the neighbourhood lined up against the fence under the flag. At the other end of the row was Wally. In one photograph, Libby was hanging onto the pole. Perhaps she was wondering when her father would come home. Even with the good news and flags flying, she'd gone on praying every night that he would return safely from overseas. As a child, that he would do so wedded to a bottle was not something she knew enough to imagine.

Some hero!

"That never crossed my mind," she said. "I do remember that when he finally did get back, he often played military music. And then he would get the three of us marching around the room."

It had taken a long time for Libby even to begin to understand the horrors of war. Of that war. Of the holocaust. And the expulsion of Japanese Canadians from Canada's own west coast. Of any war. She never knew if the vicious rounds of drunkenness came from some demons unleashed from what her father knew of battle or because he never did get to see it. Or for reasons too deep to fathom that might have fuelled his need to be at the front in the first place.

"But I loved him, too."

Michelle nodded, taking a sip from her glass. "It's getting chilly," she said.

"Shall we go back inside?"

"I guess so. I hate to see your visit end. Do you think you might come back some time?"

"Well, I could say I would. But it's a long way. I don't know." She'd found something she needed here in Ile d'Or, images, a community, maybe even the courage to go on, but the city was undeniably her home now. "Maybe you'll come to Toronto. With Marcel Blouin? I could see both of you. And Nick, too."

"You can see Nick any time."

"That's true," Libby said. "But I never do. I haven't in all the years we've both lived in Toronto except the one time Wally and Jeannie visited after they were married. And, back into our own routines, it probably won't happen. I can just imagine how busy he is with his practice."

"I guess. He seemed lost somehow, as if he didn't know if he really wanted to continue with it. Although by the time he left, he sounded as if he might have had a new burst of energy."

"I'm glad to hear it," Libby said.

64.

WHEN SHE ENTERED Guy's cabin after Lucien had parked and walked with her across the path, Libby's eyes were drawn to the envelope she'd left on the table. After hanging her coat up, she sat on the edge of the bed still wearing her new dress and slit Dan's letter open with her nail file.

Dear Libby, she read. *I miss you.*

Dan wrote that he had stopped seeing Daphne, that it was hard to admit he had treated Libby so badly. He was sorry, Libby, sorry. *Please believe me,* he wrote. *I was running away from love. I was afraid. Afraid with all you and I have in common of being drawn together too quickly.*

The letter continued as he confessed he'd wanted to meet her even before he saw her paintings at the Moritz gallery, the images of the north she often worked with already drawing him in. And then he'd been confronted that day by the horse emerging from quicksand, a sketch still, not a fully developed painting. Also by a dog with a rifle beside him, a snake in the grass the boy playing there didn't notice. *Something mysterious creeping into the landscape captivated me,* he wrote.

Had it not been for that dog her father had as a little boy in South Africa, a small white dog with black spots, a dark nose, pink pads on his feet, the snake would have killed him. The dog sniffed at the long grass, jumping suddenly in the air as the snake bit him. It could have been her father who'd keeled over and died. He would not have come to Canada as a small boy. None of the Muir family would have existed. He would not have gone overseas. She would not be in Ile d'Or now.

Libby wondered how to include some of her father's letters in the art she was contemplating, perhaps a collage of some sort with drawings and letters linked together.

The war news still seems very good, he wrote on November 26th, 1942. *Especially from Russia. However, I'm afraid there will be a lot of hard fighting before even the African show is cleaned up.*

Libby wished she had her mother's replies to this correspondence. It felt as if some important links to her past were missing. Had her father read those letters and kept them? Or had he, moving from army camp to army camp and then sailing to England, had to discard them? She knew where the genealogy charts he had drawn were and that she could use them as the basis for further research. But what she really hoped was that one day she would come across a box somewhere with all her mother's letters to him that would make the connections tangible.

As she listened to the silence, punctuated at intervals by ice cracking, she thought that when her last exhibition closed, the one Dan had mentioned, that she'd left her own life dangling.

When she stood up, she examined the photographs in the cabin again and held Guy's journal. She heard the sound of the green canoe slipping through water as they paddled across the lake together. He felt close to her here.

"Once I stole a horse," she murmured. Guy never knew about that. "I only meant to borrow it, Guy." What would she have done with a horse? She was eleven. When the time came to ride, she was too afraid. The nightmares began then. The rocky field on the edge of town where the horse grazed on one of the few farms struggling to survive on the barren land around a mining town. Then it was sinking.

"I'm sorry, Guy." As if had the horse not sunk that would have made a difference. She would explore the mystery in her art somehow; she would mine her terrain. For it was hers. Lib-BEE was what the French kids had called her, the accent on the second syllable. When she heard the lilt of the French language or someone speaking English with the intonations she had grown up with, she would always know where she came from. Maybe she had been the horse struggling in her dreams. She had never thought of that. How could she have lived so long without even the hint that she might have been the one who was caught, the one who needed to be freed?

"*Mon dieu*," she murmured, looking down once more at the letter in her hand.

I hope you'll give me another chance, Dan wrote.

When she'd finished reading to the end, Libby folded the letter and placed it back inside the envelope. It was one she would keep, she thought, with a ribbon around it in safekeeping in a drawer in the house in Toronto.

Dear Dan, she began as her thoughts started to come together. She described some of her ideas for paintings. The sketches she'd done here in Ile d'Or, the images she'd begun to capture in her drawings.

"I can't wait for you to see them," she whispered.

65

THE SUITCASE LAY open on the floor, the sleeves of a red sweater hanging over the edge. As Libby straightened it out and laid her nightgown on top, there was a knock at the door.

Her eyes moved from sink to window, from wood pile to snow shoes, from a row of photographs to Guy's journal with a sense both of déjà vu and sadness.

"Bye, Guy," she murmured. "Thank you." *Merci.*

As she opened the door, she saw Lucien cast a glance at her open bag.

"Time to get moving," he said. "Need some help there?"

"No, I don't think so," she said, unable to look at him right away. Unable to acknowledge that something final was about to happen. Something as simple as a farewell that held within it the likelihood that she would not return. Pressing the lid of the case down and fastening the zipper, she wondered if she would ever see Lucien again.

As they drove into Ile d'Or, both of them remained quiet. When they reached Pharmacie Dion, Lucien said he would be fifteen minutes or so.

"But there'll be plenty of time to get to the airport," he added.

"Okay," she said. "I'll walk around a little." As she started down the main street, she stopped abruptly at the sight of five small ceramic horses in bright colours, orange, blue, yellow, red, green, dangling on a long string from a hook in a store window. As she pushed the door open, her eyes were glued to the horses.

"*Bonjour, madame,*" the shopkeeper smiled.

"*Bonjour,*" Libby said, pointing at the mobile. "I'd like those, please," she continued in French, which came more easily now.

Taking down the horses and putting them on a piece of tissue paper, he carefully moved the strings on each horse so they did not become entangled.

"The winters used to be much colder than they are now," he said.

Libby was about to tell him she remembered the long, cold months when the plough left huge snow banks on the streets. When she and her friends built forts and igloos in them. But as she glanced at the horses, she saw a MADE IN TAIWAN sticker on the red one.

"Nine ninety-five," he said. *Neuf quatre-vingt quinze.* He looked down to see what had caught her eye. "Do you want me to remove it?"

Her laugh was a short, high-pitched sound that escaped spontaneously. Along with the plastic swizzle stick with the pink flamingo on it from the nightclub the previous evening, this might be the only tangible souvenir of her visit. She thought that had been decided when she first saw the horses. Although she sensed the old imagery would permeate everything for a while as she worked on paintings from her sketches, she wanted these dancing, brightly coloured horses to hang in her studio.

"It's all right," she said finally.

Back at the pharmacy, she opened the trunk of the car and rearranged her bag to hold the mobile, folding it gently in her nightgown. When she zipped it up again, she went inside to find Lucien just emerging from the back of the store. She took a pamphlet on hunting and fishing from the counter. Another souvenir. She would paint the Second World War monument with the twenty-seven names on it and the mine shaft with the fleur-de-lys flying, The Flamingo, l'Ange Bleu, the houses covered with insulbrick, the water tower at the end of town, the graveyards, all of it.

Lucien took her arm as they went back out to the car. At the airport, he carried her bag to the Air Canada counter. The other airline, Cree Air, flew north. She saw Al Desjardins with a dark suitcase with a strap around it heading toward the car with AL'S TAXI on the side in yellow letters. A man with a briefcase walked beside him. As they reached the car, Al turned around and saw Libby. As he waved, a smile spread across his face. She waved back.

"I'll miss you, Libby," Lucien said.

A fat woman with false teeth sat in a chair next to where they stood, puffing furiously on a cigarette. "If they delay that flight again!" she said to a small man who wore a matching wedding band, wagging her finger menacingly at the end of his nose.

"There's nothing we can do," the man said.

"Me, too, Lucien," Libby said. *Moi, aussi.* She put her arm through his and he hugged her. As she stepped back, she could see tears in his eyes and knew there were some in hers also.

"I have a clearer sense of where my roots are," she said. "Of being connected to this place." Of another trip she wanted to take, to explore the French part of her heritage. Her sense of comfort came from hearing French around her, but something more, too. Her mother's French grandmother, even though she never knew her.

"What next?" he asked.

"We'll see," she replied. "I don't know. I've wanted to go to France and spend some time there for years. I think I'll regret it later if I don't. I'm not sure I can finish the paintings I've started until I go." She was not sure why that was, but she sensed it.

"What about Dan?"

"I don't know for sure. The letter was from him. He's done a lot of thinking. I look forward to seeing him. What about you?"

"I feel better."

"And Susan?"

"It hurts. I still love her. *Mon Dieu.* The Anglo in her, too, I think. *Comprends-tu?*" Do you understand?

Libby nodded. "Are you going to Montreal?" she asked.

"I guess so. Maybe it will all just feel worse, like you said, missing arms and legs or something. But what else can I do? I have to go."

Libby smiled at him. "Would she have called and left that message for me if she didn't still love you? I think it means something."

"I don't know any more," he said. "Anyway she's so proud, you know."

"I remember."

"So," he shrugged. "I'll find out, I guess. One way or the other."

When a voice came over the loudspeaker to announce Libby's flight, she reached out to touch the sleeve of his jacket.

"*Bon voyage,*" he said. "*A bientôt.*"

"*A bientôt,*" Libby said so quietly he might not even have heard her. She turned toward the door that opened onto the tarmac. His eyes would probably follow her although for all she knew he would turn away so as not to have to watch. When she looked around once, he raised his hand.

As she waved, she imagined the sounds of French stretching back to the early settlers on the St. Lawrence, to small villages in France. These were the voices of her ancestors, too, no longer all in English, no longer only the men and women with gravestones in the countryside of England.

When she stepped inside the plane, Libby could feel the passengers who were already seated watch her as she moved down the aisle. As she sat down, she saw that the horse was no longer stuck in quicksand. It was racing down a road somewhere with wind blowing through its mane. Under a blue sky, birds sang and there were bees buzzing by raspberry bushes. And in the white house near the bush, the house on rue Champlain, she saw the oak table in the dining room as clearly as if she were ready to sit down at her place across from Sheila and Wally.

"Everybody happy?" her mother asks.

"*Benedictus. Benedicat,*" her father says.

As Libby fastened her seat belt, the pilot's voice came over the intercom, first in French and then in English.

"We expect a little chop on our way up to cruising altitude," he said.

66.

PULLING HER SWEATER around her, Michelle caught her image in the mirror on the outside door of the change room. Enough time had passed since Nick drove off through a snowfall toward the highway and Libby caught her plane that having seen them felt almost like a dream. It was quiet and outside snow was falling. Customers were unlikely to wander in until noon. They would have to shovel first, but she knew the weather itself wouldn't stop them. She thought about Nick's invitation. She would have gone to Toronto for a few days in the spring and taken Marcel Blouin with her, but Marcel had refused the invitation. Nick had written once to thank her and said he'd returned to work without too much difficulty, even with new insights. He'd asked about the boy and she thought now she would suggest Nick come up to Ile d'Or in the spring to see Marcel again. Maybe the fund could afford a camera for Marcel and Nick could teach him how to use it. Suddenly ideas emerged spontaneously. She'd let Nick know she'd be glad to see him herself. And his photographs.

Smiling slightly at her reflection, she recalled Nick's penetrating gaze when she found him looking at her. Often surreptitiously, with glances that lingered and that made her more aware of her femininity again. She hadn't tried to convince him, or anyone for that matter, that her father hadn't done anything illegal. She was relieved to have preserved the details of that bit of history for herself. That Maurice Dufresne might not have been honest about the gold no longer troubled her. It was not her doing. No one ever knew where the gold was hidden, so they could go on guessing about whether he had actually taken the high-grade. Except for Libby, whom Michelle had as much as told, albeit without any details.

It had taken her a long time to figure out that scenes she'd witnessed as a very young child were connected. A knock on the door her father answered. Frightened at the sight of two men waiting outside on the stoop, she began to cry.

"So what have you been up to?" loud voices said to Maurice in French. "Let us in." They pushed past him. "Where is it?" they demanded, looking around as if trying to decide where to start to look.

"There's nothing here," her father said.

Michelle's eyes followed them in wordless horror. Francine must have been sleeping as she wasn't saying anything either. Or maybe she'd been there, also frightened. The noise would have awakened her as they went through the house, searching through cupboards and drawers, leaving lingerie hanging from her mother's bureau, nylon stockings with the black lines down the back strewn across the floor. Coming into the living room again, they shifted the cushions on the sofa and left them upside down. One of them went down the basement stairs where he could be seen from the kitchen door, looking into the wringer washing machine. He turned away, holding his nose, appearing disgusted.

"But there's something here," he said when he came upstairs again. *Mais, il y a quelque chose ici.* "I'm certain of that."

They would return, they said.

Afterwards, her father went to the basement and moved the wringer to take something out from beneath the dirty diapers. He left the house with a package and when he came back his arms were empty. Michelle heard her mother ask if he'd been drinking.

"Just a pint," he said, starting to sing.

That was in the days before The Flamingo. Her father could drink with the best of them, but when the nightclub opened, he stayed sober for the customers and the fights and high jinks that might happen. He might have liquor on his breath when he came home, but he didn't stagger. If anything, he began to swagger.

Yes, that was her father, Michelle thought. King of the world. It was too late to tell him. She wished he hadn't died before she even thought of it. Before his granddaughters had a chance to grow into women with lives of their own to share with him. How relieved she was that Dawn had called to say she'd been hired as a translator by a large company. Soon she'd move into her own apartment not too far from where Elise lived. Michelle felt as if her family circle had been restored and she looked forward to being a grandmother. She would remember her father as someone with gumption. A gutsy guy, she might one day say about him to her daughters. Or even her grandchild. *Je me souviens,* she thought. What did it matter that she couldn't possibly have remembered the washing machine because she was just a small baby at the time? And it was her diapers that were in there. Maybe she heard her father talking to her mother later. He probably hid it in the coal chute by the time she was old enough to remember anything. And she had no idea of how he was talked into taking it. Unlike the men who didn't get drawn in at all. Like Roman Petranovich. They managed to put up with the dirty work and didn't crumble under veiled threats toward their children. Nick could be proud of that and she wouldn't hold it against him. It was Libby's lack of understanding of the dynamics that had existed in the mine that still irritated her. But she was glad they'd moved beyond whatever their fathers had been. Perhaps she would visit Libby, especially if Nick suggested it. Michelle dusted off the glass counter under the cash machine, looking down at the jewelry displayed there. There was a pale blue necklace she thought Charmaine might wear with her new dress, something that would sparkle around her neck at the New Year's dance. If she didn't happen to come into the store, Michelle would call her. Dealing with people came as naturally to her as choosing fashions, that ease something that probably came from her father.

You never knew who would be remembered and for what reason, she thought as she reached in and took out the necklace, dropping it carefully into a box with slightly crumpled tissue paper underneath it.

In the end, the Anglos who came in and built the mine were forgotten. There was a fleur-de-lys over the head frame Walter Muir designed and when that head frame was torn down, the flag flew over the gate in the chain link fence that surrounded the property. Even Father Chicoine, who seemed to run the town for such a long time, was almost lost from memory. There was a headstone for him in the Catholic cemetery, but no special dedication ceremonies were ever held. Or for anyone else Michelle remembered. The mayor didn't speak when that first priest died. And the only one who ever had a street named after him was her father.

Epilogue

EVENTUALLY THE MINE *was sold, the buyer a company that be-gan to destroy buildings, and an open pit began to encroach on the edge of town. What was left after the bulldozers and trucks were finished looked like the landscape of the moon, the buildings and houses of earliest memory gradually disappearing.*

One month the manager's house was still there and the next, except for a grove of birch trees that had run around the perimeter, you could scarcely tell where it had been. Not only was that house destroyed, but the highway was also lifted up and moved to the other side of the pit. The Catholic and Protestant cemeteries, a bit further out on the highway, were left intact for the time being. Eventually the plan was to move both of them and that had everyone fuming. Although they agreed that to put the two cemeteries together would be a good idea and Michelle thought that way her mother could be reunited with her family.

Sometimes a stray rock dislodged by the blasting landed on someone's roof or lawn. The story always was that the operation was proceed-ing according to regulations. A pile of earth and rocks was erected as a buffer between the devastation and noise of the pit and the part of town where The Flamingo still stood. It did not do anything but cre-ate an ugly line of demarcation, but after a while you could see a few blades of grass and yellow wild flowers emerging through the soil at the top of the pile.

Acknowledgments

With thanks to the Canada Council and the Banff Centre for the Arts, which at different times gave support. With extra special thanks to Adele Wiseman and William Kilbourn who always believed a book would emerge, but without whose ongoing affection and encouragement it might well not have. I am fortunate to have worked with Edna Alford, Marilyn Bowering and Colin Bernhardt at the Banff Centre for the Arts to find the soul of my material, to reclaim my voice. Thanks to Lee Davis Creal and Janis Rapaport who encouraged me to go to Banff. To James Polk and Susan Walker who supported early grant applications. To Alistair McLeod who was mentor of a workshop at the Humber School for Writers where I most recently workshopped a chapter of this novel. As well, I am fortunate that two incomparable women, my agent, Margaret Hart, and my editor, Luciana Ricciutelli, wanted to see this book published.

My family has been there to share tears and laughter and the belief that dreams matter. I am especially grateful to my daughter Andrea, her husband Mark, and their son Max, and to my son Phil. As well as to my sister Stephanie and her husband Michael, and their children, Gillian (Stacey) and Geoff (Rita) and their daughter Skye. I am lucky also to have the interest and affection of my brother John and his wife Diane and their large family.

My friends who are inspired by dance and yoga provide grounding to enjoy the dance of life. As did S. G. in giving special support during the early days of the book, the roughest times.

I am grateful to Anne Redpath, Nelson and Catherine Priske, Marcel Lefebvre, Margaret Arthur, Jay Huckle, Helen Filion, Roman Hawryluk, and all the others who patiently answered my questions. And to Brydon

Gombay, Douglas Poff, Paula de Ronde, Joy Kogawa, Deb and Ian Wallace, Elizabeth Greene, Carol Findlay, Dianne Mesh, Lee Gold, Michèle Chicoine, Ray Bennett, Ruby Trostin and Larry Crackower, Maryka Sule, Claire Croisat, Ray and Shirley Spaxman, Ila Rutledge, Barb and Bill Wehrspann, Huong Pham, Ray Thompson and Pat Louden, Myrna Friend, John Wilkinson, Gene Simon and David Florkow, Joan Burrell, Richard Bishop, Austin Clarke, Liisa Tienhaara and Gerry LaMarsh, Don Heald, Bas van Fraassen, Rosa Shand and the many other friends who, at various stages, read and criticized my work and/or provided company for the journey.

Thanks to all my colleagues in the Moosemeat Writers' Group, especially Heather Wood who manages the herd and Mike Matisko who used to, also to Edward Brown, Myna Wallin and Heather Wood who now also have books published and share that journey. And to everyone in the herd for honest, perceptive, tough critiques that as well as pointing out deficiencies, offer useful suggestions for going forward. At the risk of forgetting someone, as well as the aforementioned, this includes Katharine King, David Chilton, Beth Jones, Bill Zaget, Cecily Carver, Ben Gleisser, Sylwia Przezdziecki, Niko Troubetzky, Brian Robertson, Tessa Derksen, Max Arambulo and more, too, Joanna, Lana, Michelle, Craig, Ivaylo, Stephanie, Miriam, Kris, Ken. I have been around long enough (since 2005) that some folks have left the group and others have joined, offering new and fresh perspectives on an ongoing basis.

Also, courtesy credit with thanks to the estate of Robert W. Service.

The line from Roch Carrier is from "The Hockey Sweater," the title story in his book, *The Hockey Sweater and Other Stories*.

Photo: Dieter Hessel

Mary Lou Dickinson graduated with a Bachelor of Arts from McGill University and a Master in Library Science from the University of Toronto. She worked for many years as a crisis counsellor. *One Day It Happens,* her book of short stories, was published by Inanna Publications in 2007. Her fiction has been published in the *University of Windsor Review, Descant, Waves, Grain, The Fiddlehead, Canadian Woman Studies, Northern Journey, Impulse, Writ* and broadcast on CBC Radio. Her writing was also included in the anthology, *We Who Can Fly: Poems, Essays and Memories in Honour of Adele Wiseman.* Mary Lou Dickinson grew up in northern Quebec and has lived for many years in Toronto.